PENGUIN BOOKS

GESTURES

H. S. Bhabra was born in India in 1955 and
has lived in England since the age of one.
Until three years ago he pursued a successful
career in the City. This is his first novel.

H. S. BHABRA

GESTURES

PENGUIN BOOKS

Penguin Books Ltd, Harmondsworth, Middlesex, England
Viking Penguin Inc., 40 West 23rd Street, New York, New York 10010, U.S.A.
Penguin Books Australia Ltd, Ringwood, Victoria, Australia
Penguin Books Canada Ltd, 2801 John Street, Markham, Ontario, Canada L3R 1B4
Penguin Books (N.Z.) Ltd, 182–190 Wairau Road, Auckland 10, New Zealand

First published in Great Britain by Michael Joseph 1986
First published in the U.S.A. by Viking 1986
Published in Penguin Books 1987

The characters in this book are fictional. Any resemblance
to any persons, living or dead, is purely coincidental

Made and printed in Great Britain by
Cox & Wyman Ltd, Reading
Typeset in Baskerville

To my parents

Toronto, 1984

'Manet, sir. Short E, sounded T. Not like the painter.'

Part One

THE HORSES OF THE SUN
Venice, 1923

'As for Venice and her people, merely born to
bloom and drop,
'Here on Earth they bore their fruitage, mirth
and folly were the crop:
'What of soul was left, I wonder, when the
kissing had to stop?'

ONE

'This is my son, in whom I am well pleased.'

He laughed, and fell into the Grand Canal.

That is how I first remember him, though it cannot have been the first time that we met, in Venice, over sixty years ago, translated in air from earth to water, himself the salamander, all fire. That is the first betrayal, the inadequate treason which is memory. I have always envied those who can remember how they met, and when, and where. I have always found myself in the middle before I knew I had begun.

So it begins again. I had intended – what had I intended? An account, a memoir, even, perhaps an apologia. Something, certainly, which one day my grandson, my youngest grandson, might turn to from simple interest or complex curiosity, to discover how we lived then, we impossibly old people of whom I am the last decrepit survivor, in those inconceivable days when we were young and the world was ours for the re-making. I should know better, I suppose; I whose life has been spent in paper – minutes, accords, agreements, protocols and plans – all the instruments of the forgotten or superseded sport of diplomacy, as out of date as five-day cricket and courtesy. I have lived amongst studiedly useful, practical words, and I know how short their life is, shorter now than ever, and I would not know how to aspire, utilitarian that I am, to the unlikely immortality of art.

So how is it that, as soon as I sat down to write, I found myself remembering one who played only a little part in my life, whose troubles were none of mine, and from whom, I believe, I learnt nothing, nothing at all, nothing of any use? It is another way in which the memory of the very old betrays them, yet not, perhaps, without a purpose after all. At my age we remember, and I write, at least as much to interest ourselves as in any hope of interesting others, for curiosity is the only one of our powers which is not bitterly diminished by time, and its shabby promptings may urge my ageing flesh to go on living yet a while; and he was an interesting man.

I should, however, make some attempt to begin at the beginning, for I am an Englishman of the upper middle class, which is to say I am one

3

of the most complete creatures of convention the infinitely various human race has so far succeeded in producing. If I have any prototype for the kind of book I am trying to write it is the first book I can remember reading – *The Adventures of Robinson Crusoe*. These papers will constitute The Memoirs of an Ordinary Man.

My name is Jeremy Burnham, and I was born in the county of Worcester in England with the century. (Let us clear this up at once; whatever plenary sessions of international commissions may have said, the century and I both began on the first day of January, 1901, and as I write this I am exactly eighty-three years and three months old.) My people, without being important or ostentatious, lived the sort of life of which the slavering, slack-jawed television audience of today can only dream. I remember a vast red-brick house (I know that everything seems larger to the young, but it was big enough to be sold to the local education authority in the 1950s to serve as an art-college – whatever that is) full of silent servants and loud-mouthed dogs. My father was a gentleman, which means only that he did not need to trouble himself with anything so vulgar as work, for an ancestor had developed a celebrated proprietary treatment for colic and those other ailments of the bowel with which the nineteenth century seems to have been plagued. The rights in this particular opiate had been sold many years before, so nothing as distasteful as industry or medicine survived to stain our escutcheon, only money. My mother's people were miscellaneous landowners, though her own parents introduced an unfortunate touch of the clergy. Happily, my grandfather redeemed himself by ending his days as bishop of one of our more acceptable dioceses.

Looking back on those early years of the century, my dominant memory is not of the unbridled heat which has washed over the playing fields and parks of England in popular fiction as in fact, but of stiffness. Everyone I knew, but especially the adults, seemed to be encased in starch, and to this day I remember my mother as a sound: the stiff brocaded rustle of her skirts comes back to me unasked for, as does the splendid gleam of my father's collar in the otherwise unadorned gloom of his study or the smoking-room.

I was the fifth of six children and was put through the customary education of my class. In childhood I was brought up by nannies, which in my case meant being locked away in the children's quarters with a string of bestial Irishwomen, until at the age of eight I was packed off to that ten-year cycle at public schools whereby the English avoid their children in their most unspeakable years, to have them returned only when they have achieved some kind of maturity and the makings of possible companions. Even in my youth it was usual to

4

speak of the unrelieved horror of one's schooldays and, to be sure, for anyone except gentlemen the conditions would often have been intolerable – a combination of cold, physical exercise, scarcely credible food, unrelieved sadism and moral blackmail reminiscent of nothing so much as a Soviet psychiatric hospital for political offenders or a progressive Chinese prison – but I cannot say I was aware of any great unhappiness or that I suffered particularly from being beaten into that localised form of insensibility the English teaching profession deems appropriate to the parsing of a Latin sentence or the scanning of a Greek metron.

The Great War formed the background to my last four years at school, and though I can only look back now with complete contempt at the old fools, young shirkers and ignorant clergymen who read the rolls of the school dead each Sunday and exhorted us to do our duty and commit ourselves to a life of service each morning, I am equally glad that the accident of age kept me secure in the pieties of that antiquated community, whilst my two elder brothers were mashed into the blood and mud of Ypres and the Argonne. (Tom, the second of them, still comes back to me sometimes in dreams, still nineteen, still the tall blond innocent ruffian of my schooldays, and down the long corridor of time, four times older now than he was ever to be, I find myself unable to speak, unable to say some small word of comfort that what they saw and did was not in vain, until he fades, whistling, as he used to when going in to bat, and I am left with an inconsolable ache and only the sorry satisfaction that he did not live to see the destruction the guns of August wreaked on the world of our childhood and the way the rest of us fouled what remained.)

I scarcely impinged on my parents' world at all during my school-days. At home in the holidays I took luncheon with their party, but only rarely dinner, and only towards the end, when I would sit embarrassed and uncertain as assorted adults assured each other that Young Jeremy was waiting and eager to 'join up and join the scrap. "Hope they leave some action over there for you, eh lad?"' Only when I was at last allowed to play for the little raffish cricket-side named after my mother did I seem to become part of the adult world, and then only because of that rigorous education which ensured that if the Battle of Waterloo was won on the playing-fields of Eton, it was because cricket makes one a devilish dab hand with a grenade or petrol bomb. Though my father was an excellent shot and never so happy as when slaughtering wildlife, and though I was taught to use a gun as soon as I could hold one, I was never allowed (not until my middle twenties) to participate in his grand shoots (the King was once

5

a guest – I remember a taciturn though obviously genial figure in tweed, evidently ill at ease with the young, his subjects' subjects. I found it hard to reconcile the man I saw with t'ıe demi-god for whom, along with my country, I was supposed to be eager to die). Instead I would join the beaters as my elders set out to cause carnage on a scale unimaginable to anyone now. What I most remember about those expeditions is an elderly estate worker who used the occasions as an opportunity to exercise his primitive political consciousness of the class struggle by cuffing me crudely round the head to cries of 'Come here, you horrible little bastard'. He stank, I recall, like some appalling midden, and only now do I realise how much of my class-consciousness in my early years entered through my nose. To this day I remember with pleasure the time I finally reasserted the ancient privileges of my rank when, at the age of sixteen, I knocked him insensible with a single blow. Unimaginable miles away, across a Europe savaged by shells and snow, Lenin was even then calling the Mensheviks' bluff, but irony is an attribute of age and I would be lying if I discounted my savage delight in trouncing my enemy.

I was the first of my family to go up to the Varsity. Looking back, I assume the plans were laid early by my mother to keep me away from what then seemed an interminable and endlessly wasteful war. In the event, the fighting was almost over by the time I was due to go up, and the world was now enlivened by the spectacle of three old men – an impossibly self-righteous Yankee, a Welsh thief and lecher, and an entirely unprincipled Frenchman who, to this day, seems to me to have possessed the shrewdest tactical mind of any politician I have ever seen – carving up a continent to their own satisfaction, disposing of nations, and creating that international polity which was so ingeniously designed to blow up in our faces twenty years later.

For reasons beyond my imagining I was accepted by Oriel College, for a long time the most complete remnant of eighteenth-century idleness in the University and ideal for someone of my nature, for few days passed in which it was troubled by anything as consequential as a thought. It was a pretty place, in the literal as well as figurative shadows of Merton and The House, hard by Corpus Christi, a small dark quiet college full of gnome-like figures who laboured daily in Bodley's Library and were placed in the First class. I passed four instructively easy years reading More Humane Letters (only Oxford could have devised so grand a soubriquet for yet more Latin and Greek) and Classical Greats, finally satisfying everyone by achieving the dizzy heights of a Gentleman's Fourth, a class of degree, alas, long since banished by the University. It was not, however, the business of scholarship that filled my time or dominates my memories of it, but two other things. The first is the tiny number of undergraduates who returned from the war – out of place, contemptuous of the closed and cloistered world they re-entered, bereft of most of their friends and contemporaries, and somehow immeasurably and inexplicably aged.

I write 'inexplicably' with extreme deliberation. I have seen the children of other wars. I have known those who have passed through some of the most appalling degradations our horrible century has been able to unleash. Many of them retained that private fire which makes us recognisably human and which, presumably, bore them through their dark times. I have seen soldiers transformed by the experience of war. If you ever hear old soldiers rambling on about the glory of their war, remember that for many of them it brought a solidarity and companionship unknown outside the sports teams of their youth, and that for many of them, in an age before the package holiday and chartered aeroplane, it brought them their first and only chance to see and experience a world outside the pitifully confined and confining circumstances of their daily life.

These men, however, were entirely different. It was as though the lights which Edward Grey spoke of as going out in 1914 had been the light in the young men of Europe, which was extinguished forever, to be replaced by a hatred and cynicism which led some to early graves or unquiet voyagings, others to wild rounds of pleasure, and yet others to withdraw within themselves, pale shadows of what might once have been. I only ever saw one other man so entirely defeated by experience, so broken and so burnt, and that was many years later and was no one's fault, and in the brightness of my, and the century's, twenties when first we met, lay a future beyond our straightest nightmares, for we were young, and had more worlds to win than you have for imagining.

It has happened again. I have drifted back into the middle, and lit upon a minor figure. It was and is the greatest defect of my character, a love of minor if illuminating particulars, when what I meant to speak of was the general – for whatever the poets may say, the general is at the heart of the particular, and if we linger on a lovely trick of light, the rustle of a skirt, a whistled phrase, the echo of a single voice or a particular and inimitable limp, then we are lost. It is only what we share and what we have in common which can save us; which is the justification of our peculiarly public lives.

To return to where myself and my story belong. The other dominant memory of my undergraduate years is of that resignation to pleasure which is all the young now associate with the years to 1929.

7

What has not, I believe, been generally noticed was that the impulse towards delight was generated by the young women of our time, for many of them felt, and rightly felt, even if they could or did not find the words to say it, cheated and betrayed. The young men whom they might properly have expected to become their husbands had been killed and maimed, mentally as well as physically, on the fields of France and Flanders. They were left only with a few damaged men who were idolised into rakes, and the ignorant and callow young. It may be, as the moralists said, that we had made a covenant with hell; but as, in those delirious debutante years, we danced to the first nigger music England had heard and adopted those curious American additives to London gin which did not need them and which together made up a cocktail (you cannot imagine how saucy that word seemed then), it must be said we did so because we were in league against death and the moral domination of the uneasy dead we left behind us, in khaki graves and the feverish lives and solitary dreams of women.

I came into a man's estate, and graduated from the University, in 1922. I was then a pressing embarrassment to myself and my family. Although with the deaths of my two elder brothers I could expect a slightly larger portion of the family estate than would otherwise have been the case, and although I already had some means of my own, my surviving brother, Henry, would inevitably inherit the bulk of the capital in due course. He waited a very long time, for my father, with the longevity of our house, survived to 1952, and Henry entered into a much depleted inheritance. My sisters, who had adequate settlements made on them when they married, ultimately did better than us both. Ten years earlier no problems need have arisen, for no one would have seen any need for a gentleman to find anything formal with which to fill his days, but a chill wind of duty was blowing through the time, a compact of guilt for the past with fear for the future, and so it was that one afternoon my father shyly tackled me in the smoking-room with the gruff question, 'Any idea what you plan to do with yourself, my lad?'

The honest answer then, of course, would have been – as it would be now for someone in my position and with any intelligence (I sometimes find it necessary to point out that I am not quite the fool I usually make myself out to be) – 'No. None at all.' I sometimes think that if I had answered thus my father would have slapped me delightedly on the shoulder and encouraged me to go on squandering my time. Sadly, however, we were both caught in the stereotypes of that foolish age. It was impossible after the war to consider a career in the services; I would never have made a clergyman, even with the benefit of my grandfather's support and assistance (very well then – influence); and trade, or even the City, were beneath consideration. (What was it my father once said of a distant relative of my mother who was senior partner of my father's brokers? 'No, dear boy, can't have him to shoot. Very sad case all together, to have fallen among Jews.') In the end it was somehow decided that I should sit the examinations for entry into the Foreign Office, on the grounds that my education had taught me to speak bad French and to read two dead languages – not such foolish considerations after all, for the traditional English pronunciation of Latin was so extraordinary that at nineteenth-century conferences English statesmen had used it to converse among themselves without fear of discovery by spies, and the celebrated Rothschild cipher had been only a variant of Hebrew, then an almost moribund language. I sat the examinations in October. To this day, I do not believe I passed them, but what were fathers for?

I entered the Foreign Office as the most junior of clerks. In those days a job at the Foreign Office took up most of a morning, or sometimes an afternoon. Very occasionally it was necessary to be present at luncheon, and rather more often to dine with one's masters. Nonetheless, it left most of the day free, as was only proper in an employment designed by gentlemen for gentlemen, and it did little to interfere with the pleasures of the age. It rapidly became apparent, however, that I would never be a great international analyst or negotiator, and a series of discussions began, which it would be wearisome to recount here, to arrange for me to be offered the traditional escape of the hardly able within the Foreign Office: removal to a minor and insignificant Consulate where I could continue to live in leisure without being an embarrassment to the Department or my peers and, equally important, could do no harm.

So it was, in the spring of 1923, that I was translated to the Kingdom of Italy, to be Assistant Consul in Venice. That move was to be the starting point of my career, and with the wisdom of retrospect I wonder I was not baffled that it should have been decided that Venice was a safe appointment. Across the Adriatic lay the troubled and troublesome city of Trieste. Italy itself was in a state of near anarchy, and the Futurist Movement had declared that it was here that the future would be brought to birth. For me, they spoke only the truth: but I did not know that as I set off prepared only by a knowledge of Latin, a short course in the modern language and a piece of advice I have never forgotten: 'Remember that a Consulate has only two jobs

– to assist those citizens who call upon it, and to be the eyes and ears of its country. Leave it to the Embassy to be the tongue.'

Those of you who have grown to maturity in the age of the aeroplane (which, as far as I can see, means everyone now living except me) can have no sense of the immense pleasure travel constituted in those days. After a lifetime in the diplomatic corps my memory is filled with dozens of fragrant names which remain entirely meaningless to those who follow after. To me for instance, the sequence Paris-Dijon-Lausanne-Vevey-Brig-Domodossola-Milan-Verona-Padova is filled with a mystery and delight greater than any of those cities or towns, even Paris herself, can afford me, for it is the Pullman route to Venice and my youth. We travelled slowly in those days (and I did not always travel by Pullman – the magic always survived any local discomfort) and so we noticed change. To take pleasure in the memory of sandwiches eaten while hanging out of the carriage at the Swiss border, swallowing in great gusts of icy Alpine air, the nervous excitement at Brig, uncertain when you would at last enter the Simplon (it always took you by surprise and was always over before you knew), and the mounting excitement as, dressed and breakfasted, you stood in the corridor as the train rolled idly from Verona on the long slow haul to industrial Mestre and, a few minutes later, the first magical view of the back of Venice, the view which no one under sixty seems to know, may be the nostalgic ravings of a silly old man, but I hold any one of those journeys in greater reverence than all the time together that I have spent in anaesthetic airports and the indecent haste of jets.

I was allowed a month in which to get to Venice, so having taken leave of my family and kitted myself at the Civil Service Stores (those were the days when you could get kit for anywhere from Sumatra to the approach slopes of Everest there) I set off for Paris to make a short stay. I would like to be able to say that I rushed around the city introducing myself to the bevy of writers and painters who had colonised it, meeting Joyce and Gide, Gertrude Stein and Sylvia Beach (I discount those Americans like Fitzgerald and Hemingway who were there only because it would be good for their image and because the dollar was strong), Picasso and Dali and Duchamp. In fact, of course, I did nothing of the kind. My immediate interests were of that simple variety which had driven the previous generations there under Victoria and Edward, and I set out to investigate in greater detail than London afforded those activities which the schoolmasters of my day assured their charges would lead to blindness, impotence and insanity.

Let me say at once that at the age of eighty-three I use spectacles only to read, I am as much in possession of my senses as ever I was, and that although the opportunity has not afforded itself for far too long I am convinced that given, say, three weeks' notice and a fire in the bedroom, I could still achieve some sort of virile response, however feeble, so the schoolmasters were obviously wrong. I have always put their strange notions down to too many cold showers and too much muscular Christianity in early youth.

Nonetheless, in a lifetime of visiting Paris I cannot recall ever having seen it as defeated and depressed as it looked then. There seemed to be no young men left and it came as a shock to realise how little by comparison England had suffered. The war and the influenza epidemic which followed it had created a depopulation from which France has never recovered, and Paris in those days seemed desperate, hysterical and dispirited and, above all else, dirty. I wondered how long a country could survive such terrible shocks to its spirit. I was to discover all too quickly that my fears would have been better reserved for the Kingdom to the south.

Everyone should enter Venice from the sea at least once, but for me, now that her Empire has gone and the great argosies which sailed from her sheltered waters have been replaced by fleets of gondolas dependent on the petty cash of tourism, the sea approaches seem strangely empty, as though the dazzling image rising from the sea, so beloved by film-makers, were only in fact a glittering rococo picture frame from which the design for which it was created has been ripped, leaving it pretty but useless, a home without inhabitants. From the mainland, however, the approach was, and is, quite different.

I woke that morning to the soft light and softer smell of polished brass and oak (the recent revival of the tourist train has created images of fabulous wealth and beauty seductively enclosed on Venice trains; it ignores the fact that in those days all first class trains felt like that. You never had to travel Pullman, but it helped) and an official brought me coffee and a roll. (In the interests of strict accuracy, I must say that I have always found Italian bread virtually inedible, turning to something akin to talcum powder in the mouth.) My first awareness of the approach was the fading of the olive groves, and sudden tangy whiffs of the sea. Then suddenly we were in a small industrial town (it has grown greatly since) and a railway station called Venezia Mestre. 'Surely this can't be it?' an Englishwoman in the corridor enquired of her companion and me. Already armed with my Baedeker and the personal advice of my colleagues in London, I was able to inform her, in what I hoped then was a languid, weary, well-travelled way, but

11

suspect now was as reekingly immature as the occasional clumsy suspiciousness of a puppy, that Venice was the next and last stop. Still, the companion looked daggers till he could assume an equal omniscience. 'Of course this isn't it, darling,' (the word was proprietorial). 'Everyone knows that.'

The Englishwoman turned to me and asked sweetly, or as sweetly as a forty-year-old can manage (that is the remembered arrogance of youth, not the actual despair of age. If I find the middle-aged intolerable now, it is because I have learnt from experience that the folly of maturity is potentially infinitely more destructive than the thoughtless idiocy of youth), 'Do you know Venice well?'

'I am the Assistant Consul.'

I regretted saying it as soon as the words were out of my mouth, not because of the gratifying look of hatred from the companion, but because I could find myself being caught out as the new boy as soon as we arrived, or by the questions which I could see were about to begin. I hurried on.

'That is to say, I am newly appointed the Assistant Consul. I only know as much as I was told back at the Foreign Office' (she looked pleasingly impressed). 'But I must say I'm looking foward to the posting.'

She smiled, and though she was forty and I was a fool, I knew at once she was a woman who could be trusted. To this day I do not know what made me so certain, for I knew little enough of women and I had never felt such confidence before, and only rarely since. She slipped out a gloved hand.

'Then you must let me introduce myself to Our Man in Venice' (I admit to preening a little at that). 'Jane Carlyle' – and for an instant I had a vision of the sad woman who had married that horrible mad old Scotch writer of political romances, which faded as she turned to her companion. 'And this is John Younghusband,' – the faintest of pauses – 'a cousin of mine.'

I introduced myself, and suddenly the train seemed to be on water, the thin spit of land between the rails seemed to disappear from view, and we were in the back waters of Venice, calm and blue, reflecting a light I fell in love with then and there; the first time, I believe, I fell in love with anything in all my life. It is only now that I know enough to be able to warn young men to be wary of anything they do, or say, or most of all feel, when they fall into the company of that most unlikely of things to the English mind, an interesting woman.

The waters were studded with little fishing boats piled high with nets, some of them moored to rickety poles, and in the water first we caught sight of the workaday face of Venice, the barely adorned brick she presents to what was once her land-bound empire, a plain and practical face, reflective of the mercenary mind which paid for all the decorations she faces to the sea. Then steam and smoke and smuts flew backward, and we were there.

The next few minutes was the habitual tangle of porters and hoteliers, noise and confusion, but soon we were disembarked and Younghusband had flagged down the representative of their hotel. Mrs Carlyle turned to me and I suddenly felt ridiculously young and self-conscious, uncertain what to say or do.

'I must say good-bye.' She smiled again, and I smiled back, foolishly. 'We stay at the Schifanoia. They always send a boat to meet the train. They are ready now, I think. Shall we meet again? Soon?'

'I should like that very much.'

'Then you must call on me, as soon as you may. It is the least a lady should be able to expect from our Consul.' Then with a wave and a laugh she turned and was gone, into the crowd and the noise and the light. Even now, reflecting on the time, I remember how I felt just then, and sympathise, for it is only the young and the old, whatever anyone may say, who honestly feel their age. I looked to my bags and a porter.

I suppose I had half expected to be met by our Consul, Arthur Howard, but I had not counted on the rigidity of the hierarchy of the diplomatic corps. I was approached by a stocky Italian of middling height dressed in some indeterminate uniform.

'Signor Burnham?' he enquired, aspirating the H.

'Indeed.'

'Welcome, signore. Signor Howard sent me to greet you. This way please.'

I followed him out into the broad piazza in front of the station, and saw my first canal. Arthur Howard had the answer to it, for Enrico (he did not volunteer his name; I was told it by Arthur) ushered me towards one of the neatest, and earliest, motor-boats I had ever seen, the *Queen Mary*. Whatever else you said about the venerable Howard, and I said more than my share in my time, you had to admit that he had style, an immeasurable advantage in any national representative overseas.

The Consulate then as now was a heavily ivied palazzo hard by the Accademia, and Arthur lived above the shop. My first meeting with him was not easy. No one's ever was.

I had been warned about Howard in London. He had made a

13

career out of Venice and out of despising the inhabitants of mainland Italy. A man of some considerable means and a noted dilettante, it was rumoured that he had been removed from England to hush up a scandal involving the English vice and one of the younger sons of the old Queen. To any who knew him that story seemed preposterous, but in any case he had made Venice his own. He hated the assistants who were sent out to support him only a little less than the English visitors who made occasional demands on his time, and the Foreign Office, which he accused of incompetence and megalomania bordering on treason. He was already in his middle sixties when I knew him, and remained a Victorian, indeed a Gladstone liberal, to the end. He stood for the integrity of England, independence for small nations, and against the arrogance of Empire. He was a man born both before and after his time, but we could not know that then. Nonetheless, he looked the very picture of an Englishman of the previous century, and wore a frock coat every day, imposing himself on his territory and the Foreign Office through a combination of fear of his temper, respect for his virtues and bewilderment at a string of verbal mannerisms he had picked up who knows where.

He did not take the hand I offered him in his office on the mezzanine looking down over the noisy waters of the Grand Canal and the traffic of the Accademia bridge.

'Now look yourself here, Mr Burnham, it will be no secret to you I don't have much time for the fools those scoundrels at the Foreign Office send out to me, but if you are careful there is no reason why we should not come to some tolerable arrangement. How much Italian do you have?'

'Not very much, sir. I did a short course . . .'

'Well, you had better set about learning it. The Consulate is only open to the general British public, may the God of Battles rot their mercenary souls, three mornings a week. I do not want you mooning about here the rest of the time getting in my way. You are to learn Italian and to get to know some Venetians. You had better travel also. I take it you have funds?' I nodded. 'Good. You will find that the Venetian, both the language and the people, are very different from Italian, but you had better get to know both. That way you might actually be some use to those ignorant bastards in Whitehall when you are recalled which, as far as I am concerned, had better come sooner than later.' He paused to take his breath and rest his malice a while. 'This job unfortunately entails a lot of being polite to a lot of damn fool visitors. You will do that job for me. British visitors used to make themselves known to the Consul. Very few do now, for which I am

14

grateful, but I have an arrangement with the local police whereby they supply me with the names of all Britons registering at hotels in the city. In future that list will be passed to you, to use as you see fit. When your Italian is good enough you can take over any dealings with the authorities that may arise when our visitors get into trouble. Until then, you will liaise through me, understood?'

'Yes, sir.'

'Good. I've arranged an apartment for you in a palazzo hard by the Ca D'Oro, Byron and Wagner country. It won't be ready until the weekend. Till then you had better stay here.'

'Sir.'

'And two more things, Burnham. I don't know why you were sent here but I would guess it is because you are an incompetent but well-connected imbecile. You were probably told that Venice was a soft haven. So it is, for your kind, and you will do me a great service by taking over the social duties of my job. What those clowns at the Foreign Office will not have told you is that any Italian posting is currently amongst the most important on offer in Europe. They won't have told you, because they don't know themselves, but keep your mouth shut and your eyes and ears open, and you might actually learn something here.'

I was used to that kind of thing, of course. It was the kind of encouraging remark every schoolmaster and don I had ever known was given to making. I discounted it accordingly and I am glad to this day I did, for I had already learnt, as Howard never could, that it is unwise to be interested, at least if you are a diplomat, and safest of all to be the entirely conventional man.

'The second thing is much simpler. For some reason our people despise Italian food and drink. Very foolish of them, as I hope you will discover. For some reason, however, none of them seem to be able to resist Italian sex which, I can assure you, is more style than substance and more sweat than either. Whatever you do, a little decorum and a lot of discretion would suit me very well.'

'Yes, sir.'

'One last thing, Burnham. I have a horrible suspicion you may not be entirely a fool. That would be alarming, for fools are very much easier to deal with. However, if you continue to restrict your conversation to Yes Sir for the next few weeks and keep your wits about you, I think we might just get along. I must admit I almost hope so. Now cut along.'

It is hard now to recapture precisely the atmosphere of those first few days in Venice; so many further memories have settled down above them, and they have all of them merged and fused. It is difficult to remember what I felt and when I felt it, for everything has rolled together until I have a tight knot of memory, apprehension and regret all bundled together and labelled Venice. The city has been with me all my adult life and is so much a part of me that I can no longer be certain of anything in our shared past, any more than we can be certain when remembering incidents in our childhood whether we remember them in fact, or only because in early youth we were constantly reminded of them by others who did, and through whom we assumed a memory.

Of some few things, however, I am sure. I know that I found it beautiful, which was perhaps more surprising then than it is now. We were fastidious souls, we English then, and though no great city is sweeter than the perfumes of Arabia, Venice smelled, as it still does, in a way that no other city I had known had ever done. The smell of other cities arises from smoke and sewage. The particular stench of Venice arises from water. In those early days I was always surprised to turn a corner and find a mooring-point in some cutting of a canal where the waters gathered and stagnated in a thick wet beard of scum, a green slug oozing over stone; but it is stirring, not standing, waters which give the city her characteristic odour, the sour ozone stink of all great harbours and the ever-present mouldering of fish and the oily shit of seabirds.

Even so, it was possible to live an altogether more aromatic existence. Most visitors headed directly for the hotels and sea-beaches of the Lido, the scrubbiest rich resort I know, for we had already begun that strange belief in the mystic healing and regenerative powers of the sun which has transformed the holidays of this century (although Americans in the south of France were only just introducing the sun-tan; to us it seemed the horrible indicator of a manual occupation). Hotels could arrange for you to visit the most celebrated monuments equipped with guide and guards, pomander and smelling salts, but the relatively few who did even that were eager to see only the 'curious' and 'charming', those two horrible adjectives which I have ever since believed are master sergeants in the Company of Death.

I, however, had the great good fortune both to live and work in the ancient, mercenary heart of the city, though in fact, I suppose, I worked as much on the Lido in that most dreary of diplomatic occupations, amusing your fellow citizens.

I have jumped ahead of myself again. I am speaking as though I was already one of the city's intimates. It took much longer than that. In my own bewildered way I set about taking Arthur Howard's advice. I set myself to learn the eccentric Venetian dialect, and read as much Italian as I could. Through all that time my most certain and faithful companions were Baedeker and a dictionary. I traversed the city, learning quickly how much one depended on the two bridges and access to boat stations and the primitive vaporetti which carried public traffic along and across the canals. I avoided using Enrico and the motor-boat, to force myself to learn my way about the city on foot, which undoubtedly pleased him and, in his silent way, pleased Arthur as well, I think. The inevitable consequence was that I found myself often and irretrievably lost, but even that was an excuse to try out my primitive Italian and to learn that a wealthy foreigner (all foreigners were wealthy; how else could they have afforded the fare to Venice?) was a fair touch everywhere.

It was that posting which first gave me my love of languages, for it seemed to me that as I put on a foreign tongue I put aside myself and became merely the voice of the weary traveller calling on the international convention of hospitality to strangers which I have, over the long years, come to see as the one guarantee of civilisation, and one of the few things we could be proud of if we stood in the dock of eternal judgement. I do not know whether it should be a matter of pride or not that I first read *The Merchant of Venice* in an Italian translation with my feet up at my desk at the Consulate, but it is a memory which gives me still a ridiculous degree of pleasure. It was spring of course, and I suppose that in a way I was falling in love with the idea of myself in Venice, as Byron, who would have been a neighbour, had done a century before, for falling in love is only a dramatic affection for an idea (but that is the wisdom, or at least the exhaustion, of age speaking). I have been told that Plato believed that only ideas were real, and that in considering those shadows of particular things we discover the truth. If that is what he believed, then he was, like every schoolmaster I have ever known, in crucial respects a fool. It would be better if we were all taught to love nothing too much, and love nothing at all which could not be packaged and parcelled in good, conventional words. I have never felt the frustration other linguists express at being lost in the nuances and subtlety of another language, for I have no wish to say anything except as simply and ordinarily as possible. As it is, I know too much English, and it betrays me. I was always happiest in the set patterns of diplomatic reports and correspondence, for all of us who use them know exactly what each formulation means, while now, alone and old, I find myself driven by

17

memory and the memory of desire through the channels of language and find myself saying more than I mean.

This is meant to be a report on experience, so I must go back to where I was, trawling through the emptiness of age, into my first few days of duty. On the Tuesday, the day after my arrival and an open day at the Consulate (no one came), in the late morning, Arthur handed me the police list of Britons registered at Venetian hotels. The hotels were listed by class (quite properly from our point of view, for it meant that the richer citizens who stayed at the better hotels headed the list. It is not that we cared more for the rich, though we did, but that they had more power to complain back in England, and it was necessary to be seen to serve them well, when needed); right at the top of the list for Venice itself (the Lido was set out separately) stood the Schifanoia, and my fellow travellers. I went through to Howard to inform him I might visit them. His muttered response surprised me, who thought he had been locked away in Italy these thirty years, ignorant and careless of England and society.

'Carlyle? Carlyle? Jane Carter as was, you mean? Will Carter's daughter, of Derbyshire. Damn handsome girl as I recall. Married a fool.' At which he looked sourly across at me as though by reminding him of the husband I had somehow demonstrated the depths of my own stupidity. I half wanted to ask him more, especially of Young-husband, of whom he spoke not at all, but guessed it would be unwise to display an undiplomatic curiosity.

'Yes, of course you should call on her. Saves me from having to. Take the *Queen Mary*.' He paused for a moment, stroking his round furrowed cheeks. 'Find out how long she's staying. I'm more or less obliged to throw some sort of party to introduce you to the local bosses and the diplomatic corps, such as it is. Dreadful bad hats the most of them. Still, she may want to come.'

I sent Enrico over to the Schifanoia with a note. He returned the best part of an hour later with a reply. Somewhere amongst the appalling rummage haul of papers which my life has become, it must still exist, for I kept it, it seemed to me so stylish: a stiff cream paper with, in a strong, mannish hand, just a few words, without the chatter and whimsy I was used to in letters from girls of my own generation. 'Come to tea. Jane Carlyle.' We were impressed by little things in those long-distant days.

Three and a half hours later I stood in the bows of the *Queen Mary*, the sun and a sea breeze on my face and in my hair, the city spread out behind me like the enchanted panorama of a child's imaginings, feeling like one of those heroic fellows whose doings I had learnt in verse at school, like stout Cortes upon a peak in Darien or Horatius on the bridge, and looking, I would guess, much more like the horribly pious and stupid little boy who stood on the burning deck when all the rest had fled, churning across the waters of the lagoon towards the island of Giudecca and the hotel. For one breathtaking moment I turned round to see Enrico stiff and black against the city, and learnt a general truth; if you regard them as objects of pleasurable contemplation, cities of the sea are best seen from the quiet of their own harbour reaches (as New York is best seen not from the high Atlantic Ocean, but crossing her own domestic waters on the Staten Island Ferry) for such contemplations are the prerogative of the landsman. Sailors see no city like that; for them, all that matters is light, and comfort, and landfall, safe from the worrying storms and merciless sea. To sailors, every harbour is the same, and every city is home.

There was trouble when we docked at the Schifanoia, or rather did not dock, at once. The hotel launch was bobbing and wheeling in the water, kicking up a furious wash and spray, its screws screaming each time they lifted out of the water. Enrico hauled back on the throttle, holding us away from the confusion. On the landing jetty two men dressed in black, who looked to me entirely like nightclub bruisers, were creating tremendous argument, yelling and ranting in terrible fashion, whilst the captain of the launch yelled back what even then I could guess were the filthiest of obscenities. About a dozen well-dressed guests stood back from the fray while a doorman and a cut-away-coated assistant manager tried vainly to restore some kind of order. I turned to Enrico.

'Fascisti,' he muttered with glum satisfaction. I found myself staring. Mussolini's legions had marched on Rome the previous October, and he was now Prime Minister. I had not expected my first meeting with the shock-troops of the future to be quite like this.

'They say they are important people,' Enrico continued. 'They do not want to share the launch with the others. The captain is saying they are not even guests or guests of guests. Now he is saying that if they are so important they should walk across the water.'

At that point one of the fascists appeared to part company with his reason altogether, and turn into a frothing, sweating, raving instrument of mayhem. Looking back, I cannot understand how I had the gall to attempt what I did next. I have a vision of myself as the worst kind of parody English colonial servant, handing out justice with a firm but even hand to his ignorant and happy-go-lucky natives. I must have sounded appalling, and to myself in retrospect I look ridiculous,

19

but it must be said that, in the past, national empires and reputations have been won and maintained by less, and less worthy things, than boundless youthful confidence and a public school manner.

'I say,' I called out, 'I say, does any of you chaps speak English?'

For an instant the under-manager looked up, relieved to be distracted from the chaos which surrounded him. 'Yes, signore. I do. Be patient, please.'

'Now look here, I am the British Assistant Consul.'

The under-manager let out something between a high-pitched squeak of outrage and disbelief, which I took to be a translation, and for an instant they all actually stopped to stare at me. I do not know whether they were motivated more by incredulity, respect or simple mirth, but they stopped.

'If these gentlemen wish to travel alone, I am visiting guests at the hotel, and I will happily arrange for my launch to take them where they wish.'

There was another high pitched jabber from the under-manager, while I stood anxious and Enrico stony-faced, but at last the fascists understood the offer and regained their composure, eyeing the lines of the *Queen Mary* and the ensign at her bow. The under-manager conveyed their thanks and one of them ducked his head as though to say, 'There. This is someone who knows how to treat us.' I instructed Enrico to be back at five o'clock and to be prepared to wait, and stepped ashore to the voluble, unctuous thanks of the under-manager, convinced I had achieved my first diplomatic triumph.

I stepped ashore to the shy, admiring glances of the ladies and the frank, manly approval of their escorts and I must admit that for a while I felt the devil of a fellow. (It is strange how, even now, my retrospective embarrassment and wonder are tinged with the sense of a lift in my step and a jaunty grin of pride. Perhaps it only means that now, at last, I find that nothing is lost, nor even changed, and that in the quiet avenues to death the past is uncovered of the business and noisiness which buried it in middle age.) I asked for, and was shown up to, Mrs Carlyle's suite. In these easier and simpler days there will be few who remember the swift erotic tang that word once tasted of. Suites spoke not only of wealth (and little is more sensual than luxury) but were also the only accommodation respectable hotels would allow the unrelated or the unmarried to share. The masquerade of separate bedrooms, maid's and valet's rooms and drawing room, preserved an illusion of chastity, and no one complained at the bills, for ours was above all other things the pre-eminent age of illusion.

I was met at the door by a maid. Behind her I could see a high white drawing room (I know that height was the result of the absence of central heating and air conditioning – fuel was cheap, and height kept them cool in summer – but the lowness of modern ceilings seems to me yet one more emblem of the cramped, confining times which you, the young, inhabit). The windows were open and a breeze was lifting the curtains, but the window-bay stood empty, as though she should be there.

The maid showed me in and slipped into one of the bedrooms from which, a few minutes later, Jane emerged. Her hair looked as though she had just pinned it up in a hurry, and a single seductive curl fell loose against her temple. Her cheeks were red beneath her powder and it seemed to me she had been crying. I was so young that my reaction was neither outrage ('That brute Younghusband!') nor to dismiss the matter from my mind, but shame, as though in some way I were guilty, and involved, and had hurt her in some hidden past which had been kept from me till now, when it came out to haunt me. The smug self-satisfaction withered within me, with all the light phrases I had planned to deprecate in recounting my triumph on the jetty.

She was, however, as I said, a woman who could be trusted, and took the chair which stood before the window. The light flowed in, silhouetting her, transforming her into a creature of the dark, evening her features and cancelling the details which had so disturbed me.

'Thank you for coming to call on us so quickly. You must be very busy so soon after your arrival.'

'Not at all, not at all. I think that that was why I was sent here.'

She laughed the clear, quiet laugh of a grown and confident woman, and if I had not been charmed already I should have been so then, for it was an age when the only feminine laughter a gentleman heard was the polite insipid amusement of women refined to the point of inanition, or the mindless titter of silly girls who had been taught that giggling was fetching and that they must show off their teeth.

'I cannot believe that at all,' (and neither, for a moment, could I). 'It is much too enticing an appointment for that to be true. Why, the corridors of the Foreign Office must be filled with young gentlemen weeping with envy at your good fortune. If they had wanted to be rid of you I dare say you would be posted now to Port Said or Lhasa.'

I remembered at last where I had heard the name Younghusband before. 'Forgive me for asking, Mrs Carlyle, but is Mr Younghusband any relation of the Hero of Thibet?'

'You sound like a popular journalist, Mr Burnham! But yes, he is. A distant cousin. Half of England seem to be my distant cousins. I am

21

afraid that he is out just now. Perhaps we should start without him.'

She rang for tea and then leant forward, conspiratorially. 'Another little matter, Mr Burnham. Consider it part of your consular duty. You must call me Jane.' I dare say I looked doubtful, even alarmed, perhaps. 'I know that I am just old enough to be your mother, but I would rather not remind myself of that sombre fact. So you must call me Jane, and I shall call you Mr Burnham, which will make me feel still younger.'

I cannot remember what we spoke of in any detail that afternoon, but I remember the light failing and the darkness gathering as though it were drawn to her, until we were gathered like gems in a velvet cloth, and the distant chatter in the gardens, and the scarcely audible mournful shriek of gulls, and the faintest smell of the sea. I passed on Howard's stilted invitation and she accepted, seeming genuinely pleased. Of course I included her absent companion, though I silently cursed the arrogant young prig. (Such is the boundless confidence of youth, which does not know how others see it – which is still to be preferred to the heedless egotism of age, which does not care.) At last day drew to its end, and I prepared to go.

'I hope I shall see you again, Mr Burnham, and soon. Where are you living now? We should call on you, I think.'

How could I refuse her, and why should I want to? I suddenly felt grand, and severe, and sad, to be receiving guests in my own name, in another people's country. 'I am staying at the Consulate at the moment, but I move into an apartment by the Ca D'Oro on Saturday. I haven't seen it yet, but perhaps you could come with me to advise what I should do with it? I know so little about decoration.'

She smiled, and agreed. 'I should like that very much, but' – I was afraid for a moment that knave Younghusband was about to spoil her for me once again. I was wrong – 'I am entertaining a friend of mine that day. She has been in Venice alone a little while now. Would you mind so awfully if I brought her with me?'

I was too relieved to feel any disappointment. 'Not at all, that would be charming. What time would suit you? Shall we meet at the Consulate?'

'No. I have it. Meet us at eleven, or let us say ten-thirty, on the Rialto bridge.'

I left her standing in the window-bay, the pale grey silk of her dress still shining on the edges of evening.

Enrico informed me that the fascists had only wanted to be transferred to St Mark's Square. 'They wanted to make a big show. They wanted me to make a big splash on the seashore. I made them their big splash. I did not mind. But Signor Howard, he would not like it. Signor Howard says, in England, men who are right do not need to shout. I do not think there are many Italians in England.'

We moored at the Consulate, and I thought no more of the matter until it was time to dine with Howard. Instead, I spent an hour or so half-conscious over an Italian Grammar, boning up relative clauses and recalling the choky oppressive heat of my old schoolroom, spring in St James's Park and Easters at home at the cathedral; but even then I think I knew the country that I served and loved was leaving me behind.

Dinner with Howard was an entirely silent affair that evening. He did not even respond when I mentioned that Mrs Carlyle had accepted his invitation. Silence sat triumphant, like a monkey on a stick, until at last, dessert cleared away, he poured us both brandies and beckoned me to an easy chair. He tugged on his cigar uncertainly and, as he did so, although I had been alternately peeved by and thoughtless of his silence at dinner, putting it down as one of his legendary eccentricities, it occurred to me that what faced me was a tired and disappointed old man: a man who believed that, in some obscure fashion, he had entirely wasted his life.

'Burnham,' he began quietly, 'I am assuming that you are a fool; a fool, moreover, who probably has very little malice in him. That is the only reason you are not already on a train back to London.' Even by the standards of all the authorities I had ever known, each a prince in his own petty tyranny, this was a splendid opening and I admit I was alarmed. 'However,' he continued, 'I am also, the Lord of Battles alone knows why, assuming that you are not a complete fool, and may therefore stumble in time upon a little knowledge, though less likely wisdom. That is the only reason I will not ask you to pack your bags in the morning.'

He paused and tugged on his cigar again. I felt very small, and still feel small in memory, though now I can also admire the man's consummate technique (I have used it myself since then). 'Today you allowed the *Queen Mary* to be used by fascisti. I am not interested in the circumstances, however extenuating. Over the next couple of weeks I want you to settle into your apartment, to watch the world around you, and to read the newspapers. Thereafter we shall begin your political education. But whatever happens, I do not want today's events repeated. If they are I will have you back in London before you can wipe your arse. Good-day.'

He wheeled and left. To be honest, at the time I thought he had over-reacted, and I still do, but Arthur Howard was his own worst

23

enemy, for what in the world is the world supposed to do, and especially the necessarily mendacious world of diplomacy, when it finds itself faced by an honest man?

It was late when Arthur Howard retired that evening. I could not sleep, and sat on the balcony of the mezzanine drawing-room drinking my brandy and drawing on my cigar. It was a moonless night, and the garden and the city before me lay wrapped in blackness. In darkness even sound transforms its outlines, shifts its shape. I could barely hear the canal below me, folding and sliding its waters and slapping them softly against the city's embankments. Yet far away the bells of distant churches chimed sonorous and deep a music thick and warm as port or taffeta. At the edges of vision an occasional light still glowed in other drawing-rooms, but only heightened the stillness and sense of solitude. It is not that I was unhappy, I think, though memory is strange, so much as puzzled. I was young, you see, and inexperienced in my business, but the day had seemed a day of quiet triumph and achievement, and I could not understand the savagery of Arthur's treatment of me. I know now, of course, that he treated me more gently than any assistant before me; but then I had no point of comparison, nor could I know the growing desperation which drove him remorselessly, savaging as he went, as every attempt he made to make his colleagues understand was dissipated in polite withdrawal and knowing shrugs.

One thing again and again came back to baffle me. How was I supposed to do my job, and how did Howard ever do his, if I had to reject the simplest charitable social dealings with the fascists who now formed Italy's government? I could understand his disapproval, though in London the fascists were treated as a ridiculous aberration, figures from a comic opera who would soon be tamed, or bought, by the country's traditional establishment; but I knew even then that it is not the business of a diplomat to draw fine moral distinctions, but to serve the interests of his country. More than any other job I know (I have never mixed with tradesmen), diplomacy forces one to live in the real world of actual, substantial power. That suited me very well, for I have always distrusted the grand, heroic gesture and I do not know that I, with any certainty, can judge between right and wrong. I have always been happiest working with the world just as I found it, attempting to move forward slowly to small but certain, definite ends.

If such an attitude seems unromantic now, you must remember I was a creature of my time and class. Ours was a smaller world, and

24

we knew its wheels and motions; where to tinker, when to leave alone; nor did we have to face the torment of the modern diplomat in an age of wireless and television, when every statement, comment, action is reported at once to an eager audience at home, all shrieking for moral rectitude or shows of strength. It is the most appalling handicap, for few people, and certainly not the voting masses of modern democracies, have ever realised, or liked, or been able to endure the melancholy fact that in their international relations nations behave like gangsters, gamblers and whores, all of whom work safest in secrecy. I would not want a free and domineering press to broadcast my poker-hand to my opponents; and lovers, gamblers, perverts, hoods, none of them could endure a Freedom of Information Act.

I must sound cynical and sour, but it is not now the weary defeat of age which writes, for I knew this even then, and my doubt and confusion with Arthur Howard arose from the fact that he seemed not to. He, of course, was a creature of an earlier generation which could afford displays of moral virtue, for whatever the Company of Saints might say there always stood hard by them men who would not hesitate to use their guns, and gun-boats. It is, as others before them had more consciously discovered, a powerful combination – guns and patter. We, also, when we were young, had other, stronger, contingent reasons for facing the realities of power, which is the world, for we had seen our elder brothers shot to hell in France for windy phrases and empty intents, only to see the statesmen of Europe sit down at Versailles to tell the truth about their objects in that worst of wars. They were as they had always been – power, influence, money. We saw well how the world worked then, and set about to work it well.

Still I could not sleep, and no book could console me. I would like to paint a portrait of myself, a young romantic caught in the vivid coils of experience, musing on power and love, but that would not be true. My mind was vacant as a mob that night, and if I could not sleep it was, I think, at least as much because the schoolboy in me still saw all the world as an examination chamber (and feared that I had flunked a test), as any sense of hope or high adventure, still less outrage at my Consul's strange behaviour.

At last I rose and changed my clothes, hopeless of sleep, and set out for a walk. It must have been past two o'clock and it is not a thing that I would care to do in this unspeakable old age – to walk when the just are sleeping the darkened streets of an unknown city, well-dressed and affluent and inviting attack – but the young have a confidence the old only dream of, and do not pause for fear in circumstances which make fear itself seem bold beyond the point of wisdom.

Even now, when memory unravels with appalling singleness and clarity the slightest windings of the past, I do not know exactly where I walked that night. I have tried to retrace my steps, without success, for Venice is a city of shadows and alleys and sudden, unlikely courts which can, in life as dream, seem all the same at once, though every turn and path is different.

I know, my mind a blank, I spent long minutes watching water lapping in a little courtyard built around a drowsy square of water. Steps led in and out of its two angles and a balcony hung over its three sides, beneath which I stood in deeper shadow, a darkness in a darkness in the night; but no light came out on that balcony to snatch the oily waters into fire, no midnight-walking beauty to inspire a sonnet or a life.

In the last and sharpest darkness of the night I found myself a tiny bar, somewhere to the backward of the city, its light too garish and its patrons more than half asleep – loafers, scoundrels, vagabonds, knaves, and the one obligatory whore, grown old in her profession, her hair bleached out to a metallic radiance, her skin dried out like ageing cheese and her mouth a gash of bright, unlikely pink. I stumbled back out into darkness, half absent in my mind myself, and let my feet walk where they would. How they led me on the path they did is something I shall never know, but I am glad they did, for unromantic though I am I still have eyes to see.

I found myself at one end of the Rialto, the hooded bridge still curling into darkness, the rubbish floating and unfurling in the low unearthly wind which troubles those few inches just above the earth at dawn, and felt, instead of saw, a lightness coming in the sky; and I began to run, as I had not in years, without a thought in mind, alive and shaking weariness away, ran filled with simple pleasure at the coming dawn and living, running with youth out into a future I could not and would not ever understand. The few sad figures shifting out to work ignored me; for them the dawn was silence filled with knowledge of a day alive with heat and labour, but I knew only where my feet were leading, ducking and weaving and turning, turning always to face that glimmer, turning to meet the dawn until at last, before I had expected it, breathless, surprised at my surprise, I stood there where an empty mind had led me, before San Marco, in the place of dreams.

The Piazza still stood darkened. The light now showed through half the eastern sky as though a silk lay over it, and it was time before I realised that light would come before the dawn, because the basilica stood before the rising sun which would illuminate the sky before it rose above the swooping oriental rooftops of the church. I waited, not knowing what to expect. The glad battalions of pigeons had begun to stir, but idly, lifting and swaying, well aware that only day would bring the people out and the first prospects of a meal. In the colonnades on either side of me sweepers were shifting the litter from place to place, heedless of one mad Englishman up to see a time of day when proper visitors and people with their senses still about them still lay safe abed. The only excuse for early rising is work, except when we are young, or old, when fear of time and death makes night a torment and every further waking hour an agonising gift.

The light seeped slowly westward until the sky was one blue haze, the tender moment of the day when all the world seems perfect however terrible we know it all to be. Then at last the sky behind San Marco began to whiten, the way that skin does when you press it, and more than any church I had ever seen the basilica seemed built for display, the final vista of a square built as a stage set to show off the power of an empire long since vanished. I was too young to wonder then how later ages glory in those monuments the past leaves for them which had been most extravagant when the past was now, and monuments meant taxes and bankrupt treasuries.

Then I saw them, smaller than I had expected, against that wild, extravagant façade – four horses cast in bronze when God and the world were young, brought westward stage by stage by conqueror after conqueror, until at last they rested here as emblems of the city's wide dominion over all the waters of the east of the Middle Sea, waters which bore the traffic of the East to Europe for longer years than we remember, traffic which had drawn these horses with it, as they seemed now to draw the sun.

I had not realised, and no one had warned me (for who goes seeing sights at dawn?), how cunningly down the years the grand and terrible old men who governed the One Republic had created the eastern, unapologetic church which was the emblem of their state, trading from early years with Antioch, Ephesus, all of Asia, and Jerusalem, owing no dominion to the mighty tyranny of Rome; for here in the building which contained a slab on which was carved, in medieval Latin, the city's proudest boast – 'Here lies the body of Mark, the Evangelist' (and where, the city fathers asked, in Rome could anyone show you Peter?) – they had produced a ship, an

27

argosy, its domes the bulging sails, to accompany each dawn, in silent confidence, the rising sun, the guarantor of gold.

It was day, and light caught all the gilded, coppered, brazen surfaces of the basilica, till they were also fire, and black against them stood four horses. They are not grand, those horses. They do not rear in fierce exultation. They were cast by an early technology, standing three-square on the ground with one foreleg raised, and in the mad riot of that spectacle at dawn it is their easiness, their small dark simplicity, which makes the eyes turn away from all their cloud of witness of fire and light, and see them for what they are, the oldest things of man in that old city, five thousand years and more some say, cast far to the East in the early youth of man, and say, as I said then, not knowing what I meant (I still do not, although I know that what I said was, in some extraordinary way, the simple truth), 'These are the Horses of the Sun'.

Memory betrays us. Memory betrays our will. I had not expected when I began this account, intending to fill it with the fruits of experience, that the experiences which memory would cast up on the dusty shore of age would be so personal or so devoid of importance. I had not meant to write about myself, but about the world which made our generation and which we, in our way, re-made. I had hoped to trace events in which, although I witnessed them, what mattered was the image of the time they gave, for it is events which matter, not people, and what an individual felt or saw remains without significance. Now, however, writing, I find myself bound up in every tale I have to tell. It goes against my training, which was always to remove the personal, idiosyncratic point of view, and to generalise from fact and not opinion. I do not know how I shall sever these random individual weaknesses of age, but I must try.

The days which followed Arthur's warning were strange and artificially hectic ones. I wanted to stay out of his way as much as possible until such time as he decided to take me back into his confidence and put in hand my training. Fortunately, that was easily done. I simply took it upon myself to visit every Briton staying at a first-class hotel. The consequences of these social calls from someone so apparently grand as the British Assistant Consul can easily be imagined. I was invited everywhere, though looking back I suspect it was as much because people grew bored with their holiday companions and eager for novelty, as for any charm or rank I then possessed. Those heady days of early spring are indistinct still in my mind as they were when I lived them. Picnic and party merge into one

28

another, as do all the gamblers, idlers and invalids whose presence entertained me. To be sure, I sometimes felt guilty that, although I read the Italian newspapers, I had not followed Howard's advice by getting to know some Italians, but he introduced me to none at this time, and I was young and unused to importuning foreigners, except in Paris and then without a thought of conversation. So time slid by in that first fortnight in a haze of laughter, light and entertainment. It must be at one of those indeterminate luncheons, dinners, picnics, suppers, teas that I first came across the figure who has shadowed my recollection since I began this memoir, but I cannot remember quite and must restore him to the darkness until due time.

Two other things occurred during that short interval. One of them began to transform my career and, though I could not know it then, changed Arthur Howard's also. The other very nearly transformed my life. I wrote to Rome; and Jane Carlyle, that Saturday, looked over my new flat.

What news on the Rialto? I stood on the brow of the bridge, the morning traffickers forcing their way past me, my hands on my pockets and my heart in my mouth. I was examining the keys for the tenth time that morning when, lunged into by a trader, I checked for my money-belt and looked up at once, and caught my first sight of them, two silk hats swaying amongst uncovered Italians. I saw Jane first (I suppose because I knew her) with a look of self-mocking alarm on her face at the thickness of the crowd – and of its smell, if I am honest – until she caught sight of me and stretched out a long gloved hand. She reached out and kissed me impulsively on the cheek in the European manner, and made a fervent European of me. I dare say that I blushed, for she smiled, her eyes screwed up against the sun.

'Mr Burnham! How lovely to see you. You look quite the thing!' (I was wearing my first linen suit, and none has seemed so well-cut since.) 'I'm sorry we're late. Such a struggle to get here. Let me introduce . . .'

But I had already turned, and for an instant I was lost. I remember how she looked exactly to this day: a small, regular, almost mannish face, her dark blonde hair bobbed beneath a cream silk cloche, no weakness in her face, and the strangest pale grey eyes that I had ever seen, clear and nonetheless a little clouded over, as though she were secluded from the world. She smiled slightly, but not at me or anything about us, absently almost, as though at some enchanted garden of her own, high-walled against the world, where none could follow her. She wore the simplest of frocks, in cream again, with little flowers scattered on it, in embroidery, I suppose, and I know she wore a little string of pearls for at that instant one of the thieves who work the bridge must have tugged at it and snapped the string, and suddenly they cascaded, all three of us scrabbling to retrieve them in the cobbles and our clothes. I remember a little shriek and giggles, but I cannot remember from which of us they came, but I know at last she laid her small hand on my sleeve and said, in a lightly accented voice, an accent I could not place, her strange grey eyes transfixing mine, 'Please do not trouble now. This is enough. It is nothing at all.'

I could say nothing, but Jane could be trusted, and brushed away silence with a smile and, 'Quite an entrance. You have him captivated, I think.' (This last said without harm or malice. I do not think that sad, delightful woman was capable of anything so petty.) 'Jeremy Burnham, Eva van Woerden.' I wanted to sing.

I had bought them each lace handkerchiefs in one of the shops on the bridge, and presented them as elegantly as I knew how. (It was a long time later that I learnt to buy the paper bags from shops on the Rialto, printed with their address and a picture of the bridge, and to use them to package handkerchiefs at least as good, bought elsewhere in the city, but cheaper. I was a gentleman, those many years ago, as well as seeming one.) We walked on towards my building (nervous, I had inked in the route on the map in my guide-book) as Jane explained her friend, of whom I caught the shyest glimpses as I looked at Jane.

'Eva, as a man of your intelligence and experience in the Foreign Office will have gathered, is Dutch. Her father was a friend of my father ...'

'William Carter, as I recall, of Derbyshire ...'

She looked impressed. 'Do you know Derbyshire, then, Mr Burnham? You are full of surprises.'

I admitted my source was Howard, and apologised for my deception. 'That would make sense, of course,' she continued, 'Arthur Howard taught my father at Oxford.' She must have caught my puzzled look. 'You didn't know? Arthur Howard was a Prize Fellow of All Souls and, according to Father, the most wasted mind of his generation. But my father was given to strong opinions. As I was saying, Eva is Dutch. She has not been too well of late, have you my dear?' I looked, and felt, sympathetic, 'So her doctors have suggested the Mediterranean air. Eva, quite rightly in my opinion, chose to come here, rather than to brave the horrid, horrid English in Monte Carlo or Cannes.' She smiled again. 'I thought she needed younger company so, as you are not so entirely horrid, I thought I would risk introducing her to you.'

'And I am charmed.'

'There you are, you see, my dear. I told you you had him captivated, I own I am really quite jealous. Forgive me, Mr Burnham, but are we lost?'

'Not at all,' I replied, with more confidence than I felt. 'We turn left here, then left again.'

She led us forward, and at the second turn we came into a street interrupted rather than divided, down its length by a narrow strip of water more sewer than canal. Jane crinkled her nose. 'Oh dear.'

I stared at my map in embarrassment and uncertainty. 'It doesn't look too healthy, I must admit. Perhaps the house is better. It ought to be around here somewhere.'

Eva had gone forward and was looking into a tiny gap between two buildings, scarcely broad enough for a man to walk down. 'Is this the place?' she asked without hope. I went along the alley with the two of them trailing me. After a little way it turned to the right and in the corner, on the left, was a plain wrought iron gate. I looked through. There was a garden beyond. Jane reached past me and pushed at the gate, which creaked a little ajar. There was an old woman within in the customary black, herself all bleached and wrinkled as though she had spent a lifetime stewing in her own juices, like a prune. She stared at us silently. I did not know what to say but Jane began to speak, to my surprise in what sounded like fluent Italian. I recognised Howard's name and my own, and suddenly the old woman beamed and put aside the broom on which she leaned and began to jabber back in Venetian. 'Oh dear, oh dear,' said Jane, straining at the accent, 'this is going to prove harder than I thought'; but the old woman looked her up and down, then Eva, then me, muttered something I assume was coarse – for for the first time ever I saw Jane blush (I write 'ever'; it was the third time we had met. How quickly the young assume the world) – poked me in the ribs and put her hands out for the keys and let us in to the flat (I did not notice straightaway that Eva remained in the garden).

The old woman led us into a hall that stretched the inconsiderable width of the building. Facing us were French doors which Jane threw open on to a little paved garden trimmed with privet hedges and with another wrought iron gate, but larger this time, straight out on to the Grand Canal.

'But this is charming!' breathed Jane. 'Quite, quite charming. Clever Arthur!'

31

We eventually established that the ground and first floors were mine, the uppermost being reserved for the absentee owners; that the old woman's name was inevitably Maria; and that Howard, far from having arranged the poky little garret of my imaginings, had found me, for what seemed a ludicrously small rent, two-thirds of a palazzo more fit for royalty in exile than for an Assistant Consul – or so it seemed to me. (In fact there were three large upper rooms, two lower ones, the hall, and the customary diminutive kitchen and bathroom – the latter with miraculously modern plumbing. I felt richer that morning than I have done in all my life since then.)

'Happy?' Jane asked, as we stood by the middle windows of the first floor looking out over the canal. I was about to reply when we were interrupted by Eva walking out of the wardrobe. She had taken off her hat and there was dust in her hair, and a little grimy blotch on her nose and on the shoulder, the left shoulder, of her frock.

'Look! How clever!' she cried as we stared at the unexpected apparition, 'There are stairs up from the wardrobe in the room below.' The old woman had dragged herself up after Eva and waved her hands and made strange gurgling sounds before she spoke.

'She says it's for the floods in winter. Very often the ground floors are flooded. This is the alternative route up to this floor.'

I asked Jane to ask Maria where she lived, and the old harridan looked at me as though I had taken leave of my senses, and taking me by the hand led me down into the kitchen and opened the pantry door. There was a bed roll on the floor. Maria pointed at it and grinned toothlessly. There was more mumbling and Jane interpreted: 'She says she sleeps here because it is so convenient. She says she is only supposed to keep the place clean, and that she goes home one weekend in six, but if you let her go one weekend in four and let her do the shopping, just give her the money, then she will cook for you as well. She says she brought up seven children and thirty-six grandchildren, four great-grandchildren and two husbands, may they rest in peace, so you can see how good a cook she is ... I think you had better surrender.'

I did, and all that was left was to sign the inventory. More mutterings revealed that Maria could not read the list herself but that she would be after me in any case if I were to damage a thing. At last she looked all three of us over again, chuckled crudely, and said that, if we had no objections, she would take the rest of the weekend off. Jane was firm: No, she must be back in time to cook the lunch on Sunday. Maria looked her up and down shrewdly and agreed. 'She says you are a lucky man.'

'Tell her I need all the friends I can find, with all my new-found responsibilities.'

The information was exchanged and Maria appraised us all again and fired out a parting comment as she left, a comment at which Jane gasped at first and then fell shrieking with laughter. (Some people think loud laughter is inelegant in a woman. I learnt that day they are wrong.) 'What did she say?' I asked, baffled. Jane turned to me, grinning.

'She says it is well you are a strong young man. She hopes your responsibilities do not break your back.'

I blushed.

Eva turned in the drawing-room door. 'The furniture is satisfactory, I think.' (Her English was formal, with traces of the schoolroom on it still. I wondered how old she was.) 'Very simple. You might want an easy chair, I suppose. The pictures are dreadful, however. You must let us help you to replace them, and to find some ornaments, perhaps.'

'I would be delighted.'

'And you must always use the water entrance, as was obviously intended. The landward one is altogether ...' She paused, pained. 'Charmless. Jane tells me the Consulate has its own launch. You must make arrangements with the driver. Is that what you call them?' I said I did not really know. 'That will impress Maria, as well. You must be a little firm with her or she will be away for every weekend, but otherwise she is very good, I think. And have her warn the local gondoliers her master may want transport at any hour. That will make her feel important, and that is always good.'

'And,' Jane interrupted, 'my dear Mr Burnham, we really must do something about your Italian. All you need is confidence and practice. Anyone who survived an English public school ought to be fit for anything. Eva's is very good. Better than mine, in fact. You should ask her to give you lessons.'

'That would be delightful.'

'That's settled then.'

'Do I have a say in the matter?'

'Of course you do, Eva. Just say yes.'

'Very well then. If you could endure me, Mr Burnham, I should be glad to give you lessons.' She laughed, and tossed her head with a proud and graceful movement I have never forgotten. I noticed the fine arch of her long neck, and the dark blonde hairs that stood up on it, giving it the finest haze, like a veil.

Jane patted her skirts. 'Well, Mr Burnham, as you have obviously failed to make any arrangements for lunch I suppose I shall have to do something myself. It is a little after twelve o'clock now. You two wait here. I shall be back when I am ready.' Despite my remonstrances and invitation to a restaurant, she was gone, half-waving, to the canal gate, and calling a gondola, and slipped away, out into the bright refractive mid-day waters.

'Jane did not warn me that her friend would be so charming.'

'You are very kind. I did not know that Consuls were so young.'

'I am only an Assistant Consul, and Venice is not the most important posting in the world.'

'The most beautiful, perhaps.'

'Now it is.'

'You are turning into an Italian already! I see I must be careful with you. You must remember, Mr Burnham ...'

'Jeremy.'

'You must remember, Jeremy, that I am only an innocent Dutch girl, new to the danger and excitement of your world. I am not used to meeting powerful, important people like British Consuls ...'

'I believe that you are teasing me.'

'Perhaps. Have I offended you?'

'I doubt that you could ever do so.'

'I promise you I could. You must be careful.'

'Careful of what?'

'Don't they teach you in the Foreign Office? Beware of mysterious foreigners. I thought that every diplomat was taught to be cold as ice, to keep them safe from Mata Haris.'

'Are you a Mata Hari?'

'I may be, in my way.'

'I cannot believe it, but if you are, then any meagre secrets I may have are yours.'

'Then tell me your secrets. Tell me all about yourself.'

So I did, as I had never done before. (I suppose I had never had to in the past. Everyone I knew or met knew of my people or the people whom they knew.) It was not till many years later that I realised how seductive that one question is, unleashing so many desires. There are few things men find so fascinating as themselves, and nothing more so than the opportunity of remaking themselves in speech, reshaping their past before a pretty audience. The only advice I have ever given young women in search of a fortune is to remain silent except to ask rich men to tell them everything about themselves. In my experience, attractive women are terribly practical about their looks and see them as a commodity, security against which they can trade, and when they fade it is as much a loss to them as the death of a prize bull to a farmer

34

or arson to a businessman. Men, however, are genuinely vain and think that fame and fortune are proper parts of them and not the accidents of birth and time and place. They can, and will be, lost in singing praises. I had not learnt these simple facts so long ago, however; one of the few real fruits of wisdom I have garnered from experience. Nor can I still believe that Eva tricked me when she asked me about myself. It may be that I still look back with eyes as filled with self-delusion as they were when I was young, but if the tears which followed through a lifetime may be trusted, I do not think so. This strange, conventional shade who sits writing against the dark and death, unlikely though it may seem to those of you who demand strong individuality, has been liked, as well as loved, and it is perhaps the greater honour. So I talked and she sat listening, her thin frock catching in the breeze alternately against and away from the contours of flesh, her grey eyes translucent as the sky, until the light against the water-gate thickened as a gondola moored hard by and Jane stepped from it, a basket on her arm.

'Are you two still in the garden? I had quite expected you to be in bed by now!'

Eva looked up alarmed, and shocked, I think. I must have done so too.

'Oh really, dear boy, there's no cause to look shocked. I didn't bring you both together for the good of my health, but what you do hereon is your affair entirely. Now, lunch!'

She smiled and passed it off, but I wished, as I wish now, wondering what difference it might have made, she had not strayed so closely on my secret thoughts.

She had bought early fruits, and sausage, and cheeses and some of the rough red wine of the Veneto region. 'Nothing much to win a prize in international fairs I'm afraid, but it should serve, in default of warning. Let me get some plates and glasses. Knives as well.' She rose and disappeared into the house. I turned to Eva, who sat composed but withdrawn.

'I'm sorry. I'm sure she doesn't mean the half of what she says.'

'You have nothing to be sorry for, and Jane means everything she says, as she has always done; but you and I need not concern ourselves with that.' She turned away, and I noticed how short her eyelashes were, almost stubby, and how much younger that made her seem. Her hands, too, set on strong and slender arms were rounded, like a child's. 'Let us not speak of it further.'

Jane returned and we began. It seemed a little strange at first (you must remember that in the age of servants eating was a much more

35

formal business than it has now become) but Jane Carlyle converted the world to her manners of proceeding; whatever she did seemed right, and in retrospect that meal has always seemed a part of the great unbending which Italy added to my education. I took advantage of her own indiscretion to ask after Younghusband. A sharp glance was her first response, but her voice was gentle. 'You don't like him, do you? Why, I wonder? Just the natural rivalry of young males in the spring? Don't be surprised. I should have been desolated if you had not found me just a little attractive, though not as handsome as some ... Or is it something else? Quite possibly. He isn't very bright, poor dear, and I think that he resents it, which, I have always thought, is a mark of the most profound stupidity. That doesn't answer your question, does it? Well, it will have to serve for now.'

Eva helped her clear away while I idled over a cigarette. The day had begun to turn and was drawing a shadow across the garden. I was surprised when they came out, already hatted and ready to go. Jane spoke.

'Have you two arranged your first Italian lesson yet?'

'Not yet.'

'I am also staying at the Schifanoia. Perhaps you could come on Monday, after lunch?'

'Monday then.'

'Oh and Mr Burnham, forgive a tiresome older woman, but could you invite me to lunch tomorrow, now that you are settled?'

'Come to lunch. Tomorrow. Noon.'

'I should be delighted.' She went to the gate, to the gondola she had kept waiting. 'San Marco. Vaporetto Schifanoia.' They stepped in, and I watched them drift away, bobbing on the still-bright water, almost indistinct against all that light, Mrs Carlyle and her dear, disturbing friend.

She was early. I had struggled with my dictionary and grammar for most of the evening to construct a sentence for Maria, to tell her I was expecting a guest, and she had seemed to understand, for money had changed hands. I forget exactly what we ate but I know it was my first Italian meal and that Arthur Howard was right. I enjoyed it. I also know it cannot have included spaghetti, for I would have remembered the embarrassment of trying to eat it elegantly before that kind, sardonic woman.

She came to her point quickly. 'I haven't seen much of Eva since her marriage, nearly three years ago. I thought you would want to know. I make it my business never to comment on other people's marriages, Mr Burnham. They are always inexplicable to outsiders and, like icebergs, most of them is submerged. I do not know if Eva's is happy and it is no business of mine or yours. I do know, however, that she is unhappy, and unwell, though what the cause of that is who can tell? She needs patience, and friendship and company. Whether she needs anything else or not, I cannot say. Yesterday I introduced you, I also embarrassed you. That was only to prevent either of you doing anything as stupid as falling in love simply for the sake of it, simply because you are young and in Venice, and were introduced by a fond and scandalous old woman. Anything that either of you do from now will be conscious, which is always to the good. All I would ask of you is two things. Be careful with her, Mr Burnham. She is still only twenty years of age, and younger in many ways than that, and is not well. In particular, do not grow over-possessive, for I intend her to meet as many suitable people as possible. The second thing is, do not enquire too closely about her past and background. I know that does not come so easily to the English, but she is – with every cause – a very private person, and I would not want her disturbed or alarmed. There. That is the end of my sermon.'

'Thank you for telling me all this.'

'Do you mind?'

'I don't know. She seems too young to be already married. Is he a brute? Is that why ...'

She waved a finger. 'No questions, I warned you. And even if I were prepared to make an answer, what way would I have of knowing? Very often the couple concerned have none.'

'Why did you tell me, then? I should have been happier in ignorance.'

'Because you would have pried, and I have told you I do not want that to happen. You are a fool, Mr Burnham. Most men are, though you are more amiable than most. Sometimes it is better to tell even fools the truth, to prevent them doing damage.'

'Is Younghusband a fool as well?'

'Good Lord! The biggest fool I know. My husband was a fool as well. Arthur may have told you ...'

'We are not so close as that.'

'The more fool you. I know about Howard. I know he is a joke in Whitehall. I know his strong opinions have left him stranded. I also know he is one of the few truly clever men I have met. Learn what you can but keep your counsel and you will gain both ways. But you were asking about Younghusband. Some people think I have always been unlucky, partnered by fools. They are wrong, of course. You can have no idea, Mr Burnham, how unpleasant life is for an intelligent woman. It is getting better now, but slowly. I have worked on the principle that foolish men can easily be led and controlled. They take up less of my energy and leave me free to be myself. Since my father and my husband died I have had means of my own. John Younghusband offers certain satisfactions – do not blush, Mr Burnham, and do not pout; I make no comment on you – without the outlay of too much intelligence. Clever men, on the other hand, are dangerous, demanding and generally disliked. They are also often poor, and though that matters less to me than once it did, I do not wish to become a charitable foundation. I can do that when I am dead. Ever since I realised the world was not so organised that I could live the life I wanted ...'

'What life was that?'

'Yours. Or rather Arthur Howard's.'

'A diplomat?'

She grinned. 'Not primarily, no. I will explain one day, I promise. All I wanted to say is that I have tried to organise my life so that it offers me certain considerable comforts and certain unexceptional pleasures. In the meantime, if my money and my age allow me sometimes to play the fairy godmother, I take the view it can do me little harm and may do others some benefit.'

'I do not think I understand you.'

'I do not imagine you do. I promise you, Mr Burnham, that I pray for only two things, whenever I pray at all, which is more rarely every year. I pray for a world where no one would need to understand me, and I pray for a world where Englishmen could learn to like women.'

'But I do like ...'

'No you do not, Mr Burnham. You like what you think women are, which is what you usually make them. The English know much about sex, though they are embarrassed to say so, next to nothing about love, and nothing at all about friendship, with women at least. Enjoy your lessons, Mr Burnham.'

Of the week that followed I remember only the silent disapproval of Arthur Howard, a confusion of visits and parties, and the rare stillness of my visits to Eva van Woerden. Her Italian was indeed remarkably fluent, especially in one so young. On that first Monday we spent most of our time in laughter as I tried to mask a grievous ignorance of the language beneath an accurate accent. (I have always been lucky in my ear for the rhythms and shapes of a language – its tune – for much will be forgiven you, I find, if you show you have actually listened attentively to native speakers and can sound a little convincing.) Our classes grew more serious every day, however, and I found myself more and yet more taken by her quiet gravity; a gravity I did not learn until much later grew from shyness and fear. She would not let me use any English in those first days together. Everything I wished to say had to be translated, however haltingly. I have ever afterwards been convinced this is the best and only way to learn to speak a language. That would not have been enough in time, though, for what do strangers have to say to each other when one of them has been forbidden to ask about the other and has, in any case, only a halting command of the language they share? Eva's answer to the problem was both simple and shrewd; she took me shopping, for prints and ornaments, and encouraged me to brave Maria's extraordinary accent to speak of food prices and cookery. It seemed to work, and I began to grow in confidence and to use the language as much as possible. Newspapers helped too, providing me with a basic standard to aim for and avoiding what has always been my fault in languages taught more formally – an over-elaborate, fussily educated speech. I even impressed Enrico, and thereby Arthur, by giving him his instructions in Italian, something which still had me wracked by minutes of nervous preparation with paper, pen and dictionary. I began ordering early-evening drinks in Florian's in Italian, to impress the wealthy riff-raff who gathered there, and I do not think I flatter myself if I say the new Assistant Consul soon came to be well known amongst the idle and affluent visitors on whom the modern city's wealth is built. In those post-war years, in a Europe whose currencies were mortally ill, there was always a floating population of people with too much money and too much time, drifting from city to city and country to country looking for amusement, a population which battened on and used the ancient itinerant communities of artists and scholars and diplomats. I suppose that even Jane and Eva, and I too, fell into this parasitic category, pumping out a minimum of money in strong and over-valued currencies in exchange for company and glitter, attempting to seduce bohemia and all too often succeeding.

I cannot remember exactly how I came to invite a dozen or so of my new acquaintances to drinks that Sunday afternoon, desperate, probably, to fill the city's one sleepy and undernourished time, the long narcotic hours between masses we did not attend. I cannot even remember most of their names though I suppose I could check my notebooks, if I cared, for a diplomat's life is filled with names and faces. I had thought I would come to write about them all, to add my marginal notes to the gossip which is history, but I find I do not care to now. The older I grow, the fewer people who fill my recollection, expanding into the space left by all those other wasted faces, names and unspeakable chattering tongues.

I set a table up in the garden out on to the Grand Canal, I remember, dressed in new-bought linen and laden with bottles and glasses. I know I invited Eva to lunch with me beforehand, and that Maria clucked about us approvingly. She told me then, perhaps for the very first time, that she had learnt Italian as a result of a love of opera, and that she had once aspired to be a singer. I asked her to sing to me that afternoon but she turned away from me, her small head heavy on that long and slender neck, and murmured it was foolishness and she had put aside such childish dreams. The memory of that day is filled with stillness, almost sadness, and I cannot have proved a very good host, for no detail remains to me of most of my guests. Like so much of that time, all that comes back to me is a diffuse awareness of light and warmth and a strange quiet pride in possession. I know that as the afternoon drew on I came out into the garden to find Jane Carlyle speaking urgently to John Younghusband.

'No, John, no. I will not have you spoiling Burnham's party. He is a clever and charming man, and you are to leave him alone.'

I wondered whom she meant, realising by now she could not possibly mean me. Before I had a chance to think any further she had turned her habitual smile upon me. I noticed how her face had aged as much as it was ever meant to do, the skin a little coarser than it must have been in youth, but otherwise the deep fixed lines and crow's-feet of her face were lines of laughter and the wry amusement with which she faced the world. If time had turned out differently she would have always been the same.

'You have been hiding from us, Mr Burnham. You must be careful, or I shall feel it my duty to warn the Foreign Office you have become a recluse. Come and support me. I was giving John a wigging for affecting these silly black shirts.'

Younghusband bristled. I should have mentioned before; he had taken to wearing the high-collared black shirt of a fascist.

'I must admit, now Mussolini says fascism isn't for export, I don't see much point in apeing his fashions. Useful in this climate, though, if you can't find a laundry.'

Jane smiled broadly and Younghusband turned on me, furious. 'When in Venice, Burnham ...'

'That has never seemed a very appropriate attitude to me. Not for an English gentleman.'

'Listen here, Burnham. Let me tell you something they won't teach you in your precious Foreign Office. I say these people have got the right ideas. We've had enough shilly-shallying these last few years. If our sort of people don't make a stand we're going to lose the fight for life. Life's a battle. Burnham, whatever the soft-hearts say, and if we don't keep the working man and the coloured races in their place, then we're done for. Thousands of years of civilisation gone to waste. Look at them! The world has always been ruled by the strong and it's up to us to prove we have the power and will to keep the others in their place. They would be nothing without us anyway. Leaders are what the superior races need, and Mussolini knows it.'

Jane stood half in shadow and her response was barely audible. 'You disgust me.'

'Oh really, my dear? That wasn't how you felt last night. Or have you forgotten?'

'I despise you, Younghusband.' She was quiet still, but quiet with rage, a terrible paleness in her cheeks. 'The only mind you have is between your legs, and even that is not as clever as you think. Don't touch me, sir! Either you amend your ridiculous behaviour or you leave me entirely.'

'Be careful, my dear Mrs Carlyle, or I might take you at your word, and where would the Merry Widow be then?'

He turned smartly and veered across the garden, looking more than a little drunk to me. Jane swayed suddenly and swooped in through the doors, off right into the drawing-room. I followed her, not certain what to say or do. She was crying.

'I'm sorry, Mr Burnham. I am truly sorry. Our behaviour was insufferable, brawling like guttersnipes ...' She paused, sucking at breath as tears rolled down her cheeks.

'Please don't, Mrs Carlyle. It was my fault for interfering. He's taken a bit more drink than is good for him ...'

'Why? Why are men so ridiculous? To take such absurd pride in the possession of an organ which is dwarfed by a donkey and made ridiculous by a whale? And why am I so weak? So foolish?'

I did not know what to say. All my upbringing taught me that Younghusband's behaviour had been unspeakable, but Jane's reaction had been to speak of terrible things, things we tried not even to think of in those days. To me, in my sheltered orderly world, strong in the ignorance of my youth, it was as though I had been forced to endure the squabbling of a zany and his whore, and all the public puritanism rose up inside me, rebelling and revolted, doing battle with friendship and real affection.

41

Jane wiped her face, with her fingers, like a working woman, trying to compose herself. 'You are shocked, I think, Mr Burnham, quite rightly. It was wrong of me to involve you. Quite despicable. How can you possibly forgive me?'

I was silent, not even daring to think.

'Come. Take me out, and I'll try to get him away from here.' She took me by the arm and placed her free hand over on my biceps, leaning in to me as though she needed all the support I could give her, and led me to the garden. At the doors I felt her stiffen; I realised why as I saw Younghusband swaying before Eva van Woerden and a man I knew only slightly. Younghusband's behaviour thereafter is the stuff of my nightmares, as it is of any diplomat's: a man out of control, without manners or thought for the feelings of others. In my case that apprehension was heightened by the previous scene and by the simple fact that, as a man as well as a diplomat, I have always found excess and immoderation intolerable. I cannot abide extremes, and nor, I think, can any ordinary man.

'Listen to this everyone! This funny chap here, pretending to know about pictures, trying to impress our little Eva. "You ought to see the Tiepolos in I Frari," he says. Gosh, just fancy that! I know your sort, don't you just bet I do. I'll give you Tiepolos. I know what you're after, you filthy animal . . .'

I tried to look imposing. I was certainly angry. 'That's enough, Younghusband.'

'What's got into you, Burnham? Drawn along in my lady's apron-strings, are you?'

'Shut up, John.' She was almost queenly in her rage, her colour heightened, as I had seen it that day at the Schifanoia.

'What's got into you, my dear? Englishmen not good enough for you?'

She slapped him, hard. I stepped between them and hissed in his ear, 'Get out, Younghusband, and sleep it off. I will not have my guests insulted.'

'What's got hold of you, Burnham? Can't you see what he was doing? Why are you defending him? Can't you see he's only a filthy, filthy, little Jew?'

Eva's companion spoke quietly, a broad, dark man with glittering eyes, 'Not filthy, Younghusband, nor so small . . .'

'Keep out of it, Jew . . .'

I stepped forward, meaning to take hold of Younghusband, but the other man lifted a hand to warn me back.

'Mr Younghusband is quite right. I am a Jew. I know my kind, and

42

his. I know the kind of weakling who drinks to give him strength. The kind of fool who likes to shout his shabby opinions out in public, and I assure you nothing he could say could possibly offend me.'

'Bastard!' Younghusband threw a wild punch the other fended, pushing out so Younghusband rocked backward.

'I know the kind who wear black shirts and talk of the battle of life. My kind have known about them for thousands of years. What is it you're waiting for this time? What saviour are you expecting, to rescue your stupidity?'

The gleam in his eyes was one of tolerant contempt. There seemed to be no anger in him. There was enough in Younghusband for both. He bellowed and let fly again. The other swayed, out of harm's way, and began to laugh, in loud ironic amusement at ignorance and rage. For a moment he seemed the calmest man I had ever seen, his composure infuriating Younghusband.

'Waiting here by Jordan River for a pigeon to perch on your head . . .'

Another attempted blow and he reached up and outwards, at the edge of balance.

'Telling all the world This is my son . . .' and then the laughter once again. The Englishman lunged forward. 'In whom I am well pleased!' As Younghusband came at him he launched himself into the air, still laughing, seeming to levitate, hovering in the bright blue air. Then he was gone, and all the outrage with him, lost in the dazzling breakage of the waters as he dived away, at home and free, Jane pulling Younghusband away, Eva and all the other guests stony-faced as sphinxes.

As he broke up through the waters and (even now it seems ridiculously assured) flagged down a passing, baffled gondola, he broke into our lives, unstoppably.

Yes. That is how I first remember him. His name was Anthony Manet.

TWO

I would like to be able to say that my chief reaction to Younghusband's outburst was one of outrage. In particular, outrage at his hatred of the Jew. That would, I know, be the acceptable, polite reaction now. It is not true to say it was mine. As much as anything, my reactions were a compact of embarrassment, amazement and an uneasy sense of stupidity. I had not realized Manet was a Jew. I felt I should have done, and was bewildered. So deep did the institution of anti-semitism run in my class in those days, that for some time after my feelings about him were confused. I felt in some obscure way that he must have been my guest on false pretences. It says something about how complete their disbarment was from any but trading or raffish society (including politics, of course), that I had only rarely encountered Jews. I expected them all to be a caricature of Shylock and Disraeli: ringleted and jewelled, with oily skins and high hook noses. I knew nothing of middle-European Jews and their entirely different cast of features. Only time taught me that Anthony would have been immediately recognisable to a German or Pole by racial characteristics.

He was a man of medium height, darker skinned than the average Anglo-Saxon (in those days, at least. Now in the summer, with the world's obsession for lying on beaches, the streets of London, Munich, Paris all seem filled to me with so many piccaninnies); but instead of the aquiline nose of legend his was long, straight, broad and fleshy. His hair may have curled, I suppose, but he brushed it straight back from his high forehead. (You have seen the kind of face a thousand times, in photographs of Einstein.) He was broader built than the average Jew, but the most striking thing about his physique only became apparent when he moved; he had a slight but very definite limp. I cannot describe his exact motion, but found it unnerving, for every second footfall came slightly later than expected. I am trying not to presume knowledge which came only later, for that would be to falsify the time (I am bound to falsify, I suppose, for I cannot entirely remove the weight of decades of later experience as I write, but I am trying, like a good public servant, to report without commentary). Nonetheless it

44

must have been quite early that he explained his peculiar gait to me.

'It disturbs some people, I know, but there is nothing further I can do to remedy it. I was born all out of kilter. When I was born, every tendon in the left side of my body, from the waist down, was a tangle, pulling me out of shape. It was a difficult birth, and my mother once told me I was born looking like a wrinkled banana. The fact that I can now stand straight, and walk, and swim, is the result of fourteen operations in my childhood and early youth to unravel the mess.'

There was a further aspect to the suspicion of Jews in my time. Somehow, we had come to believe that all Jews had evaded war service. That Anthony's physical disabilities had caused him to do so seemed only to justify that dark suspicion. I wondered sometimes why he was not dead, like my two eldest brothers. (He was twenty-eight when I first knew him, though all his life it would have been difficult to guess how old he was, until the very end, and then all guesses would have been wrong.) I am glad to be able to write, even after all these years, that his answer to such doubts, when it came, left me ashamed; I am not entirely a scoundrel.

'My family life is rather more eccentric than yours, Jeremy, for my family covers more nationalities than yours. There are few of us left now. Perhaps that is the price we pay for being scattered. Not only running other peoples' banks and parliaments, and being hated for it too, but also fighting other men's wars. Two of my Russian cousins died at Tannenberg. The others, and my uncle and aunt, we have not heard of since the Revolution, and though we can hope I also fear the worst. My father was an Alsatian Jew by birth, in his time both French and German, but most of his adult life he spent in Frankfurt, trading in commodities. My brother, three years older than me, died of trench-fever fighting for the Kaiser. My sister married a Dutch Jew, and I am glad to say lives safe and happy in Amsterdam even now. My mother was an English Jew, but for reasons of her own spent much of her time in Paris with her cousins there. All but two of their sons died fighting on the Western Front. The War was not a successful few years for our blood line. I am glad to say I got no nearer to the fighting than driving an ambulance in the summers of '15 and '16, on the French and German sides respectively (it depended on which of my parents I was visiting). I should also say, Jeremy, that if – the Lord forbid it – you should find yourself injured and I arrive in an ambulance, wave this particular Samaritan by, for you are less likely to die of your wounds, be they never so grievous, than you are to die of my driving.'

He did not tell me then (I think it was Jane who told me, later) that his parents were also dead, killed by the influenza epidemic of 1919. They were not good years to be a Manet.

He belonged to a type I fear we shall not see again, despite a recent easing of Western European borders. The strangest thing about our world (no, it was never ours, not we of the English upper middle classes – I should say that world) to those of you who come after, was that there developed for a while an international body of scholarly gentlemen, children of the wealth and apparent security (fractured by a few revolver shots at Sarajevo) of the late nineteenth century. Knowledge recognised no borders; it could usually, somehow, pay its way; and it did not suffer yet from the pompous professionalism, in love with aeroplanes and jargon, of latterday professors.

He had been schooled at the Lycée Louis-le-Grand in Paris. His first degree had been in history at Oxford (the University still had a proper faculty in those days, before being colonised by pygmies). He had taken his doctorate at Göttingen (only Prussians ever called him Dr Manet) and was now, as far as I could ever establish, loosely attached to the research staff of the Collège de France. If you were to ask me what he did, I am not sure how I could answer you. He belonged to the last great age of polymaths, who took all speculation and endeavour as the proper field of their enquiry. I know he spoke an alarming number of languages, and read their literatures for pleasure. On one occasion he explained how he came to be the most natural linguist I have ever known. 'When I was very small my parents lived in Paris, and at home I heard three languages. I never knew, when a sentence began, what language it would end in, so more or less since birth I have spoken English, French and German as mother-tongues, so languages have never frightened me. Anyway, I hate it when I cannot talk to people for a reason so stupid as ignorance. I just battle on until I have picked up the language. It seems to work.' Another time – I cannot remember why – he looked up from a book and muttered, 'This is really very tiresome. I must get round to learning Sanskrit.'

There was another factor as well, of course. One of the things most people hate about learning foreign tongues, myself included, is that in the early stages, with only a minimal command of speech, it is impossible not to sound as though you are very stupid. In a native, the competence you possess would be a certain mark of idiocy, and all of us hate seeming more foolish than we know we are. Anthony seemed to have no trace of that perpetual and sympathetic fear. It may have had something to do with the fact that he was the most obviously intelligent man I have ever met. He could lose a half or more of his apparent intellect in the traps and mazes of a new language and still come through as being more intelligent than almost anyone that you knew.

The reason for his presence in Venice, however, could not, in his terms, have been simpler. They became apparent at a luncheon party Jane gave a few days later, in apology and remorse. There were just the four of us present – Jane and Anthony, Eva van Woerden and I.

'It's quite straightforward. Really. I think. I have a client, a private collector in Dresden, who possesses what is thought to be a Veronese, a *Circumcision of the Infant Jesus*. It was bought authentically classified. Since then, however, some German scholars have cast doubt on its authenticity. Fortunately, my client is that rare thing amongst collectors, someone who is more interested in scholarly accuracy than in value. Though there is also the possibility that he might have to sue the dealer. He has asked me to validate, or expose, the attribution.'

'Who authenticated the painting in the first place?' Eva asked. A look halfway between distaste and pain crossed Anthony's face.

'Berenson.'

Even I had heard of the great American, who had more or less alone rescued the science of attribution from the realms of fraud and corruption. 'Well that should settle it, shouldn't it? No one alive knows more about Italian art than Berenson. If he says it's a Veronese, that's surely an end to it.'

Anthony rubbed a finger across the broad bridge of his nose, in what I was to come to recognise as a characteristic gesture. He still looked pained, choosing his words with care. 'Mr Berenson and I have had our disagreements in the past. It isn't very safe to say it, as well as being illegal, but I'm not altogether sure that all his recent attributions have been entirely unimpaired by financial interest. He is retained on a permanent basis by at least one major New York dealer to make attributions – an inevitable, but not entirely healthy practice. But leaving that aside, we disagree on fundamental grounds of methodology.'

'Oh dear,' said Jane, refilling our glasses (she had ordered the hired servants to wait without that afternoon), 'is this going to be terribly difficult to follow?'

Anthony grinned, boyishly. Almost to the end he had an almost childlike grin, a grin at once self-deprecatory and delighted in the things he cared about. 'I hope not. If it is, I'm doing something wrong. You see, Berenson begins and ends with paintings. He has a more complete knowledge of the styles and manners of the great figures of

Italian painting than anyone I know – greater perhaps than anyone since the great dealers and collectors of the seventeenth century. That kind of knowledge can be enormously useful. You can use it to say that a Virgin the colour of mud and drawn as though by a four-year-old is unlikely to be a Raphael. However, most of the great painters we're asked to identify ran studios. Their apprentices were trained in the master's style. Sometimes, often, more than one hand worked on a painting. Also, in middling works by middling masters it can be very hard to tell between an original and a really good fake. The Italians haven't lost their skill of hand and native cunning over the centuries – only their eyes.'

'So what do you do instead?' Eva asked, and I too interrupted:

'Yes, and what are you doing in Venice? Why aren't you where the painting is – I think you said in Dresden?'

'Good questions. Unlike Berenson, unless the painting is an obvious fake, I go to work on the physical and financial evidence. Let me give you an example. Suppose you came to me offering to sell me the Stuart Crown Jewels of England, the ones that were lost in the Civil War, presumably melted down to pay for troops and harlotry. I'd be very suspicious of their authenticity. I would certainly have them tested for indications of age at the very least. If however, you also supplied me with a bill of sale signed by King Charles, and with records of their being owned by specific people since then, and if I could check all the papers and demonstrate *their* authenticity, checking the paper, the inks and the signatures, then I'd be very much more likely to believe you. Of course, it's always possible for the documents, or the bulk of them, to be genuine and the objects themselves a fake, but I could make a reasonable guess about the likelihood of that, taking detailed questions of style and technique at that time into account as well.'

'But what has that to do with your being in Venice?'

'Veronese and his family, and his studio, were based in Venice. Most of the records dealing with the initial sales and early history of his paintings are in the archives here. I am here to do the paperwork.'

'What if there are no records?'

'Then I have problems. I'm not yet sure how happy I would be to overturn an attribution simply because of an absence of records. Paper is quite as fragile as canvas. More so, if anything, because most of it is less likely to be as carefully preserved down the centuries as a painting. How many of your letters do you keep? At the very end, I may be thrown back on the Berenson method of judging by style and manner.'

'And what will you decide?'

He frowned at me, self-mockingly. 'I think I probably agree with Berenson,' he said, as though with a heavy heart. 'The palette, at least in what seems to be so early a work, is highly characteristic. The canvas, too, is contemporary, though it's not unknown for fakes to be painted over less good works of the appropriate period. I hope that one day we shall be able to use the Roentgen rays to settle doubts like that.'

Jane teased him with the thought which had occurred to us all: 'You don't seem to like Mr Berenson very much.'

He looked shyly round the three of us before answering, rubbing the bridge of his nose once more. 'It's true we've had our disagreements, but there's no belying his intelligence or importance. At bottom, I suppose, he believes that if I'd spent more time on a donkey searching out examples of old master works in isolated churches and monasteries and houses round Italy, as he did at my age, then I would know a great deal more about art. He is probably right. I would argue that if he had spent more time in libraries poring over financial records, as I have, then he would know a great deal more about fraud.' He sat back in his chair, swirling the wine round in his glass, started, hesitated, and spoke at last. 'There's more to it than that, however. I don't like his language.'

Jane laughed. 'What a very silly way of putting it, Mr Manet.' He grinned back broadly in reply.

'It was a bit pompous, I suppose. I'm sorry, but it's true.'

'What is it about his language, Mr Manet? Is he a foul-mouthed, filthy-tempered old man?'

Anthony rushed in to correct the impression he feared he had given. 'No, not at all. A charming, equable man. It's just he uses a sort of priestly language. Not as bad as Ruskin and Pater, who simply raved on about the things they liked – lessons in elementary moral philosophy and political thought, masquerading as art history and criticism – but he will suggest you need an almost religious dedication, and that mere mortals cannot understand the way he works. It's true he knows more than anyone about individual masters' palettes, brush work, tricks of design, but he will not see that the things he fixes on have been chosen, chosen by him, as significant. There isn't any universal truth about them or special virtue in the fact he notices them. There are quite as many things he chooses not to notice, and sometimes they may be just as important. I'm against scholars setting themselves up as anything special in any case. If our first duty is to know and understand, our second one is to explain – even, when possible, to popularise. I am the phantom democrat.' He grinned again, lop-sidedly, defusing the seriousness of his statements. It was Eva who interrupted the silence.

'Then perhaps you have come to the wrong country, Mr Manet, and come at the wrong time.'

'I fear you may be right.' He cut himself a slice of mozzarella, chewing thoughtfully before speaking again. 'I hope I have not put you off Mr Berenson. Perhaps you ought to visit him at I Tatti. I'm sure that Jeremy could arrange it in his official capacity.'

'But Berenson's an American,' I interjected.

'True. But his wife is English.'

I did not go down to I Tatti at that time to see the old man, nor for some time later, while Kenneth Clark was his assistant. I had known young Clark at the Varsity, a languid Trinity man who had haunted the Ashmolean, though I had not known him well. We would not meet again till the years of what he called the Great Clark Boom, when he was Curator of the National. If I had done, perhaps I should have learnt more about the dislike which soured relations between Anthony and Berenson. I might even have been able to check a suspicion that arose a little while later and may have been entirely wrong. Still, I sometimes wonder how much of Berenson's dislike of Anthony arose from his being a Jew and a native European, and how much of Anthony's dislike of him arose from his being a Jew and an American. I am probably doing them both a great disservice, or doing Berenson one, at least.

Jane rang to have the table cleared. Once we were settled with coffee (a European habit I have always approved of thoroughly) she turned to face us, her back to the afternoon light (was it the vanity of middle-age, or is it just an accident of memory that I always seem to remember her as a creature of the shade?), and spoke.

'For once, I find myself not knowing exactly what to say. You know, I think, that I invited the three of you here to apologise to you. To you Mr Burnham, for ruining your party. To you, Eva, for spoiling your afternoon. And to you, Mr Manet, for the terrible things which were said to you. I do not know how to make amends. I hope that your presence here today indicates that you might find it possible to forgive me.'

Anthony spoke for us all. 'As far as I am concerned, Mrs Carlyle, you have nothing to apologise for, and we have nothing to forgive. Your behaviour has always been unimpeachable where I am concerned,' (is it only hindsight which settles a smile on his voice?) 'and your company entirely charming. There are others for whom that cannot be said, but they are not present in this suite today.'

Jane examined her fingernails, as though they were no part of her, imposed on her flesh by someone else, as she replied. 'Nor are like to be. The person of whom you speak left this suite at my request two days ago. I am afraid there is nothing I can do to drive him from Venice, unless Mr Burnham has unknown exceptional powers, but I have no wish to tolerate his proximity after what has happened, nor to impose his company on my friends.'

Eva rose, and in a gesture which would seem impossibly dated now, I fear, took her friend by the arms and kissed her cheek. I must have been bewitched, for I noticed no other movement in the room, but Anthony must have slipped to the piano (if that curious walk could ever describe so graceful a movement) for almost without our realising it the silence and stillness of the moment was disturbed, or rather rearranged, as a painting is by the addition of a figure, by a gentle, reflective, melancholy music, music which caught at itself as though with a perpetual sob, music coming to defeated terms with loss and sadness so that sadness itself was transformed and loss became the presence of sound, as in the promise of the apostle, 'We shall all be changed, changed utterly ...' The music died away. I did not recognise it in those days, but forever after it has been associated in my mind with those three people, with that afternoon, and most of all with the brave, inviolate figure of Anthony Manet.

His voice was distant, and dry, like paper sliding over itself. 'I'm sorry. I wanted to wrap you up as you stood against the sunlight, and carry you away for ever, and I didn't know how else to do it.'

There was nothing we could say, in a silence that seemed too valuable for breaking. At last he spoke again. 'May I ask if any of you have appointments for this afternoon?' We shook our heads. 'Then will you come with me?'

We left the suite, in silence still, were silent in the lift, and were silent as we came out of the lobby into a tidal wave of sunlight. Jane frowned, and Eva raised a hand against it. Even I screwed up my eyes. He stood before us, in a linen suit and panama, his polka-dot foulard being tugged by the breeze, and looked – as he always looks to the eye of memory – ablaze. Venice stood all before us in her marble and pink and orange-red, between an endless cerulean sea and a sky as blue as longing, all the vacant elements, and he seemed to light it up as the sun beat off his clothes. He seemed like the restless spectre of an ancient Doge, come back to claim his inheritance. We would have followed him anywhere.

We did not have to follow him far. He beckoned, and led us with his curious syncopated step along the waterfront, a little way from the

51

hotel. The day was the first precursor of summer, and heat irradiated us, thin moustaches of sweat on our lips (even Jane and Eva too wearied to brush them away). The light from the water and the blank-faced houses at our side seemed to narrow our vision into a tunnel which, in angry retaliation against the air, seemed to darken, an artificial corridor created by the mind and eye for us to walk down till we arrived.

'This is it,' he said quietly. The unbroken building wall on the north side of Giudecca stood before us, but here it was a pattern of herring-bone brick, cut into by huge high painted doors, painted black, and above them, recessed from the wall, a balcony with fat stone balustrading.

'What is it?' asked Eva.

'My grandfather's house.' He pushed at the doors and let us in. Before us stood a long brick corridor (or it seemed long, in contrast to the product of the blazing light outside. I do not suppose it was much more than twenty or thirty feet in all), and beyond was a garden or courtyard filled with cypress and laurel, dusty in the sun. Doors let in to both sides of the corridor. 'Come.' He led us through the one on the left. It led up dark, narrow wooden stairs onto a small brick-floored landing, from which we walked through an arch into a large high airy room. A matronly old woman in black entered through the facing door.

'Signore.'

He replied in Italian. I was beginning to be able to understand. 'Susanna. I have some guests. Bring us something cold, please.'

Eva had gone to the balcony, a single pool of light in the gloomy coolness looking out on to the grand façade of Venice, half way between and facing the Salute and the Campanile.

'This is lovely,' murmured Jane, and I could only agree. It was everything I wanted my own house to be, in time. The furniture was the local dark stained wood. All of it heavy, little of it attractive but with a sturdy rightness about it as though it were meant to be here and would not be shifted elsewhere. On one wall hung a fading tapestry of a mythological scene (Perseus rescuing Andromeda, I later learned) with a figure like St George battling a dragon in the foreground and in the background a picture of Venice, its harbour filled and bustling with galleons, three-decker frigates and carracks, all of them flying ensigns bearing the golden lion of St Mark. On the other wall facing it were glass-fronted bookcases filled with early printed books (almost all of them printed in Venice, Anthony told me afterwards, except for a few from Amsterdam and Leiden, and including a copy of Aretino's much-banned sonnets on the Postures of Love, with engravings taken from the drawings of Giulio Romano). The chairs and sofa by the balcony had rattan seats and backs and were filled with heavily embroidered cushions. At the back of the room stood an immovably solid dining table permanently set for twelve.

'Please. Sit.'

We did, except for Eva, who continued on the balcony. Susanna returned with fresh-pressed lemonade, and spoons and caster sugar.

'How have you managed to hide this place?' Jane asked.

'None of you ever asked me where I live.'

'So this is your home?'

'In a way. It was never really mine. My grandfather's certainly, and all the family have used it since then, but I am the last one alive who comes to Venice and it is much too large for me. It can sleep thirty quite comfortably. I am going to sell it.'

'But you mustn't!' cried Eva, turning back into the conversation.

'But I must,' said Anthony gravely. 'It is wasted on me. Susanna, who has worked here since before I was born, and her son want to buy it, to turn it into a small hotel. I think it is the least my grandfather would have wanted done for them. However, I propose that, should I sell, the master-suite be permanently reserved for my use, so it would not be entirely a loss.'

'How did it come to your grandfather?'

Anthony smiled as though to himself, excluding us for an unpitched moment before replying. 'The sort of way that people hold against the Jews, still. My grandfather was in the Levant trade, dealing in everything from musk and civet to dates and pomegranates. In those days, the later 1850s, his principal offices were here in Venice, in Constantinople, and in Tyre, Sidon and Alexandria. The Alexandria office was closed after the building of the Suez canal. In those days this house was owned by a man called Giuseppe Santi, the head of one of the few families to have held on to its wealth and its trade during the long decline of Venice. The house itself was built in the late sixteenth century by his maternal forebears. Santi more or less controlled the sea trade in black pepper and the import of cloves from Zanzibar. My grandfather, who spent half his life establishing contacts in the Indian Ocean as well as the Mediterranean, was offered contracts in pepper and cloves. He came here to see Santi to explain the position, and to reassure him he posed no threat to the senior merchant. Santi not only threw him out, but also had him beaten to a pulp as an upstart.'

'Because he was a Jew?' Eva asked for all of us.

'Oh no. The Eastern trade has long been riddled with Jews. It's the Russians no one can stand. Well, it took my grandfather twenty years, but he grew to monopolise those trades. The Santis went bankrupt and grandfather bought their house.'

'Do your family still control the trade?' I asked, professionally, I hoped.

'Good Lord, no. The old man got out quick. He knew some sorts of competition could not be defeated.'

'What competition was that?'

He smiled, in his odd, ironic way. 'The British Empire, I'm afraid.'

'Do you mind?'

'No, not really. I travel under British papers half the time myself.'

'Why half?'

'I have German and French ones too. I suppose that, if I wanted, in the war, I could have fought myself.'

'He sounds fascinating, your grandfather,' Jane interrupted. (Was it the talk of money she objected to – a distasteful subject in our day? Or did she simply think I was prying?) 'Like the hero of a nineteenth-century novel.'

'Or the villain. Yes, he was, though I would not have trusted him beyond the letter of his contract if I had been trading with him myself; but at least he honoured all his contracts, which is more than many did. When I was little I thought of him as being like the Count of Monte Cristo.'

'Does that make you some sort of baron?' I asked.

'We were never rich enough in any one place to buy a title. Not every Jew is a Rothschild, you know, though most of us act as though we were.'

'At least he didn't sell his soul.' It was Eva, on the balcony still.

'Neither did the Rothschilds, I think. In fact, I don't believe that anyone has for a very long time, though many of them tried to give it away.'

Eva pressed on. 'It's still a wonderful story. Was he tall and dark and handsome? All the story needs to make it perfect is a woman ...'

'He was five foot five and fat, in the days I knew him, though I gather he was a handsome man in youth; and his wife's name was Giulietta Santi. It caused quite a scandal at the time, and there are still those amongst the orthodox who refuse to account my father a proper Jew. That mattered less in Germany, where the family mainly comes from, than it does round here.'

'Why don't people sell their souls anymore?' Jane asked mockingly.

'Most of them don't have to. They can give them away to whatever set of ruling beliefs they want and be told what to do and think and feel.

54

For most of them the price of selling is too high. You have to stand against the operating order and faith of the world, knowing you do not know what is, what may be, or even what you want. Faust was driven by curiosity, not desire.'

Eva came back into the darkness of the room and settled by me, her arm up on the seatback, her face to Anthony, catching me in the pale shallow curve of her cheek and throat. 'What kind of man would you have to be,' she asked softly, 'to sell your soul today?'

He thought silently, for a long time, so long the pressure of thought behind the conversation slackened. All of us, including him, were almost absent-minded when he answered. 'In an age of enthusiasm and popular democracy, you would have to be the one entirely reasonable man.'

Memory fails me hereafter, every time. I wanted to catch the rest of that afternoon, spent talking to Eva while Anthony showed Jane about the house – but all of it has gone, lost against the early brightness of the day. I want it back, but simple happiness always seems to return, drenched in sameness, undifferentiated as the days. All I remember is her final question to Anthony, as we left. 'The music – the piece you were playing in Jane's suite after lunch – what was it?'

His face was turned away, to Jane, as he answered. 'You might have heard the original in Amsterdam. Nowhere else but Vienna, I think. It was a transcription . . .'

'I guessed as much.'

'Of the orchestral score of one of Gustav Mahler's Songs – "Songs on the Deaths of Children".'

Memory is a thoughtless tyrant, recalling fragments of the past unasked for yet failing to bring back those things we want to remember, even though it is only memory itself which torments us with the knowledge that we want to recall them. So it is with those afternoons with Eva. All I have is balloons of memory, filled with insignificant gas. All the detail and particularity has gone, and I am left with the sombre partial truth that nothing happened between us. There is a further tyranny of memory. I am an old man now, playing back and forth on the surfaces of a superficial life. I have been a happy, conventional man. I have been successful in my career, and honoured by the nation. I have been married twice; the first time for sixteen years, and we had two sons. After my first wife's death, and a suitable period, I married again. We were married for thirty-five years and had a son and daughter. My second wife died last year. Everyone dies before me. It is the least supportable part of my fate. My children are successful, after the fashion of our time and class. I have happy, healthy grandchildren, and even three great-grandchildren at last. I am the envy of poorer conservatives and the loathing of socialists. I am, according to one group, a representative of everything that was best in Britain. According to another I represent the worst, a child of hell who battened on the healthy flanks of radical, syndicalist Britain. The great joy for me is that I am too old for either party to do anything about it. My life is over. I have had the joys and honours and no one can take those, at least, away from me. Except myself, it seems. Memory betrays me. Why am I haunted by these distant shades of Venice sixty years ago, instead of by my family and my success? Why am I driven back to times which did not affect me? Is it the freedom which is the spur, perhaps? The knowledge that I, alone unaffected, alone can make a record of the times, to the honour of fact and the glory of truth? I have been a long time remembering.

The postal service, at least, worked reasonably well in Italy in those days. Old fascisti will attribute that, like every other efficiency, to Mussolini. I do not know. I had not been in Italy before the March on Rome of October 1922. (That March has always struck me as a characteristically Italian propaganda achievement. Whatever apologists may say, it was not until he had been invited to become Prime Minister that Mussolini dared to risk his legions on the March. Nonetheless, he suppressed news of his appointment to make it look as though his rag-tag rebels had carried off a coup.)

There was a letter waiting for me at the Consulate next morning, from Rome. Protocol within the service in Italy in those days was rather more eccentric than it is now. As a hangover from Italy's centuries of disunity, consuls in Genoa, Venice, Naples operated almost completely independently of the Embassy in Rome, reporting directly to London, as well as to the Embassy. As much as anything, this was a pragmatic admission of the still largely regional structure and nature of Italy, and though it led to some duplication, and sometimes to disputed interpretations, in the main it worked very well. In a sense, therefore, I reported directly through Arthur to London. Protocol demanded, however, that I should at least pay my respects to the parent Embassy in Rome. During Arthur's long silence I had taken the risk of writing to an old school chum (Tim Carmichael – we were to work together again during the Second War) to ask him what the form was. It was his reply that awaited me. I can quote it from memory for it inaugurated my rise.

56

Dear Burnham,

Delighted to receive your letter. Most of the chaps before you haven't had the sense to get in touch – presumably under Howard's influence. Not good form. It only guaranteed that Howard and the Old Man here were racing to see who could get them recalled to London first.

The F.O. sent your accreditation on to us, of course, so I knew you were lurking about, and would have written to you anyway.

The pukka thing would be to write direct to the Ambassador, asking to be allowed to call and pay your respects. The letter will be intercepted and passed to me anyway to make the appointment. It would be good fun to see you here in Rome, so set about it pronto.

You ought to inform Howard, of course. He may not like it, but cannot stop you, so don't take fright. We're more important than he is!

So get on with that letter – it will be like old times to have you hanging about the bootstrings for a few days.

Yours etc.,
Carmichael

I wrote the letter straightaway, but did not (I cannot now say why) tell Arthur about it for several days. He did not look entirely happy when I told him, but he took it in good part. I can still see him looming over my desk, forbiddingly frock-coated, his hands behind his back and his round cheeks puffy and red, like a brightly-coloured waxwork of Gladstone.

'Quite right, of course. You ought to call on the Ambassador. Call on him, mind. No more than that. You would be paying purely social respects. You report direct to me. If the Ambassador has any worries about this Consulate it's a matter for him and me and London. Don't go forgetting who calls the tune in Venice. Still, clever of you to remember. Most of your predecessors didn't. Terrible badhats, some of the chaps they sent me. Sometimes I think Whitehall treats this posting as a cross between a luxury resort and a sanatorium for the deeply disturbed.'

'Are you on holiday or disturbed?' (I do not know where I found the courage to joke with him. It seemed to work, however, for he smiled and reddened further.)

'Less of that, young fellow. I hear quite good reports of you. The Italian's coming along I hear, and you seem to be getting out and about amongst our bloody visitors.'

'I'm doing my best, but it isn't easy to meet the right sort of Italian, and I don't suppose I've met a single member of the British merchant community here.'

'You leave the right sort of Italian to me. As for British merchants, there aren't any, not any more. You're living in a city living with decline, old fellow. The British and Dutch empires, long-distance ocean-going shipping, and finally the Suez Canal, all did for Venice's stranglehold on the Eastern trade. Most of it was lost between two and three hundred years ago. What was left was largely moribund, waiting to be picked off by northern-based shippers and traders. The bigger London stores send buyers out here once a year to buy glass and lace, but Venice cannot live on glass and lace alone. It lives on visitors and industry now – industry on the mainland, at Mestre. The waters are finally losing to the land and are taking their revenge on the old city. You wait till you see the autumn and winter floods.'

'You said something about meeting Italians.'

'Oh yes. There isn't much to be gained by it now, not now the fascists are in power. Half the people are frightened and the other half are place-seekers, hangers-on and arse-lickers. Still, I'll make arrangements for a consular reception. Terribly dreary shows. I'll have to ask you to support me through it. Know any amusing visitors we could add to the guest-list, along of Mrs Carlyle?'

I mentioned the names of some of the richer visitors I had met. 'No, can't have them. Frightful shits the lot of them. Foreign money grafted on English titles. They don't have the brains or class to handle all the money and power. Just like our people in Ireland used to be. And in India, now, of course. Result will be the same. They're looking to a damn good kicking. No, they won't do at all. What about your pretty Dutch lady?' I was shocked, as much as surprised, that he should know about Eva. 'Giving you Italian classes I understand. Good idea. Damme, wish I'd had a pretty girl to give me lessons when I was learning.' He was one of the very few people I have ever met who really did put their tongue in their cheek when they were teasing.

'I'm sure she would be delighted. There is someone else. I don't know if you'd mind. He's Jewish.'

Howard seemed to take the announcement without discomfiture. His qualms were simple: 'Orthodox chap, is he?'

'I'm sorry?'

'Orthodox Jew, I mean. Kosher and all that. Bit difficult, that's all, being in Venice, if he is, and we can't serve shellfish.'

'I honestly don't know. I've never thought of it. I think I've seen him eating shellfish.'

Arthur grunted. It was he who taught me the simplest rule about

58

arranging meals for guests who may be of varied religious persuasions – stick to poultry and lamb, except when dealing with Poles, in which case stick to poultry and let them be bloody well grateful (I quote). 'Suppose we can risk it. What's the chap's name.' I told him, and his big round face suddenly filled with creases, a child's cack-handed drawing of a smile across his face. 'How in hell do you know Anthony Manet? And what does he think he's doing in Venice without calling on me?'

I was beginning to be unsurprised by Arthur's range of acquaintance. 'I might ask the same of you. How long have you known him?'

'Never met him.'

'But ...'

'No no no no no, dear boy. All I know about him is that he wrote a splendid article on the spice trade between Venice and southern Germany, appeared in *Historia*. All a bit modern for me, of course. He's a fifteenth- and sixteenth-century man, I gather. Mediaevalist myself, but I know he knows my book. Well I'll be a kaffir! Of course you must bring him along. Jot down the names for me, and I'll organise something.'

So it was arranged. We did not know it would turn into a nightmare. There was another matter yet to be arranged, however. 'Italians, Howard, and my political education. You were threatening to begin it.'

'True. Well, we can begin with the most obvious facts. Be a good chap and get me today's *Corriere della Sera*.'

We had an enormous number of newspapers delivered at the Consulate, although press-cutting was taken care of at the Embassy. I went into the outer office to find a copy of the great Milanese daily. There was none there. I checked with Enrico. None had been delivered that day. I reported the fact to Howard. He was in turn apologetic. 'I'm sorry to have sent you on a wild-goose chase. I knew it had not been delivered. I know that copies which arrived at the railway station were seized and burnt by the local fascist authorities. Only a few had got this far in fact. Most copies were destroyed in a raid on the newspaper's printing works.'

'But why? And how do you know all this?'

'I have friends in Milan. They telephoned me. So now the Venetian authorities know I know. In case you hadn't realised, the telephones in the Consulate are tapped, as are most foreign missions and the telephones of all leading politicians. We live in what the Chinese call interesting times, Mr Burnham, and even spying is slipping into the twentieth century.'

'But that's monstrous!'

'Oh, I don't know. In London we have intercepted foreign diplomatic mail for four hundred years. We're very good at it, and historians like Mr Manet are duly grateful. This is much the same. I am only suggesting you should be careful. In the same way, Enrico is in the pay of the fascist authorities.' I was appalled. Howard only smiled. 'I shouldn't worry. Local staff are often paid informers, a few of them. Enrico is very good at the job he does for us and, fortunately, it is usually possible to count on the cupidity of the ordinary man. He's in my pay as well.'

'But why has the *Corriere* been impounded?'

'The usual reasons. It made the mistake of carrying an interview Mussolini gave to an American journalist without clearing it first. Mussolini will say things abroad he does not want repeated in Italy, yet. Such interviews have to be edited for domestic consumption.'

'What sort of things?'

'Oh, that the police is the state. That democracy is a farce and that next year's elections will be the last that Italy will ever see.'

'I thought his supporters agreed with that kind of thing.'

'They do. The thing is, his power base is still very fragile. He can't be certain who his true supporters are. He tends to play both sides against the middle, very successfully too, but it's barely three months since he united the fascist movement with the nationalists. The nationalists have a lot of able men, who serve real interests, and he cannot be certain of them yet. There was the usual thing as well.'

'And what is that?'

'A report of a socialist deputy being beaten by a fascist squad. It happens all the time – not just socialists, liberals too. He's in hospital I gather, and lucky. An MP was killed earlier this year. Last year a death squad ran riot in Turin, so much so as to become an embarrassment. Eighteen months ago they killed Di Vagno, the socialist deputy for Bari. They've been attacking MPs openly for years and the communist Misiano was even ejected from the chamber so they could thrash him, but now that Mussolini's prime minister things are getting worse, quickly.'

'But it seems so peaceful.'

'This is Venice, remember, at the beginning of the season. No one can afford to frighten the visitors, so most of it is fairly quiet here – kept underground for the moment.'

'Even so, it can't go on much longer. Mussolini's bound to be paid off by the establishment. He's such an obvious fraud.'

'That, I am afraid, is where the Embassy and I disagree. The best advice I can give you is to use your eyes and make your mind up for yourself. If you have a mind, which no one else in the service seems to.'

'You still haven't said who you are going to introduce me to.'

He rocked back on the steel-capped heels of his heavy boots, his mouth puckered in a frown. I knew, although I could not see them, that his hands behind his back were twisted round and clasped, pulling down against the ache which sometimes affected his upper back, in his standard pose of contemplation. 'I think I am going to take a risk. I think we had better start your education at the very top. It is about time you met Matteotti. Let me know when you have a date for your trip to those pedants in Rome. I will see if I cannot tempt him up here for a little holiday.'

I visited Anthony that afternoon (Eva and Jane had gone shopping on Burano) to tell him that his reputation had preceded him to Arthur Howard. He seemed to be pleased, though a little bashful, as though he wished that such matters had not drifted out to me, a diplomat, beyond the comfortable walls of scholarship and the reticent, nocturnal community of learning.

'Will you give him a message for me? Will you tell him that I did not call because I did not want to impose or take up his time, but it would be an honour if I could do so now?'

I stretched my legs out on the settle by the balcony. Beyond us the waters of the lagoon lay a dark cold blue. 'First Jane. Now you. Is Howard really so terribly clever?'

I always seem to remember him smiling. He smiled again now. 'Terribly. He wrote the standard work on the effect of the crusades on eastern Mediterranean trade. It caused something of a scandal at the time. A few people had already begun to write about the crusades in terms of power struggles within Christendom, instead of their being holy wars, but Howard was the first person to examine their economic basis and effects. Venice, amongst others, comes out of it very badly, as only looking after its own trading interests. I suppose at the time people didn't want to be reminded that missionaries and the white man's burden were only aspects of empire. Howard might as well have called his book *Trade Follows the Flag, or Stealing from the Darkies*. Right book, wrong time. Remember that if anyone ever tells you scholars can or should inhabit ivory towers.'

'Was that what made him leave Oxford?'

'Mainly. They were terrible times, the years before and after the Wilde trials, and rumours were circulated about Arthur Howard as well. Quite falsely, but by all accounts they so disgusted him he never wanted to go back. Almost everyone who settled in Europe about the turn of the century had rumours about unnatural practices – silly term – spread about them, particularly if, like him, they had been friends of Wilde.'

'But is he . . .?'

'A bugger? By all accounts quite the opposite. What really mattered, though, was his impatience.'

'They say the same about him now.'

'Do they indeed?' His eyebrows rose, in time-honoured fashion. 'That is not good to hear. He put in for the Chichele Chair of History. He would have been a wonderful choice, but he was too young. He would have held the Chair for over thirty years. The long and the short of it is, he challenged the decision of the faculty board. He has never really been forgiven for it.'

He seemed relaxed, isolated in his own home and in his scholarship. I found myself curious as to how he knew so much, and how he knew so many people. The English society of my day was a small affair; anyone who was anyone knew everyone. Manet, on the other hand, seemed to know all kinds of people without being anyone very much at all. It was to be years before I grew out of my imperial ignorance, and by then it was too late; the world to which Anthony belonged, of European intellectual society, had vanished, to be replaced by people on bursaries and grants. Two wars and a depression handed his world over to faculty committees and arts councils. There is almost no one left who is admired for unbribed intelligence, but cleverness alone was the key to Anthony Manet's world. The very word now seems, as it has always done in England, an insult. The best and worst thing anyone ever said about him was that he wore his mind on his sleeve. I pressed him further. 'How do you know all this?'

He sat back and lit up a cigarette. (He rarely smoked or drank, but when he did, did so expensively.) 'How much do you know about your contemporaries at school? Since you were schoolboys, I mean.'

'Quite a lot.'

'And your contemporaries at Oxford?'

'The same.'

'And about the right sort of people generally?'

I stiffened, under what seemed an attack. 'I'm pretty well informed, I suppose.'

'And how often do you, or did you, see all those people?'

'Well, it varied, depending on how well I knew them.'

'Of course it did. And how did you fill in gaps? Gossip.'

'I don't gossip.'

'Everyone gossips, Jeremy, though they sometimes give it different names. Howard and I are known in the same eccentric dilettante circles. We are gentleman amateurs. My tutor at Oxford was a contemporary of his, and I gossiped.'

'Then what about Jane and Eva?'

'They don't gossip much.'

'I mean how do you come to know them? I mean, at least I know now that Jane's related to one of our neighbours. She won't be related to yours, whatever city you choose to live in.'

'Perhaps you're right. Not many Jews in your home county, I take it? Which is it, by the way?'

'Not many, no, and it's Worcester, but you haven't answered the question. How do you come to know them?'

'I didn't pick them up in Haymarket, if that's what you mean.' I reddened. 'Why, my dear Mr Burnham, I do believe you're jealous. Well why didn't you say so? Which of them is it you care about?'

'You still haven't answered my question.'

He exhaled a long aromatic column of Turkish smoke. 'Jane's father was a long-standing friend of my mother's parents. Her mother rather less so.'

'He must have been an extraordinary man.'

'He was, but you had best ask Jane about that. I've known her slightly all my life. She and her husband sometimes had me to stay when I was an undergraduate, but I suppose we only really became friends when we met up again in Paris, after the war.'

'And Eva?'

It was his turn to stiffen. 'Eva lives a very quiet, and private, life. She would not want to be talked about.'

'You said you were a gossip.'

'I am, but even I can choose to draw lines somewhere.'

'It's a simple enough question. How did you meet her?'

He stubbed out what was left of his cigarette. 'I told you. My sister married a Dutchman.' He rose and stood stretching before the tapestry. He was distant, as though lost in the picture before him. 'Whatever happened to the dragon, I wonder?'

I thought he was trying to distract me, and was brusque: 'Perseus killed him.'

He dug his hands into his pockets, grimacing. 'No. I don't believe it. In the real world dragons never die.'

I was impatient, and therefore foolhardy. 'Do you love her?'

'Who?' I remained silent, hesitant at my own audacity, almost not wanting an answer. He half-turned towards me, his eyes closed, frowning. 'No. I am much too reasonable for that.' I felt an uneasy relief, and both the relief and the uneasiness were heightened by his next remark. 'Jane and I are only friends.'

Jealousy is strange. We all affect to despise it, yet it is the strongest and truest emotion I have ever felt. I have only rarely been transformed and transfigured by love, yet even in the quieter, more stable affection of my marriages I have found myself racked by jealousy. I suppose it is simply that it exposes the weaknesses in our image of ourselves. There must always be a slight sense, and at times an overwhelming one, of the unlikeliness of affection; and in the honest moments which come uncalled for (and come more often now, in the uneasy hours before dawn, when I lie awake against the darkness, hoping to achieve the day, desperate for – yet desolated by – the weary continuity of living) of our own unworthiness, we are prey to jealousy, which is only a desperate cry to be liked and loved and has little to do with its object, until we are filled with fear that, like the child that sits abed at nights crying for the moon, we too must cry in vain.

I was half-relieved that Anthony had not realised I spoke of Eva, but half-suspicious, too, uncertain that he had not simply drawn a false scent to dissemble his feelings. If I am a little honest, I suppose there was also a little part of me that was outraged that a man such as he should even link his name with that of a woman like Jane Carlyle, if only to deny any association.

I walked back along the quay of Giudecca, and as I walked I could hear the sound of Anthony playing the pianoforte in his upper drawing-room, smaller than the one he entertained in. It occurred to me for the first time that part of the difficulty and distance I sometimes felt in his presence arose simply from the fact that in this new unharnessed world in which I found myself he always seemed to know what to do, and it only seemed to be the things he wanted to, and would have done whatever came. I, on the other hand, felt constantly uncertain, far from the easy formalities of English society. I felt his easiness was unfair, and that in my world it would have been he who stood at disadvantage. In my youthful way I was right, for I belonged and he would never have been allowed to believe he did; but I did not understand, in those distant youthful days of callowness, that he had stood at an angle to the world all his life, and would have found some way of coping, some place he could fill, as he always did. His great composure, growing from the mind which was his visiting card, was an answer to movement, and loneliness.

I walked on to the Schifanoia, thinking to take the hotel launch back to San Marco. (After Howard's revelation I did not want Enrico with me everywhere. It takes time to develop the watchful carelessness Howard himself possessed.) I found Younghusband disembarking as I arrived, with some of his fascist friends.

'Ah, the little Consul! How are you, Burnham? Where's your nanny today? Slipping off the apron-strings?'

I stared at him, eyes screwed up against the harsh, flat light of an overcast afternoon. Part of me despised him, but part of me, part of my very youth and Englishness, felt called to his arrogant easy manner, the gawky blond good looks of the captain of the First XI and boxing Half-Blue. His languid grace contrasted absolutely with Anthony's stammering step, and I felt drawn to taste both halves of the afternoon.

'Cat got your tongue, little Consul? Or are you afraid of my big bad blackshirted friends? You shouldn't be. This one's the police chief.' He pointed one out with a stab of the thumb. 'I thought your sort were supposed to search out all the important people in case any innocents like me need help. Do I have to do your job for you as well? Come in for a drink.'

I had not meant to, but curiosity, and the call of his odd charismatic charm, turned me to the doors. I followed them into the lounge, though one small, sane corner of me prayed that Jane and Eva would not return too soon. There are times when we are drawn to that which makes us feel guilty, and I felt guilty then.

He ordered us all whiskies, to the evident delight of his ungainly companions, who looked as out of place as monks in a bordello, and quite as grateful. Younghusband introduced us. His own Italian was competent, but bore no trace of an authentic accent. He continued to speak in a lazy London drawl, as though to underline the point that there was only so far he would go for foreigners. He never made more concessions than he had to.

'This is Jeremy Burnham, and this is Federico Capodimonte, chief of the police. Umberto and Alfonso, two of his men.'

I realised at once I had nothing to say to them, and conversation frittered into banalities about the weather, and how I liked Venice, and the forthcoming season. One point, however, the policeman was urgent to make. 'Mr Younghusband, he will tell you, how fond we are of helpful foreigners. We want to be of service, we are simple people, very friendly. If you help us, then, if there is anything you want, all you have to do is ask. We are always ready to help visitors who want to live in peace. Not like some troublemakers, always complaining, always picking on little things, wondering where the newspapers are.'

I said nothing, for I did not know the right thing to say, and realised

65

that my presence this afternoon was an added bonus for the chief: as much as anything, an opportunity to show off his new toy attached to telephones. I was angry as well, wondering if Younghusband knew, but decided he could not. I guessed he had called me in entirely for reasons of his own, not at all associated with his curious friends. He called for more whisky and eyed me over as though I were some strange new insect, or a new boy at school, scarcely worthy of interest.

'Do you still see the Merry Widow, Burnham?' I remained silent, staring into my whisky. 'Sorry. Keep forgetting you're a diplomat.' His head shook slightly, side to side. I wondered if he could be already drunk, or if he had a touch of the sun. 'Tell me, Mr Burnham,' he continued slowly, struggling for his words, and I began to wonder for his reason, 'have you seen Mrs Carlyle, Mrs Jane Carlyle, recently?'

'I see her from time to time.'

'Do you? Indeed? And how is the mad old bitch?'

I choked on my whisky and set down my glass. 'Go to hell, Younghusband.' It was, till then, about the most demonstrative thing I had ever said as an adult. I left, and his long loud caustic laugh followed me across the lobby, catching in the swift click of my footsteps.

As I came out on to the quayside I found Jane and Eva coming in to land. They waved at me but I was too distracted to respond, even when Jane called out to me. 'Mr Burnham! How lovely! Did you come to search us out? What luck!'

I handed them ashore; then taking both Jane's hands in mine (her eyes were peppery with fire), whispered, 'Younghusband's in the lounge, drunk, or addled, or something.'

Her face hardened, and her long eyes darkened. 'I will not allow myself to be harried from pillar to post by that tiresome young man. Would you be an angel, Mr Burnham, and walk us in?'

I took them on my arms. I would like to say we swept into the lobby triumphant, but our progress was more sedate than that, and I more nervous. We got to the lift cage unharrassed and unimpeded, but there Younghusband saw us as he swayed against a pillar of the lounge.

'Two ladies is it now, little Consul? You'd better watch yourself, especially with the old one. A Jew-lover that one, and it really won't do.' He fell wheezily against the pillar, laughing and breathless, and Jane almost forced us into the lift, a box of cool stained darkness, far from John Younghusband's mockery. Jane had coloured, and her eyes had closed, and all my thoughts fell into tangles in her hair. I did not know what Younghusband meant, or whom he had spoken of, and for one appalling and appalled moment I wondered about Eva van Woerden and Anthony's sister, and my spirit was repelled by her, and even my thinking darkened.

Jane turned to me. 'Thank you, Mr Burnham. You don't have to come any further. Thank you for your help'; but I could not be put aside. I followed them from the lift to Jane's suite. I would not be gainsaid. All undiplomatically it fell from me as they stood waiting, stiff and unbending, angry at further intrusion.

'There is one thing I have to know, and then I'll leave you. I promise not to ask another thing, but I have to know. Is Eva Anthony Manet's sister?'

Both of them stared at me for a long moment, as though I were dressed in harlequin; then both of them together, as much in release of the tension of the last few moments as anything, let out long helpless whoops of laughter, reaching out for chairs, for anything to support them, and in that laughter was mixed, to my confusion and relief, the one word, much-repeated:

'No!'

I was young, and now I am not. I was foolish, and I have gained a kind of wisdom. I was innocent, and I have been spoiled. I was in love, and will not be again. I do not even know what that strange emotion is, and can scarcely recollect it, until an old man's memory throws a whole world back at me which I had thought had passed away, and the old confusion of desire and hope and longing sits like a jackanapes triumphant, a fool ascendant in the seat of kings. Looking back, we were always too peculiar a partnership to be conceivable. I knew almost nothing of her, and was now even more uncertain than ever. We belonged to different nations which might as well have been, for all I knew, different worlds. Love is perhaps only a deluded conception of what the world might be. All revolutionaries are in love, as much as the fond young man who hopes the light hair on a forearm – or the curve of a neck, or the turbulence of eyes – can be held an emblem, though the whole world come in force against them, to make the universe anew. Every lover sighs, and knows it to be true, 'I was present at the creation, and we shall all be changed.'

I spent as much time with her as I could, even trying in my way to play the piano and to encourage her to sing. Such efforts retired her to a grieving silence I could not break and grew to fear. Her eyes seemed always patient with suffering. It seemed appalling one so young could be so bruised. I wanted to wrap her in tissue and voile, to box her in my heart against the troubles of the earth. I did not know then that we murder to preserve, and what I dreamed of would have been an annihilation.

Still, absent from her, I hardly lived at all, the world a sepia photograph which only filled with colour if she were there. (That is the mendacity of love. Memory restores the times, and I know I only felt as I have written when I had time to think it. I was too full of living, and my strange new existence, to dress myself in monochrome. Lovers are only ridiculous because they make claims no mortal form could endure.)

Work filled much of my time, much of it socially. I seemed, too, unwittingly to have arrived at some compromise with Howard. We spoke more – sometimes, to his great delight, in Italian. He began to feed me books and, before my eyes, turned to the don he should have been, outrageously inspirational and generously attentive. Nonetheless, he often seemed distracted. As his trust in me grew, he would leave me alone in charge at the Consulate. Increasingly he would vanish for the day, claiming meetings in Bologna, Ravenna or elsewhere. I exaggerate, of course, for I am writing of the passing of only a few weeks, but when we are young and happy occasional events come to seem habitual, and single ones, endless.

I did not see so much of Anthony at that time, for he would disappear into the archives, returning with his hair dishevelled, his linen suits creased and his mind elsewhere. He seemed to carry about with him at those times the bright delighted schoolboy, golden with mockery, he must once have been. I had always thought of scholars as wizened and dry with longing and frustration faced by the vast sea of the unknown, but he was hope incarnate, anxious to learn and to achieve the world. There seemed to be nothing he did not know, or had not thought about. He was that rarest thing, a man who understood the limits of what he knew and never stopped trying to push them back. I still possess a slim volume of poems by an unknown American called Eliot, in a mottled cover with a handset pasted label (the label is misprinted on my copy, reading 'Ara Vus Prec') he gave me then, inscribed 'For Jeremy, because he ought to know'; and I recall a lunatic, laughter-ridden occasion when he tried to explain the Relativity Theory to us (I think we must have been drunk, for he rarely spoke of his degrees, but he mentioned his doctorate then as he explained what little he knew of physical science he had learnt at Göttingen, where the quantum physicists reigned). I think it must have been that afternoon he announced his greatest sadness.

'Sometimes I think I was born too late. Two hundred years or even a century ago, people like us, with time and leisure, could still hope, with a little patience and much effort, to know everything there was to know. The whole realm of knowledge could be bounded by one man, although it might take a lifetime. Men who wrote like angels, because like angels they knew, and bore the invincible armour of knowledge against the sad defeated armies of ignorance. Give me the world, the whole of it! Is it so unreasonable to want to know?'

His enthusiasm was his greatest virtue, with his mockery of his own inflated aspirations. I remember one early evening, the late light harsh and razoring the shade, I sat in Florian's at the farewell party for an arrogant young English remittance-man starting out on the next stage of his mission to drink the Mediterranean vineyards dry. Europe was full of the jetsam of England, America, Brazil and Argentina in those days, the idiot children of plutocrats shipped off to countries where the drink was strong and the currency weak, to effect their inane destructions out of sight. I was bored. I had had my brief moment as guest of honour, representative of the already fractured might of the greatest empire the world had seen; I had been looked over by ambitious mothers, excited daughters and randy divorcees, and been found wanting by all but the shallow, lubricious last. I was good at being bright and gay and vacuous, but even for those who make a life of lying for their countries the effort sometimes palls. There is something to be said for friends and silence, which perhaps only those who are paid to talk and to distrust all they meet can properly appreciate. I could not have been much happier to see Anthony Manet come in. I hailed him over to me.

'Hello, Jeremy. What are you up to?'

'Being the Consoling Consul. The chap over there, the loud one with the laugh, is off to Capri tomorrow, if his kidneys last that long.'

'There are worse places than Capri.'

'Only if he is in them. Can I introduce you to some of our fellow inhabitants?'

'Not for a wilderness of monkeys.'

'You'd never make a diplomat.'

'True. A one-man League of Nations perhaps. I could spend the sessions talking to myself.'

'Have a drink.'

'Cappucino.'

'No, never make a diplomat. Couldn't stand the pace.'

'That's what comes of being a humble bookworm. Too busy reading to learn to live.'

'You don't believe that for a moment.'

'No. I don't. But I see why Howard needs an assistant. If only your contemporaries in London knew, they would be livid with envy.'

'Do you really think so?'

'I know it. Imagine – an honest man sent abroad, to drink for England.'

'Drink for England!' I raised my glass aloft, to the cheers of my party. Anthony let a shallow heap of sugar fall slowly from his spoon so it lay on the surface of the coffee, colouring before sinking, then stirred it with long upward strokes, the coffee draining back, so the foam coloured evenly.

'How are you finding the new authorities?'

'We have as little to do with them as possible.'

'So Arthur said.'

'You've met him then?'

'Briefly. He was very kind about my research. He called on me in the end.'

'How is that going?'

'Slowly. I've been in the archive all day. There's a gap in the papers. I think the Este family may fit into it, but that's only a guess.'

'Do you think the painting's authentic?'

'Most of me says yes. A little selfish part, however, would like to prove Berenson wrong, just for the fun of it.'

'You don't like Americans very much, do you?'

'It isn't as simple as that.'

'What is it, then?'

He paused before answering. 'The only things I really know anything about are books and European history. You must remember, I come from a peculiar, and very ancient, people. A hundred years ago I would have been a rabbi, but liberalism happened to Jewry, too. In some ways I am extraordinarily lucky. I can study the things I like, but carry the canniness of my people with me. Nothing is very new to us. We see the world in the context of the past, which is humbling as well as consoling. What I object to in Americans is a jackdaw passion for newness, and the terrible certainty of their faith, faith in themselves and in their ability to make the world again. Berenson returns to the ancient practices of art scholars and is hailed as a saviour – but I'm being unfair. The practices had lapsed, and he did all the work which lets me carp.'

'I thought faith was a good thing.'

'Sometimes. It has to include doubt, though, and question itself and its tradition. Eliot, who's an American himself, published an essay about tradition a few years ago – a very fine one but the work of a man who quite obviously stood outside it, who had acquired tradition, not learned and lived it. While I'm here, amongst my sources, I can fight and argue and change. I think they're in danger of erecting a monolith called culture, immutable and built of individual, disconnected bits and pieces. I don't want to live in a monument, and I don't want a dead encrusted faith. Books I could now find anywhere.' (He was wrong, of course, as I have since learnt in my travels.) 'But not that attitude of mind. Do you have to stay on here?'

I shook my head, and he took me by the sleeve and led me out into the sunshine. The square was busy with pigeons and hawkers and early-season visitors. It was one of those days when heat and glare and the pale stones of the city make it difficult to see, painful to focus. He turned me towards the basilica.

'What do you see there?'

'Well, San Marco.'

'What you see is tyranny made stone. This city was once the liveliest in Europe. Titian and Aretino lived a walk from here. Books were published here which were banned throughout the rest of Catholic Europe. Galileo set up a telescope in a bell-tower on the same site as that one. Look at it now. Baffled, broken, declining; living off memories and the hand-outs of visitors. And do you know why?'

'They lost the trade ...'

'They lost the trade. Why? Because this city lost its mind. In the days of its confidence and its greatest trading success, this city dominated science as well as art. It developed the technologies of navigation. Galileo built a telescope for maritime as much as intellectual reasons. Anyone of intelligence travelled here, to be in the company of their peers, in the most serene republic. What happened? That happened.' He stabbed at the basilica with his hand. 'A belief without the confidence to doubt, to be uncertain. Galileo was silenced. Within a century Venice was in decline. The scientific revolution passed to the north, to Holland and England.'

'So? They stood out against the new, like you with Americans.'

He grinned at the gibe. 'True. I shouldn't speak against newness, still less against the truth. All I mean is that I cannot help grieving. Just think what this place could have been, without the dead weight of applied tradition. Tradition fought for as a monument, a pedestal for a frightened few. Think what Europe might have been without religious wars. I know, as part of my tradition, the world could not have been other than it was, but I do blame them. There were men here and throughout the enclaves of the Church who knew better. They might have trusted themselves, and others, and let the tradition grow and change. They failed, and this failed with them.' He swept his hand

71

about to indicate the city. 'All that I object to is a world which will embrace only the old or new, dispatching the other, but cannot live with both.'

'Do you really think that's possible?'

He stood deflated, looking down at his shoes, his hands in his pockets. His reply was quiet. 'There is nothing I would like to believe more.'

'That isn't an answer. As far as I can see they're embracing a new tyranny pretty quickly.'

'Perhaps. And I suppose the old one is teaming up as well, which seems to deny what I was hoping for – the new and old together for freedom, not silence. Have you ever been to mass there?'

'Me? No.'

'You ought to, once.'

'Strange advice from a Jew, with your beliefs.'

'To a communicating member of the Tory party at prayer?'

'I'm Church of England.'

'Exactly. Go. One high holiday. It's the most beautiful spectacle in the city, and it's dead.' (A few months later, on All Saints' Day, I took his advice; and am glad I did so, for he was, as he so often was, right.)

'You don't like Catholics too much either, do you?'

He suddenly looked immensely weary, and fretful, as though he doubted he could ever explain. 'It isn't really that, I promise you. My grandmother was one after all, in her way.'

'So your father was brought up a Catholic?'

'No.' He was sombre. 'They excommunicated her for that. She never really forgave them, or us. Sometimes she would slip very quietly into the back of a church and listen to a service, but as far as they were concerned she died apostate, and damned.'

'Was there nothing anyone could do?'

'Sometimes the asking price is much too high.' I did not ask him whose.

He rocked back on his heels, his hands still deeper in his pockets. 'I really shouldn't let my enthusiasms run away with me. It only leads to sadness. After cognition . . .' He laughed to himself. 'Most of all I hate tyranny, whatever form it takes, because it corrupts the mind. That doesn't make me too orthodox a Jew either, for we have a tyrannous God.'

'There must be something you believe in.'

'I believe in those.' He unfolded an arm and pointed at the horses, stiff on the basilica. The western sun caught the rooftops and they had begun to blaze, more softly than at dawn, but the matt bronze horses absorbed the light, dark against the gilded domes. 'I believe in the phenomenal world. I believe we have to act without any certainty of success. I believe that underneath the arrogance of empire and power and the glitter and tawdry wilfulness of humankind, and against its desperate pleas for bread and circuses and certainty, there remains the ability to think, to make, to act and to learn. Four horses against the darkness of the sun, as well as of the night.'

'Is that a voice of hope?'

'We are alive . . .'

I laughed and stepped in on his thought, for I had heard him speak it before, like a motto, 'And everything may be achieved.'

'May be,' he murmured, as if in correction or monition.

'It doesn't seem so very much against a new-born Roman Empire.'

He smiled and turned into the setting sun, his eyes half-veiled against the brightness and in a tone akin to mockery said, 'It may be all we really have.'

Time passed, both quickly and slowly at once. Looking back at my diaries, all the events of this time seem crowded together into a narrow space of time; but then it seemed as though minutes were hours, and hours were days, especially in her company, when time appeared to stand on points, revolving slowly, without any forward motion. Again, and again I wanted to speak, to tell her something of what I thought I felt. (Again, that is the wariness of age. I felt it well enough. It is only afterwards we doubt, and doubt the depth of feeling.) I was not made for those words, however. I am a practical man with language. I can make it tell a story, or explain, in simple words that anyone can understand, or special ones known only to the appointed. Simple words, however, can only tell simple stories, and jargon conceals. I did not understand when I was young that what I had to say was simple. I thought there was a special language of the affections, taught or handed on to poets. I did not realise it was only a deep attentiveness and scrupulous truthfulness – those, and the lying love of form and the shaping of tunes. All I am capable of now is compromise.

I seemed to be busy with Howard as well, though he delegated very little, at least of the duties he cared about or which interested him. I was his social dummy, what Americans call a front-man. He kept all the arrangements for the consular reception and Matteotti's visit to himself, muttering amongst his papers and rubbing his high bald forehead.

I begin to understand why writers write so little about work, and people's jobs, although they constitute so large a part of most people's experience. Most of my own working life has grown indistinct, as even and undistinguished as custard, though that may partly be because it is nearly twenty years since I last worked for the state. In age as in youth I have been a gentleman of leisure. Only the prospect of my own extinction has driven me back to my desk, to fiddle with language. Or is there, after all, another thing? It may be only the precipitate fearfulness of age, but sometimes I feel hounded through these reminiscences as though I stood with my back to a mirror and caught, out of the corner of my eye, a vision of something reflected there which is not proper to me or my comfortable surroundings, something fell and ancient, grinning, satisfied and ruthless. There should be something else to fill the hours of age, something other than myself, something like the work which was my occupation and – more than I can know, I suspect – helped to make me what I am.

It was not long before I received the letter Arthur and I had been waiting for, and I could make my preparations to travel for the first time across the long peninsula, to Bologna first, then on to Tim Carmichael, the Embassy, and Rome.

May had turned over on its side to June, and the spring morning mists scattered before dawn. The heat rose early now and stayed unchanging, with the fixity of a baker's oven, until night came with the chilling cold no season robs it of. I took the early morning train to Bologna, the dampness of night still itching under clothing and glistening on the long squat casing of the engine. The station was exiguously alive with grubby-costumed railway workers in the habitual oily blue of their craft, and only a handful of travellers. I had chosen a train with only first and second class carriages, avoiding the cacophony and dirt which spread from the other classes, with their wooden seats, and families travelling with livestock. (I have always found that the prospect of having a shoe eaten by a disease-ridden goat, or being shat on by chickens in wicker baskets in the luggage-rack, tends to distract from enjoyment of the view, and detract from the pleasures of voyaging.)

I settled into my compartment, and glared at anyone who passed in the corridor. The sun had not yet cleared the mists inside my head and I poured myself a thimbleful of Maria's unimaginably strong coffee from what was then one of my proudest possessions – the vacuum-flask of the seasoned traveller. My spirits rose with the temperature, as we set out into the dusty scuff of the Italian summer. A little after nine we passed the preposterously regular, artificial-looking slopes of

74

Monselice and slid on in a curve to Rovigo, the access point to Emilia and the soggy landscapes of the often flooded Po valley. We crossed the Po about a half hour later, the river and all its floodwaters flat as glass, flat as a funeral announcement for the water-meadows the river flooded again and again, to the despair of legates, dukes and administrators down an endless flow of centuries. I did not know we were passing through one of the heartlands of fascism, one of the regions Mussolini feared, where bands of agrarian squadristi felt loyalty only to their region, their manhood and the *ras*, the local chief. It was here his most aggressive, most vicious lieutenants came from; men like Dino Grandi, Italo Balbo and Roberto Farinacci. (I learnt this later, but not much later. It is a falsification I will let pass.) I learned where foreigners belonged, in the hierarchy of fascism, a little way on, in Ferrara.

I had reserved my seat to Bologna and another on to Rome, but when the train drew in to Ferrara, a body of fascist militia (in their teens and early twenties most of them – younger, even, than I was then, that distant brilliant summer) piled on to the train, commandeering the first class compartments. They tried to eject me, and I protested, until the conductor arrived and made it plain these brave lads took precedence over any foreign diplomat. I moved with an ill grace into a crowded second class compartment (the trains fill up as they proceed in Italy). I settled down with a book for the last hour or so to Bologna, then as now the focal-point and principal junction for the Italian railway system. (It was a book by Forster, I recall – *Where Angels Fear to Tread*. Jane had lent it to me. I could not make much of it.)

I lunched on the station at Bologna, for fear of missing the train to Rome. The station looked busy, and the people confident – but stations usually do, as do the people on them, wrapped up in their own affairs, so I could not make a judgement on Mussolini's state from that. The afternoon arrived, and the special express to Rome (I had to pay a surcharge) and I was off, over the grand divisive hog's-back of the Apennines, drowsy in the bright, well-fed afternoon sun, on the four hour journey to the capital (so much, and so unfortunately, quicker now).

That afternoon, I saw my first Italian summer storm, up in the mountains. The sky covered over in moments, as though someone had drawn a lid across a pot; and there was silence for a while, before the winds rushed in, slapping in rain, low and lateral and fast – so fast it did not have time to run into rivulets on the window, but splayed out into sheets of water travelling all ways at once – upwards, backwards, down. Then the lightning, the thunder directly above us, the great candescent forks of dreams and films, fired down, to gasps and little enchanted cries from the crowded compartment. The train slowed to less than a walking-pace, but in less than a quarter of an hour the storm was gone and we slid and steamed back into motion, the hillsides black and glistening, like horses in a sweat.

'Lucky,' said the old man next to me. 'Sometimes they last twelve hours up here, and the land slips underneath the rails. If that had happened we would still be here next week.'

As it was, we pulled into Rome late on a clear wet afternoon, the streets all silver, and the traffic almost unbearably loud. That was the first great shock after Venice. I had grown so used, so quickly, to that watery city, that I had half expected the streets of Rome to be canals as well, but filled with gilded, stately gondolas. Instead, I found myself in the quotidian modern world of motor-traffic and smog, devil-may-care pedestrians and drivers like duellists. I took one look at it and hailed a taxi.

I was being put up in the Embassy flat that night, and Carmichael was waiting for me. He hardly seemed to have changed at all since the day he got his place at King's. I could still imagine him in the autocratic uniform of Pop. He settled me in and fixed me a scotch and splash.

'Well, old man, you look pretty fit. How long can you stay on? I think we ought to be able to arrange a few days' sport at least.'

I grimaced. 'I don't think that's in order, I'm afraid. Howard's arranging a consular reception for me next Saturday, and so far he's cut me out of everything. I'd like to get back in time to make sure I have some say in things.'

He shook his head sympathetically. 'He doesn't change. He doesn't tell us what he's up to half the time. Not that it matters all that much. It's not the most important posting in the Kingdom, with all respect to you.' He tilted his whisky at me and I waved him on. 'We keep an eye on Trieste ourselves, but it can sometimes be a bit embarrassing not knowing what one of our junior envoys is up to. Anyway, how long do you think you might be able to stay?'

'Really, I'd like to take the night train tomorrow – there's one straight through to Venice, just after midnight.'

He reflected. 'It's a bit tight, but we ought to be able to manage it. You're due to see the old man at nine tomorrow, for half an hour. Did you bring the rig, by the way?'

I had. My morning coat was already hanging in the wardrobe, the creases dropping out. Carmichael had warned me the Ambassador liked to meet new officers dressed in full fig, tricorne and all, to put the fear of God and him into them, and expected them to be as formal.

'Righto. After you've seen him we ought to get you into the Vatican and show you the sights. The old man's lunching in mess tomorrow, so we ought to be there. We could do a taxi-ride around the ancient sites tomorrow afternoon, if that suits you?'

'That would be fine.'

'Doesn't leave us any time to introduce you to local society, such as it is. I find them a pretty tawdry lot, to tell the truth. The women are handsome enough, but out for the lucre and not to be trusted. You ought to come back down for the Corps Ball, though. Introduce you to the King. Nice enough fellow, but paper-thin – hasn't an idea in his head and won't stand up for himself to anyone. Are you sure it's only Howard you have to get back for?'

Despite the inquisitive gleam in his eye, I did not tell him about Eva. We did not speak of such things in those days. I did, however, tell him about Matteotti's visit, scheduled for that Thursday. I had not seen him so appalled since a housemaster tried to discipline him last.

'How dare he? Really, how dare he, without asking our permission first?'

I was mystified, and asked him what we had done wrong.

'Do you know who Matteotti is?'

'All I know is that he's an opposition deputy.'

Carmichael fumed. 'He's *the* opposition deputy, and a socialist, what's more. It's bad enough having that riff-raff elected in England. They're ten times worse over here. Little better than Bolsheviks, most of them. It isn't just that, though. It's the principle of the thing. Things are difficult enough in Rome as it is. Mussolini's a fool and an actor, but he is the Prime Minister, and he's new and nervous in power. He's already teamed up with the nationalists, which is a real step forward, ever since he made an ass of himself abroad last year. The liberals are waiting in the wings. You don't know Italy as well as we do, and Arthur Howard, whatever he may say, doesn't either. Even if he did, he has no right to fly in the face of the Foreign Office's collective wisdom. Italy's Rome, not the provinces. Things are going quite well over here. If no one rocks the boat the liberals will be back in power in next to no time, even if Mussolini remains the figurehead. With a little luck, however, we might even get Giolitti back into power – he wants it, and he's the only man in Italy who knows everybody's price. The last thing we need at a time like this is to have a socialist – damn it, the man's virtually an enemy of the people – being dined in a British Consulate.'

I began to understand Arthur Howard's machinations. 'It won't be at the Consulate. He's asked me to organise it at my place. Apparently, Matteotti's travelling up incognito.'

Carmichael snorted and reached for the glasses. His reply came over his shoulder as he refilled them. 'That's ridiculous. You or I or any private citizen can still travel round Europe incognito – the borders and the paperwork haven't got so bad as that, thank God – but Matteotti can no more travel about Italy in disguise and unnoticed than could Mussolini or the Pope. I'll have to tell the Ambassador.' It was the first time I had heard him refer to his chief by his title.

'Can he do anything to stop it?'

'He could, I suppose, but not without making matters even worse, this late in the day. No, I think our best bet is to let the authorities know on the quiet, and tell them it's happening without our approval. If we lean on Howard to withdraw the invitation at this stage it would look as though we were submitting to external pressure, and we can't allow that either. Why is Howard such a damnable fool?'

I remained silent, an admirable policy, I find, when in doubt. Carmichael sighed and tapped his fingers against the arm of his chair. He was enjoying his seniority as the Ambassador's secretary, and the edge and information he thought it gave him. 'Well, old man, no good fretting about it now. What say we go out and eat? Can't stand the Italian muck, myself, but I've found a little place where they do some decent French.'

We dressed and went out to dinner at a restaurant I have avoided ever since, where we had the filthiest French meal I think I have ever been subjected to. It was some solace, however, to be talking to a contemporary and a kind of friend. I had not realised how isolated I had been since my arrival in Italy. I was glad that Anthony was not there to hear my gossip.

The rest of that first brief stay in Rome occurred too fast for me to remember much, for I barely had the time to take in anything. I remember being more nervous before I met the Ambassador than I had been at any time since I first met my headmaster (for a thrashing, I regret to say). I need not have worried. Our conversation was restricted to those safe and formal pleasantries the English should have patented, so perfect are they at allowing social intercourse without any fear or risk. (I later discovered he had been mildly impressed, which is the effect I have always hoped to achieve.) I strained my neck in the Sistine Chapel, pretended to be disgusted by the opulent excess of St Peter's, and gawped at Raphael's Stanze (I have always liked Raphael – he is such an easy painter). We drove around the Roman ruins, and I found them strangely dusty and unimpressive, as though they had been mislaid, left there by mistake. I could not feel the frisson a classical education had prepared me for, which Gibbon had once felt on these hills. The remains continued to seem, as they had done in museums (and would do even after I finally got down to Pompeii and was shocked into a sense of this past) curiously dead, as Greek remains have never done. I could not help remembering the rhyme of my schooldays – 'Latin is a language,/As dead as dead can be./It killed the ancient Romans,/And now it's killing me.' (At school once, as a punishment I was required to translate it into Latin and write it out five hundred times.) Even then, however, I knew I was being unfair. I always enjoyed Latin much more than Greek, perhaps because it is the perfect bureaucratic language – concise, and with a place for everything, without the murderous freedom of Greek. It was, I suspect, only the ancient Roman virtues I abhorred, their heroes made of marble and patriotic sentiment.

Lunch in the mess, however, was a delight. The Ambassador sat me on his right, and for an hour, as the new boy, I was the object of interest and afforded them a change. I have always liked first meetings with my kind; it is a game I know, and I play it well. To my delight, I even discovered that Anthony had been right; some of the younger officers, in their manner, displayed something very close to envy. None of this is important, however, and none of it made so strong an impression on me as my conversation over dinner with Tim Carmichael that first night. (I returned to Rome that autumn – missing the Venice floods – for the Diplomatic Corps Ball, and stayed ten days, ingratiating myself with the city and growing at least to like it. It was not until the following year that I experienced Venice at her worst, in fog and snow and hail, gun-metal grey waters rising and spewing filth wherever they go, the whole city monochrome with water, on land and in the air, a stiff widowed bleakness I grew, however, to care for as expressive of my darker moods.) I do not know how much of what he said that evening was pre-arranged, or if he had discussed it with his superiors, and I have always wondered, and suspected that he had. That evening was the first indication I ever had that my personality as the steady, unexciting man had been noticed in the service. It is an invaluable reputation to acquire, and led me to success where other, more intelligent or more charismatic figures stumbled and failed. I had an advantage, of course. In my case, it was true.

It began over the brandy, or rather over Carmichael's brandy. I drank grappa, for I wanted something yet more disgusting to erase the taste of the filthy meal he had just enjoyed.

'We're very glad to have you in Venice, you know.'

'Who are we?'

He continued without answering. 'We wanted someone solid, dependable. A reliable type. I thought of you at once.'

I knew he was bragging at the very least, and almost certainly lying, but I let it pass.

'Howard's very able, of course, and he's been in the post a very long time. Too long, some cruel souls would say, but I'm not one to be party to back-stabbing like that. Still, he is quite old, and he's always been a little eccentric, shall we say.'

'He's certainly has strong opinions.'

'Exactly. I see you take my meaning. It doesn't matter too much, of course, not in Venice. It's not as though he were involved in making policy.'

'I sometimes think he would like to be.'

Carmichael looked rueful. 'True, old boy. He doesn't seem to realise that things have changed since the telegraph and wireless came along. There are no plenipotentiaries now. Even the old man has no real freedom of action. We're just the poor bloody messengers. Ours not to reason why – that kind of thing.'

I pushed more confidently than I felt. 'But what has this to do with my being in Venice?'

I thought at first I had pushed too hard, for he paused to consider his response, if any. In the end he tried being evasive. 'Nothing sinister, old boy.'

'I didn't think so.' I feigned indifference. My silence encouraged him to continue.

'It would be nice to know, now and again, what Howard is up to. Useful for us to know about Matteotti, for instance.'

'I thought you were against his visit.'

'Never as simple as that, you know. More a question of concerting our action, to get the maximum effect. Doesn't do to have our batteries firing off in different directions. Have to concentrate our fire.' Like so many, he had picked up a smattering of military diction during our excitable schooldays of the war. I relaxed a little, giving him an opening.

'I don't suppose there would be any harm if I kept in touch, just now and again. Chew the cud with an old chum.'

He was duly grateful. 'That's the sort of thing we had in mind.' I let the tell-tale pronoun pass. In other circumstances, I have taken single words like that and rammed them down my interlocutor's throat, but here I was patient; I had too much to learn. 'We're always happy to be of help,' he continued. 'But if we are to help we have to be kept informed.'

'There might be one problem, as I understand it.'

'Nothing, I'm sure, we can't clear up.'

'Perhaps. My Consul believes our telephone in Venice is – tapped, I think the word is. He mentioned others might be, too.'

'I think he may be exaggerating, but it shouldn't worry you unduly. I'm sure there's nothing we might have to say we would not want anyone else to hear. Who knows? There might even be some benefit if certain people understood the broader range of our position.'

'I have to trust your better judgement.'

'I think that's very wise. I'm sure our people here will be very pleased that you've taken such a co-operative attitude.'

'I think it would be wisest if I knew exactly how we stood. As you can understand, I only have one source of information and policy at the moment. It would be helpful if I could be told how I can best serve the interests we represent. It's safer if I know exactly where I stand. I'm sure you understand that.'

He had relaxed, and was perhaps more confident than I would have been in his position. 'Oh, quite. Quite. It wouldn't do for there to be any misunderstanding.' He paused, going over the outlines of a prepared statement, I suspect, wondering exactly how to phrase it, what nuances to emphasise to ensure my sympathy and support. 'Things are very difficult here at the moment. Some people don't quite understand that. They are a little hastier than we would like. We don't believe, however, it serves any interest to be precipitate. We are envoys, after all – foreign guests and visitors. There is the principle of national self-determination to be considered. We don't want to interfere, or seem to. We don't want any fuss.'

'How far should we take that policy, I wonder?'

'Right now, we don't want any fuss at all. There are disputed matters at the international level. It would be such a shame if our position were jeopardised by hasty action or trivial disputes.'

'Of course. I quite see that. The question does arise, however, given that there are people who wouldn't necessarily agree – people who take a more ... puritanical view, shall I say? – the question arises, where does my responsibility lie, and whose support can I expect?'

'I understand your worries, naturally, but I assure you they are groundless. I have been instructed, quite specifically instructed, to inform you that should there seem to be a question of – jurisdiction, say? – that you can always count on the highest level of support. Why,

81

yes, of course. All that we ask is that we should be kept informed. We would not want any surprises, nothing to upset the delicate balance of policy. But you understand, I know.'

I was silent, in acquiescence. He pushed through, certain he had gained his end.

'I'm sure I don't have to say how grateful ...'

'Oh, quite.'

'It's not the sort of thing our principals forget. I'm sure you can rely on them, in every way.'

He settled the bill and walked me back to the Embassy, leaving me at the gates, repeating himself for surety.

'I'm so glad we had our little chat. Of course, we knew we could rely on you. One of our own, so to speak. You'll be in touch quite soon, I expect. After Thursday.'

'Oh, certainly. As soon as I safely can.'

He picked the word up gratefully. 'Safely. That's the ticket. No point in troubling people who wouldn't understand. Best keep mum to them. We don't want any arguments after all.'

'True.'

'So glad you understand. After all, it's keeping the peace we're after. No ... upsets.'

'None.'

'Well, goodnight, then. See you just before nine.'

'Indeed. Goodnight.'

The night train pulled in to Venice just after eight in the morning. I went home first to shower and change and breakfast. It was after ten o'clock before I arrived at the Consulate. Enrico informed me Howard had a visitor, and it was not until they both came out, two hours later, that I realised it was Anthony. Howard affected to be surprised to see me.

'Hello, Jeremy. I hadn't expected you back so soon.'

'I thought I had better come back.'

'How was Rome?'

'Dull.'

'And the Ambassador?'

'Duller.'

'Does he still do his silly business about dressing in full fig to meet new officers?'

'Oh yes.'

'Silly bugger. Discover anything interesting from our enemies?' (He should not have spoken like that before an outsider. To this day I believe Howard's enthusiasms were unprofessional. Diplomats should be unemotional men. In my day, that one requirement would have excluded women from the service. Now, however, the few, few girls I meet seem tougher than the men. Perhaps they always were, without our knowing.)

I was cold. 'Nothing. I wouldn't expect them to keep the other ranks informed.'

He chuckled to himself. 'Sorry to have excluded you. Manet and I fell talking about some problems he's been having.'

'Nothing serious, I trust?'

It was Anthony who replied. 'Nothing diplomatic. Just two dilettantes' gossip.' He turned back to the old Consul. 'Howard, have you finished with Mr Burnham for the day?'

'Nothing to start on, sir. He's yours.'

'Doing anything for lunch today, Jeremy?'

'I thought I might go over to the Schifanoia, to see if Jane were free.' I had meant, in fact, to call on Eva, but for reasons of uncertainty and doubt which still remain obscure, I did not want to tell this new scholastic alliance that.

'Good idea. Would you mind if I came too?'

'Not at all. It's your island.'

'Hardly.'

'Take the *Queen Mary*,' Howard grunted, ruining my afternoon.

As we came out of the lift at the Schifanoia, I sensed, rather than saw, someone I thought I recognised turn down the stairs. Anthony, too, perceptibly stiffened, but the half-thought was gone before it turned to words. The door to Jane's suite stood open. She sat on the chaise-longue, her bodice torn, her hair tattered loose, weeping, a great bruise swelling over her right eye and cheekbone. Anthony was gone, with a hellish roar.

'Younghusband!'

Jane began to reach out imploringly, but I turned back into the corridor. I learnt that afternoon that there are certain advantages in not being an English gentleman. Anthony was racing down the corridor, head down, his left leg trailing. I followed him. He threw himself down the stairs. Younghusband stood on the landing, grinning wolfishly. He drew his right arm back, fist clenched, his left up on guard. Anthony's bad leg snaked out. He seemed to be falling. Then his left foot slapped, with all his weight, between Younghusband's legs. Younghusband went down like a tub of wet cement. Before I knew it Anthony was racing back down the corridor, his face still dark as murder. Younghusband lay there, pale and stricken, without a sound. I decided he had slipped, which was no concern of mine. I went back to help Jane.

Anthony was holding her head up, under her chin.

'It doesn't look too healthy. Wait there.' He went through to her bedroom, and through the open door we could see him rifling through her wardrobe, pulling out dresses, dark ones – black, magenta, purple, indigo, navy, olive and brown. He pulled a maroon one from the pile and came back into the room, thrusting it at me. 'Be an angel, Jeremy. Get hold of Eva, get Jane a drink, and get her into this. I'll be back in an hour.' Out into the corridor he went, diving back a second later, the pile of dresses billowing in his arms, into the bedroom, catching up a pair of her shoes, and then he was gone again, a cry of 'Back in an hour. Promise!' echoing behind him.

I did my best to follow his instructions. Eva excluded me in calming Jane, not even asking what had happened. I got her a whisky and Eva got her into the maroon dress.

Anthony was as good as his word, returning an hour later, his arms still full of dresses to which were added a miscellanea of paper bags. He dropped them in a pile on the floor by Jane, who sat looking into a glass, murmuring 'Horrible! Horrible!' as she fingered the mottled blue and purple cast which ruined her face. Anthony straddled across her knees and lifted her face gently.

'It isn't very pretty, dear. Good job he didn't get your mouth. Couldn't have done much with broken lips.'

'Bastard! Bastard!' she muttered slowly and in pain.

'Don't worry. He won't be able to walk for the best part of a week. Now, let's try this.' He seized one of the paper bags and pulled out a long maroon sash. 'With a face like that you'd look damn silly in pastels or anything light. Dark colours for you, dear, until the swelling's settled down.'

He began to swathe the sash around her head, pulling it down occasionally over her eye and cheekbone. When he was done, he seized another paper bag and rifled amongst lipsticks till he found the shade he wanted, a toning purple. He began to apply it quickly, deftly. He ruffled through other items of make-up (I cannot be expected to know their names). When he had finished, he reached for the biggest paper bag and pulled out a pair of high brown boots. I was almost shocked. In fact, shocked silence had reigned since he began his performance. He helped Jane pull on the boots. When they were done, he helped her to her feet with a cry of 'There!' and stepped away from her.

She did not look demure or ladylike, but she did look beautiful, a beautiful cossack princess, high-spirited, haughty, and dangerously foreign.

Jane looked at herself anxiously in the glass. Slowly, a shy smile curled the corners of her mouth. Manet spoke quietly, his hands crossed before him. 'It isn't very English, I know, but it should keep you out of purdah till you're better. There are turbans and make-up to match all your darker frocks in those bags.' She turned to him, smiling. All of us were smiling. At last she admitted a kind of acceptance.

'It's certainly striking.'

Then all of us started to laugh, and I slipped my arm round Eva's waist, and Jane curled up almost girlishly in Anthony's protective embrace, her bad cheek against his shoulder, muttering with a smile, 'You are a love, you are a love.'

Federico Capodimonte came to see me at the Consulate the following morning. The police chief was brisk.

'Signor Burnham. I understand you may have been present yesterday when Signor John Younghusband was viciously attacked by the Jew, Anthony Manet?'

I remained silent, wondering what he wanted. He made it plain soon enough that he was more embarrassed than I and did not really know what to make of the situation.

'I wondered if you might have some more information for me?'

'You seem to know as much as I do, Chief Inspector. As far as I know, this was a private matter between the two gentlemen.' (I trusted to Younghusband's dubious good sense, hoping he had not involved Mrs Carlyle.)

'Perhaps you are right.' The police chief was sympathetic, unctuous even, but a vague sense of menace seemed to travel in company, like a foul personal odour (he sweated heavily as it was). 'You ought to know, I think, however, that some of us are very fond of Signor Younghusband. He is a very sympathetic man. He understands us and our cause. He is alive to the New Italy. I told you we are always happy to be helpful to sympathetic foreigners; and, besides, he is rich.'

'I don't believe the other gentleman is a pauper.'

'Indeed. Please do not misunderstand me. We have no history of anti-semitism here, but he is a foreigner twice over and one, I understand, who goes around devaluing Italian art ...'

'That isn't strictly true.'

'I think it is. When he has done, the pictures sell for less. Some people even take our dealers to the courts. We do not like that. Some of those men are our great supporters, but fortunately we are the courts now. And as I say, I do not think the police need to be too closely involved, but perhaps the Jew should be warned to be more careful. Some of my men are very enthusiastic, particularly when it comes to protecting friendly foreigners. We do not leave everything to the courts. They are a refuge of everything which is weak and feminine.'

I ignored the threat, convinced it was only Italian bluster, but took up the salient point he had let slip. 'Does that mean Mr Younghusband will not be pressing charges?'

'It does not seem so.'

I tried to trip a line between firmness and understanding. 'Well, Chief Inspector, if Mr Younghusband chooses not to lay charges, embarrassed, shall we say, about being beaten by a crippled Jew, I can only concur with his decision. Dr Manet is a British subject too, of course, and as such has as much right to my assistance as Mr Younghusband. It is, however, my duty to advise our citizens also, and I shall certainly have words with him. Can we let the matter rest there, in my hands?'

I still remember the uniformed bandit's smile, aped from cinema heroes, which seemed to show more teeth than any mouth has room for. He was sardonic. 'I knew you would understand. It is good to have a Consul one can work with. We bureaucrats must work together.'

After Capodimonte had left, Howard came through into my office, his lips pursed in evident distaste. 'What did he want?' I explained. Howard was puzzled. 'But what was it all about? It doesn't sound like Manet at all.' I did not know how much to tell him, and stalled him with a compromise.

'I believe it concerned a lady.'

'Damn!' For once he seemed at a loss, his usual composure gone. 'Could make it dashed awkward on Saturday.' I did not understand. He explained. 'I've invited them both.'

I was annoyed. I should have known that something like this would happen if I did not keep a firmer hand on the arrangements. 'But why, Howard? We never even mentioned Younghusband.'

'When you wanted to invite Mrs Carlyle I naturally assumed we should invite her companion too. This is a Consulate, after all, not a convent.'

'But where did you get his name from? What made you think they were companions?'

He looked baffled, and hurt, as though I was questioning his intelligence (which I was, I suppose). 'But damn it,' he protested, 'they're booked into the same suite at the Schifanoia. It's on the hotel list.'

There was nothing I could say. In the end I settled on the simplest version of the truth. 'He moved into rooms of his own some time ago.' We were both silent for a while. We knew that someone had blundered. I tried another dose of firmness. 'You'll have to withdraw his invitation.'

Howard was scandalised. 'I can't do that. It would make us look like fools, or knaves, I don't know which is worse. No, we'll just have to count on them behaving. They're gentlemen, after all. They had a proper education. They should know how to behave at a consular reception.'

I let it go at that, taking some consolation in the fact that, if Anthony was right, Younghusband might still be bed-ridden on Saturday.

Thursday came, the day of Matteotti's visit. Howard was as restless as a kitten with a ball of string, reviewing the arrangements when we met in the morning.

'He's arriving on the six o'clock train. I shall meet him at the station. We don't want people gawping on the concourse so I've arranged for Enrico to pick us up further down the Canale Grande.'

I thought of Enrico's links with the authorities. 'Does he know who it is you're meeting?'

Howard grinned, like a schoolboy with an inky secret. 'What do you take me for? All he knows is that it's one of my particular friends, and that I'm taking him for a walk to stretch his legs before Enrico picks us up. We should be at your house no later than seven o'clock. Are all the arrangements made?'

'Everything's done. Maria's been hiding herself in the kitchen for the last two days. I defied her to do her worst. Actually, she's a very good cook. Matteotti should have no complaints on that score. He is still staying overnight?'

Howard nodded. 'Taking the six forty-five to Milan.'

'Fine. I've had Maria make up the beds in both the spare rooms, so you can stay as well if we run on late.'

He was gleeful. 'If I have anything to do with it, we will.'

In fact they arrived at the house only a little after six-thirty. What do I remember of Matteotti? Two things most of all, for he was not greatly physically distinguished: he had the most beautiful almond eyes I had ever seen on a man, and powerful long hands, brown, with startlingly pale broad palms and long strong fingers. He was the perfection of a statesman: eyes and hands were all you noticed: eyes to see, and hands to make and do.

Maria scurried out from the kitchen as soon as he arrived, wiping her hands on a dish-cloth, yeasty with curiosity. She recognised him at once, and I realised the truth of Carmichael's assertion that he could travel nowhere in Italy unnoticed. Maria knelt down painfully and tried to put her arms around his ankles. Without any affectation he helped her tenderly to her feet as she went on repeating his name, imploring her to stop, calling her 'Mother'. I still find other people's political allegiances baffling, especially in foreign parts and most of all in countries as diverse as Italy, but whenever I have doubts I have only to remember the look of trust which passed between that autocratic, patrician politician (socialism used to be good at producing noblemen) and that tough, embattled old peasant woman, to know that once, long ago, in a city of dreams, my house and table entertained a hero. (I remember something Howard once said, when I mentioned a doubt about entertaining a prominent opposition deputy – it was the day after my return from Rome. He said, 'But damn it, Burnham, Matteotti's a socialist, not a tyrant; whereas Lenin is a tyrant, and a communist.' It is a distinction I have tried to remember.)

After Matteotti had washed, I led them in to dinner. Arthur Howard believed my political education began that night.(It began at school, where I first learnt the strange but vital relationship between promises, delivery and support.)

'Arturo and I are old good friends,' Matteotti explained. 'There are many things we take for granted. You must stop us if we confuse you, or if you do not understand. And would you be happier in English or Italian?'

I thought it over and plumped for Italian, silently blessing Arthur's stern didactic ways (I have always found most people are more open, and more honest, in their own language. I cannot say the same), but promised to stop them if they should lose me.

Howard began without small talk, over the antipasto. 'Things are quiet in Venice at the moment, Giacomo, now the season has begun. The usual trail of rumours from Trieste, to be sure, and uglier ones from the Adriatic, but how are things with you?'

Matteotti ignored the question. 'You have heard the Mediterranean rumours, also?'

Arthur nodded. 'What rumours are those?' I asked.

The deputy waved a fork at me. 'Mussolini dreams of a new Roman Empire. Like every imperialist before him he thinks he can use a war of conquest to export his domestic and social problems. There are rumours he is planning a new adventure, something to eclipse the memory of D'Annunzio's attack on Fiume, two, two and a half, years ago. That still rankles. He did not join in that attack because he was too weak in those days, and did not want D'Annunzio to get all the glory. Also, he was frightened it might fail. It didn't, and D'Annunzio got the glory anyway.'

I was genuinely curious. 'What sort of adventure?'

'Many rumours,' Matteotti replied, brushing his mouth with his napkin. 'All the reliable ones concerning Greek or Turkish territory. Some say Cyprus ...'

'Some,' Arthur interrupted, 'say Corfu.'

'I have heard this too, and I can believe it.'

I, on the other hand, was incredulous. 'It sounds too fantastic for words. There's an international boundary commission in Corfu now. The last thing the League would stand for is another power simply stepping in and taking over. He'd face international obloquy.'

The Italian was cynical. 'Disapproval fires no shells.'

'But the Royal Navy does, and the Mediterranean is still a British sphere of influence.'

'That, my friend,' Matteotti smiled, as he sat back to let Maria clear the table, still awestruck by his presence, 'is Italy's best hope.'

I was dumbfounded. 'You mean you want war with Britain?'

'I don't want a war with anyone, and it wouldn't come to that. Mussolini would back down if faced by strong opposition, and, to be entirely honest, I think it is only a chain of overseas fiascos which can now dislodge him from power. It is not something I could say in public, and hate having to say at all, but I fear we must be humiliated before the nation will see the folly of Mussolini's ways.'

'But I don't see why it should need to. When I was in London after Mussolini's visit, the general impression was - and Amery and Nicolson at the Foreign Office were saying - that Mussolini was a megalomaniac and an actor, but a fool, and that your establishment would soon tame him.'

Howard was contemptuous. 'Nicolson's a charming bugger without an original notion. He's too much of a ninny to understand or deal with men of blood, and Amery hasn't had a thought outside the commonplaces of his class and background since the day he was dropped squalling on to the planet.'

The Italian was sombre. 'Arturo keeps on saying things like that, and I keep hoping he exaggerates. We have to count on the intelligence of the Chanceries of Europe - not so easy after the past twenty years, but we have to hope. Are there no Young Turks, you called them once Arturo, who understand what is happening?'

It was Arturo's turn to be deflated. 'Our service has an unhappy record with brilliant young men. It gets enough of them, God knows, and then ignores them. Look what happened before the War when Eyre Crowe and his German desk kept up a flow of detailed warnings about German aims, and were ignored or reviled. Now they've emasculated him by kicking him upstairs. It is a depressing prospect. The only one in London I trust is young Kennard. He knows the mad-dog type, and that you have to shoot them, but he has no influence alone. Nor do I.'

We were silent for a while over our carp. I remained puzzled by it all, and finally addressed a question to them both.

'Forgive me, but I don't see why anyone else should become involved. Isn't it Italy's problem?'

The deputy pushed his fork to one side and searched his teeth with his tongue before replying. 'For the moment, yes, but it will not remain so long, and it is my belief the Powers should act quickly to prevent unnecessary slaughter. We can no longer defeat this scoundrel on our own.'

I was unrepentant; Howard, I suspect, was furious with me. 'Why not?'

He chewed over a fresh forkful. 'Mussolini is many things, but not a fool ...'

I pressed on regardless, heedless of protocol. 'He's also weak. Arthur himself told me how much the administration had needed the alliance with the nationalists, for their credibility and exper-ience. I won't believe an alliance between your socialists and the liberal power blocs couldn't stop the fascists if you really wanted, without our interference.'

'Liberal power blocs?' The Italian seemed amused.

'Yes. Arthur was telling me about them. The parliamentary groups round Salandra and Giolitti.'

Suddenly the two of them burst out laughing. Howard groped for his napkin to wipe away mock tears and even Maria came back into the room to see what her idol's merriment was about, but it was Howard who replied, sitting back and beaming, trying to restrain his laughter. 'It's a lovely idea, dear boy. The only trouble is, Giolitti and Salandra haven't spoken to each other for eight years – not since Salandra took Italy into the war when Giolitti was against it – and they're not about to invite each other to breakfast now.'

I would not be stopped. 'But that's appalling. A country's future shouldn't rely on two men's whim.'

Matteotti agreed, firmly. 'It is appalling, you're quite right, but it is the case. There's more to it, of course, but you begin to see the problems, the problems of division we face.'

I could not understand. 'I thought Giolitti wanted to be Prime Minister again? He's had the job more often than anyone else and seeme to be prepared to do anything to get there. Why shouldn't he settle with Salandra?'

'Salandra is ambitious, too. He wouldn't agree.'

'But they say that Giolitti's the only man in Italy who knows everybody's price.'

Matteotti smiled sadly to himself. 'That's almost true, though the truth is more subtle. Giovanni Giolitti is the only man in Italy who can remember everybody's price.'

I hoped I was being implacable. In fact, I was only querulous. 'And what is your price, Signor Matteotti?'

He raised a hand to stop Howard butting in in anger. His reply was measured, almost formal. (It occurs to me in retrospect that if I had not liked him so much, immediately, I would have written it off as a prepared statement for foreign consumption.) 'My price is the restitution of Italy's constitution and her parliamentary democracy. My price is the inheritance of Cavour, who created everything that is best in Italy.'

'It sounds very noble. I thought you were a socialist. Would you do any better in Mussolini's place?'

'I don't aspire to anything like such a pedestal. That is for statues of the dead. And I don't think I would destroy democracy, no.' (I remembered Howard's distinction, and knew he was telling me that least simple of things, the truth.)

Maria had excelled herself, and now brought in highly-sauced veal with rice. Mattcotti looked at the chafing dish and put his hands on his stomach and shook his head, saying sorrowfully and in mock disapproval 'Oh madre, madre ...' I swear she giggled.

Howard served, and the deputy took up the argument again.

'If I may say so, I think you underestimate the depth of the divisions in the opposition, of which the Giolitti-Salandra quarrel is only one example. Mussolini's genius, and he has a kind of genius, lies not only in setting the factions off against each other, but also in rendering their arguments and actions meaningless. It is the administration which lies at the heart of what he has done.' I admitted I knew nothing about Italian bureaucracy and added, with unnecessary rudeness, that I felt little need to.

Howard could restrain himself no longer. 'Then you're a damn fool – '

'Arturo, please.' Matteotti raised a pale pink palm again, and once again laid down his fork. (He can have eaten very little that evening, though he drank as much as the rest – and yet Maria raised not a whimper of complaint. She would shout the house down if I left a thing. Such is real power.) 'You must know,' he continued, 'that for fifty years and more now, the Italian administration has been rotten to the core, in the grip of regional interests which express themselves through personal and factional ones. Mussolini took over that administration as it stood and learnt to use it, learnt to give each region a sense of preferential treatment and local advantage. He is a master of feudal patronage, and that makes him a master over all. As long as patronage and benefits are seen to flow from him, he can ignore the parliamentary opposition, for he knows what Giolitti also knows: that Italian politicians vote for their bank-balances. He also knows what Giolitti never has, which is that the faces may and can change so long as the money flows out to the regions. What's more, by keeping on the administration he has avoided Lenin's problem after his revolution, of having no civil service, no apparatus of state.'

I remember being shocked. 'Do you mean you think a revolution is happening in Italy?' (Remember, it was the dirtiest word in the English political vocabulary.)

He was quietly adamant: 'I think it has already taken place.' He paused to take a mouthful of veal and broccoli, and to sing praises through to Maria, squirming delightedly in the kitchen doorway. 'He has even finally taken control of the fascist movement.'

'I had assumed he always had it.'

He shook his head. 'No. A common mistake. As much as anything, fascism developed from regional, agrarian forces, answerable to local *ras* or chieftains, particularly in Emilia and Sicily. Mussolini gained his position by force of character, by the brilliance of his propaganda journalism, and through those chieftains. Last December, however, he turned the fascist squadristi into the national militia with their own officers – centurions and consuls he calls them. The squads are paid now, by his government, so the chieftains retain a nominal authority but he has the power. So much talent gone to waste.' He seemed genuinely saddened. 'And he has the Church.'

I had been expecting some such comment, and had done my homework. 'That I find difficult to believe. He has publicly spoken out against the Church.'

'Until recently.'

92

Arthur stepped in. 'Giacomo doesn't care to be reminded of it, but Mussolini began on the left of Italian politics. He's trimmed and trimmed, however, to get himself into power. Italy still has a Catholic majority and he needs their docile acquiescence at least. His government have opened negotiations with the Vatican to work towards what they are calling a concordat. It may take years, but that doesn't matter from his point of view because the fact that the Vatican is talking to him implies he is the only politician in Italy the Church trusts or regards, and that is enough to satisfy potential or actual Catholic supporters. And from the Church's point of view he has the advantage of being a new man, not an old liberal, because the liberals – as well as the socialists – have always stood up to the Church and held out against its presumptions. It's said, as it happens, he also has the Cardinal Gaspara, the Papal secretary of state, firmly in his pocket.'

'That seems to be true,' Matteotti agreed, 'but an even clearer sign of the way things are going is that the Pope is ordering Don Sturzo – a priest, a conservative and a *populari*, but an opponent of Mussolini – out of Italy. It looks as though, so long as Mussolini stands out against divorce, bashes a few heretics and pays a little restitution, Pius will do anything for him.'

Their case appeared to grow overwhelming, and deeply depressing. I suppose the difference between us was and remained that I have never been certain there is any justification for one country's interfering in the internal affairs of another unless its own interests are directly affected. I began to understand how difficult Howard, with his naive enthusiasm for direct involvement, must be for the Embassy to deal with. (It seemed they could not hope to control him.) I tried to say as much.

'I sympathise, I think, Signor Matteotti, but I don't see there is anything else I can do. Britain cannot interfere, especially when there is supposed to be an election forthcoming here. If things are as bad as you say, Mussolini will be voted out of office.'

He pushed his plate aside. 'That is extremely unlikely now. You won't have heard, Arturo – I have only just found out myself – but next month he proposes to put a bill before the parliament stating that, if the fascists achieve twenty-five per cent of the popular vote in the next election, they should be awarded two-thirds of the seats. It is the end of Italian democracy.'

Howard slumped forward, looking suddenly tired.

I protested. 'He'll never get away with it, surely? It will be voted out.'

Matteotti shook his head quickly but slightly, like an old man, but his eyes were stern. 'I don't think so. He has enough people in his pay now, and there are enough politicians who see him as the road to power instead of the road to destruction, to make sure he gets almost anything he wants.'

'Why not take your case to the people?'

'We try, and we will go on trying, but most of them seem to assent to his rule, even if they do not support it. He pays his bills and speaks of greatness. It's a very powerful combination after the last few years. And anyway, they're frightened.' His head drooped forward, as though it had become too heavy for him. Maria came in and·put a hand on his shoulder. He looked up and she pointed to his plate. He nodded. She began clearing the table. When she had gone he continued. 'We need him to be embarrassed abroad; if necessary, defeated by force of arms, because we cannot beat him on the ground at home. We could have, once. Now it is too late.' Maria came back in bearing a tray laden with glasses of a hot, sweet, sticky, semi-solid pudding (it was delicious), fruit and a Cona of coffee. 'Ah! Madre!' Matteotti cried, clapping his hands. 'Zabaglione!' He teased her and thanked her all at once, and she simpered and preened like a fifteen-year-old before promising to leave such busy men in peace, but only so long as we called if we needed anything more. (With most politicians I have known, the common touch has been something vile and specious. With Matteotti it seemed to be no more than being an Italian.)

He took a spoonful of zabaglione and waved his spoon at me. 'Two years ago, take a month, a fascist squad led by two of Mussolini's most vicious deputies – Albino Volpi and Amerigo Dumini, remember their names – ran riot in a little town called Sarzana. For once, the police took action. They opened fire, killing some of them. The fascists fled. If we had reacted with force then, the fascists would never have come to power; but we did not, so now we need another power to do it for us.'

'It seems a great deal to ask.'

'I can't say I think so,' said Howard gruffly, 'to save the crucible of western civilisation.'

The deputy smiled his melancholy smile. 'Arturo is one of the greatest patriots we have.' I did not say he had another country he should look to. 'I know it is a great deal to ask – but he is killing our people. On average, five political killings are reported every day. The true figure may well be higher. Three deputies have already been murdered, including Di Vagno. Two years ago they sent squads into the Chamber to drag out the Communist Misiano, to give him a

94

beating. Then, it was a scandal. Now, attacks on politicians are commonplace.'

'Including,' said Arthur, fingering his spoon, 'attacks on you. A dozen beatings it must be now. Or is it more?'

He shrugged his shoulders. 'It is the price I have to pay for speaking out. The squads – I'm sorry, the militia – are being run by some of the most notorious gangsters in Italy – Volpi, Dumini, Farinacci, Bonaccorsi. Take Farinacci, now. He is supposed to be Mussolini's brightest legal brain, and he copied another man's doctoral thesis word for word and presented it as his own. On behalf of the sansepolcristi, his early supporters – and their numbers grow daily by retrospective appointment – corruption is endemic, in every walk of life. You don't know the latest on the Amendola affair I think, Arturo. Amendola, a conservative liberal, was walking home and was set on by five of Mussolini's thugs, including Volpi and Dumini. He's an old man, but he fought them off with his umbrella. Do you know what they propose to do now? They're threatening him with proceedings for criminal assault.'

I could not help laughing. They remained silent and I wondered if I had done something wrong. Howard explained. 'No, it isn't your fault, Jeremy, you're new to the situation. All we were thinking was that the next time they come for Giovanni Amendola – and they will come – they will come in their hundreds.' (I think it may be worth, in the interests of truth, recording that, although it took some time, they were right, and Amendola died of his injuries.)

Matteotti stirred sugar into his coffee with a broad graceful movement. (I like the way some foreigners eat and drink, so different from the dainty pecking and sipping of the English.)

'The saddest thing of all,' he said, 'is that those Italians who aren't bought or frightened by the government are impressed by it. Even Croce, the best historian we have, thinks we ought to give this government a chance. And now Arturo tells me there are even Englishmen who are impressed by Mussolini and are queuing up to buy black shirts for export to England. Is there really no one at the Foreign Office we can count on?'

Howard looked humble, for he knew the truth as well as I. 'No one important enough. Kennard can do nothing alone, and I, even with my experience, am only a Consul. In better days young Toynbee might have been with us too, but as it is even he is considered to be too much to the left to be invited to join the service.'

Matteotti looked saddened but unsurprised. 'I can't say that I blame them. We have enough men of our own who underestimate the threat and who are prepared to enter into pacts with our enemy. The blackest news of all, in some ways, is the rumour that at the next election Salandra himself will put his name forward on Mussolini's list of fascist candidates.'

It was growing late. Thereafter, my education begun (as Arthur would have seen it), they had very little use for me. They spoke of friends, potential allies and specific problems and incidents of which I knew nothing. I did not interrupt their conversations, but ferried them alcohol and coffee. Maria sat watchful in the kitchen, although the night dragged on, as though her wakefulness could keep the great deputy safe.

It was well past midnight before the two of them looked as though they might be flagging. Howard became solicitous at last. 'It's late. You have an early train to catch.' Matteotti agreed wearily. He went to thank Maria, her face shining with pride and tiredness, and then I took them upstairs to show them to their rooms. (Arthur gave every impression of meaning to be present until Matteotti was safely on his train.) The exhausted quiet of the night was interrupted by a stamping of feet and general crashing in the front garden out on to the canal. I heard Maria scurrying to the door, and the deputy threw himself down the stairs with Howard and myself behind him. We found Maria in the garden, yelling in Venetian (I made out 'Fascist bastards' and 'Murderers', but the rest was too highly specialised). From the open gate to the canal I saw a motor-boat pull away. I cannot be certain, especially after all this time, and it was very dark, but I had the impression it was a police-launch. Matteotti nearly fell over a body slumped in the corner. It was Anthony. He had been beaten unconscious. There was a piece of paper pinned to his sleeve. It read, 'This is how we deal with Bolsheviks and foreigners.'

Matteotti helped me to lift him. 'Get him upstairs,' was all I could say, thinking to get him away from danger. 'We can put him in my bed. I'll take the couch.' We got him upstairs, a dead weight, and stripped him off. Matteotti looked him over with a practised eye.

'Professionals. Intended to damage and frighten, but not to disfigure. No injuries to the face or hands, for instance. They didn't want him to be believed if he talked. Who is he?'

I was angry with fear by now. 'A friend of mine.' The deputy looked as though it were only to be expected. I would not let myself believe his scare-stories. 'Don't be ridiculous. Damn it, is he all right? That's what matters.'

'It doesn't look too bad, but we had better call a doctor. There may be internal injuries.'

Somehow Howard got hold of a doctor, even at that time of night. While we waited Matteotti and Maria, with barely a word, prepared astringents, lemon juice and vinegar in hot water, and bathed his body with a steady, gentle nursing efficiency, the skill which Englishmen look for in their women.

Manet was semi-conscious when the doctor arrived, though he never could identify his assailants. Before long we were informed that though he was badly bruised there were no internal or permanent injuries save for a broken rib. The doctor bandaged him up and gave him a sedative and told us to keep him rested for a day or two. (I remember that the deputy stayed in his room while the doctor was calling, not wanting to be seen.)

It was three o'clock before we were done and Anthony was settled. We did not go to sleep, but stayed up drinking coffee until it was time for Matteotti to go. Enrico arrived with the *Queen Mary* in time for breakfast, looking pleased with himself I thought, and was told the events of the latter part of the night without our visitor being identified; but he knew well enough. I last saw Matteotti standing with Arthur in the *Queen Mary* as Enrico pulled away. He turned, smiling, and waved a long strong hand. Then he was gone, away into the fading dark and mist. (Almost exactly a year later, on the tenth of June, 1924, he was murdered, and buried in a field, by Albino Volpi and Amerigo Dumini, on orders direct from Mussolini's principal lieutenants. I know such tributes are meaningless, particularly from solemn, old and sentimental men, but it means something to me, at least, that I record the fact that he was one of the bravest men I ever met, and amongst the best.)

It is also worth recording what I felt at the time and have felt ever since: that in his relations with Giacomo Matteotti and other politicians, Arthur Howard massively exceeded the limits of authority and involvement of a consular official, denying thereby the primacy of the elected government and compromising the integrity of the British diplomatic service. What he did was wrong, and had to be prevented.

Later that morning, I called on Chief Inspector Capodimonte to report a vicious, inexplicable attack on a subject of the British Crown. He was sympathetic, but did not hold out much hope of finding the perpetrators. Many such, he explained, had recently eluded detection or identification.

'A common assault, the work of thieves or hooligans. There are many such, I am afraid, and the number rises all the time. We are doing our best, but it is difficult, to make Venice safe from these Bolshevik scum.'

I left him on that ambiguity. Then I telephoned Rome.

Honesty is difficult in retrospect about those next few days, for in every event I know what followed after, what came next, and I must try to shave out hindsight and recall the local gesture and response. I left Anthony in Maria's care that day; she seemed delighted to have someone to fuss about. In an obscure way, I suppose I was almost glad to know he was immobilised under my roof. Over the weeks I had developed a nagging jealousy of him, without foundation as far as I knew; jealousy of his easiness with Eva, as well as with Jane, and of the time I was sure he spent with her. That is in the nature of jealousy, arising from ignorance, self-doubt and fear. I was troubled also by the fact that his relations with these women seemed not to fit any classification I had previously known. It was only later that I learnt to suspend judgement and to ignore the turbulent hither-and-thithering of human beings, a discretion which allows the truth to manifest itself but which is often mistaken for indifference. I was not indifferent then, and knew enough of cunning to manipulate my opportunity.

I called on Jane, to tell her of the attack on Anthony. Herself still bruised from Younghusband's assault, she nonetheless decided to call on our friend at once. She thought of taking Eva, but I lied and said I had a pre-arranged lunch appointment with her I wanted to fulfil, and that I would bring her on thereafter. Jane set off at once, at my request in the *Queen Mary*.

At the desk they told me Eva had gone out, to Dr Manet's house nearby. I was baffled and a little angry, wondering if she had somehow heard of the attack, but dismissing the possibility. What business had she at the house, I asked myself, and how often had she called there unattended?

Susanna let me in to the old Santi palazzo without so much as a glance or murmur of surprise. I did not then identify it as an aspect of his Jewishness that Anthony kept a more or less permanently open house, wherever he travelled, wherever he lived. Traditions of desert and ghetto hospitality died hard. The old woman left me to myself, and finding the main drawing-room filled only with sunlight, furniture, books and a tapestry, I went up the dark narrow stairs to the upper day-room where Anthony lived and worked. As I climbed the stairs the silence thickened and turned into music. She was playing the pianoforte, and I realised that the troubled stillness I had sensed in the house on my arrival had been only the rest between music, the air still shimmering and resonant with the ghost of sound, expectant of its resumption.

As I entered the room Eva turned at the piano, as if in anticipation, and smiled. I cannot say now if it is only the cynicism of youth or of old age which registers a subsequent look of disappointment and of faded hope on her recollected features, or if she was discontented in truth. It seems I cannot hope even now to be absolute in judgement, for all the world, except for memory, changes as it is considered, and even memory is troubled by past failures of attention and the broadcast interference of what we, all of us, were.

She returned to the piano and took up the music. It was the song Anthony had played in Jane Carlyle's suite, what seemed a lifetime before (and it was a lifetime, too, for though I did not know it then the start of my travelling was my emergence from the chrysalis of youth. In certain senses I was born on a foggy day as the boat-train pulled out of Charing Cross). The transcription score stood grubby on its stand, covered in pencilled annotations in Anthony's strong sprawling hand and Eva's neater, more delicate one. The desolate chromatic sequence sobbed across the day, and I wanted to still it, and to restore the thoughtlessness of tumbling pearls and amicable afternoons on balconies. A little tooth tugged at her lower lip as she strained at a passage spread too wide for her small childish hands, and she stopped.

'It's no good,' she explained sorrowfully. 'I can never reach it without tearing at the legato.' She shook her head, and shrugged and worked her fingers.

'Do you come here often?' I asked, and we both laughed for, even then, it seemed a foolish question.

She shook her head once more, and I noticed yet again the dark blonde hair at the top of her long, slender neck, like swansdown. 'Sometimes. Anthony lets me use the piano. I don't like to disturb Jane too often.'

'It was lovely. You're very good.'

She disagreed. 'No. Too scholarly. Anthony says I play as though every piece were an examination.'

'Is he a good pianist?'

'Not really.' I was almost relieved. 'But he does know how to listen and explain, which is what teachers ought to be good at.'

'Is he your teacher, then?'

She was emphatic. 'Oh no. I'm too old to take it too seriously now. It's more of a hobby really.'

'But what all Venice is asking,' I teased, 'is when are we going to hear you sing?'

She turned, and fiddled with the piano-score. 'I ... no. Never, I don't think.'

'That is a pity. My father once told me that if I ever had to choose between marrying a beautiful woman and a woman with a beautiful voice, I should choose the singer, because voices never fade. He didn't tell me there were women who are both.'

What almost seemed a blush almost seemed to tinge the hair on her neck and the little of her cheek I could see, as she sat still turned away from me. 'Some of them don't – fade, that is – if you really believe in them, but voices can and do get tarnished, and it isn't worth the effort to polish them back to a shine.'

We sat in silence for a while and then she practised her scales and arpeggios, like a dutiful child. When at last she paused I invited her to lunch, and in response she played the first few bars of 'For He's a Jolly Good Fellow'. We both laughed, but she declined, saying, 'Susanna said she would fix me lunch here. Would you like to join me?' I wanted to very much, for this was an afternoon I knew I would not be interrupted in her company, and did.

It almost embarrasses me to remember how little we had to say to each other, but I would not have exchanged that time for a mountain of diamonds, enchanted to see blank air displaced by her pensive presence, as grateful for her company as parched earth is for water. When at last I told her of the attack on Manet, although a flicker of alarm passed over her, she showed no passionate distress. It saddens me that I was glad.

'He will be all right, though, won't he?'

'Oh yes. The doctor advised a couple of days' rest, but otherwise he's fine. He's staying at my house. I suppose I could get Susanna to pack him some clothes. Would you like to come back with me to see him?'

She shook her head in the small, troubled way I came with time to recognise as a sign of a condition of nervousness. 'Not today, I think,' she said, and although I was pleased she did not race to his bedside, I was sad to lose her company on my return. She turned and smiled, patting the back of my hand, a hand I found myself stroking involuntarily afterwards. It almost became a habit. 'Give him my love, won't you? Will he still be able to attend the reception?'

'I should think so. He's amongst the good Samaritans, so we'll try to have him up and about in time. I don't think Maria believes in people being ill.'

'Then I shall see you both there tomorrow.'

'Can I call on you beforehand?'

I wanted to reach out and take her hand, but for some reason I dared not. She sat, her arms close by her, as though defensively, still and self-contained, and perhaps a little troubled.

'I don't know. I hadn't thought about tomorrow. You must let me think. I might even call on you.'

She did not do so, and if she had done her journey would have been wasted, for the following morning, against all my advice, Anthony insisted on getting up to go to work in the archives. Maria rallied to his support, obviously believing that no young man, however grievously beaten, had any cause to lie abed a second day. Somewhere she found him a gnarled old knobkerrie of a walking-stick and he hobbled off gingerly, on foot, not trusting himself to a gondola.

I passed the day with Howard at the Consulate, unnecessarily checking his arrangements for the reception. For a time I hoped that Eva would call at the house and be sent on by Maria, but as the day turned into an overcast afternoon all hope subsided, and I was left as empty as the chill wind shifting the corrugated waters of the canal.

My presence was pointless; Arthur had arranged this kind of reception far too often before to need any help or advice from me. All day, caterers arrived, ferrying in trestles and banks of food. Much to Arthur's dismay, I suspect – given his affection for most things Italian – we were only to serve champagne (an uncompromising Krug, as I recall) to manifest the wealth and splendour of Britain and her Empire. (I learnt quickly that the entertainment budget is the only budget which is never underspent in the Service, though once or twice, when supplies were bad, I have been reduced to bottled beer – but it was British bottled beer.) He had even arranged for lanterns to be strung up in the Consulate's small walled garden, a relic, I think, of the Chinese and Japanese fashions of his youth. Sometimes he reminded me of the raffish, bohemian uncle of French comedies or Viennese farce. Though systematic himself, he seemed to despise the imposition of systems. The only thing I could find to complain about were the paltry displays of cut flowers. (Under normal circumstances there were never any at all.) Before I could raise the matter with him, it was taken out of our hands. Two florist's assistants arrived by gondola, a gondola laden with spray on spray of imported flowers. They came with a card, which read 'For the Consul and Mr Burnham, lest they should have been wary of seeking assistance – Jane Carlyle.'

'Damn the woman!' Howard cried.

'I thought it was rather a charming gesture.'

'Oh it is, it is! Charming. Unless you suffer from hay fever.'

'And do you?'

'How the hell should I know? I've never liked flowers enough to get close enough to find out.'

By late afternoon we were as ready as any hosts have ever been and the hired servants had begun arriving. I went back home to change. Anthony had not returned by the time I had to leave again, so – assuming he had made his own way to Giudecca – I departed, tie starched and tails pressed, feeling at last like a diplomat. For the instant, only the admiration of Maria and a distant faint unease about Younghusband disturbed my placid mind.

Whatever else I may say about Arthur Howard, it became obvious that in his thirty or so years in Venice he had made himself a prince of the local society, and that in a country which, except for a few Cavourian liberals, had never had much cause to stand in awe of Britain and the Empire. I must not exaggerate. It is not as though he had single-handedly conquered the stifling formality and rigid hierarchy of Austro-Hungarian Vienna or ancient Susa by force of personality alone. This was a small provincial centre, and by the beginning of the century one would have been hard pressed to find sufficient numbers of the right sort of people to make up the guest-list for one medium-sized English country house weekend. The local Veneto society, as I discovered that evening, consisted largely of impoverished aristocrats still living off memories of the grander families their ancestors had once been related to by marriage or intrigue, self-conscious bourgeois tradesmen and their over-decorated wives (wives who made sure their husbands' fortunes showed in their attire – dresses designed for opulence rather than skill or style, an even more grievous sin in Italy than in England), peripheral diplomats (like Arthur and myself, I suppose) shunted off to this safe haven where all hoped they could do no damage, and a scattering of clerics and lawyers. (I have despised all lawyers for as long as I can remember – nit-picking mercenary charlatans who will not even stand by their opinions, and who have confected a profession from legislators' deliberate incompetence with language. They are knaves or jackasses all, and they seem to be everywhere.) Italy was even fuller of lawyers then than it is now, for the law was seen quite rightly as the easiest route into the money-trough of politics, and most of them there that night were politicians.

'He is a remarkable man, the Consul. So very English, don't you think?'

'How long do you think your posting will be, here in Venice?'

'Such a lovely city, our Serenissima, so much more enchanting than Paris or London, I think, and such a home for genius!'

'Of course, on my maternal great-aunt's side we are Roman Colleoni, and my cousin almost married a cadet Fitzalan-Howard. But alas, it was not to be. Even so, we have always felt close to the English. Are you a Catholic, by any chance?'

'I can't say I approve of the dresses young girls are wearing now. So short, as though they cannot afford a proper length, and no substance to all the modern fabrics. I like a heavier material, made to last, like this brocade for instance ... You are too kind!'

'I have a manufactory now, in Mestre, for corkscrews, cruets, tin-openers – that kind of thing – and some vineyards, though farming is very bad, very bad in Italy now. The peasants do not want to work, or want to come to the cities. They do not know their place. I blame it on the liberals and socialists, and all the changes of government.'

'You must visit us, Mr Burnham. In the summer, when Venice is horrible with visitors. I have two daughters, you know. And a son.'

'The trade, the sea-trade, is very bad in Venice now. The only consolation we have is that even the Genoese are suffering!'

'We need, like England, to have laws which defend our rights of property.'

'Venice is free, like a sea bird, don't you think, Mr Burnham? Or like a galloping horse on a race-track, although it has a rider. Freedom to do what is natural, and what it enjoys. That is the real freedom, don't you think? The freedom to take pleasure.'

After about an hour of this, even my patient and well-trained head was beginning to reel. Howard would whisper encouragement whenever he passed, of the 'Chin up, laddie' or 'Remember, you're an Englishman' variety. So I did, regretting only that protocol forbade me from conversing more honestly with the French Consul, the one sardonic ironist amongst the party. Nonetheless, I almost cried with hope and anticipation, as a castaway would on sighting a three-decker on the horizon, when variety arrived in the forms of Anthony, Jane and Eva.

Howard and I were holding court in the garden when they arrived, the evening sky turned purple but not yet inky, the lanterns lit, and conversations only just beginning to turn to fine fronded mare's-tail plumes of frost in the air; so we did not hear them announced. They must have walked straight through the long hall which traversed the

103

Consulate, and I suppose we first became aware of them by the silence which grew in the building as they passed towards the garden, a lame man helped by the two most handsome women there that evening and, as far as I was concerned, in Venice.

I remember turning towards the house. The lights were already blazing, and a steady chink and chatter of glasses, forks and conversation came from all the rooms; but in the hall there was silence. They stood in the double doorway, silhouetted against the electric light, the tops of their heads shining, Anthony in tails, Jane in a black silk version of her cossack outfit on his left arm and Eva in cream crêpe-de-Chine on his right, and the words froze in my mouth. Howard went over to greet them, both his arms outstretched, the right hand leading, like Garrick as Hamlet. 'My dear Manet, Mrs Carlyle, Mrs van Woerden, so good of you to come.'

'I'm only sorry we're late, Howard. My fault entirely. I'm a little unsteady on my pins today.'

The general chatter broke out again over Howard's insistent 'Not at all', and I noticed with envious amusement the French Consul disengaging himself from his companions to cross to the doors to be introduced to the ladies. (I discovered in time that he had a refreshingly unworried, guiltless approach to affairs of the flesh – or so it seemed to an innocent Englishman – and always contrived to disentangle himself without scandal. His motto was that of an unnamed French General – 'On s'engage, puis on voit'.)

Much of the time thereafter I recall only as a tangle or kaleidoscope of gaiety, as though the world were improved by their simply being in it, though it seemed an age before I got the chance to speak to them and I hardly seemed to speak to Eva at all. I know, however, that early in the evening Jane swept dramatically past me, stooping to whisper, 'Congratulate Anthony. Berenson is wrong.' So it was that, having spent an appropriate time talking to the other ladies invited, all of whom seemed quietly furious about the most recent entries ('Where are their husbands?' was the commonest question), I found myself before the fireplace of what had been the drawing-room when the Consulate was a house and which was still furnished as such, where Anthony was holding forth to Howard. He spent the rest of the evening there, one elbow on the mantelshelf, and all the party appeared to revolve round him, the guests all circulating before him like satraps before the High King of Persia. He always seemed to have that effect at parties, and it was not until long experience later that I realised not all of it was the result of his force of personality. Having passed a lifetime on the cocktail circuit of international good manners

I know at last that people in a crowded room always circulate about what seems its focal point, which is always on the periphery and never in the centre. In rooms of a certain age, it is provided by the fireplace and the painting or looking-glass which conventionally hangs above it. Anthony's maimed and damaged leg prevented him from standing unaided for long, so he always made for support like mantelshelves, and found himself the centre of attention. It is a fact I turned into technique a long time ago, and it is frustrating now to be so old that I must sit wherever I go and be shunted off beyond and below the range of anyone interesting's vision. I always seem to be saddled with sweet young things (which is anyone under fifty) who bend down to be nice to me, the dear old man, not realising that what I want more than anything in the world is for everyone in the world to forget that I am old, myself included.

He gave me the opportunity to congratulate him, his dark eyes glittering. 'Have you heard the news?'

'I have, Jane told me. Congratulations. But how did you do it?'

'I was just telling Howard. I think I mentioned there was a gap in the papers, and I thought the Este family might fill it. Well, it seems they do, but as dealers; the confusion arose right here in Venice. The catalogues of the time don't give exact descriptions, but it seems that two near copies of the painting, or possibly just very similar paintings on the subject of the Circumcision, were ordered from Veronese's studio. I believe I can prove from the sales records that the Dresden painting is one of them. The truth, inevitably, seems to have been a little more complicated than either Berenson or I first expected. I'm almost certain, about as certain as anyone will ever be able to be, that the cartoon, the original drawing, was made by Veronese, but that the painting itself was by an assistant and pupil of his, a man called Palma Giovane.'

'So what happened to the original *Circumcision*, the one that Veronese really painted?'

He grinned, and Howard grinned with him, delighted at his protégé's success. 'The old, old story of confused descriptions. I know it was originally in the hands of the Giustiniani family, but after that – until the misattribution of the Dresden painting in the mid-eighteenth century – it disappears. Except that I've found a marriage contract for one of the Giustiniani daughters to an Austrian count. The contract lists, as part of the dowry, a painting 'from the studio of the great Master Veronese' of the *Presentation of the Christ Child at the Temple*. I haven't been able to track that one down anywhere in the Veronese studio records. I suspect our painting, the real Veronese, is still

105

hanging under the wrong title in an Austrian castle. Anyway, I mean to find out, and I don't suppose the owners will be too distressed to hear that far from getting a studio painting, one of their ancestors married a missing Veronese.'

It was impossible not to be cheered by his delighted enthusiasm, and I suppose I always shared his passion for paper, for contracts, for records. What I have never understood was how they seemed to come alive for him, as though issues of the past were issues of the present and – due allowance made for circumstance and the age, both then and now – susceptible to the same excitement, reverence, outrage or standards of judgement. I have never felt so secure myself. I am not saying that to understand everything is to forgive everything, merely that I am glad that as a diplomat and impartial public servant I have stood apart from the desire or duty to decide, or establish or judge. I am happy, on instruction, to execute a sentence, but I do not know if I could reach one.

'I was just telling the Count here,' Howard said diplomatically, bringing a bystander into the conversation, 'that one of the reasons I have been so glad to serve His Majesty's Governments here in Venice is that although the modern world goes on unabated, as it must and should, it is also still possible to live here in the manner of a gentleman of the nineteenth century, when we were young and enthusiastic. There are parts of the modern world we must leave to you and Manet.'

The Count was mournful. 'I am not so certain of the modern world. Everything is noisier and faster than when I was a boy, when everyone knew their place. When I was a boy the year was divided by the festivals of the Church, and the local priest depended on the local nobleman. Everyone knew where authority lay. Now there are even priests who encourage the common people to vote and become involved in the business of their betters.'

I tried to divert the Count from his gloomy and, to Howard, infuriating, train of thought. 'Will it be a good opera season this year, do you think? I gather the opera is one thing which never changes in Venice . . .'; but he was not to be dissuaded.

'Nowadays every day is opera, and the servants cheek their masters. It is impossible to find good servants now. They believe that all men are equal.'

Howard could control himself no more, though he was firmly polite. 'But hasn't the Church always believed all men were equal?'

The Count was obdurate. 'That is a nonsense. All men may be equal in the sight of God,' (he crossed himself reverently) 'though one may hope there will be a separate queue for his greater servants on

Judgement Day, but we are not God, and neither is the Church. Do you honestly believe the Church considers this waiter' (oblivious to offence, he indicated the man who was even then serving us drinks) 'equal to the Pope? No, the world was better when I was young. We should put a stop to this farce of democracy and elections.'

'In Venice?' asked Anthony quietly. 'The first of modern republics?'

'Which had a government chosen by and run by perhaps a hundred families.' The Count was brutal. 'I would have no objection to that.' I hoped that Howard would not be taunted into saying anything injudicious, unworthy of a diplomatist, but it was Anthony who would not let the matter rest.

'There was a time, in the days of the city's greatness, when those hundred families stood for many of the things you most disapprove of. There was a time, like this one, when Rome tried to impose conformity on half the world, in a mean-spirited and coercive Counter-Reformation. Venice stood alone then against the authority of Rome, although there were sympathetic powers like France which did not dare to act. There was a time when one Venetian theologian, an abbot called Paolo Sarpi, on behalf of his city and freedom, denied, by using the law and teaching of the Church itself against the presumption of Rome, the right of any power to impose its will on the freedom of the people of this city.'

'I think you mean the freedom of the hundred families.'

'I mean that as well, but he based his argument on that ancient doctrine that the voice of the people is the voice of God, which Marsilio of Padua had raised against the comprehensive petrifications of Aquinas, and declared that the people of Venice would not bow before the tyrannous throne of any Roman pontiff without the doctrine of supremacy being called before a Council of all the Church, such a Council as no tyrant has ever wanted to call. While that one man was alive – despite three attempts to murder him – hope lived here in Venice, the hope of all Europe for a settlement to set at ease the rifts which drove the continent into her most terrible, most religious wars a few years after Paolo Sarpi died, died with prayer for his beloved city on his lips, died in an agony of doubt, his greatest supporters dead before him and the rest broken by cowardice or cupidity. Is Venice so stupid, so selfish and so blind that she forgets her greatest son, the canon lawyer, historian and monk whose memory should endure though all the palaces of the world sift down to dust? Why have you forgotten Paolo Sarpi?'

'Because he lost, and memory resides with the victors. When you are older you will understand the importance of power, and wonder, as I do now, how to drag it back and cast aside the influence of the foolish many who have neither the desire nor the ability to learn of men like Paolo Sarpi. The only question in the world is who has power. I want it for myself, to make a world for my comfort, and one day you will feel the same, whatever you may say now about one mad monk. All monks are mad, and most priests. It comes of being neither men nor women.'

The old man turned away from argument. I was glad, for I had not known how to restrain Anthony; and Howard, I suspect, was too much a partisan to try. (Ever since then I have done my best to avoid historians or patriots at parties; they are forever bringing up ancient quarrels, and there is no way in the world an averagely well-read man or woman can diconnect an argument about a monk who has been dead for three hundred years or more.)

I was relieved of any responsibility for finding casual or soothing things to say by Jane's arrival. She protested that we had allowed Anthony to monopolise us, and bore us away. Within an instant Howard remembered his duties as a host, introduced Jane to three new people, planted me on the French Consul and recommenced his round of guests. I moved more slowly than the Frenchman, who explained he had just remembered the answer to a question of Mrs van Woerden's and that he ought to seek her out at once. He said he would return, but realising that was too much to expect (I would have done the same if I had thought of it first) I joined Jane's little group, doing my best to conceal my second-bested temper.

What followed is as indistinct as all the other parties of a long career have become, though I seem to remember Howard telling someone something which seemed insane and self-parodic even then: 'If I had had any say in the matter, I would have wanted to be born an English gentleman of the eighteenth century, revolving round London and my estate, studying the politics and literature of the seventeenth century and collecting the pictures of the sixteenth. That would have been bliss. Instead, I am a relic of the nineteenth in the twentieth, and console myself with the books of the century I should have been born in.' I remember wondering if he had taken leave of his senses, or had too much to drink, or merely spent too much time recently with Manet.

The evening drifted down towards its end (we had called for gondolas at eleven), and the few of us left (the hardier guests included the French Consul, who was to be able to reassure me a month or so later that I had made a suitable impression on the Veneto's parochial world) gathered in the drawing-room. Anthony had taken a chair and

Eva, to my and the Frenchman's dismay, sat on the floor at his feet. Jane stood with Howard by the fire, which should, in retrospect, have been lit, for the nights are cold in Venice, but which had been overlooked. She stood with a glass in her hand, interrogating Manet (who had been holding forth again) in a tone of gentle mockery.

'I did not know you were an incurable optimist, Dr Manet.'

'Not incurable, and not so much of an optimist either, but it does annoy me when I hear people say things are merely as they are and cannot be changed. They change all the time. This Consulate has electric lighting, everyone here knows how to write.' (I remember wondering about the servants.) 'And it is a long time now since human beings were obliged to dress in skins.'

'I don't imagine they would suit my colouring,' Jane interrupted tartly.

'No, madam. But I'm not an optimist. I don't believe the enemies of mankind can be destroyed – merely defeated, and must be, time after time, in place after place.'

'It sounds terribly dramatic, terribly violent.'

'It isn't. It's usually a private matter in private lives. The only absolutely evil man I have ever met was a minor civil servant.'

'Who was he? Do tell.'

He put up a hand to stop her. 'And you know from your father how strange the decisions of wisdom and justice may seem to a conventional world.'

She coloured, and turned away. Then John Younghusband crashed through the door.

He stood swaying in the mouth of the room, straining on two heavy ebony walking sticks, Capodimonte behind him, both of them blackshirted, and the servants who had been unable or unwilling to prevent their violent access. He walked with immense difficulty, almost bowlegged, towards the fireplace. He had been drinking.

'Sorry I'm late. Forgot my invitation, too.' He tossed his head back at the servants. 'Didn't want to let me in. Bad show, I reckon. Brought a chum. Burnham knows him.' Howard was speechless. Younghusband turned his gaze on Jane, then Anthony, and back to Jane again.

'See the lesson I tried to teach you hasn't sunk in yet.'

She was quietly angry as she had been that afternoon in my garden. 'I have nothing to learn from you.'

'I think otherwise. I think all of you have something to learn from me. I think that you' – and he swayed towards Howard – 'should learn to keep away from things that are no concern of yours. I think you' (here he pushed his reeking face before me) 'should grow up; that the

109

pretty little Dutch lady should learn a trollop gets recognised by the company she keeps;' (if I had not been so shocked, I know I would have hit him) 'and the Jew had best get back to the ghetto where his kind belong. And you,' (he straightened himself, peering at Jane) 'you, madam, had best study the manners appropriate to a whore' (he almost fell with his own vehemence) 'before all of you find out we have ways of dealing with people who don't know what's good for them.' He turned and hauled himself from the room. We continued to hear the scratch and drag of his progress down the hall, while Capodimonte stood expressionless in the door. Then he shrugged, and turned, and they were gone, leaving the Consulate silent except for Eva's muffled sobs.

Anthony put an arm about her shoulders and murmured, 'It's all right. He's gone. Come on, I'll take you home.' He helped her to her feet, still crying quietly, and a servant brought both their coats. He helped her on with hers and threw his own over his shoulders. Jane turned back from the fireplace.

'I'm sorry. This is all my fault.'

Howard would not hear of it. 'No. Not from what I hear from Mr Burnham. That young man needs a damn good thrashing.'

The Frenchman came over to us. 'You must not blame yourself, Mrs Carlyle. There have always been men who never stop being boys. I am afraid you have only been the occasion for one such to practice a childish sense of theatre.'

'You are very kind.'

'Not at all. May I attend you to your gondola?'

'No, thank you, I think I would like to talk to Mr Burnham.' The Frenchman clicked his heels and bowed, like a Prussian, and left, as did the two or three remaining Italians, and I was glad that at least the Police Chief's temporary presence was likely to limit any tendency to gossip. Jane told Manet and Eva to go on without her and they left arm in arm, supporting each other. Gently, tactfully, Howard withdrew.

'The servants can see to this in the morning, Jeremy. I'll send them home. See you about ten? Goodnight, Mrs Carlyle, it was a pleasure to renew our acquaintance. Goodnight.'

Jane looked up at me, the electric light too bright and direct, her face looking older than I knew it to be when transformed by movement and daylight. She looked tired and emptied, but she placed a hand upon my sleeve, saying, 'Come, Mr Burnham, take me to supper.'

*   *   *

It was growing late, and I could not think of anywhere – or anywhere respectable, besides the Schifanoia and Danieli Hotels – which might prepare us a supper without notice at such an hour. Jane was not unduly troubled.

'If John Younghusband is right,' she said ruefully, 'then I won't be allowed anywhere respectable, whatever the hour.' I was pained on her behalf, and took her hand. Her eyes glowed in the weary mask of her face. 'It doesn't matter. I'm not really hungry. I just wanted to get away and get that filth out of my nostrils. You can take me for a walk instead, a midnight tour of the city. You'd think a woman of my profession would have got to know it by now.'

I wondered what depth of bitterness lay behind her words, not realising in my youth that she was not wounded at all, but merely weary, of the folly and ignorance of the world.

'We could go back to my house. I'm sure that Maria could throw together something.'

She smiled, grateful for my solicitude. 'It really isn't necessary, and I'm not sure Maria would take too kindly to being woken. If she didn't sleep in the pantry I could cook us something myself.' (I was surprised; it was the first time I had heard a woman of my class admitting she could cook anything except, perhaps, cakes and pastries. Even that was rare, for of course they did not have to trouble themselves with such labours. It is difficult for you to imagine, I suspect, how much of our living was done for us by servants.) 'But as it is, let us go for that walk.'

We threw on coats, and I took her by the arm and we went out into the chill Venetian night, the hall lights of the Consulate blazing briefly behind us before we were swallowed up into darkness in the back-alleys and courtyards of the city.

She walked tall and erect and her grip was strong, and in the cloudy, refracted moonlight she seemed almost to vanish except for the touch of her arm and side, the light scent of perfume and hair washed and brushed repeatedly, and the sound of her footsteps and her sad, honourable voice. Sight faded, and our talking danced down the darkness as the irregular, ill-timed midnight bells began to chime, not even in a geographic sequence, now here, now there, around the ancient city speckled with loud mechanical reminders of mortality. I did not know how to begin, though I wanted to talk, but at last found an inadequate opening.

'It really wasn't your fault, you know, not at all. Just bad organis-ation on our part. Howard shouldn't have invited him at all, and I didn't get to see the guest-list until it was too late to do anything about

111

it. When he didn't show up I thought he must be hurt still, or had decided to be a gent, but ...'

She squeezed my arm in consolation. 'But he turned up like the wicked fairy.'

I did not know if I was being teased, but stopped and turned to her. I have always been too impressionable, though I am too much the diplomat to succumb to my impressions. In that midnight, alone with her and proximate, I wanted to kiss her but knew I could not do so, and asked a question as a kind of retaliation or recompense. 'What was it all about, do you think? I couldn't make any sense of what he said.'

She began walking again and I followed her, attentive as a drone, though for a while we walked apart. 'I'm not sure Younghusband can answer that himself. I don't imagine he knows himself. Part of it was play-acting, I think. Part of it was just wanting to be the wicked fairy. We went to *Swan Lake* once,' (in the darkness I sensed her toss her head, as though to hold back tears) 'and at supper afterwards he could only speak of Von Rothbart, the wicked enchanter. There is a part of him that wants to be a sorcerer, or an evil genius of crime.'

'How very silly.'

'How very pompous, Mr Burnham!' (I was relieved to hear something almost like a smile in her voice.) 'You would be surprised to know how many men who ought to know better think of themselves in the privacy of their own imaginations as Sherlock Holmes or Professor Moriarty, or, in these days I suppose, Bulldog Drummond or Petersen. It isn't so very unusual.'

I learnt with time that she was right and that those imaginings are amongst the strongest part of men, from pot-boys to princes. Even though I have never shared the habit of mind, I have seen how it can be unleashed to make a hell of certain places in certain times, and how easily it takes up and uses men who have the fantasy I also share, the dream of steady dependability, the freedom never to dream. That night I did not know such things, but I had the boldness of ignorance and of curiosity masquerading as concern. She had sounded so attentive to him that I dared to ask a question I would rather choke on now.

'Did you ever think of marrying him?'

She almost laughed. 'Oh, my dear Mr Burnham, sometimes you are such a fool.' I stiffened. 'No, no, you mustn't resent it. I do these things for the good of your education. I thought I had made it plain that I would never consider marrying again.'

'Why not?' (We were two generations from the mid-Victorian straitjacket of decencies, and I could not understand why any healthy woman should not wish to re-marry as soon as was proper after her grief was assuaged.)

Her voice was soft and gentle and low in reply. 'I know it is not generally believed, but I liked my husband dearly and, in my fashion, loved him. It is true that he was a fool, but unlike most fools he knew it, and he was kind enough to know I could not be satisfied with the county and field set he moved amongst and was revered by. There are not so very many husbands who make the effort to understand their wives, even if they cannot help them. Most Englishmen prefer to take consolation in notions of the mystery, the unfathomable irrational mystery, of womankind. In fact, we are much more practical and reasonable than men. There were imperfections, of course. There always are in marriages, which only the people concerned can understand, because we are only people, not saints.'

'How did he die?'

I was amazed by the lightness in her voice. 'Of a heart attack on board his mistress.'

I hardly knew what to say, and stammered at last, 'Didn't you mind?'

'Of course I minded. Don't be silly. I know I was not supposed to, and that infidelity was expected of men of his class, but I minded. I had been faithful to him, you see.'

'What happened to ...'

'Maggie Kneller? It came as a terrible shock to her, of course. Well, can you imagine? It would have frightened me off for life. It wasn't her fault, poor girl. After all, she had to make a living, and being a mistress was better than being on the streets – or any kind of life she might have found amongst her own class, come to that. I let her keep the house Harry had bought for her, and set her up with a little capital. The last time I heard from her she was running a house in that line of business herself, off Haymarket. I could let you have the address if you wanted. I'm sure she would arrange suitable terms with her girls ... Oh, dear, what must you think of me? You will be agreeing with John Young-husband next. I only meant to say that, though I minded, the fault did not lie with her but with Harry, and perhaps myself.'

'How did you explain his death?'

This time she did laugh, low but deeply, and stopped to lean against a wall to catch at her breath and compose herself. I knew (although I am not sure that I could see) her eyes were shining. 'Harry would have liked that. He used to say he thought the best death would be a fall out hunting, to break his neck and go out like a gas lamp. The doctor was all for heart attack on the death certificate, but I honoured my husband's memory more than that. I insisted on the truth: that he died of injuries sustained in a riding-accident.'

'I still don't understand why you haven't thought of marrying again.'

'It really isn't so attractive a prospect, you know, to a woman of independent means. Not if she is prepared to endure the calumny of other, envious or disoriented, women.'

'But why?' (I was genuinely mystified. I had not read any Lenin in those days, and only a little Marx. I had not begun to consider how absolutely the world was affected by the twin absolutes of money and power, the private world included.)

She began to walk again, briskly, and her manner was as definite and purposeful as her pace. 'Most men, both before and after they marry, affect to despise the institution of marriage. They are liars, if only to themselves. The one thing that any woman in danger of an infatuation must remember is that, whatever they may say in whatever they may think is the heat of passion, most men want to go back to their wives. They want the security of home, with an occasional licence to travel. Sub-consciously, most men are desperately grateful for marriage, if only because it guarantees them sex.' (I blushed in the darkness. In those days the word itself still had a faintly obscene odour.) 'Affairs and mistresses are a bonus, for those who can afford or attract them. Women, on the other hand, usually have to go back to their husbands, a fact unscrupulous lovers count on and the few rare honest ones can be destroyed by. Most women are tied at least as much by their purse as by their heart- or apron-strings. I have a purse of my own. That is the principal reason I have not married again. I would rather be thought a loose woman than know myself to be an imprisoned one.'

I felt myself under attack, on behalf of all men. 'But what about children?'

'I have yet to meet a man whose children I would be prepared to bear. I am lying of course. I have occasionally met such a man, but all of them would have been intolerable to pass a lifetime with; and, leaving aside the issue of legal status, I happen to believe that children should have, and know, a father. And now it is too late.' She stepped out briskly again, and I saw in half-obscuring darkness that we were passing I Frari on the way to the Rialto. 'Will you walk me back to San Marco?' she asked.

'Yes, of course, but how will you get back to the hotel?'

'It's all right. The Schifanoia runs a boat service through the night, at half-hourly intervals.'

114

'You would be welcome to stay at my house.'

She turned and held the palm of her right hand out to me, as though to hold me back (I had not moved at all). I could only make out the outline of her uptilted head in the darkness, and her voice was distant with emotions which, although she spoke of them, I did not understand till many years later. 'No. You are kind, kinder than you know, I think, but you are too young to be able to cope with the loneliness, and the intensity of need, of this old widow.' She turned, and put her hand in mine, her voice brave, and bright and young once more. 'Come. I must get back to San Marco.'

I was foolhardy in the darkness, and with pride at being spoken to as a grown man by such a woman, of things we did not speak of then; and as we crossed the Rialto, the outlines of the shops ghostly in the spectral, retarded light, I asked her, 'So why Younghusband?'

She was better, now, in command of herself and able to answer such a question. 'That was my folly. He was, he is, handsome, and foolhardy, and headstrong and reckless and brave. I was lonely. There was no more to it than that, though I do not think he likes to believe so. Young men are dangerous, Mr Burnham:' (her voice soared) 'as dangerous as intelligent ones. At least intelligent ones know themselves, but young ones are half in love with an idea of what they think themselves to be. They wrap their insecurity up in pride and valour and ask to be told how wonderful they are. They want a mirror to see themselves reflected as they would like to be, and I am too old and too unkind to spend a lifetime as a looking-glass.'

I was stupid, and did not understand what she had said (so much time I wasted, learning what she tried to tell me then) and blundered on. 'What came between you?' She did not answer. How should she have answered, it being so evident I had not comprehended her at all, not even her intensity of feeling? I thought only of myself, and of my hope for Eva, and asked, 'Are you and Anthony . . . ?'

'Oh no . . .' Her reply was absent and disinterested. I wish now I had understood her better. She deserved more highly than a fool for company that night but I could not stop the flow of my unworthiness. 'And Anthony and Eva?'

'I do not know, and I do not greatly care.' Her voice thinned back to normal, to an English drawing-room voice. 'You must not be so possessive. Nor must he. She is not yours for the possessing. Only she can decide where she belongs, and to whom, if anyone. I do not think she will trouble you very much longer. I think she will go home quite soon.'

'I won't let her.'

115

'You cannot stop her, and you would be a fool to try.'

'I would follow her. I would go to Holland and seek her out.'

'You would find that very difficult.' I was silent, puzzled. I began to frame the question, Why. 'Oh Jeremy! Why are you such a fool?' Her voice was kind with disillusionment. 'It isn't her real name.' I could think of nothing to say, and we walked on in silence.

We walked down back-streets and alleys, past and over domestic canals, unwinding down the tangled skein of Venice to the square. I knew that somewhere, through my ignorance and self-regard, I had lost her, I had damaged beyond repair the ties of affection to the slight strong figure who walked before me, a black pad on, against, the heart of dark. I was company now, only company, small comfort against the careless days or solitude or the stars behind the night-time's envelope of cloud.

'Wait.' She stoppèd, one hand raised. 'Do you have any matches?' I passed her my box and she struck one, the stench of phosphorus sweet and stifling in the still cold air, and was transfigured by it, as though her face and hair and bodice all burned with a cold, malevolent flame. 'It's all right,' she said, 'I know where we are' – and vanished down curving steps. I followed her, but the light had guttered before I reached the foot of the stairs, and I strained to catch her footsteps. There was another grating noise, and another match flared, and I knew we were in a courtyard I had passed through before, built round a square of water, with a balcony on three sides and stairs in two corners. I had dreamed of a Juliet or Portia heavy-eyed with sleep, coming out on to that balcony, a candle and her heart alight for me (and it still comes back to me in dreams, until its square of water grows troubled, and all images fade); but instead a woman I had lost somehow burned on the water in the light of a common lucifer. 'This way,' she said, and led me on.

As the darkness rearranged itself about us (though the outline of the match-lit image glowed in the retina for minutes after, as though seen from behind the eye), she spoke again.

'John Younghusband sometimes can't ... Well, sometimes he just can't. There isn't anything to be ashamed of in that. It happens to all men sometimes.' (It was only then I understood what she was speaking of, and was silent in embarrassment, prurience and dismay.) 'But he is not the sort of man to understand that. I thought if we had a change of scenery, if we travelled somewhere far from England and fog it might help. It did, for a while, but I had not realised why he wanted so much to come to Italy, or how much hatred and fear there was in him to work its filthy way out once

116

he was here. Tell me, Mr Burnham, why are men so ridiculous?'

We passed the Fenice, and a few turns later stood in the far colonnade of the Piazza, a package of darkness. There seemed nothing more to lose; the night had shaved away the reticence of day and we had already spoken too openly for wisdom, so I succumbed to my curiosity. 'Tell me about your father.'

She was still. 'There isn't any secret. It's just most people don't talk about him any more. They don't want to be reminded.'

'What did he do?'

'He killed himself.'

I could not think of anything compassionate enough to say. 'I'm sorry' was all I could manage.

'You shouldn't be. He wasn't.' She set off across the silent piazza, motionless now except for the dreaming flutter or preening of a pigeon. 'My father was an exceptional man, like Anthony in many ways, but he never forgave himself for murdering my mother, as he saw it. She died in child-birth, bearing me. I was their only child, and he never married again. He turned reclusive. Perhaps there may have been something wrong with him even then. I had a strange childhood. He loved me very deeply, I think, and would not let me be brought up to the silly pursuits of women of our class, but there were times when he could not bear my company. I think I reminded him of mother too much and the memory tormented him. I was taken away from him, in fear for my safety, and I was miserable. They were right though, I suppose, for he had a kind of madness in him which worsened as the time went by, until in his periods of insanity he was a danger to everyone about him. In his lucid times he knew what had happened to him. In the end it seemed inevitable he would have to be restrained in an asylum. He asked to see me.'

We had reached the Campanile and a stiff sea breeze shifted the darkness, airing it with travel, and longing, and hope. There was a kind of delight in her voice as she remembered the mad old man. 'He was so gentle when I saw him, so kind; the father I remembered from my childhood. He knew what had happened, and what was likely to become of him, and he knew that when he was sane he would not be able to bear the institution. He asked to see me to ask my forgiveness, as though I had anything to forgive him for, as though he were tormenting anyone but himself with the foul dreams which troubled his days as well as nights. By then they would not let him near fire-arms or other possible instruments of offence, so he did the only thing he could. Two nights later, less than a week before committal proceedings were due, on the chauffeur's day off, he let himself into the

117

garage, and locked the doors, and started the engine of his motor-car. He was dead when they found him in the morning.' She cleared her throat and led the way down to the jetty. 'After his death, all hell broke loose. He had broken the law, of course, and the attentive relatives who had removed me from him in the first place contested his will on the grounds that the balance of his mind had obviously been disturbed. Some of them even thoughtfully suggested I may have encouraged him to take his own life. In the end, however, the main clauses were effected as he wished, and I became an heiress – and an outcast for a while, until my fortune registered.' She coughed again. 'I must be catching a cold.' She thought before continuing. 'I have always thought my father, once he had seen me, did the best and bravest thing he could. Suicide is usually cowardice, and destroys the lives of the survivors, but I believe he had no real alternative and knew that I would understand. I think that is why he did not even write a note. What was there he could possibly have said? That is what Anthony meant tonight.'

She turned to me, her arms folded. 'You had better go. It's late, and the boat will be here shortly.'

'I would rather stay.'

'No, please go. There is nothing you can do, and I want to watch the water for a while.'

I left her, on the jetty, that brave, high-headed woman, her turban and skirt both tugged at by and streaming in the cold wind from the sea.

I could not sleep the rest of that night, and sat up in my bedroom with a dictionary and the Ariosto Howard had given me. Dawn came, and Maria rose with it, thin grey lines striated across both their faces. She brought me coffee, and at last a desperation of restlessness and boredom drove me to wash and dress. I did not know what to do with myself, for I wanted a fresh Alpine wind to blow down through my mind and scatter the cobwebs that seemed to have gathered there in the weeks since my arrival. The winds never came, and I set out for San Marco, to look at the horses instead. But the horses brought me no pleasure that morning, and some part of me must have felt and must still feel that that was a great and absolute exception, an exception which went against the proper, orderly organisation of the earth, for it has taken me eighty-three years to start a sentence with a But.

They were grey that morning, and the sky was grey, and the stone was grey, and the sea and even the domes of the basilica, heat seeping through greyness to begin what would be that summer's first

118

stifling day. I took the Schifanoia boat across to Giudecca and asked for Eva.

'She is not available, sir,' I was told.

'What do you mean she's not available? I only want to invite her to breakfast.' I was given no answer. The reception-clerk kept ticking his files. 'Mrs Carlyle, then?'

'She is not available either.'

'What does not available mean? Look, you know me. I'm the Assistant British Consul. Look, I'll go up and call on them myself.'

'No, sir.'

I had turned to go, but his tone was firm enough to turn me round. He was staring at me over his half-spectacles. Then I noticed that the keys to their suites were still lodged in their pigeon-holes behind him.

I think I must have run out from the hotel, but I cannot remember if he called after me. I know I half-ran, half-strode along the quayside, oblivious to the day and the growing heat, the whole world a tunnel of greyness down which I raced until I came to a high, herring-bone brick house with double black wooden doors. High above, through an open window into a kind of drawing-room, I heard the sound of a piano, and of something else I had never heard before, a voice I recognised, a voice I had never heard sing, now singing, a 'Song on the Death of a Child', the two sounds twining and drifting out over the lagoon and the tarnished majesty of Venice, sad, and throbbing, and mournful. I knew then, as I would always have known if I had not been young and foolish, that Anthony Manet and Eva van Woerden, whatever her true name was, were lovers, and I would have cursed Jane Carlyle for a bawd, if I had been capable of any strong emotion. Instead, I stood breathless before the house, gasping, evacuated, deprived of sense and motion, the whole world contracted to a pair of sounds. All feeling dropped away from me, and all understanding, too.

I cannot remember how I made my way back to the Consulate. I cannot even remember if I took the public vaporetto or the Schifanoia boat back to San Marco. (On later investigation I discovered I had taken the public boat.) I know I spent what seemed like endless time (perhaps an hour) in a faded, peeling estaminet drinking grappa and coffee to the confusion of a proprietor unused to serving Englishmen, much less to serving them alcohol at that hour of the morning. I suppose I got to the Consulate a short time after ten. The servants had already been and cleared away the debris of the previous evening. Only the old cleaning woman remained, scrubbing the marble floor of the hall.

I climbed the stairs to my office, still tired and empty, and I suppose

Howard must have heard me for he opened the door of his own. Through the open door, behind him by the desk, I could see the black-clad figure of Capodimonte.

'Could you come in here for a moment, please, Jeremy?'

He closed the door behind me, and leaned against it, his face a horrible pallor, grey as the city about us, before saying, 'Jane Carlyle has been found murdered, in a sack.'

THREE

'Is this an interrogation, Chief Inspector?'

Capodimonte was casual; he knew himself to be entirely in charge, for the first time since I had met him. He perched on a corner of Howard's desk, one leg swinging, and shrugged.

'Nothing so formal, Mr Burnham. We have a fairly clear picture of the events of last night. We are pretty certain of what happened. There are just some gaps in the chronology we would like to settle. And of course arrangements must be made for formal identification.'

'What would you like to know?'

'After the reception last night, you saw Mrs Carlyle back to her hotel?'

'No. I walked her to San Marco. She was going to take the Schifanoia boat back to the hotel. I was going to wait with her, but she wanted to be left alone.'

'What time was this?'

'About one o'clock this morning, I should say. I was back at my house a little after one-thirty.'

'Were there any witnesses to this?'

'At what stage?'

'At any stage.'

'I don't think so, no. Mr Howard here knows when we left the Consulate – it was a little before midnight – but I don't remember seeing anyone, or anyone who could identify us, after that, certainly not in San Marco.'

'I see.'

He was silent, and I was silent with him. Howard appeared to be in a state of shock, or at least distress, and I remember wondering how well he had known the family and if Jane's father had ever become a friend. (I have since decided that all that ailed him was age. Consulates become inured to scandal and outrage; they exist, at least in part, to deal with them. In his thirty years in Venice Howard must have dealt with cases as distressing before, but now I think the world had ceased to make any sense to him, and to offend him whichever way he turned. I may be rationalising in hindsight; it is equally possible he was frightened of death.) I seemed to be calm; in retrospect I appear to myself to have been that day a puppet imitating tricks of feeling and expression, whilst inside I was so much sawdust and rag. Something went out in me, and kept me sane and dutiful that day, while Howard let slip three decades of training and practice and responsibility. He allowed himself to be a man and not a diplomat, and made the greatest error a Consul can make; he allowed himself to feel personally involved.

Capodimonte spoke again. 'What route did you take to San Marco?'

'Up to the Rialto, past I Frari, across the bridge, then on to San Marco. I don't know the exact route; Mrs Carlyle led most of the way. I know we approached the Fenice from the west.'

'Did your servant wake when you got home?'

'No. Not to the best of my knowledge. I couldn't sleep so I read all night. I went over to Giudecca, to invite Mrs Carlyle to breakfast, but . . .'

Capodimonte waved a hand. 'The reception-clerk at the Schifanoia will remember you, I expect. You did not come straight here?'

'I went for a walk. I had breakfast in a café.'

'You seem very fond of walking.'

'I don't know how to fly.'

'Please do not lose your temper with me, Mr Burnham. I am not suggesting you are under suspicion.'

I still felt tired, and already the heat of the day was almost intolerable (and heat and exhaustion are how I remember that interminable day); I suppose I had also taken too much coffee, and too much alcohol for that hour of the morning. I was not to feel fully well again until several days later, and for a while Maria's cooking went straight through me, to her annoyance and dismay. At last I tried what seemed a rational question.

'Where was she found, Chief Inspector?'

'In an alley-way, tied up in a sack.'

'On Giudecca?'

'No, over here, nearby the Salute.' (I have never known how he managed that, unless he had assistance; it would not have been wise to ask in 1923, and now it is too late.)

Howard had roused himself at last, his face flushed and his manner distant, in a voice thin with anger. 'I don't understand what all these questions are about, Capodimonte,' (he should have used the police-man's title; always use a policeman's title, when you need something from him). 'You have already told me my assistant is not under suspicion, and you know as well as we do that there is an obvious suspect.

122

You were here last night . . .'

Capodimonte put up a hand to stop him. 'It is true there is an obvious suspect; someone who had opportunity and possible motive. One has to be careful with motive in cases like this, for, as any policeman will tell you, domestic murders are often sparked by the little thing you are not looking for, or do not suspect. We must act circumspectly, especially in a case involving foreigners. Nonetheless, as you say, there is an obvious suspect, and we must decide today if we are to arrest the Jew, Anthony Manet.'

For a moment the two of us stood in appalled silence. Howard was off the mark first (and if there is one thing that can be held against Howard it is that he was always off the mark too quickly, compromising the strategic interests he was supposed to serve): 'This is outrageous! How dare you, you of all people –'

I broke in at once to stop him before he said something foolish to the detriment of all parties. 'Arthur, please!'

He stopped, breathing heavily. I turned to Capodimonte. 'The Consul is understandably very distressed by this whole affair. Perhaps I could have a word with you in private, Chief Inspector?' He nodded, and I glared at Howard, who kept himself mumchance. I took the policeman into my own office, overlooking the canal.

'Chief Inspector, what is going on . . .'

He cut me off abruptly. 'Mr Burnham, I am very glad you asked to see me alone, as I do not think I am likely to get much co-operation from that old man. I have no reason yet to believe you are an enemy of the Italian state, and some cause to believe you may be a friend. Whatever the true state of affairs, I will speak honestly with you, as I cannot to that man.' He stopped and pulled a chair up by the window. He was calmer when he continued.

'The murder of a wealthy foreigner, a visitor, is the worst thing that can happen to Venice, especially at the start of a season when enemies of Italy are spreading rumours abroad about anarchy and a reign of terror. In the interests of this city's principal business I must do everything in my power to avert a scandal.'

He took a cigarette and offered me one. I waved him on. 'If there has to be a scandal,' he continued, 'it is better for Venice if the murder is committed by a foreigner, and not by an Italian. Fortunately, that appears to be the case, but even so I would rather prevent the publicity. Mr Howard has begun making scandalous accusations about Mr Younghusband, a friend of the New Italy, and a personal friend of mine.' (He almost smirked at this last thought.) 'He insists we arrest this man,' (I bit back my concurrence) 'claiming him to be the obvious suspect.' A thin curl of smoke slid from his lips, followed by a stream of it. 'I have told you before, Mr Burnham, that we look after our friends, people who understand us and support our ideals. I will not throw this man into a cell to satisfy the hysterical suspicions of an acknowledged enemy of the Italian state. I would rather make no arrest at all, but if anyone tries to force my hand, I have an obvious suspect too, obvious to me, at least; the seducer, enemy of Italian art and Jew, Manet. If necessary, I can have him arrested, tried and shot within the space of hours. As I have told you before, we are the courts now; and whatever Mr Howard may say, I suspect that if we have to try an Englishman, your newspapers would prefer it if we shot an alien rather than a respectable English gentleman like Mr Younghusband.'

He had me, and he knew he had me, but I tried, too hard, to be cunning. 'But what if I know that Dr Manet has an alibi?'

He was unconcerned. 'Dead men tell no tales. Dead men have no friends. Nor dead women, either.'

'There is Mr Howard. He may protest. He may insist you charge Mr Younghusband.'

'It is your job to stop him. I think even your Embassy would agree with that: for if Mr Howard protests, that would be a major diplomatic incident, a scandal, and I believe that your country wants that a great deal less than we do. We know what to do when countries complain about our nation of the future. And there are hundreds, maybe thousands, of British citizens in Italy without the benefit of diplomatic immunity.' A smile crossed his sallow face, and I knew that I was powerless.

'I will do what I can, if you can promise to arrest no one until I have explored all other possible avenues.'

He nodded. 'Twenty-four hours. Thereafter, I shall have to do something, just in case Mr Howard begins to make a noise.'

'I understand.'

'Someone will have to formally identify the body.'

'Of course.'

'I take it you will delay notifying the family until matters here have been drawn to a conclusion.'

'She was a widow. There was no immediate family.'

He nodded again, and exhaled another shaft of smoke. 'So I was led to understand.' I did not ask him by whom.

I went through to Howard's office and, before I could say anything, he started with, 'They can't arrest young Manet.'

'They will, Howard, unless you let me deal with this. You have offended this government enough already.' He blinked, dumbly. 'Just give me one day and I can sort all this out. Will you give me twenty-four hours?' He was mute, so I left him, and Capodimonte took me to the morgue.

Time collapses. Fragments of it expand, displacing everything that really matters, the daily duties and contentment of a normal life. That day, and those preceding weeks, have filled the space meant for the memory of the ordinary times of my successful existence. The recollection of them betrays me and everything I have ever cared for. This is time's own tyranny, and its revenge on extreme old age. This mind, which should be dead and has lived beyond the reaches of due time, where memory stops, is forced to play back over trivial things.

Capodimonte stopped me at the door of the mortuary. 'The doctor is very amenable. She will have died of whatever I decide.' I nodded, and we went through into a long, high room whose stench I have never been entirely rid of. It had the usual smell of extreme cold and formaldehyde, but it was a cellar in Venice in summer and the walls were alive with damp, with fungus and lichens, and the bodies brought to it had begun to decompose before their arrival. I think I almost fainted, for Capodimonte took me by the elbow, saying, 'It is not pretty.' I shook my head, my senses protesting, not daring to speak lest I gag at the smell.

'She is over here,' said the doctor, leading us to a slab with a sheet thrown over it. 'Did you know the deceased woman well?' I nodded. He turned to the police chief. 'In these conditions, in the summer, we cannot keep her here long or there will be nothing left to bury.'

'A day or two at most,' Capodimonte agreed.

The doctor frowned. 'If you have any questions you had better ask them now. Post mortem investigations after two days of this heat will tell us nothing.' He pulled back the sheet. I threw up.

He patted me on the shoulder and called for an orderly to clear up the mess. 'She was beaten, with a heavy, blunt instrument. Perhaps more than one.'

'A walking-stick?' Capodimonte asked.

'Possibly, a heavy one, or even crutches. With so much damage it is impossible to tell. The corpse was assaulted, sexually, after death, probably with the murder weapon.'

I wanted to throw up all over again but there was nothing left inside me and, if anything, my vomiting had cured me of the stench of the place. My mind was clear, and had to endure the spectacle and description.

'Then she was cut, repeatedly. Although the damage looks bad, and indeed is bad, it could have been inflicted with something like a sharp, long-bladed pen-knife.'

'Aren't the Jews supposed to do this kind of thing,' the policeman suggested, 'in their ritual killings?'

'Please,' I gasped, 'Chief Inspector, spare me the Elders of Zion.' The doctor shrugged his shoulders.

She was no longer the indomitable, unillusioned woman I had known. What faced me was a tangle of damaged bones and ligaments, integuments and sinew. Her skull was smashed open, and a rubbery grey portion of the brain had spilled out. The top of her head was a crushed tangle of bone and hair and blood. Where eyes should be there were purple-black bruises. The face had been slashed, and one cheek had peeled back from the bone, a high white pyramidion flecked with black specks of blood, and I could not help but ask myself if all the loveliness in the world came down to this, this carcass, this worm's-meat. I remembered Anthony's tender attentions to her bruised face scarcely a week before, and wondered why any of us bothered, with silk and cambric and pearls, if this was all we came to, at the end, this butcher's pantry on a slab. I cannot describe the rest. It has soiled my imagination ever since, and although I have subsequently seen things as bad or worse, they did not affect me as this did, they were not attached to me as Jane once seemed attached, and they have not so contaminated my dreams.

'Will you make the identification?' I nodded, beyond speech, even beyond tears or grief, for this bombed, empty building gave no indication of its former occupant, the woman whom I have since mourned. 'What is the cause of death to be?'

'Cholera,' said Capodimonte firmly. 'It is one problem we may never solve, in Venice, and it is dangerous to open its victims' tombs.'

I went back to the Consulate first. Arthur was still in his office. He looked broken, empty, a shell or split pod of a man. His voice was small and seemed to rise from some far past within him. 'I telephoned the Embassy, to let them know. They didn't want to talk to me. They said I was to do nothing. They said you were to call them.'

I looked at my watch (on my wrist, unlike Howard's). It was too near lunch-time to think of telephoning Rome at once. 'I'll try this afternoon. Please tell them if they call again.'

'Where are you going?'

'It doesn't matter.'

I called for Enrico, to take me to Giudecca.

*   *   *

Susanna let me into the house without a word and I made my own way up to the drawing-room. Eva sat by the open windows reading, frowning slightly in the mid-day heat. Anthony lay languid on the settle. He looked up first, and motioned me to the chair beneath the tapestry, facing the bookcase. They must have sensed my mood, or rather my lack of one, for Eva asked, 'What is it?' gently.

'I have some bad news, I'm afraid.'

Anthony put aside the book which had lain open on his chest, and pulled himself into a sitting position with a single, still painful, movement. They were both wearing white that day, I recall. His shirt-sleeves were rolled back, and she wore a tight-bodiced, full-skirted, high-necked frock, all gauze and lace. They could have been at Henley or Lords, but we were not, and beyond lay heat and water and sky, and alleys behind the Salute and the smell of the charnel-house I had risen from.

I did not know how to break the news gently, and have never done, for any gentle way of speaking of death is a lie and I had enough lies of my own to maintain, not knowing how much of the truth I should tell them.

'Jane Carlyle died last night. There is a little evidence, a suggestion, that she may have been murdered.'

They said nothing. What could they say?

'It is only a suspicion, however, and may be completely wrong. I hope it is.'

It was Anthony who spoke. 'It was Younghusband, wasn't it?'

'If it was murder, it may have been. On the other hand, it may equally well have been you.'

'That isn't possible,' Eva said quietly, and I knew I was right and that Anthony had his alibi and the woman I believed I loved, or had done, for that day I felt nothing at all.

He tried to prevent her with an impulsive 'No,' putting his hand out as though to withhold her, to restrain her from incriminating herself.

'It could equally well have been me,' I continued. 'I was the last person to see her alive. But we don't even have a cause of death as yet.'

'Where is he?'

I could not blame him for asking. I had asked the same myself, though without the same motive. I had passed into a wilderness far beyond the luxuriant shadow of revenge.

'He's at his hotel, I understand. Please don't try going to him. There is a policeman with him all the time. You would be prevented.'

127

'How, when, did it happen?' Eva asked, the summer freckles bright against her sudden pallor.

'Some time last night, after the reception. We don't have all the details yet. I wanted to tell you because you were friends, and I thought it was better you should hear it first from me.'

She nodded, working to control her emotions.

'That wasn't the only reason I came myself, however. I have a job to do as Assistant Consul, on behalf of British citizens, like Anthony. Whatever happens, whatever seems to have been the cause of death, inquest proceedings could get quite ...' – I groped for a word – 'traumatic. I don't think you ought to talk to anyone about this. I think it would be wiser, if privacy is important to you, if you Eva, were to leave Venice immediately, as quickly as possible.' She had started, and Anthony put out a hand for hers, and cradled it. It did not move me at all. If she took my advice I knew that this was the last time I would meet her, the grave, frightened woman I had dreamed of through the spring, and whose temporary absences had been a torment. Now there was nothing. My spirit had vacated me, and all I was aware of was the darkness of the room in the oppressive heat and the stroking of the breeze. I was formal.

'I think you ought to go as well, Dr Manet, as soon as I can arrange permission, which I hope will be by the morning. I can't promise any inquiry will be gentle.'

He seemed not to have heard me, as though he were elsewhere. He was watching Eva. She had crossed her arms beneath her breasts. She began to rock backwards and forwards, very slowly, very slightly. He was watching her as though he was frightened she might break.

'He will be arrested, won't he?' he asked in a whisper, watching her all the while.

'I don't know. I don't even know if there has been a crime. I'm not a policeman. I am a British Consul, and my job is to protect and advise British subjects, and to avoid scandal. I am advising you to leave.'

'I can't do that. I'm staying till I know the truth, and Younghusband's been dealt with. I owe it to Jane. We are alive ...'

Desperation made me truthful (it was only heat exhaustion, but it felt like desperation). 'Yes, we are still alive, and Jane is dead. For her, now, there is nothing to be achieved. Let me make this plain: if you make trouble, if there is the slightest whiff of scandal, you will be arrested. If you are arrested, you will die. It is really very simple. You must leave Venice, in silence, as soon as it can be arranged. Eva should go sooner.'

'That is ridiculous!'

'I promise you it is anything but ridiculous. I have it from the chief of police and, in case you had forgotten, let me remind you they are not democrats here.'

There was silence in the room, except for the occasional drifting mew of gulls, and the honk of a steamer far out in the harbour. At last he spoke again.

'Why? Why me?'

'Why not? The world is not required to give us reasons.'

'But why branded as a murderer?'

'Only if you do not leave. Only if you make a fuss. And there may have been no murder. It's only speculation. I am only trying to advise you in your own best interests.'

'I couldn't go at once in any case.' He was pensive. 'I have to complete the sale of this house.'

'How long will that take?'

'A few days, at least.'

'Today is Sunday. Have it done by Wednesday morning at the latest. I think we should be able to guarantee you that.'

Then Eva at last began to cry, until she was ugly with weeping, her face blotchy and purple, her mouth a parallelogram. Anthony crossed to her and held her to his breast, rocking her back and forth like a child. She choked for air, pummelling feebly at his chest with one curled hand. Then she turned away from him, rejected and rejecting, pushing him away. She wailed like an infant through her tears.

'You're letting him get away with it.'

He reached out feebly, into empty air, and turned to me and said, as her sobbing softened, 'I will stay, Jeremy. As long as is necessary, if you will only help me find the truth.'

I ticked off my replies on my fingers. 'If you stay you will die. There may be no murderer. The case is hopeless. And what is truth?' For an instant I felt almost amused at my own apophthegm, and turned to go, not wishing to hear an answer. I knew he would do as I asked. I knew he was a most reasonable man. As I left, over her weeping, I heard Anthony muttering in a language I did not know. It was to be many years, and much experience, later before I realised that it had been the Kaddish, the ancient Jewish requiem for the dead.

By the time I got back to the Consulate, Howard had recovered some of his composure, enough to ask in a tone of injury, 'What is going on here, Jeremy? What is all this about?'

I pulled off my jacket and began to roll up my sleeves. 'Impossible weather, isn't it?' He remained glowering mutely in his frock-coat

129

and embroidered waistcoat, his pin-stripe trousers stiff and sharply pressed beneath the desk.

'Answer my question. I am still Consul in Venice, and do not take kindly to acting as your messenger-boy from the Embassy. What is going on?' (I remember looking at my watch and thinking I had time to settle matters with Howard and still call the Embassy later, with all the problem resolved. It would seem more impressive.)

I sat down heavily in the chair facing him and wiped my neck with my kerchief. 'Mrs Carlyle died of cholera.'

His fury was quiet, but real enough for all that. 'What in hell's name do you mean, sir?'

I liked him, I admired him, he had been a generous and, in his own way, kind mentor. He had forced me into Italy's language and her life. He was one of the cleverest men I had met in the service. I wanted to support him and console him, but I believed (and I still believe) he had been in the wrong in the operations of his Consulate, and I knew that Rome's instructions were issued to be obeyed.

'Exactly what I said. Mrs Carlyle died of cholera.'

'But Capodimonte ...'

'Capodimonte has changed his mind, provided we change ours – and I have. I have identified the body. In this heat a proper autopsy isn't really possible. I am prepared to accept the decision of the mortuary doctor.'

'People don't die of cholera in sacks, not people like Jane Carlyle.'

'Capodimonte must have been mistaken.'

His rage howled. 'Damn you!' He turned to the window, scarlet, a vein in his balding head throbbing. 'I am going to make a formal protest to the authorities, and demand an investigation. I shall make a statement to the newspapers.'

'Stop it, Arthur.' He turned to me, outrage and contempt mingled in his face. 'I'm tired, Arthur. It's too hot to argue. Can't you see it's over? Victoria's dead, Arthur. Consuls can no longer act alone. It's over, all your playing at politics. We take our orders from Rome, and they take theirs from London.'

'What do you mean, sir?'

'Arthur, am I right in saying that we are here to protect British subjects?'

'Of course we are.'

'Fine. Well, we failed. One of them was murdered last night. Do you know who did it?'

'Of course I do. So do you.'

'Who did it?'

'Younghusband.'

'Very well. Is he a British subject?'

'Of course he is, but that has nothing to do – '

'Arthur, John Younghusband is the one British subject who will not be charged with the murder of Jane Carlyle. He is the one British subject whose safety we can guarantee. I have Capodimonte's promise of that.'

'That bastard!'

'Very probably. But if you can accept, as I have accepted, that Jane Carlyle died of cholera, then no British subject will be charged, and we will have done something to make up for our failure to do our duty. But if you can't accept she died of cholera, do you know who will be charged? Charged, tried and shot before we can do anything about it? Anthony Manet. You heard Capodimonte this morning.'

'I will protest . . .'

'He will already be dead.'

'They dare not do it, they dare not!'

He was hunched over the desk, puffing, on the verge of tears of frustration. I kept my voice low; I wanted to be gentle with him, to let him down lightly, but I did not know how to do so.

'This is not the nineteenth century, Arthur. Palmerston is no longer Foreign Secretary, and Anthony Manet is not Don Pacifico. No one is going to send a gun-boat to his defence, and if they did he would already be dead. No one will go to war over an incident like this. You cannot give Matteotti what he wants, or what you think Italy needs. London wants peace. Rome has been telling you that for five years now. Let it go, even if it means freedom for John Younghusband. It is the price we have to pay for Anthony Manet's life. One Briton is dead already. Do not sacrifice another.'

He looked about himself, wildly, aimlessly, like a cornered beast or recalcitrant child, spited in what it wanted. 'I am the Consul here. I can act on my own initiative. I can insist the authorities arrest Younghusband . . .'

He was beaten now, but to tell him tasted like defeat to me. I had wanted to keep it from him, but I saw it was the only way to silence him and still his dreams of freedom and justice, of an England which stood as a beacon, bastion and arbiter amongst nations. I told him the truth. 'I'm afraid you can't, sir. I have Rome's authority, in writing, to override your actions if I believe them to be detrimental to the interests of Britain, or to policy as laid down by London. That's why they didn't want to talk to you on the telephone. Will you do as I ask, sir, so I can go back to being the Assistant Consul?'

131

He said nothing. I slid the letter I had insisted on in Rome before him. For once he seemed to be anywhere but Venice, his eyes darting all about him and his tongue flickering feverishly over his lips. At last, with a groan, he buried his head in his hands. There was nothing more I could say. I went to my office, to telephone Carmichael in Rome.

I arranged with Capodimonte that she should be buried on the Tuesday morning. Even Arthur, disenchanted, despondent, with his thirty years experience of dealing with Venetian administration, could not resolve all the formalities in so short a space of time. She was an Anglican, and Venice is a Catholic city. It is a city built on water, and land is valuable; burials take place on the mainland for the poor, or on one small island cemetery for the rich. It was not possible, in a day, to arrange for special clearance for her to be buried in a Catholic cemetery. It was agreed that she should be buried in unconsecrated ground at the edge of the island. In the end, it did not even seem worth arranging for an Anglican priest to mutter the ritual words over the grave. It was a burial, not a funeral.

We had to do almost everything ourselves. Enrico hung the *Queen Mary* in black crêpe, in the baroque Venetian fashion, and we set out early in the morning to collect the coffin. It was already hot that morning (it was just before eight o'clock) and I remember Arthur sweating in his heavy, black, anachronistic clothes. I deliquesced myself, and bore a neck-rash for days thereafter from the fretting of my high, stiff collar.

They were waiting for us at the mortuary. The coffin was on a sort of tumbril waiting for us, and I was glad that I would not have to enter that terrible cellar again. Arthur, as Consul, signed for the corpse (he paid for the burial himself) and the orderlies shifted the simple, rough-cut plank box into the launch.

Enrico turned the *Queen Mary* back down the canal towards the lagoon and open water, and the boat crawled down the brilliant waters of the morning. As they passed us, seeing Arthur and myself standing in black in the bows, other launches fired their sirens, and silent gondoliers slowed and crossed themselves in the waterways' traditional salute to the departed.

We were a long time getting to the cemetery and the heat grew stifling. I feared I would faint and wanted to sit down, but Arthur remained silent and erect in the bows as a kind of recrimination and I somehow bore the heat, humidity and glare of our passage. When we arrived Enrico, without a thought, held out his hand for the customary

132

coffin-bearer's tip. Arthur was ready for him, and palmed him a gold half sovereign.

The sacristan was waiting for us and led us to a shallow grave scooped out of a grass verge beside the cemetery's railings, boarded over with planks. Arthur asked for helpers with the coffin, and the sacristan beckoned to his subordinates. They dropped their mattocks and shovels where they stood and slouched towards us. There was a further exchange of coins, and they went off with Enrico to the launch. I can still see them, re-emerging through the brightness of the day, carrying the box on their shoulders as though it were light as match-wood, an impediment only to their footing, as they slid and picked their way through ruinous paths, unfinished graves, and a presiding litter of dust and grass.

The interment took only moments, I suppose. Arthur stood with his head in his hand throughout, to the slushing and scraping of shovels and the rattle of dry earth on the wood, replaced at last by the pat and squash as it fell only on itself. When it was over the sacristan looked at us as his men clapped the sweat and dust off their hands. We had nothing to say or add or instruct; we had not even had time to think of ordering a memorial or head-stone, and I doubt one would have been allowed in that illicit ground. The sexton shrugged and waved his men away. There was another exchange of coins, then he too was gone, his head down and his hands in his nonchalant pockets. As we left, I saw Capodimonte, black in his uniform, standing in the middle distance. He nodded swiftly, and it was done.

I do not know when or how Eva left Venice, but when I got back to my house after the funeral there was a letter waiting for me from Manet. It was brief. 'I am leaving Venice tomorrow on the morning Zagreb-Vienna train. Could you meet me, for breakfast perhaps, in the station bar, at seven? Anthony.' I could do better than that, and sent him a note to tell him that I would pick him up at his house in the *Queen Mary* at half past six.

We did not speak much on the journey. His belongings were packed into two expensive, battered suitcases.

'Is that all there is?' I asked, surprised.

He nodded. 'The house is sold with fixtures and fittings, except for the books. They will be packaged and sent to me as freight in time.'

'You'll miss the house.' He did not reply. 'Do you plan to go on to Dresden, now you know about the picture?'

He shook his head wearily, as though he no longer cared. 'I think I might stay in Vienna for a while. I suppose I ought to try to track down

the original Veronese, if I'm going to declassify the one in Dresden.
The world is not so full of honest paintings that it can afford to lose one.
I promised some friends I would call on Dr Freud again, as well. They
want me to introduce them.'

Even I had heard of the already legendary Viennese witch-doctor
and dope-fiend. 'You know Freud, then?'

He nodded in assent, and a pale, watery smile crossed his features.
'They know me quite well in Vienna. I always go there when I have
cause to feel morbid.'

He did not expect a reply, and we passed the rest of the short journey
in silence except for the race of water and Enrico's tetchy grunts at the
deemed incompetence of the other early morning boatmen. We slid
into berth at the station and I helped him ashore (his bad leg always
made stepping in and out of boats a tricky manoeuvre).

'Breakfast?' he inquired.

'Why not?'

We sought out his train first. It was a long journey in those days, and
he had booked a sleeping-compartment. (They converted into sitting
rooms during the day, for those of you who do not have my generation's involvement with trains.) He put away his cases and handed his
travelling documents to the guard, and we headed back towards the
bar.

Then as now, there was a ridiculous system at the bar at Venice
station; you had to order at a cash-desk, and pay, and take a ticket to
the bar to be served with what you had paid for. The tickets had a
time-limit, too, so you could not build up a reserve for future use. I
told Anthony what I wanted and he went off to queue for both of us.
When he returned, a surly waiter stepped over to us and slapped his
napkin down on the counter. Anthony ordered our coffee, rolls and
mineral water (I should never have ordered the roll. I have yet to
finish an Italian roll) and while the waiter was away I turned to him
confidentially.

'Has she left Venice yet?'

He sat unblinking. 'Yesterday. Early in the morning.'

'Good.' I was relieved. I was also curious and, in a way, resentful.
'When will you see her again?'

He seemed to be under some enormous strain, but I felt no
sympathy at all. 'I don't know. I don't know that I ever shall, not
now.'

'How did she take it, in the end?'

'Badly. Hurt. Angry. She wanted, she still wants, something to be
done. I can't say I blame her.'

'I can. She is not so very much younger than I am. She has to learn we have to live in the real world, as it is.'

He turned back to me as the waiter returned, a strange expression on his face I could not fathom or reckon. (It is only now I recognise that it was pity.) 'If I had been present at the creation . . .'

'I'm sorry?' I was puzzled, not recognising the reference.

'It doesn't matter. A random quotation. One of the academic vices.' (Many years later, Dean Acheson, in Washington, supplied me with the whole remark, by Alfonso of Castile: 'If I had been present at the creation I should have given the Good Lord some advice about the better ordering of the universe.' I am quoting from memory, and I am falsifying in another way, again, by raising things I did not know of then.)

'When are you going to tell me the truth about her?' I asked, my curiosity recovering.

He was sombre. 'Jane Carlyle was not my only conscience. I hope I never shall.'

In its way, and with its evocation of Jane, it was the sternest rebuke I had ever received. There seemed nothing to say and I sat in silence trying to chew the powdery dough before me. I left it to Anthony to resume the conversation.

'There ought to be something we can do.'

'There isn't, and please don't ever think of trying. Anything you may say will be officially denied by both the local and the British authorities.'

He smiled, sadly, inwardly. 'Is that why I am running away?'

I wanted to, I tried to, change the subject. 'Shall we meet again some day?' It was only as I asked the question (and I do not know what brought it into mind) that I realised how much I hoped that we would meet once more, in better and less alien circumstances. I do not know if I saw him as an available reminder of Eva and Jane; or if I hoped secretly, without realising it myself, to meet him on my own ground without the nagging inadequacy I had felt in his presence here; or if by some strange intuition I foresaw that that stray, brilliant, gentle gentleman would one day seem to become amongst my closest, if my most errant, friends.

'I expect so,' he answered quietly.

I tried to make him laugh; something in his melancholy made me feel guilty. 'Then when shall we two meet again?'

His answer, even now, still puzzles me – although it was simple enough on the surface – as though it were runic or mantic or a mystery. 'Whenever and wherever you can find me,' he said. 'I will have to send you a map of my travelling, at the Consulate, I suppose.'

'Yes. That would be safest.'

'Yes, safest,' he repeated. He queued for another ticket and ordered us more coffee. It was nearly eight when he was settled again. He checked his watch (he carried a fob-watch in his breast-pocket, strung from the buttonhole of his linen lapel, a habit he never changed). 'I should be going soon. The train leaves at twenty-five past.' (He never used the fashionable inversion of 'five-and-twenty past'. It was one of the small, un-English things about him. Whichever middle class he came from, it was not mine.)

He still seemed troubled. His next question went some way to explaining why. 'You said you were the last to see her.'

'After the reception, yes. I walked her to San Marco.'

He went off on a private tangent of his own. 'The worst thing about death is how little there is to remember a person by. So little tangible worth preserving, and memory so fragile against time; at most another lifetime's grace.' He was thoughtful, before returning to the subject he had raised. 'How did she seem to you, after, after ...' He could not bring himself to speak Younghusband's name.

'Sad, I think; and bitter.'

'How, bitter?'

'About everything, I think. About men mostly, and marriage. Things like that.'

He shook his bowed head, his eyes closed. I noticed how long his eyelashes were. 'Oh Jeremy, Jeremy, no. That is the kind of thing she got sick of hearing from men. She wasn't bitter at all, like that. She was simply too honest to subscribe to the prevailing illusions of the world, or to the fruitful lies which make it work. It left her without a place to fill, that's all. She had no conventional niche.'

I was pompous in my disagreement, which was also, I now understand, a kind of disapproval. 'I think I believe in conventional things. They make life easier for everyone. You can't hope to stand out against them.'

'No, of course.' He was sober, academic. 'Illusions are part of our material world. They are as solid as mountains.'

'I believe in material things.'

He looked away and fumbled in the inner pocket of his jacket. 'Arthur came to see me last night.'

I was surprised. 'What about?'

'He told me you had buried Jane, as best you could.' I shied from what appeared an implicit criticism. He understood. 'No, please – I didn't mean to offend. I realise how difficult the arrangements must

136

have been. I suppose she must stay in Venice until the body has decomposed?'

I nodded and, inexplicably, felt my first real, sudden pang of grief. 'That's the idea, I gather.'

He did not look at me, but slid an envelope along the counter. It contained a cheque, drawn on his London bankers' correspondent in Venice, made out in my name, with the amount left open but crossed 'for an amount not exceeding one hundred guineas'.

'When the time comes,' he said quietly, 'will you arrange for what is left to be shipped to England, and to let me know? I've written my addresses on the back; mail is always forwarded.'

'But it won't be as much as . . .'

'Whatever it costs. Just date it and make it out for the appropriate amount in sterling. The bank will arrange the rest.'

'But we can ask her family to deal with this.'

'Her family will do nothing, beside squabbling over her will,' he snorted sourly. 'And you can hardly ask Younghusband to take care of it. No, when the time comes, please get in touch with me. She ought to go home. Someone should see she is properly buried.'

I was strangely moved. 'Thank you' was all I could think to say.

He shook his head violently, gnawing at his upper lip, and said, in a voice full of pain and failure, 'It is entirely inadequate.'

He rose and left for his train. He left without saying goodbye.

Arthur retired that summer. His resignation was supposed to be effective from September, but he chose to go on leave almost at once. He never returned. He would not even let me throw a farewell party for him.

Months later, he wrote to me. He returned to Oxford, it seems. Somehow his ancient quarrel with the University must have been patched up, though not the one with All Souls itself. Brasenose, his old house (he had studied under Pater), took him in and gave him some unspecified position (I know it was not a fellowship; he would have said) and he eked out the last ten years of his life on the periphery of scholarship, though the book we all expected never materialised. (I am overdramatising, of course. There was no eking about it; he was a moderately wealthy man.) We never met again, however, for my occasional visits to Oxford never seemed to coincide with his terms of residence, so I never really had the chance to tell him how much I owed him.

I was appointed Acting Consul in the interim, of course, and when September came I was confirmed as Consul. That was always to have

137

been a formality, but I suppose it was the real beginning of my career. As I wrote before, I built the success I had in the service on an entirely accurate reputation as the dependable, conventional man, and it was at this time I proved my worth to the powers that be. I have always thought it wiser to make accommodation with the princes of this world.

In time, Capodimonte agreed to release Jane's body. As he had asked, I got in touch with Anthony and shipped the body back to London. He arranged the burial, I believe, in the same vault as her husband. (He wrote to say that he had thought of burying her beside her father, but that he, an undeniable suicide, lay in unconsecrated ground, and he had not wanted her to suffer that indignity twice.) He arranged a proper service as well, though her family were not best pleased. I got the impression he was almost the only mourner, but I was beyond sympathy or anger, consigning my emotions to a foetid cellar in Venice.

At the last, the arrangements were surprisingly easy to make. I suspect that that was some kind of covert reparation to the British representative in Venice by Capodimonte, for that summer Italy had invaded Corfu, to international calumny, bombing Armenian refugees and killing children on the pretext that an Italian general, Tellini, had been murdered there (almost certainly by Mussolini's hired bandits, shipped over from Albania). The troops retired after a month, but – as history knows – things got steadily worse thereafter.

I did not choose to live in Arthur's Consulate (I thought of it as that for a little while at least) and kept on my house, and Maria; but it was at the Consulate that I had my first occupational caller, a little while after Howard's departure. John Younghusband called on me.

He looked as self-contained, even smug, as ever. I suppose he had good cause to be. He continued to affect black shirts, and sank into my visitor's chair as though he owned the building. I could not even find it in me to hate him, or despise. He wanted my assistance, as though he had not had enough already, but I knew it was my job to help him.

'Seems I have a possible problem with my bankers here,' he explained. 'Running a bit low on funds. Any way you could arrange a cable to London for me, to my bankers there, to have them wire me more cash?'

Part Two

THE GOD HERCULES
Amsterdam, Winter 1945-46

Then they left you for their pleasure: till in due
time, one by one,
Some with lives that came to nothing, some with deeds
as well undone,
Death stepped tacitly and took them where they never
see the sun.

ONE

'LONDON 19.12.45. ARRIVING AMSTERDAM WEDNESDAY TEN
A.M. ON FORCES POSTAL SERVICE FLIGHT STOP SEE YOU
QUERY MANET'.

That is to jump too far forward, however, and to do so too fast. It is
to betray, to do insufficient justice to, the time between: a time in
which, although it took ten more years, for twelve years thereafter,
Europe fell apart. What I remember most about those unrestorable
years the locust has eaten, is fire. That is itself a kind of treason, for my
senses revolt and tell me that what I should remember are happier
times, times like long summer holidays up in Norfolk on the open
cheek of earth, with water flat and calm to beyond the utmost edge of
vision, under an English sky. What I remember, nonetheless, and
remember most of all, is the darkness beyond the edge of vision, filled
with wailing and grinding of teeth. What I remember is fire.

I must try to scoop out all the cinders, ash and clinker, to recapture
the residual gleam from hours that were once golden, before the
conflagration of our middle years. I must reach back, as I have done
every day these past few weeks, back sixty years. I must put aside the
peculiar people whom I knew for a while and remember I am an
ordinary man who has lived many ordinary years. This is still the story
of an ordinary man.

I was married in 1924, in April, on St George's Day (my wife's idea)
at Norwich Cathedral, to Amanda Montague-Williams. She was
nineteen years old, the daughter of long-established, respectable and –
in my case importantly – wealthy Norfolk people. What can I tell you
about her, before the darkness restores its filthy hold over memory and
imagination? She was charming, fresh, frequently silly, surprisingly
serious, capable, kind, amusing and English. She was an absolute
change from anything I had known in my hasty ejection to maturity.
England lived even in the smell of her, a smell of milk and freshly
laundered linen. We met ducking for apples at a New Year's party my
people gave to celebrate my first Christmas leave from the service. Our
heads clashed over the barrel, and as I babbled apologies she began to

141

laugh – at me, at herself, at the world in general, out of simple happiness in the world and all its ways. I proposed to her before the end of that vacation, was accepted, and returned in the spring for the wedding.

They were simple, simply happy, years. It seemed most sensible to honeymoon in Venice, and the small, and sometimes shabby, local society performed wonders to welcome the new Consul's bride. (Amanda's delight in travel recovered the one possible drawback to marriage; the service does not care for officers who cannot or will not be relocated because of their wives, but a wife who can cope with and enjoy varying environments is seen quite rightly as a positive advantage.) Before long, the younger sort in Rome – and even once the Ambassador – were calling on us in Venice, where we provided the perfect location for supposedly working holidays, and friends came out to see us, too, in the three summers we spent together there. Fortunately, also, she always had a way with servants. Maria was a little suspicious at first, about losing the mastery of the house to another, younger, foreign woman, but Amanda captivated her, and soon I was convinced the two women were in conspiracy against me, a mutinous compact intended for my happiness. Our first son, Michael, was born in the May of '25 (I insisted that Amanda return to England for the confinement. She protested, not wanting to leave Italy or me, finding my fears ridiculous, but he was nonetheless born in Queen Mary's; all my children were delivered at Queen Mary's). Nineteen summers later, the same age my younger elder brother Tom had been, he was so much mud in the fields of Normandy without the shattered walls and refuges of Caen. He was scarcely out of school; and I had scarcely known him. It ought to be some consolation to you now, but for some fool reason it seems not to be, that for forty years or nearly, no young man has had, for European causes, to go for a soldier. I do not think I am being merely sentimental if I say I think we lost some of our best, as well as bravest, in those lunatic years when Europe heard great argument.

We did not know that then, though clouds like a man's hand stood on the horizon. Over three years we saw the creation of the kind of Italy Arthur Howard had feared, in the grip of squadristi and the rule of terror. There were great convulsions, of course, and despite his African adventures it seemed as though Mussolini might be toppled in '25. He was more cunning than his enemies or rivals in the end, however, and knew that inertia stands at the shoulder of the incumbent power. It came as something of a relief when, at the end of 1926, I was transferred to Riga. It was not so attractive a post as Venice, but an excellent one in terms of my career (designed, I suspect, to further test my mettle). Amanda bore it well, and another son, Alan, in celebration, and we grew in time to love the stark chill waters of the Baltic round whose possession the ugly history of northern Europe has so often revolved.

We were well rewarded for my patience on the Russian marches, for my next promotion, in 1930, brought with it translation to Peking. I assume my masters worked on the principal that anyone who could cope with the Italian Machiavels and the complexities of Slavonic languages should have no difficulty with the Orientals. They were nearly right. I developed a crude working knowledge of Mandarin, which is hopelessly rusty now (only enough remains to charm the waiters on my rare excursions to a restaurant). We fell in love with China and travelled as widely as we could. It was obvious to anyone with eyes that the administration was collapsing under the weight of the country's problems and that only a radical restructuring could save it. Even so, I am glad that I did not have to witness the excesses of the Japanese (a people I have, like every China-hand – and indeed all Chinese – always considered barbarians prancing beneath a lacquer of chivalry and tea), or the imperial carnage of Mao. (Unwittingly, however, that posting gave Alan his career; he trades with China now, and that it should be that vast fascinating state is some consolation for the fact that I have been unable to save my children from the indignity of lives as common merchants.) As I say, I missed the worst, and the beloved country of my memory is, I fear, long vanished, like dragons, wise counsellors and kings. In 1933 it became apparent even to our masters that the service needed everyone who had experience of fascism. I was recalled, and slammed through a course, and shipped out to Berlin as deputy in the Consulate to the German Republic.

My recollection may be scarred and partial, but I hated my six years in Berlin; and I hated the Germans. I found them pompous, stupid, cowardly and greedy after my dear Chinese. They also had, as many of them still do, a relentless devotion to the state and a belief in the probity of all its actions. (I remember a story Howard told me, from one of James Joyce's unreadable books, about an Irish cardinal who opposed the declaration of the Infallibility of the Pope, until the Pontiff took the throne and proclaimed it against all argument. At once, the Irishman got to his feet and cried, 'I believe, O lord, I believe!'; he should have been a German.) I have been accused of similar faults myself, in my time, but for me the state has seemed only the best of available evils, and acceptance of the realities of power a necessary adjunct to sanity.

143

I have little fresh or new to add to the endlessly documented tale of Hitler's imposition of his own anarchic authority. I was only glad that Michael was old enough to be sent to school in England that autumn, and early in '34 we agreed that Alan should be sent to live alternately with my and Amanda's parents till he was old enough for prep school also. Strangely, the single thing which most shocked me about those brutal years and most persuaded me that Hitler was unstoppable except by force of arms (I did not advocate war; none of us in the German service did, for England was weak and unready, and there are some things one cannot advise his political masters, for the good of his career) was the occasion I returned to Germany from my younger sister's wedding in '36. (She was twenty years old, the dearest of my parents' children, the unexpected child of their old age; he was a shit; it ended in a messy divorce, four years later.) I was carrying a copy of Anthony Manet's book *The Politics of Romanticism* with me. It was impounded at the Customs-post as an anti-German tract (yet Göttingen had awarded him a special prize when it was published in '29) and burned before me, on the spot. It was the first book-burning I saw with my own eyes. In retrospect it seems too small a thing to have been shocked about, whilst pogroms, mass-arrests, executions without trial, bribery, barratry and the corruption of children, the good intentions of the totalitarian state, took place all about me; but I set it down in the eccentric interests of truth. I was shocked by the burning of a book.

They were not, however, such bad times to be English and middle-class. Rentiers, our money now more in government stocks and blue-chip shares than in land, we were largely unaffected by the Great Depression, except for the fact that it made servants everywhere easier to find; and in Germany a little peculation by officials was understood to be the way to have anything you wanted arranged – as long as you stood aloof from politics, which I always tried to do, away from my desk, perhaps because I found the new régime too unsavoury to contemplate. I was, I suppose, lucky in that my early years in the service had disbarred me from that admiration for the strength of tyrants of both left and right so many of my contemporaries displayed, fawning before Mussolini, Stalin or Hitler. I merely learned to live with them.

I was lucky in my private life as well. By whatever strange chance we had met, I was fortunate in my wife. Both of us the children of large families, we opted for a smaller one ourselves, though I grant I yearned sometimes for a daughter. Amanda, a great hostess – even in the days of rationing – was the perfect diplomatic wife. We were a handsome couple (it is true, if immodest) and there were already those who spoke of us ending my career as Consul-General in Washington or Paris. She kept me sane by mockery through all the minor crises of a consular life. Though Berlin was more sombre under Hitler than it had been in the days of Weimar, it still drew half the buggers in Europe (the other half were in North Africa) and my staff spent an inordinate amount of time bailing them out from blackmailers and the police (often the same people). We also had to register great numbers of marriages of convenience as Britons tried to get Germans in danger out of the country. At one stage it amounted to a healthy trade, though we did our best to discourage it. Fortunately, Amanda could take none of this or me seriously, so we bowled along, dancing towards destruction, in a kind of happy mist.

Our departure from Berlin in '39 was fast but not unexpected. I lobbied unashamedly (with Tim Carmichael's help) to be placed with the team in London co-ordinating relations with allied European nations and partisan groups in occupied territories. Like everyone else, I had to take my turn dealing with the mulish, extravagant pride of the Free French (oddly enough, I rather liked De Gaulle and Gamelin); and afterwards, after the collapse of the last great alliance to partition Poland, which had tumbled us into war in the first place, with the paranoia of the Soviets – but at last I was seconded to assist the Adriatic Desk, which tried to exercise a measure of hopeless control over our Italian, Greek and Jugoslav friends (bonny fighters the lot of them, but about as disciplined as crabs).

My work kept me in London much of the time, so Amanda and I wanted a house close by, with good transport services. Property was ludicrously cheap during the war, when it came on the market at all – particularly in that uneasy period when the fighting was all in the east, and all England (whatever may now be said) suspected the war would be over in blitzkrieg, bombing and the mass destruction of our cities in a matter of months, at most. We bought a large house in a little village south of London called Coulsdon (it is a waste land and by-pass now), hard by the edge of Farthing Downs. I do not care to admit I once lived in Surrey, and I rectified the fault as soon as I could when the war was over by buying the house I live in now, in Hampshire.

It was at Coulsdon, one winter's night in '41 (January the thirteenth, a night of infamy in my memory), while I was trapped in London by a random air-raid, that a German pilot cried off too early, mistaking his target, or through fear, and unloaded his bombs on the village before scuttling for home. A stick of incendiaries marched up Downs Road and three of them fell on our house. What happened thereafter I have replayed again and again in fancy and dreams, and every time I cry for it to stop, to rewind, to play again with a different ending; but it never changes and it never goes away.

Amanda was by the cellar doors, locking them for the night (they opened on to the garden, a general lumber-room and store). The elms beside her burst into flames as one of the incendiaries skipped tumbling from the roof. Somehow a lick of flame must have jumped the narrow pathway and set her clothes on fire. In unimaginable fear, in pain, in shock, she must have struggled into the cellar for cover, or without the capacity left for thinking, thrashing about and screaming until her hand fell on what may have seemed to be one of the jerrycans of water we kept stored, not seeing the white cross meaning 'Petrol' painted on it.

Here the dream slows down as though in an attempt to make me suffer as she suffered, as though any suffering I may endure could ever compensate for what she must have gone through, or palliate her pain. I see, each time, her struggling with the top and in her unimaginable panic pouring the contents, despite all warnings, over her clothing. I hope beyond hope or reason that she never knew what she had done, but my dreams inform me of an agonising realisation and a slow, tormented death as she, the cellar and half the house were transfigured, as one, all one, by fire. What I remember is fire. This is the filthiest of the nightmares which infect my age.

I have wondered ever since if it was such an anguish for his mother and hatred of her murderers which drove Michael on heedless, to his unnecessary, early death. I have wondered if Alan entered the China trade in a desperate attempt to recapture the years when he was a scarcely conscious child, but his mother was still alive. I have asked myself such questions again and again through the ever-sifting night; but no answer comes, as no answer comes to slake the agony of the thought I might have saved her if I could have somehow made my way home. No thinking, however, and no remorse, can be a recompense or restitution for what she lost, all human being and reason burned from her. I do not know why, but one of the greatest sorrows of the night for the old man I have become, is the remembrance she was barely thirty-six years old.

I survived, though I do not know quite how; survival is a human being's business. Fatherhood became a necessary agony. The boys were evacuated to my or Amanda's parents during the holidays (their school, in any case, was outside any of the areas deemed dangerous). Seeing them brought her back, yet gave me some cause for continuance. I found the worst, the most horrible aspect of grief not the

146

steady almost insupportable pain – for that lessened in time to a dull numbness of spirit; not even the tormented memory of things unsaid or left undone, of meanness or folly or anger for which I had never apologised or spoken my shame and told my affection; but the unguarded moments when life took on a kind of tolerable emotionless calm, when I would find myself turning as though I sensed she had just come into the room, or thought I had heard her calling, or came across things I wanted to tell her about, before realising, stricken, that I would never tell her anything again. Over the years, she had become, as I trust I became to her, the landscape of my life, the home to which I returned, the guarantee that somewhere I belonged and had dignity and value. After her death I was a kind of refugee.

Almost the worst of it was the inability to burden anyone else with my grief. Loss was a constant factor in the lives of all those about me. The young, the old, the middle-aged, died stupidly through the years, and no one I knew remained untouched by sorrow. We all developed a carapace of reticence, a particularly English refusal to mourn in public or to burden others with our suffering, for all the others we knew had their own wounds to bear. I withdrew inside the curtain-walls of work and privacy and self. Behind those walls I died a little every day.

They were years of glittering desperate cold romance in London, whole sections of the city sheared and shattered, ineluctable reminders of the proximity of death and the imminence of termination. We inhabited a world without a future in it. The young turned, as they had turned before, to the consolations of passion and sex, and I am not now so old or yet so wise that I can deny the virtue or necessity of what they did. Those war-time marriages, those leave-time couplings, were expressions of vigour and hope against the insanity and darkness their elders had let a whole world slide into; I have never found it easy to deny or criticise the young, however vacuous or foolish they might sometimes seem to be, how empty their protestations, how foolish their hopes, and how selfish to the cynical eyes of age their aspirations and desires. It is not as though their elders, in any generation, have done so very much better. It is not as though we have done so much with our greater knowledge and experience. Perhaps it is only and desperately true that the increase of knowledge is the increase of sorrow. The tragedy of the young is that they turn into their parents. The tragedy of the parents is that they forget they have done so already, except for those of us who unweave the wind in age, when we are forgotten, above and beyond the argument and anguish of the earth, outside the combat and released from the fray. I can understand the old who

147

choose to forget it all and pull back into the querulous selfishness of age; the most wonderful thing about age is that I am no longer required or expected to pretend; with so little time left to me I can sometimes get away with the irascible or urgent demands we conceal when there is still a future before us; I try not to do so too often, for it seems my fate is not to demand but to wonder, to read the riddles of a lifetime, and to see the world we made and acted in through the unpitying eyes of memory. Not everything is forgotten. Not everything is lost.

Even then, however, I was no longer young; and without Amanda, her loss as violent as sulphuric acid, I was reduced to desiccation. Work became my only respite from the nightmares which pursued me and the desperation which arose from the simple absoluteness of her absence. Everything I felt, the controlling shame and waste and emptiness of those years, resolved into those things which may be meant by the words, She should be here. In the end, I have come to realise, it is always ourselves we grieve for, it is our own suffering we mourn. There is no end to the selfishness of men.

Only in recollection do I begin to understand what seemed to be one of the worst and most defiling aspects of that season. Looking back, I see myself as the handsome dutiful servant of the state, noble in enduring the weight of his loss, transfigured by sorrow, acquainted with grief, master of the destinies of brave men and women throughout fallen or hostile territories, a captain of our cause. The world was full in those distant days of the impressionable, lonely and fearful young. There came a time when I found myself rejecting the timorous advances, wet-eyed, dry-mouthed and hesitant, of some of the young romantic women I worked with or knew. I did not know how to be kind in those rejections, though in my way I tried, for my emotions on such occasions were a confusion of desperate need and loathing. There remained within me a longing for physical consolation, and a certain knowledge that if I reached out for it the intensity of that need would overwhelm its fragile young surrogates, for they could only be transformed in every touch, in every intimacy, turned into her. I would have destroyed them in my mind and with my flesh, for what my body cried for in irrational, unpredictable stabs of longing was the presence of my wife, and nothing could restore her to my company, my arms, my bed. I laboured in the heat of her destruction; they were playing with ready embers, those innocent, foolish young women, and if I had reached out to touch them they would have burned. I began only then to understand what Jane Carlyle had tried to tell me so many years before, one distant night in Venice, when she had said I could not have

148

endured or coped with the loneliness and intensity of need of that ageing, still-passionate widow. I was become a widower myself, and I grew to know the fires she spoke of. It was to be years, not till the conflagration of the world had ceased, before I achieved anything resembling her simple, frank acceptance of her own desires, and more time yet before I gained her astonishing (it seems to me no less than that now, knowing what I know, having become what I have become) capacity for affection. She must have loved her husband very much.

Throughout the nearly five years more of warfare which remained to us, the nearest I found to consolation or understanding was in the letters Anthony wrote to me. (I have kept them all, still having the bureaucrat's passion for paper; and it is a sign of how quickly a scholarly or literary reputation may diminish without the pressure of new work, that I have only been troubled once by a graduate student asking to see them whilst researching the more celebrated figures Anthony knew. I let her see them, of course, but I am glad in some ways that I have not been often troubled, for something inside me still revolts at the thought of the impartial disinterestedly raking through dead leaves which are still alive to me with the memory of a man.)

No one could hope to free me of my burden, nor was it true that time would do so. Time displaces nothing, in my experience. It merely continues, and we continue with it, adding to what we have already been until at last the griefs or joys of time gone by do not lie so near our surface, nor so easily command our attention, until a single incision comes, and cuts through to the heart of them. He was not so foolish as to try, however, to placate or diminish what I felt. Instead, he wrote simply, directly, affectingly of loss and unhappiness. He had the wisdom to deny that he knew what I felt, for there is an arrogance in suffering which insists on its own uniqueness and angrily rejects any notion of understanding on equal terms; rather, he accepted that I was inconsolable and could not foresee a time when life would ever be tolerable again. He offered, without having to say so, to listen, to accept the buffeting and gales of my anger, fear and pain. All the while, he wrote with his usual dark-eyed gaiety of the folly and ignorance he witnessed all about him, of the endless inventive knavishness of men, of the world as it had been and the world as it was, of his work and his surroundings and of the simple pleasure he took in light and landscape and music and books. (To the very end he was the most peculiar scholar I ever knew. He read very slowly, and never lost an almost childish delight and glee before books. 'Suspension of disbelief?' I remember him once saying. 'I have never found it a problem. I'm hooked from the moment I reach to the shelf. I'm one of those simple souls a writer actually has to work at losing, and I hate it when it happens.' That was nothing but the truth, for even in his darkest days, when the spirit and passion seemed to leave him, he could be reduced to helpless laughter – or racked with tears – by books.)

In his very first letter after Amanda's death, he sent me the addition to my education for which I am most grateful (though in his unthinking way he made many such); he sent me the little pamphlet of Eliot's *East Coker*; he had marked the second part of the second section, and the opening of the fifth (you must look them up yourself – I am too old and too weary to be bothered with arranging for clearance of the copyright) and I found their clear-sighted, brave and honest refusal of consolation becoming a kind of litany for me, as they did for thousands of others whom I joined in buying the two remaining *Quartets* as they were published.

His letters came from the United States, where he had taught – to the surprise of all who knew him – since the autumn of 1937. In the years since Venice, his travels nearly as extensive and eccentric as my own, we had kept in touch mainly by letter. We met in London on several occasions, including the great Italian Art exhibition he had helped to put together; in Berlin once, briefly; and before that he had come to visit us once in Riga, when he was working in the Hermitage (it will always be the Winter Palace to me) in Leningrad. Amanda had never met anyone like him, but he was always good with women and soon charmed her so that she came to refer to him to others (in his absence) as 'Jeremy's half-tame bohemian' – although he was one of the least bohemian figures we knew, and would never have been guilty of the crass bad manners which were more of a characteristic of our class at that time than of any world he belonged to. After he left us in Riga she said something I did not understand, but began to see the truth of later. 'He likes women. Most men don't.'

'What about homosexuals?' I asked her, teasing. 'They're supposed to be good with women.'

She was serious in reply. 'Yes they are, because we feel safe; but they find us funny. They don't see what all the fuss is about. He does, most certainly, but he likes women so much he's never got round to marrying one. It's such a pity.'

Throughout this time we kept in touch by correspondence, though he never once referred back to the spring of 1923, even when I tried. He was mostly a remembered voice and limp, and I would see these stalking even through his scholarly papers (he sent me off-prints) and his frequent reviews and articles. There was a time in the Twenties and very early Thirties when he seemed to be everywhere, writing funny, informed and erudite articles on history, art and literature, in any number of languages for the press (it seemed) of a dozen countries. He translated the Russian revolutionary poets into English, French, German and Italian. He translated the writers of each of those languages into all the others. He was one of the first translators from Lorca's Spanish. For a while he seemed to be a whirlwind of wit and knowledge, but in his late thirties the work-flow eased off rather. I suspected he wanted to spend more time in original research, thinking and writing, and certainly the books which came out in 1929 and 1934 gave evidence of being the products of much labour. In '29 he wrote to me saying he feared he would never be forgiven in England for *The Politics of Romanticism*. (It was his second book; I had not realised when I first knew him in Venice that he had already published a volume of essays on the use of poetry as an inspiration by painters, with a wonderful, scathing Afterword about poets who describe paintings. I remember one line in particular – 'For painters, poetry is an occasion; for poets, painting is an excuse.') *The Politics* was the book in which he tried to demonstrate (to my untutored satisfaction) that the early Romantics did not effect a technical revolution in the way the arts were made, but what he called a broadly political one, by changing the objects of their attention and concern. As far as I could tell, he was right in believing that he would find no forgiveness – if only because he wrote so well that people remembered his gibes.

His next book, *Re-Inventing Love (The Translators of Petrarch)*, is still widely used and quoted. I found it even then almost impenetrable, referring to more languages than I choose to be burdened with; I did my duty with Mandarin.

All I mean by all of this is that it came as an immense surprise, not least since he had spoken to me of his fears and doubts about America, when he decided to take up a post in the United States, without warning, in '37. He seems to have moved from university to university, never quite achieving tenure. I know he taught at various times at Columbia, Yale, Williams, and even Vassar, but I heard from him less in those next few years, and the flow eased off again two years or so after Amanda's death. (I wrote that sentence with something approaching equanimity; it is some tribute to his remembered kindness that, even now, to write of him eases my remembered pain, although it is always the pain which most readily endures.)

So time drew on, and a time came when we could see the war might yet be achieved in under a lifetime. I had laboured on through its dark middle years, losing myself in work; and my masters, both as a reward for my endeavours and because aware of my capacities, I believe,

151

made me part of that team which was intended to oversee the liberation of the occupied territories and their return to civilian government. At first I was incensed that I was not placed with the group which followed our troops up through Italy, but a conversation with my mother-in-law made me realise the silent wisdom of the service. As she pointed out, I was (and am) still uncertain how easily, if at all, I could have borne being returned to the landscape of my early married life. Throughout that time, in fact, both my parents and parents-in-law, with enormously judicious tact and gentleness, began to wean me from my grief back into the world. I know that they were precipitate and that I was to take my own time returning to the community of common men, but I acknowledge their kindness in first beginning to suggest, if only for the sake of their shared grandsons, that I ought to consider marrying again. Then, however, the notion still revolted me, and the violence of my reactions must have caused them volumes of unspoken hurt. Michael's death that summer pulled me back yet further from the world.

With 1945, however, times changed. Allied troops fought their way through France and Belgium and Holland, through Eastern Europe and Italy, and into Germany itself. By my forty-fourth birthday it was clear, except to its leaders, that Germany was defeated, that the outlines of the post-war world were already taking shape, and that all parties must begin to organise the new governments of Europe. I had eventually been assigned to the staff intended for Holland, but was, in the end, one of the last to travel across the Channel. There were not many of us with appropriate experience, as governments in exile flooded in entreaty to the Western allies, and the vexing problem of Eastern Europe and what might be done after the Red Army's long advance took up many of our best. I spent most of '45 in London, coaxing, cajoling, pleading, begging, trying to create – or at least evoke – some order, or sense of order, whilst military authorities held an unrelaxing power, whilst civilian, local authorities bayed to have it given back to them, whilst the wishes of each country's population remained unknown.

At last, at the end of September, I handed my duties over to other unfortunate unhappy civil servants, and travelled from Harwich to the Hook to take up my unasked for duties in the Netherlands.

I have never forgotten that time in Europe after the Second War, for in time I had the opportunity to travel widely, through most of the West and some of the East. I had seen destruction, degradation and waste at home, but nothing prepared me for the totality of the destruction the Continent endured, and most of all Germany herself.

No newsreel had succeeded in preparing me for the sight of cities not partly but entirely in ruins – rubble and shards the bombers had picked over night after night, displacing and disturbing the dead, the most elementary of goods or services unavailable, the whole of what it is now fashionable to call the infra-structure laid waste; and, most affecting of all, the unimaginable numbers of missing and lost. In all, millions of people vanished, their fate unknown to family or friends, leaving only a terrible, gnawing, futile hope; hope which was only rarely answered, or if it was, was answered too late, when the world and all of us in it were unrecognisable, or for the worst.

When I first saw Rotterdam, the docks no longer existed. I do not mean they were in ruins. It was worse than that. Nothing recognisable as a dock remained. There was water, there was shattered concrete, there was tangled metal, there were rotting half-submerged carcasses of what might have once been ships in what might once have been a harbour; but for the city to work as a dock again, it had to be cleared and rebuilt from the beginning – as though there had been nothing but ruination there before, as though the trading history of northern Europe had been deracinated, eradicated, in not quite six years. The same was true all along the northern seaboard, making it desperately difficult to move goods in bulk. What we saw most of that winter was starvation.

As always happens, the armies and the occupying powers (including me) took first priority when it came to the distribution of such goods as were landed. The local populations had to make do with whatever was left over. Whatever may be said about the Americans, one thing is certain: without the generosity and wealth of the United States that winter, death would have ridden triumphant and the old turbulent western shelf would have seen depopulation unequalled since the Thirty Years' War, or even the Black Death.

As it was, babies died in their thousands because young mothers were too starved to make milk and we had too little powdered milk to hope to satisfy all the demand. People starved because too little had been planted in the death-throes of the war. Animals were slaughtered because there was insufficient feed. There were few enough animals left after the years of need, but even so there was not the manpower, equipment, will or time to preserve every one of them; their remains rotted on the land, picked over by the needy, black-marketeers and carrion, spreading disease, until we were faced by protein-deficiency malnutrition on a massive scale.

Holland was relatively lucky, as were France and Belgium. They had been conquered early by Germany, and not too inefficiently

153

administered. Their agriculture had remained largely intact, and though food was short the situation was not as grievous as it was elsewhere. That was one of the main reasons why, once six months were over, I asked to be transferred to Tim Carmichael's team of travelling administrators and specialists who went wherever help was needed, wherever the problems were worst. (I was given permission to join them. That, however, was another, different, future, and did not affect what happened here. Carmichael had a nose for jobs with good publicity value and high exposure; it served him well, for he achieved the great heights of the service, in the end – Paris and Washington.)

In the meantime, it was the destruction of industrial Holland which was my immediate problem. Her ports, railways, bridges, roads had been bombed to paste in the Allied invasion and by the Germans' desperate attempts to throw it back. Till then Holland had endured, unhappy but mainly peaceable, so it was not surprising that some of the citizens treated us with a distaste at least the equal of their loathing of Germans. It was we who had caused the damage, and were now doing what seemed like an inadequate best to remedy it.

The scale of even Holland's problems meant we could not retire behind the safe, conventional structures of a diplomatic mission. Although the Ambassador and the Chancery staff were officially based at the Hague, where the civilian government was being cranked back into operation, the great trading cities of the country remained – insofar as trade was possible under those ludicrous conditions – Rotterdam and Amsterdam. Our first priority was to get both cities as much operational as possible, and the mission kept staffs in both. It was in Amsterdam, the historic administrative centre of the Netherlands and the location of their greatest merchants, that I set up my consular staff. I have to admit that in those days the divisional titles were virtually meaningless. We all did whatever seemed necessary, liaising and keeping records as best we could, and it was to be months before the system was working anything like normally. In those days we were making everything up as we went along for, in the West at least, the Great War had been largely static, and none of the services had any experience in dealing with mass destruction on such a scale, affecting so many people, in so many places.

Even the simplest aspects of running a mission became a trial, especially one scattered in three locations with many of its principal officers moving from one to the other. The telephone system was in ruins. Wireless communication between great cities was not feasible. We relied largely on our own and on military messengers, but even so things went astray, got lost, mislaid. Even accommodation was a problem, with the military having first choice. From London I had cut through the red tape surrounding premises in Amsterdam by the simple expedient of commandeering an office-building on the Damrak by the Central Post Office (the postal service was one of the more extravagant jokes in immediate post-war civilian life) and promising to settle the rent, and compensation for the original lessees, at a later date. (Long afterwards I discovered that that process had taken four and a half years.) Accommodation for staff was even more problematical. Army officers were put up at the better hotels, as their German counterparts had been before them. (If I had ever had the misfortune to live through another conventional war, I would have moved heaven and earth to raise the capital to buy a stake in the biggest hotel in town.) We, however, expected to stay longer than the officers, and discovered, in any case, like other peace-makers before us, that there was no room at the inn. All we had was the confidence of victory, hard bargaining and harder currency. Even so, my Second Assistant spent six weeks before my arrival sleeping on my First Assistant's floor. As for myself, I managed to arrange a tiny flat built into the upper floors of an ancient merchant's house, hard by what is now the Jewish Museum, close to one of the safest but least savoury red-light districts in the world. (That is not written in any sense of puritanism; it is simply an old man, born in slower, more spacious, and less egregiously democratic days, sighing for the privacy and elegance of his youth.) I had two floors and a separate entrance. The lower floor had a small sitting room, a smaller dining room, an apology for a kitchen and, behind a curtain, a bathroom. The upper floor was the customary high but unconverted attic; a single room, above whose solitary window a block and tackle still swung in the breeze, rattling me awake at night, left over from the great days of the Dutch Republic centuries before, when the house was built, when merchants had used their lofts for storage of the goods lifted from barges on the canals. It became my bedroom and study. By the standards of the time, I lived in luxury.

I did not know the city well in those days, but I found it making me almost nostalgic for my youth. I have always loved water, a wet-bob since boyhood, and Amsterdam is more filigree with waterways even than Venice, and has more water in it – though the absence of that city's broad vistas, its liquid boulevards and the amphitheatre of the lagoon, do not make it seem so. In water, everything changes, even light on the clearest, strongest, brightest day. It is a perpetual reminder that even the strongest and most certain things decay, and are eroded, by the shifting happenstance of time and circumstance, and that nothing we do can deny the irrevocable, undeniable, unanswerable lapping of events. We shall all be changed, when earth and air are one and the world is left to its final consumption amongst the elements which gave it birth, in water, and in fire.

Although barely October, it was already winter when I arrived. The leaves from the tall black trees (where are the elms of yesteryear?) which fingered the thin slivers of urban sky lay thick and rusty along the wet, cobbled, treacherous streets and on the clotted water of the canals. I came into the city by train (itself a miracle, made possible by the splendid labours of Dutch railway-workers and the Royal Engineers; it was the one service which kept working almost all the time, though replacement track and sleepers had to be pillaged from smaller, local lines) and my arrival was a hardly registered disappointment. Scarcely anything shifted my desolation in those days, although I did my best to ensure my dejection did not show; but throughout my life there has always been a tiny part of me, unaffected by grief or pain or joy, which lifts at the prospect of entering another city and rises like migrating geese at the first sharp sniff of the sea, smelling the simple joy of journeying and the prospect of new nourishment.

It was already almost dark when I arrived that afternoon, and all I saw from the train was the usual sad accompaniment of sidings, locomotives, ash-heaps, rubble and rusting machinery, tired and run-down tenements, their cladding peeling or, here, their vital members shattered, doors and beams jutting from the fractured sides of buildings, eloquent with life gone missing like the rag-dolls and tin-soldiers of dead children.

The huge station echoed with our arrival, so little traffic was there in those days, not even enough to disturb or feed the scrawny, ruffianly pigeons who sheltered there; old, tough, piratical ones, who had avoided the fate of hot cooked pies.

I was glad there was no great celebration or ceremony for my arrival (there rarely is for Consuls, except in places starved for celebrities or gentlemen) for my approach left me unmoved. I was met only by my First Assistant, Christopher Harkworth (he had been invalided out of the Air Force three years before, when he had lost a Mosquito and most of his left arm. He was returned to the service, a serious, diffident, intelligent young man I had worked with almost ever since). He smiled when he saw me, and ran his one remaining long white hand through the lick of light-brown hair which fell over his eyes, before pushing it out to greet me. I looked down at the newly grubbied object and set my face in a mask of feigned disapproval. He looked down at it himself, and wiped it sheepishly on his heavy special-issue Diplomatic Corps greatcoat (an affectation I never shared; I would not even wear the buttons). He tried again.

'Hallo, sir. Good to have you over here.'

I looked him up and down, his open intelligent face hopeful and expectant, his left sleeve empty; and found myself thinking of the son I had lost fifteen months before, whose mother's death had left me without the energy to control his lust for combat; and felt oddly paternal. I took him by the hand.

'Glad to be here. It looks as though my staff need looking after already.'

Christopher walked me to his flat that night. There were no taxis yet and the tram service still closed down early, and I needed to stretch my legs – though I discovered that the main streets of Amsterdam, deceptive on the map, are wearisomely long. The city was shabby and deserted, with minimal lighting, and as our footsteps echoed through the darkness down the Damrak and Rokin towards the Bloemen Markt area where Christopher lived, he explained the problem of accommodation.

'I think we've found a suitable place for you, sir. Very central. A German colonel with the permanent staff had it before. Trouble is, the old man who owns the place doesn't want to deal with people he thinks of as lackeys. He's agreed in principle to rent the place out, but he's waiting to meet you. We can go see it tomorrow. I think you may have to lean on him pretty hard, and a cash gift would go down pretty well – we can take it out of the general expenses fund ...'

'I know how the finances of my own Consulate are run, Christopher,' I reminded him, I hope gently.

'Sorry, sir. Comes from trying to kick this rabble into shape for you.'

I smiled, though he would not have seen me. 'Don't push it, Kit. I'll see the old man in the morning. How are things shaping up?'

'It's still pretty much of a mess, sir. Part of the problem comes from our not being military, and having to work with the civilian authorities. The military would have commandeered this place we've found for you, but I've been working on the principle that we have to maintain good peacetime relations with the locals so I've avoided that kind of thing.'

'Very wise.' He nodded gratefully. 'Have we had any come-back on the offices?'

'A little. We passed them back there, just before Dom Square. Did you see?'

I was grave and humoured him. 'I did notice, yes.'

157

'The owners aren't overjoyed, and the original lessees have kicked up a bit of a fuss. They haven't really got a leg to stand on, though. Most of their warehouses were bombed out during the invasion, and until compensation is sorted out they aren't even trading – so I don't see why they should need an Amsterdam office. Any instructions on that front, sir?'

'Kick it back upstairs to the Embassy staff at the Hague. It was their job to requisition us quarters in the first place, and it isn't our fault if they were slow off the mark. They'll be authorising compensation claims anyway. All we should have to do is prepare and submit them.'

'Fine, sir, I'll have that done tomorrow. We turn right here.' We turned from the broad Rokin canal into the Singel, the innermost of the city's radial canal streets. Kit's house was tucked in between the university library and the old Lutheran Church. 'We're on the first floor. It's only a couple of rooms, I'm afraid, but it does me handsomely.' He helped me with my bags. The flat, as he had said, was two small rooms, so small that he kept the door between them permanently open to create an illusion of space. It was meant to be like an Oxford set, I think, a study and a bedroom, but it was hard to tell with papers scattered everywhere which was which.

'Shared bathroom on the landing, sir. They keep it pretty clean, but best to get in early if you want hot water. There's a proper truckle through there.' He pointed vaguely through the connecting door. 'I'll take the camp-bed tonight. We'll have you fixed up in the morning.' He was pouring us both a stiff drink; I raised my eyebrows, wondering where he had laid his hands on anything so valuable. He smiled shyly in answer. 'Only, bourbon, I'm afraid, sir, from the American Army PX Store. I have a friendly major.'

'Then I had better find myself a colonel.'

I settled into the one armchair with my glass and Kit leaned against the desk. We were both still in our coats, for there was no fire burning and frost was creeping up the window-panes. Kit's breath formed nacreous ribbons in the air.

'As you've probably gathered already, sir, things are pretty bad over here. Insufficient fuel, which means a lot of the old folk will die of cold this winter. Food's rationed, which means there's just enough to go round. We could try going out to eat, a few places have re-opened since the curfew was lifted, but I don't hold out much hope of finding anything worth what we're likely to pay for it. Most of the good stuff goes to the officers in the big hotels, hence the importance of making friends with the military. I've still got some cold meats and cheese left over, if that's all right.'

158

I coughed agreement and buried my head deeper into the warmth of my coat lapels. 'It's pretty much the same at home.'

'So I gather. I'm only glad I'm not in Germany. I gather the big cities there are unrecognisable and conditions ten times worse. The Russians don't give a damn, either, which doesn't help.'

'I can't say that I blame them' (and I still cannot). 'They've lost more people than all the rest of us put together, and to some of the chaps they've brought in from the steppes even a bombed-out public lavatory must look the height of luxury and engineering.'

'I know, but ... How are things back home, sir?'

He was thinking of his wife. I tried to reassure him, being beyond reassurance myself. 'They're all right. Really. We won after all. The government's doing its best.'

He nodded earnestly. 'They seem a pretty decent lot, all things considered.'

'Yes. Not too many Bolsheviks amongst them.'

He smiled. To most of our class the election of a Labour government with a massive majority had come as a profound shock. I had hardly registered any reaction at all. Looking back, it sometimes seems that I, traversing the world, was less cut off from the reality of England than many of my contemporaries who had stayed at home and seen (though not experienced) the Depression of the Thirties. I know, however, that that is hindsight. At the time, and ever since, the expropriations of the socialist government seemed to me little short of theft; but I did not whimper as others did, for during those years I worked on a shattered continent, in Holland first, then in more grievously injured places, and I could understand – although I could not share – the desire to change the world.

We spoke of the work my staff had been doing over the past two months, trying to co-ordinate the military and civilian administrations, trying to help organise the rebuilding of roads and bridges and damaged canals, trying to oversee the regeneration of industry and the provision of jobs, helping the circulation of emergency relief. He spoke of the immensity of the disorganisation; and, as he spoke, I found myself for the first time in years beginning to feel proud of the work I was involved in, and proud of the people who worked for me. Outside, blackness enfolded the city, and we sat in the flickering brightness of a hurricane lantern, two figures out of a painting three hundred years old.

As we chewed over cold meat and cheese and tough three-day-old bread ('Freshest I could find,' Kit told me), there came a knock at the door. He went to answer it.

159

I could not make out the figure who entered behind him in a clatter of boots and indistinct conversation, until they both stood in the light of the lamp. Our visitor was tall, well over six feet (six-four at a guess) and dressed in workman's boots and tough industrial hopsack trousers. He wore some kind of fishing pullover, heavy and greasy and yellow, and a flapping mackintosh turning green. He seemed genuinely painfully thin, as though his frame had been artificially elongated in some hideous torture. He was also the palest man I have ever seen. He was pale to the edge of albinism, his hair almost peroxide white, his face and hands bloodless, his eyes the palest washed-out blue and his eyelashes startlingly blond against the raw, strained redness of his eyelids and sockets.

'This is Adam Altdoorp, sir. He works sometimes for our people at the Hague,' Kit explained. 'My chief, Adam. Mr Burnham.' He turned to me again. 'He's come looking for Bill Carstairs. I was just explaining that Bill moved out a couple of days ago. Just hold on, Adam, and I'll give you his address.'

He scribbled it on a scrap of paper and handed it to the tall, emaciated young man, who never once averted his almost colourless eyes from me. Altdoorp stuffed the address into his coat pocket, apologised for disturbing us, in flawless English, and was gone, his heavy boots thumping the old, unyielding wooden stairs.

'So it is true,' I said. 'The Dutch do all speak English.'

'Seventy per cent of them, sir. It's one place where you won't have to learn the language.'

'That is almost a disappointment.' That was not my main reaction to the young man's visit, however. 'Tell me something. When I left London there was still a ruling in force saying this mission should not employ Dutch nationals. I admit it strikes me as a foolish rule, but what is that young man doing working for the Embassy?'

'I couldn't really tell you, sir. It struck us as odd, too. He doesn't seem to have any regular job there. Bill might know more. They've become quite good friends. Apparently he's come over specially from the Hague to see him; that's why I gave out his address.' Kit stood with his hand thrust in his pocket before hazarding a further guess. 'I wouldn't mind betting his father had something to do with it.'

'His father?'

'Yes. You probably didn't recognise the name out of context. His father is David Altdoorp, of Jordaens-Altdoorp, who are still the fourth largest industrial conglomerate in the Netherlands. That young man may not look very impressive, but he stands to be one of the richest men in Holland one day.'

'Interesting, but not as interesting as what I really want to know about, which is how the hell did you and Bill Carstairs manage to share this mouse-trap for six weeks?'

He grinned, as he began to roll off his coat with his one whole arm. 'It wasn't easy, but anything's possible after the RAF.'

I did not sleep easily that night, but when I did I slept more heavily than I had done in months. One thing, I remember, kept me awake more than any other; the realisation that I had almost ignored – or at least forgotten – my son's death in the immensity of the loss of my wife, as though there is a limit to the pain one person can feel, or perhaps more truly to the attention he can give. I felt guilty, and guilt is perhaps the beginning of recovery, for it is an entirely selfish emotion unless it persuades us to change what we are, and it is that selfishness which helps us survive. I was too old to be changed (perhaps I was always too old) and it was not until long afterwards, after my second marriage which brought me new children, that I realised the priorities of my grief had been entirely normal and entirely sane. We grieve most for that which is irreplaceable, and the loss of an adult we love is the loss of something finished, formed and active in the world, something of its own particular kind and class that we shall never see again, while children are all potential; we cannot know what they might be. Others will take their place, and grow in their own way, into whole and completed creatures, capable and worthy of love. As long as we can hope to have more children, the death of a child cannot be the most absolute of tragedies. This is a fact which, for simple biological reasons, must be more wounding to women than men. It is the mature we should most honestly grieve for, not the young. Michael, nineteen years old, could not, should not, have been the equal of my wife.

Christopher woke me just as the thin winter sun pushed aside the last damson traces of night tucked into the fringes of the sky. It was bitterly cold, and I pulled the coat I had thrown over the bed closer to me. He cleared a patch of window with his sleeve and clouds of breath.

'Bad frost last night. We shall have snow before the month is out. We only have ersatz coffee, I'm afraid, but if you'd like to catch the last of the hot water I'll have some ready by the time you're out of your bath, sir.'

I nodded, unwilling to speak lest my teeth rattle. It was like being back in school again. The bathroom, which had no window except for two panes of frosted glass in the door, was running with condensation, as was the tiny bath. I turned on the hot tap and waited for the exhausted plumbing to rattle and belch and throw up a nasty piddle of rusty brown water. Instead, after several seconds' wait and much noise, it heaved a cascade of boiling water into the bath, splashes flying. Ten minutes later I began to feel as though I was human again.

Kit's description of his coffee had the virtue of honesty; the dull brown sludge he handed me in a mug (he used the mug without a handle himself; such are the small privileges of rank and age) had no virtue at all besides heat. Like all of us that winter, he used a single-ring Primus stove, with bottles purloined from military stores by sympathetic quartermasters.

It was with some gratitude that I left to do battle with the mad old man who wanted an extra two hundred guilders a month rent for his flat, and a sweetener of a thousand. After I had ranted and raved and haggled for the requisite half an hour (it is necessary in such situations that the vendor should feel that he has done long, mighty and arduous battle with you) we agreed on the sweetener and a rent increase of seventy-five guilders a month (I should have held out for fifty). I went back to Kit's for my bags (never have them with you; it makes you look desperate) and by lunchtime I had begun to acquaint myself with the streets and canals of central Amsterdam and made my way to my office.

I have to admit that in those months I had relatively little to do (which was as it should be; the less a head of station has to do, the more efficiently that station is being run – unless all the staff are asleep, of course). By this time I had a staff of seventeen, not counting Christopher and Bill Carstairs, a quiet young East Anglian, who between them divided up most of my work. That was in Amsterdam alone, and the figure was almost doubled over the next six months. In other centres, including Rotterdam, I had another twenty-nine staff. Most of my time was divided between travelling round all my stations, dealing with any problems requiring mediation with the various powers that were (though Bill took over much of even this work), liaising with the other divisions of the mission, and being brought in as the heavy gun when relations between the military and civil powers, common citizens and businesses, grew acrimonious or intractable. I travelled, I talked, I sat in meetings and approved minutes, I shouted down telephones on the rare occasions we established a connection, I wrote stiff letters and I submitted memoranda, but I find it difficult, even embarrassing, to claim that I worked.

Kit Harkworth, in particular, was the fulcrum of the Consulate (he ended his time in the service as our man in Kenya, where he retired; he died last year, only sixty-seven years old) round which the circus

162

turned. I was educated never to use the word 'nice' unless in commination, or to mean a small, fine measure, but I have to say he was one of the nicest men I have ever known. His injuries had somehow left him mentally undamaged (though that must have had something to do with Sarah, his wife, who survives him), and in his cool, calmheaded way he ensured the rest of the staff maintained a proper sense of perspective. It was essential that everyone be aware of the importance and urgency of the work we had in hand, for the fortunes and happiness of the populace depended on the reconstruction of a country we were trying to help with; but it would have been foolishness to deny that on many occasions that work was fouled or muddled or delayed by the egotism or arrogance or sheer tomfoolishness of mortals anxious for status, wealth, or the proper completion of forms (soldiers are even worse than bureaucrats in this last respect). Heading the Consulate, we made no attempt to deny such things left us frustrated or angry or simply looking incompetent, inane or mendacious. Often we existed merely so that some party directly involved should not have to take egg on its own face. The only sane defence was self-mockery and laughter in our submission to the will and dubious wisdom of men. We lived through those times on the basis of Kit's working hypothesis, one of the few sane remarks I have ever heard from any man who was ultimately to achieve a knighthood, and an excellent means of ordering any life.

'This is not a country,' he cried, in the full mockery of his exasperation; 'this is a mental hospital for everyone too damaged by war to live a normal life. We are being kept here to avoid our infecting the whole of the rest of the world.'

There were times when it was impossible to disagree with him. One battle, however, I did fight on their behalf. Everyone in the mission was doing more, and different kinds of, work than those for which diplomatic stations are designed. We, in particular, were trying to encourage and nurture the re-emergent Anglo-Dutch trade, and to facilitate the movement of civilians. Like every other part of the mission we were desperately under-staffed and, more than most others, we would have benefited from the forbidden employment of local staff. One morning in November, my assistants came to see me. They were fierce, for I think that at the time they believed it was my resistance they had to fight rather than that of my superiors.

'What can I do for you, gentlemen?' I asked the sullen pair.

'Local staff,' was Bill's guttural reply.

'What about them?'

'We want them,' said Kit, more muted. 'There's very little point in shipping out typists when the locals speak such good English and we're not exactly over-laden with state secrets.'

'They're not sending them out to us anyway, clerical staff,' Bill concurred.

Christopher continued, 'There's even less point in sending us British trade or finance specialists. What we need are people who know conditions here and the local industries.'

Bill handed over a slip of paper. 'We've drawn up our requirements, and costed them. They come cheap.'

I looked at their requisition and smiled. I handed them a piece of paper of my own. It was a memorandum I had drawn up to the Embassy and to the Foreign Office. It was brief:

Re: Local Staff.

It has come to my attention that the Embassy is already employing local staff in the person of Adam Altdoorp. I assume therefore that the objection in principle to the recruitment of local personnel has been withdrawn.

Whilst the streets of Amsterdam are not awash with the heirs to fortunes seeking employment in the British Consular Service, this station and its sub-station in Rotterdam urgently require the service of both local technical and clerical staff, not least those drawn from the business community.

I attach a minute of our requirements. I am beginning the process of recruitment immediately.

Until such time as the attached budget is approved I intend to pay salaries from the Central Contingency Fund.

Both of them laughed out loud. 'This is wonderful,' Bill offered at last.

'Well, gentlemen,' I agreed, 'thank you for drawing up this requisition. It saves me from having to do one. This memorandum will go to the Hague this afternoon. I suggest you start recruiting before they realise what's going on.'

'Do you want to be involved in the hiring process, sir?'

'Good God, no,' I replied, looking over their requirements once more. 'Not at these salary levels. What are you two for?'

As they turned to go I added the one essential proviso: 'Temporary contracts, please, gentlemen. All of them.'

It caused merry hell between London, the Hague and Amsterdam, of course, and it took a fortnight of temper tantrums, threats and bullying before the formal budget was approved, but even that haste was a miracle. I suppose that, without realising it, I had gained respect and clout during my years in London. I had certainly gained seniority, confidence, and that measure of intolerance which is necessary to get your way in large organisations. I also still had my reputation as the steady, dependable man This was the first time I had stood against a ruling, and it was obvious I would not have done so unless there had been good and pressing cause.

Kit and Bill seem to have had most of the local staff they wanted in mind already, for within days the formerly sparsely-populated building was scarcely big enough to contain us all. My assistants worked with irrepressible gaiety during that time; it has become hard with the passing of years to establish if we achieved so very much, but it seemed as though we were doing so, and at the time it was enough.

I suppose that it was during this period that the burden of my misery eased and shifted, sliding from view as new experience grew over it out of the exigencies of our work, the stubborn cruelty of that winter and the destruction around us, and Kit's refusal to be rejected, dissuaded, diminished or defeated. Whenever I looked at him I was reminded of Anthony's youthful motto: We are alive, and everything may be achieved.

That dark November I found myself taking delight in my surroundings and circumstances as I had not done for many months. The tiny cold flat I inhabited became a haven and refuge for me. I took long walks throughout the slumbering penurious city, acquainting myself with her light and ways. Even frost began to charm me, stippling glass and coating the weeds and grass which struggled between the cobblestones of the undressed city, ruined and unattended through years of occupation and war, with blue steel edges. In late November the first snows came, out of a sky which thickened over, swelling the hidden sun, clouds like back-combed hair blowing and tangling and filling with grey, and black, and fatty deposits of white. The roads became almost unwalkable (walkable distances trebled in the duration of their journey). We all went to our beds wondering how anyone could sleep at all in cold like this, and before we knew awoke to even colder, sharper mornings.

The city, my work and my colleagues were restoring me to the world. I was not yet alive, but I began to feel the stout bands of my mummification beginning to tear and strain. Without realising it, like the winter itself I contained for the first time the possibility, the forward memory, of the ice-break: an unforeseen but inevitable spring when the earth itself would be riven open and the long denied greenness of life slice upwards like sabres.

165

The time was not yet come, however, and would not come properly – despite false starts, brief thaws and ice's hesitation – for much time thereafter; but I knew, without admitting it to myself, that although scar-tissue never disappears or changes, the scabs themselves must break and peel and fall. I achieved a kind of steady, uncertain, still restless equanimity during that time. The salt had not regained its savour, but it was no longer gall or wormwood either.

My younger son Alan wrote to me then, to say that he intended to do his military service before going up to Oxford. Even that news, which re-evoked loss and pain and remorse, was not intolerable as it once must have been. The loathing, the guilt, never parted from me, but I was able to present myself to myself – and not merely to the world – as a reasonable, rational man for the first time since Amanda's death. I wrote to him to wish him well.

I wrote again to Anthony also (I had written to him from London months before, giving him my consular address in Amsterdam and asking for his news, but had received no reply) to ask once more for the address of his sister and her family, that I might call on them. (He had referred to them often in his letters, Ruth and Pieter and the children, but I did not even know their surname.) I wanted more than ever to hear from him and to read his mutinous derision of the world and the self-importance of its inhabitants, but, as for many months before, the American mails were empty of him. I was not surprised, for civilian post was no great priority at that time; but in some strange sense I felt he had been for many years one of my few constant points of reference. Excluded by age and rank from the company of my assistants, I found myself simply wanting an old face and friend I could talk to, in whose hearing I might unravel the excitement and adventure of this time and the misery which had preceded it. No answer was allotted to me then, however; and when the answer came, it was as they must always be, a different one from that which I had expected. The gulfs of time and space had brought him into places I had never journeyed in, and when the time came for us to meet again it was hard to know which of us would be filled with stranger travellers' tales.

Winter continued its remorseless way, biting through our shoe-leather and other people's lives. (Cold and damp cracked ordinary shoes open; army boots were one of the most valuable commodities on the Dutch black market that season. People died of cold feet.) With winter came the final accounting of the crimes of our enemies and the inadequate reprisal of judgement at Nuremberg, and a conviction amongst men of good will that an evil had stalked the world, un-equalled in human memory (our memories were brief, and we did not

166

know what evil was, for that is a knowledge which comes with age and the memory of the face seen indistinctly reflected in a pool, or forming in the kitchen fire, or glimpsed when unexpected in a looking-glass). We believed we could extirpate this dream, this nightmare of destruction, but forgot we had been dreamers too.

None of this was conscious in me, however, one winter morning as I stood in the doorway of my office yelling for a file. The frost had completely coated the windows, I remember, except for one low in a corner which had cracked in the extremity of the cold and been filled with putty and brown paper. All my staff were wigwams and igloos of woollens and mittens, their eyes like waterfalls and their fingers frightened Esquimaux. The light caught in the watered windows grew there, refracted, and then glowed into the room.

My call was wheezy with cold. 'Christopher, Bill, where the hell is the Entertainments File?' (We were planning a day-trip to Amsterdam by British businessmen to meet their Dutch opposite numbers, with a reception at the Consulate; that was the occasion on which I was reduced to serving bottled beer; the Dutch were polite about it, though they evidently preferred their own cold frothy lagers.)

Christopher came to the door of his office grinning, and folding the cow-lick out of his eyes. 'It's with your secretary, for indexing.'

'I don't have a secretary.'

'Now you do. Wait here.'

He vanished down the stairs, taking them three at a time. (I always wondered how he did that, without one arm to help him maintain his balance.) Bill remained at his desk, the door open and a frank, indulgent smile on his face. They both seemed pleased with themselves.

'There's no allocation in the budget for personal secretaries,' I began, but stopped as I heard footsteps on the stairs.

She was startlingly pretty, with short dark blonde hair, brown eyes and a slight, boyish figure. She was wearing a tailored tweed suit and a high cotton blouse with a purple stock. She wore woollen knee-socks and stout, efficient, expensive brogues. She handed me the file and disappeared.

I was confused, surprised by features I seemed to recognise as though I had seen and desired them before, and I was troubled by that desire, as though I were being unfaithful to the dead. It had been what seemed like endless time since I had even been troubled by need, and to find that need given a form and face was more than I wanted to be disturbed by. She had been silent and self-assured in ways I was not used to in the young, and her self-possession troubled me, as

167

though she had no right to it. My confusion came out as anger.

'You know we can't afford personal secretaries with all the other staff we've taken on. If you haven't got a proper job she can do, get rid of her.'

Bill joined us on the landing. 'I'm sorry, sir. We meant it as a joke about the secretary. We've hired her to liaise between the industry and finance teams. She's very good at the job. That's why she had the file.'

They mumbled their apologies and I turned scowling back into my room. Something pulled me back, however, some nameless curiosity and longing. I called to them, 'Who is that girl, anyway?'

Kit smiled secretively; I frowned to mask my own uncertainty. He was humble again. 'We thought you wouldn't mind if we took a subtle slap at the Embassy, sir.' I waited, refusing to commit myself, though part of me was already suspended tremulous on the end of want. Kit was almost diffident. 'Her name's Elena, sir. She's David Altdoorp's daughter.'

I know why some men slide into old age preternaturally early. It is out of fear, fear of the knocks and injuries committing yourself to the hurly-burly of the world may bring, a desire for peace, and the assumed tranquillity of abdication. They are all false reasons, for only by acquiring the armour of cynicism can the crab-apple old hope to hold themselves from the windswept tumult of the world. In crucial ways we are all of us always young at heart, our emotions untutored by the strange duplicity of wisdom. It takes an appalling weight of anger and frustration to cancel our contract with the things of earth, except for saints, or madmen, or those few like me who are old in fact, on borrowed time, dragging the sputtering pen of memory across and against the blank sheet of our own impending destruction. Let me tell you now that there is no grace or glory or even peace in this armistice with the world; there is only an almost overwhelming sense of pity and loss, for I have come to realise that, like trees or empires, we die unless we grow.

Nearly forty years ago, however, to find myself being drawn back into the world of company and flesh was an agony to me, heavy with guilt and self-disgust, and it was time before I began to understand that I had allowed grief to corrode me, to become part of my image of myself and my image to the world, a rotting stook against the cornflower sky, a thing of pride, not properly, no longer keenly, felt.

For over a week I avoided that young woman, though her presence in the dusty, institutional building on the Damrak, alive with the clatter of typewriters, the chatter of clerks and the occasional explosions of my assistants, seemed to tag behind me, more often sensed than seen, a shadow of desire. Something inside me moved, disquieted, as though something had arisen from before the years of my contentment to face and accuse me with things unsaid or left undone, or said and done without realising the import of their malice. I felt guilty for something I did not know, as though a grinning figure chased me down the alleys and precincts of my dreams, assuring me in monotone, over and over, that my sins would find me out. Worst of all at the time, though I know now they were the beginning of a restoration of sanity, were my dreams of Amanda. For the first time since her death they reached back beyond the night of fire to times when we were young and happy together. I dreamt of her in a pale blue frock one chill spring morning in Riga, wind pressing the fabric against her, till I was almost crazed, eyes streaming, by cold and wind and desire. I dreamt of her heavily pregnant with Michael (and that itself brought with it no darkness) calling me a silly silly man for wanting to send her back to London, before falling giggling and understanding into my arms. I dreamt of picnics and parties and her calm quizzical smile after love on cool white sheets. I dreamt all these without pity, or rancour, or longing, and the absence of the adder's tooth of grief was itself a cause of guilt. It was as though by dreaming of her alive instead of dying I was persuading myself of that hardest and most callous truth: life does go on, after all, however careless and cruel that may seem. Like children we sometimes cry for our own extinction, not knowing that we do it only out of a sense of the unfitness of the world, not knowing that the world is all we have and that there is only silence and defeat, not mercy, in the grave.

In that time, however, I did not know such things, and did not want to know them. It occurs to me in retrospect that Amanda would not have been so foolish; there is a kind of a sturdy realism in women, which men who expect them only to be soft yielding flowers are appalled by; they bear too much already, in bearing men, to be too much disheartened by the way the world is made, or to move in an individual atmosphere of self-pity. There came a time, though, when I could no longer avoid her. My assistants came to see me. Kit spoke first.

'We need your help, sir.'

'What for?'

'Something a little out of our depth, it seems,' Bill butted in, always incautious and in a hurry.

'Good of you to admit I have my uses. What do you want done?'

'It's Jordaens-Altdoorp, sir,' Bill continued.

'What about them?'

'We haven't been able to get hold of them. As you know, I've been going round all the major Dutch companies, introducing myself, trying to arrange introductions for British businessmen, and trying to establish exactly what help they need now the war's over.'

'I know all that, yes.'

'The fact that I'm liaising with the Americans,' Kit took over, 'has been proving especially useful. I don't think it was meant to happen, but I've more or less become the link with our official commercial people at the Embassy' (I saw Bill grimace; he had a word for his opposite numbers at the Embassy; it began with W) 'and the Marshall Plan group.'

None of this was new to me for, without interfering, I have always believed in keeping a close eye on my staff. In Amsterdam, as elsewhere, I had instituted a post-opening meeting for senior staff which allowed us to discuss work in progress, traffic and new calls each morning. Nonetheless, I let them run on, for they were young and enthusiastic and doing my job.

'We're in close touch,' Kit continued, 'with Royal Dutch Shell, Phillips and the Lever operations. They've all been very helpful and co-operative, especially in providing help and supporting services for smaller companies.'

Bill had grown impatient again. 'But the one major company we haven't managed to see are Jordaens-Altdoorp. Everyone we talk to tells us they've always been a secretive company, particularly since the old man took over ...'

I was curious. 'Took over?'

'Yes sir. Sorry, sir, no reason why you should necessarily know. Until about twenty years ago the famous company was Jordaens N.V. It was bought out by David Altdoorp's firm. It caused quite a stir at the time. Major success for Netherlands' brightest young business-man, that sort of thing.'

'Yes,' said Kit, eager to show teacher he had done his homework, too. 'Since then, apparently, the old man's run the place under a cloak of secrecy. It's still a private company, not listed on the Stock Exchange. Except for a couple of banker friends the board of directors are all his appointees and yes-men.'

'And what am I supposed to do?'

'Well sir,' said Kit, folding back his empty sleeve and patting it, 'the commercial people at the Embassy have been trying as well, without success – but then, they're rather out of it, being at the Hague. They haven't had the gumption to raise it with the Ambassador yet, so we

170

were wondering whether or not a letter from the Consul-General in person requesting a meeting might not smoke the old man out.'

'We've drafted something for you,' Bill interrupted, hawking a leaf from his file and sliding it across my desk. I swear there were times when I thought of them as Tweedledum and Tweedledee. In a better and more fortunate world they would have been promoted together, to become the best commercial team the service ever saw, but we cannot plan for the hour-glass's accidents.

I read through their draft. 'This looks fine to me.' I signed it. The two of them glanced at each other, nervously, I thought.

'There was one other thing, sir.' Kit started hesitantly, coughing against the back of his hand. 'Bill has already mentioned the matter to Adam Altdoorp – you met him, sir, that first night you were here – David's son. He knows him quite well. Adam didn't hold out too much hope. We were wondering if you'd mind doing us a favour? It would come better from you than us, we thought. You are the Consul-General ...'

I smiled. 'Sometimes, gentlemen, I think you forget it.'

They both looked sheepish. Bill put their request: 'Anyway, sir, we were wondering if you'd mind raising the matter yourself, with Elena Altdoorp?'

I did not want to, and yet I wanted to more than anything else which seemed possible that bitter winter season. What I was afraid of, of course, was myself. There was something else as well, which perhaps only the very old can admit to themselves; for even though desire is endless, enduring as long as the mind survives, the ignorance and fear of age of those who have not achieved our extremity exempts us from the hubbub of flirtation. We are no more devoid of longing or the spurs of flesh than are the very young, but those still in their prime like to think we are. Secretly, I suspect, many of them look forward to the day when they can stop trying (Jane Carlyle believed that was one of the secret, unadmitted attractions of marriage; but I am falsifying the record again, for I never thought of her in those northern, unromantic days). They do not realise that trying is the template of our experience. In more ways than one, the end of trying is death.

The day after being importuned by my assistants, I invited her to lunch. Kit had made arrangements with a local restaurateur on Spuistraat behind the Dam which resulted in our being offered something resembling a decent meal, provided we did not ask too much, too often, for provisioning was difficult, and his other customers complained. (To tell the truth, I think Kit had helped to arrange the

171

restaurant in the first place, under the guise of helping local business; we shared an awareness of the importance of the style in which a mission entertains.) It was not the finest restaurant I have ever eaten in, and it was certainly not my finest meal, but it was clean and fresh and we were treated as important personnages: and from the moment Elena had first taken me by the arm, as we approached the door, I felt like one.

I remember all the details of that hour. The restaurant was small, with less than a dozen tables, each dressed in ageing but newly starched white linen. The only other people there were two earnest, silent businessmen and a prosperous-looking family of four. (They would have had to be prosperous to eat out at all, for supplies remained both intermittent and expensive; occasionally, hungry passers-by would look in over the lace curtains, their stomachs rumbling with envy. I had grown inured to that additional guilt.) I think Elena must have been a cinema fan (I should know; I should have known; it is strange how little we learn about the people we believe we care for), for she was wearing one of the broad-shouldered, stiffly-cut black and white check suits I associate with a cinema star of the period (would it be Jane Crawford?) and a loose black blouse and bow. She had a brooch at the heart of the bow, I remember, an oval crossed by a bar of silver, all decked in diamond chips and pearls. She looked what she was, rich. We ate some sort of chicken casserole, which I remember being tolerable. I cannot remember any vegetables at all, so they must have been disgusting. We both drank local beer, all froth. Conversation was desultory at first for she was entirely self-contained and volunteered nothing. I was kept going forward by the remembered pressure of her arm on mine, which held my distaste for myself in check, and fed my hunger. We had spoken of her work at the Consulate, and at last I asked her why she worked at all. Her answer surprised, even shocked, me.

'It's very simple. I think a young woman should go where the power is. Only powerful men are interesting. Before the Allied invasion I worked for a colonel on the German staff, for exactly the same reason.'

'Weren't you afraid of being branded a collaborator?'

'I am too rich to be a collaborator. I am free to do as I choose. Only the rich and powerful have any real freedom; you ought to know that.'

'I am not so rich.'

'Perhaps.' She gulped down a small piece of chicken, without the exaggerated daintiness I hate in most women. 'You are powerful, however, here, now. It is remarkably attractive.'

172

I stirred uneasily. 'But if you're rich, why do you have to work at all?'

'Not having to is an excellent reason, and it would be intolerable to work for any member of my family. When families work together, all but one of them usually end up crippled. Sometimes all of them.'

'What a very shrewd young woman you are.'

'I think so.' She laid down her fork. 'Thank you. That was the nearest thing to an edible meal I have had in Amsterdam for some time. Now, Mr Burnham . . .'

I behaved with what still seems an unforgivable lack of professionalism. 'Call me Jeremy, for now.'

She paused, smiling slightly, her napkin half way to her mouth. She finished wiping the edges of her dark red lips before continuing. 'You will regret that lapse a little later, Jeremy,' (she paused over the name, struggling with the first letter; I found it charming, but I already knew she was right, and wondered what folly had driven me to the suggestion – as though I did not know). 'As I was about to say, why did you invite me here?'

I could not resist the temptation. 'Because it is far too long since I took a beautiful woman to lunch.'

She laughed, and in her laughter my middle-aged bones lost some of their brittle defeatism, and the ligaments of my emotions softened. 'One of the dearest things,' she said, and hope rose, 'about men your age,' and hope died, 'is that they still know how to turn a compliment.' Hope hoped again. 'But you still haven't answered my question. What else is it that you want?'

I was mock-serious. 'I have an important mission, an embassy, a request to you from my two assistants . . .'

'No,' she said firmly, tossing her head, and her cherry lips pursing. 'They are not powerful enough.'

'Nor rich enough?'

'Certainly not rich enough.'

We both laughed, and once the owner had taken our order for sludge (I mean coffee) and the fierce plum brandy which was the only liqueur he carried (Kit did something about that shortly, with the help of his major and the PX Store) I returned to her in earnest. 'It's more embarrassing for them than that, I'm afraid. They've been trying to get to see your father. They've written to his office and had no reply. Now I have written on their behalf. Mr Carstairs has also spoken to your brother Adam, who didn't offer much hope . . .'

She was defiant. 'Adam is a fool and a weakling and unfit to inherit anything; but my father knows that already.'

173

I was faintly disgusted by her honesty, but would not be diverted. 'We are not questioning the terms of your father's will, merely seeking an interview.' (I almost said 'audience'.)

There was strain, and some bitterness, in her reply. 'One day I will be rich and powerful enough in my own right for people to want to know me for myself, and not for my father's sake.'

'I think I do already.'

Her anger abated, and her voice was soft. 'Yes. I think you probably do.' She turned her small oval face away from me and fingered her coffee spoon, toying with it, examining the gleam shifting on its dull criss-crossed surface, almost matt from years of scouring. Her mouth opened a little, and the high gloss of her lipstick frosted in her delicate breath. The pink point of her tongue crept out and licked over her lower lip. 'As it happens,' she said, still not looking at me, 'the matter had occurred to me already.' She turned to face me at last, her dark brown eyes shining. 'I raised the subject with him last weekend.' (She made it sound like a Privy Council meeting.) 'You will be receiving a letter shortly, inviting the three of you to join us over the Christmas holiday. I would cancel any other plans if I were you. My father is not the kind of man it is wise to cross.'

I walked her back to the office, wanting all the while to take her by the arm but not daring to lest we be spotted and gossip begin its maculate journey through what was still a happy and contented office.

I soon discovered she had been speaking the truth, for the following day a letter arrived for me by hand messenger, inviting me and my two assistants to spend the Christmas break at David Altdoorp's house in the country. That created one problem immediately. Kit was in torment.

'I can cancel my leave if you really think I should, sir.'

'When is the baby due, Kit?'

'Late December or early January, sir.'

'Then don't be such a damnable fool. It's your first, isn't it?'

'Yes, sir.'

'Then take your leave, and my blessings with it. Your wife needs you a good deal more than we do. It will give Bill a chance to step into your shoes for a while, anyway.' Bill smiled; Kit looked glum.

'But if you really think I could be of any use . . .'

'No. I most certainly do not. The last thing I want is you mooning about David Altdoorp's house with sympathetic labour pains putting a damper on the festive season. Go home, damn you! and if it's a boy you can call him Jeremy. I want you out of Holland by dawn on the twenty-second, at the very latest.'

174

'Yes, sir.' (He did as he was told. They always did as they were told.)

The matter was settled, and I wrote to the old man (it is strange; only now do I realise that almost everyone knew David Altdoorp as 'the old man', even before they had met him) to accept on behalf of Bill and myself, and to apologise for Christopher, who also wrote to the old man (I have done it again) independently.

During those days, however, I did my best to evade Elena. Something had been engaged inside me, emotions I had thought long quiescent, somnolent, but now like old volcanoes they were rumbling and straining, testing their channels and their lava, and I shrank from the possibility of their eruption. I was unprepared, therefore, for her arrival in my office one afternoon. She seemed prettier than I had ever yet seen her (she was still at an age when it was possible to be pretty, before beauty or handsomeness or the common fading strain of most of us establish their possession; she was only twenty-one, and the difference in our ages terrified me). The intensification of the winter's cold had left her soft cheeks flushed, like rose-water trapped under ice, and her eyes seemed deeper than any I had imagined. She was entirely emotionless when she came in, her step steady, and her not-too-perfectly mannequin features in repose. She sat down without invitation and passed an envelope to me. I did not open it, but sat looking at her, almost frightened to speak.

'What is it?' I asked at last.

'My resignation.'

I was honestly surprised. 'But why? Aren't you . . .'

She was smiling wickedly, knowingly; her eyes were arch with amusement. 'I merely thought,' she said in a low breathy voice, 'that I should no longer be working for you when I invited you to lunch. On Sunday, at noon. The address is on the back of the envelope.'

I tucked her letter into the top drawer of my desk, and smiled back at her with unfelt confidence. 'We can discuss your resignation then.'

I was almost relieved. I am no puritan, but I have always been against affairs between colleagues – not out of any moral disapproval or ethical doubt, still less out of any misguided feminism, but because the colleagues are rarely equals and the affair can never be kept private, and causes tensions and distortions of behaviour so that all respect and discipline in the work-place breaks down.

I was almost relieved. On the Sunday morning, however, bells ringing for services in churches of every denomination, I was foolishly nervous. I left the flat at eleven thinking that would give me time for a gentle stroll to Elena's flat on van Eeghen straat, overlooking the

175

Vondel Park. Once again the map deceived me. Frost and snow slowed me down yet further, and I began to realise that, in such conditions, anywhere beyond the limits of the central canal system might as well be in Kathmandu. I arrived, hot, sweaty and ridiculous and, looking at the building and back at the address, thought at first that I must, even so, have come to the wrong place. I had some notion that Elena was rich, at least in prospects, but I had not expected an apartment building of such obvious luxury.

It was an enormous Jugendstil edifice looking over the Park, one of the few buildings to abut directly on to the Vondel, and even in those days of privation and penury it still had its own uniformed doorman.

He looked me over with evident contempt. I cannot have been a very impressive sight, my clothing tugged awry and my face alive with steam. I explained my business. He raised his eyebrows and made a telephone call. Then I was in a mahogany and mirrored lift-cage, its door-frame in the form of blowing, twining willows, about the size of the average family house. It released me at the tenth and topmost floor. I padded down thick pile carpets. Before I could knock on the door it was opened.

'I'm sorry I'm late . . .' I began lamely, but before I could get any further her hands had rushed up like swallows to her mouth and she began to laugh uproariously. She disappeared, leaving me unattended as I heard her laughter echo off the high walls and ceilings of the flat, passing from room to room, like the evening flight of nesting birds. I followed her in. She was in the drawing-room, her hands still covering her mouth, still whimpering, exhausted with merriment.

'I'm sorry,' she coughed out at last, 'I really am sorry, but you look so silly!' That set her off again, and I did not know if I was more angry, embarrassed or amused myself. She staggered to her feet and took me tenderly by the wrist to lead me to a marble bathroom. She handed me a heavy towelling robe and left me to shower and change.

Twenty minutes later I joined her in the kitchen. There was a half-ham on the table and fresh potato-salad and even a decent claret. I fingered the bottle in wonderment.

'How did you manage all this?'

She put her arms around my neck and pushed herself close to me, rubbing rough towelling against my skin. She was serious beneath her smile.

'I told you. Only the rich and powerful are free.'

We were lovers before any of it was eaten.

*   *   *

176

I remember that for the first time in longer than I could remember I forgot myself. There was an absolute selfishness in her abandon which seemed to release all kinds of responsibility from me in the urgency of her pleasure. I remember the pale clear porcelain of her inner arms and the chalcedony of her skin. I remember the way she threw her head back, mouth open, eyes closed. I remember the way she loomed above me before lowering herself on to me, saying in a low humorous voice, clear with fondness, 'This really has to be my resignation.'

I was late into the office that Monday morning, her unanswerable letter of resignation still in my pocket. I had left her curled up like a child in her bed (one of three; we had padded through the flat that night, bearing candles, examining all the opulent fixtures and fittings of the apartment which had been, she said, the loveliest part of her mother's dowry) and I had left more of myself with and within her than I knew. I did know, however, that I felt lost, as well as found; disquieted, as well as content. I was, I suppose, still romantic enough to have expected that one love would last forever, even against death, and I felt I had betrayed it. Only now, with the singular vision of age, do I realise that I was right about love, and that it does survive, unchanging, whatever may come to cover it, no matter how necessary further, other, loves may prove to be. Then, however, I felt only weary, confused, and more than a little ashamed.

I was certainly in no condition to take in the full import of the three messages which awaited me when I arrived. The first was borne to me by Christopher, who leapt reckless down the stairs as soon as he heard my footfall, his one hand thumping against the stairwell wall with every jump until he caught himself at the final landing, swinging himself over the railing, his face bright with the coming season and his impending journey homeward to his wife and child.

'The Ambassador's already been on the line, sir. They must have been working all weekend to make the connection.' He was almost smirking, but checked himself and became serious. 'He wants to see you at the Hague immediately. He wouldn't say what it was about. He's sending a staff car over to collect you. It should be here by lunchtime.'

I was incurious, and hardly cared. I dragged myself up to my office. I thought of her youth and my middle-age, I thought of Amanda and Michael, I thought of Alan departing on military service without his father to see him off – though part of me knew that is no loss to the young, who do not like to fuss over partings; for, being young, they cannot foresee a time when partings are finite, and every leave-taking

177

may be the last. I thought of her, and Amanda; and, for the first time with fear, of the possibility of loneliness stretching out before me like the Steppes, featureless and unchanging. I wondered what I had become. Now I know that question is never answerable, for by the time we know, we have already changed. When did the Prince of Day tumbling from Heaven's Gate first realise what he had become? When does a dragon, in its own hot breath, first understand what it most truly is? There is no understanding, unless at the end of things.

The other two messages were waiting for me on my desk. The first was Anthony's telegram. I was even too confused to wonder why it had been accepted and how delivered. I suppose I assumed that his arrival two days hence in the week before Christmas had been cleared as critical information.

The third message was a letter from him, post-marked Boston, six weeks before. It was long and witty and informative as usual, full of shrewdness and delight, but I could not take it in except for the warning that he might be visiting Europe shortly. I supposed that it was a reply to my first, from London. The postscript confirmed as much, in answer to my latterly repeated question to him, and brought me back into the daylight world of other people and work. It was brutally brief:

'I'm afraid I cannot give you Ruth and Pieter's address nor that of any of their family. To the best of my knowledge, every one of them is dead.'

TWO

The staff car was an emblem of power, power I was meant to feel, for the driver slammed us down the long flat roads of provincial Holland as though he were still a fighter pilot. We were at the Hague by four, and I was taken directly to the Ambassador's office. I did not even have the opportunity to indulge myself in one of the few real physical pleasures of that worthy, wealthy, soporific town: standing by the great pond before the Binnenhof and allowing the slight invisible spray from its single mighty fountain, too light to soak, strong enough to refresh, to play over me. The Ambassador came straight to his point.

'I understand you know a chap called . . .' (he riffled through his papers; he knew the name perfectly well, but it is a technique we all used to establish the fact that we were too important to remember the names of lesser mortals, and to re-establish the necessary periodic contact with the proper object of our faith – paper) 'Anthony Benjamin Solomon Manet.' He pronounced the surname like that of the painter.

'Manet, sir.'

'Beg pardon?'

'Manet, sir. Short E, sounded T. Not like the painter.'

'I see you do know him.' He pulled off his half-moons and returned them to their case, leaving it unclosed, one arm still standing spikily in the air. He seemed distracted for a while, his head towards the window but his eyes focussed on some invisible object a few inches before his nose. 'I understand he's due in Amsterdam shortly.'

'Yes sir. On Wednesday. I only heard from him this morning.'

'Yes. Wednesday.' He turned back to me, essaying a hesitant smile. I should have wondered what was so important about Anthony Manet's arrival. I should have been more suspicious or surprised, but I had enough confusions of my own to deal with, and my mind and response were bland.

'Is that why you asked me here, sir?'

179

'Yes, really.' He seemed grateful for being reminded of the subject in hand. 'Funny chaps these writers, professors . . .'

'I don't quite follow you, sir.'

'Perpetual students. Never had what you might call a proper job, not even a fellowship somewhere decent. Can usually rely on the fellowship types . . .' I let him meander on, talking to himself. 'Never quite know what notions they might have got into their heads. Bit dubious about having one of them we don't know, straight from America too, stumbling round Amsterdam so soon after the war. Never know what mischief they might get up to. Quite radical, some of them, I understand. Got enough troubles of that kind back home, right now.'

'I don't think Holland is ripe for revolution, if that's what you mean sir, and I'm not at all sure Manet would be the man to start one if it were. Isn't this a matter for the British Council?' I suggested. 'Their people know more about his line of work than anyone in the regular service. If you wanted to keep an eye on him, that is.'

'Oh, quite, quite . . . I agree. Just the chaps to do the job. I only thought, you seem to know him quite well . . .'

'Twenty years or so, on and off.'

'So I was led to believe. Will he be staying with you?'

'I don't really know. He hasn't mentioned it. I know he used to have relatives in Amsterdam, or in Holland anyway,' (I thought of his postscript, but although the words were clear enough, I still wondered what it meant) 'so he may well have made arrangements of his own.'

'Yes, I see. You will be seeing him fairly regularly, however? Being an old friend, all that?'

'I would expect so, yes.'

'Yes, yes of course you would. Not so much social life in Amsterdam yet, eh?' I nodded, with the expected subservient smile. 'We do a little better that way here, of course, being the seat of government. We must have you up for a decent length of time one of these days, instead of all these flying visits. Introduce you to some chaps.' I smiled inanely. 'So you'll keep a weather-eye open for him, will you? Nothing too serious. Proper consular care and attention, that's all. Make sure he keeps out of mischief. Let us know if he looks as though he's up to anything.'

'Sir.'

'Good. Should be quite easy for you, as it happens. Gather your chaps have been doing rather well. Off to stay with David Altdoorp, my commercial people tell me. They seem rather peeved about it.'

'He's invited us to stay over Christmas, yes.'

'Good. Any decent game, that neck of the woods?'

180

'Only some wild-fowling, I gather. We might get a day or two's shooting in.' (I said it only to cause envy.)

'Very good indeed. I almost envy you. Should make things that much simpler, as it happens. This Manet chappy's invited as well.'

I should have wondered how he knew so much, but I was beyond all care. He was avuncular again.

'Some tea?'

'Please.'

He rang for it, and a typist arrived in a blue-green woollen suit, bearing a wooden tray, quite decent bone china, and a silver teapot filled with filth from the stewing urn in the canteen. The Ambassador raised his heavy eyebrows over his steaming cup.

'Make your way back by train all right?'

We were interrupted the following day, as Kit was bemoaning Elena's departure to me ('Very rare to find staff that good. Damn pretty too,' he had said; I let him rattle on, concealing my own vexation of spirit, without comment or interdiction), by the sound of yelling and revelry from lower in the building. I looked at Kit bewildered, but he was already laughing.

'It must be here,' he cried. 'This I have to see' – and led the way hopping, skipping and jumping down the stairs.

Bill Carstairs was in the street, dancing and ululating, hands above his head in a kind of parodic Scottish reel, like an urchin who has stumbled over a sovereign. The object of his ecstasy stood directly in front of the Consulate. It was low, and open, and painted in British racing green. It had wire wheels, two bucket seats, a pull-up roof and a bog-standard Morris engine. It could achieve no very great speed, but as it rattled and careened it felt as though it did. Bill patted its bonnet, his pride and joy.

'Bloody hell!' was all I could say at first. Bill began leaping about again, hugging Kit and almost hugging me, chuckling to himself and rubbing his hands with glee. 'Have you entirely parted company with your senses?' He fell silent, aggrieved and bemused, as I had intended. Then I smiled, and he relaxed. 'What in God's name do you want a racer for? And how did you get it shipped over here?'

'Easy, sir. I said we needed a car, senior consular personnel, for the use of.' He saluted smartly. 'And if they wouldn't let us have a service car they'd better let me ship my own across. Care to take a spin in her, sir?'

'I wouldn't get in that thing if you paid me. Consular car, indeed! More like a spiv's, if you ask my opinion.' He looked hurt. I was merciful. 'Still, all very well for you commercial-type johnnies, I dare say.'

'Yes, sir. Lovely little goer, sir. Smoothest ride of any small sports car on the market. Leaves the Yankee racers standing.'

'I'm sure that will do so much for inter-alliance relations.'

He ignored my sarcasm. 'Not all that thirsty, actually, either, sir. Well within our petrol ration. For the three of us together, that is.'

'I see, Mr Carstairs. I have to give up my petrol ration so that you can swan about Holland looking like a pimp, or the Incredible Mr Toad?' He was crestfallen again. 'Be off with you, Bill. I want that infernal engine on the road every day, one way or another. I'm not giving up my right to commandeer service cars simply because I'm supposed to be able to use this tin can. Keep it away from anywhere I might have to use it, and you're welcome to my ration.' He executed another skip of jollification. 'I reckon that has to be worth a bottle of decent whisky – decent, mind,' and I wagged a minatory finger at him. 'None of your junk from the backwood stills of Friesland.'

He performed a florid, Restoration bow, right there before me on the pavement. Passers-by crossed to the other side of the reassuringly wide street. 'Your servant, sir,' he said as he rose, 'so long as my life shall last.'

I met Anthony the following morning, at the scramble of tarmac and prefabricated huts, brick towers and bomb-sites that was to grow into Schiphol, the only tolerable airport I know. He arrived on the little Dakota forces' postal flight as he had promised, and although I had not seen him for nigh on nine years his appearance came as a shock. He had aged immeasurably. His long hair, still swept back, was almost entirely grey, with only the faintest reminder of its former pitch blackness. He looked tired, his skin coarse and weathered, his eyes stitched into lattices of crows'-feet and satchels. Great lines scooped down from his nose past the edges of his mouth. He looked like a battle-worn cross between an eagle and a lion. With the schadenfreude of middle-age, I was pleased to see he had put on weight; but even so his big brown herring-bone greatcoat swung loose about him, as though his frame had weakened and diminished. His old brown eyes were steady as he embraced me on the tarmac and picked up his single battered leather suitcase, one of the same ones, I guessed, that I had seen him with over twenty years before. He looked fifteen years older than his fifty years of age. I was still glad to see him, the kind clever man who – even at a distance – had been my counsellor, confidant

182

and confessor over the years, back at last in my company, in yet another foreign land.

His voice was so low with fatigue that I could barely hear him. 'Hello, Jeremy. You haven't changed as much as I expected.'

'Nor you.'

'Don't lie. It doesn't become us.'

I had hitched a lift from a friendly American captain (I supplied him with books of chess problems; in my early days in the city I had haunted the chess-cafés, an institution almost lost in Western Europe). We piled in silence into the back of his jeep.

Anthony was exhausted and his eyes closed almost as soon as he sat back, although he did not sleep. On our journey into Amsterdam I screwed up the courage to disturb him and ask what he was doing here. He shifted himself, shaking out the weariness, and drew a hip-flask from his coat. I waved it aside and he took a swallow. Even then he was not ready to answer, and pulled out one of the small cigars I came to realise had replaced the expensive cigarettes of his youth. At last, after several wasted matches, some scowling and a cough, he was ready.

'I have a commission to fulfil.'

'What kind?'

'Official enquiry?' He raised his eyebrows.

I shook my head. 'Just old friends.'

He closed his eyes again. 'I've been invited over by a collector, a man called David Altdoorp. Mean anything to you?'

'A little. He's very rich.'

'He would have to be, given the terms he's offered me.'

'Which are?'

He sat back, warming to his tale, and drew on his cigar, scattering fine ash over us both. 'He says he has a Rubens. A small one – an oil study for a *Deposition from the Cross*. He wants me to authenticate it, or otherwise.'

'And the terms ...?'

'Are extraordinarily generous. Whatever decision I come to, whether it be genuine or not, I receive ten thousand dollars plus all my expenses for as long as it takes. Unheard of terms. They allow me not to have to worry about telling the truth. The fee has been paid already.' He smiled, and for an instant I caught a glimpse of the young man I had formerly known, when God and both of us were boys. 'On top of that, however, should I find the painting genuine, there will be a further authentication fee of twenty thousand dollars.' He was grinning broadly now. 'I have to admit it's the most elegant bribe I've ever been offered.' (You would not recognise it now, after the latest great inflations, but the sums he was speaking of were not inconsiderable fortunes.) I left him in peace until we were within the city.

'Anthony?' His head remained thrown back, in an attitude of rest, but his eyes opened. 'Where are we going?'

'Oudezijds Voorburgwal,' he said, in a voice distant and strained with tears, 'near the Oude Kerk.'

The captain stopped at the corner of the Damstraat bridge. 'Sir?' he asked politely. (Americans, like Etonians, are either very charming or utter pigs.)

'Speak, Lord,' said Anthony, opening his eyes once more, 'for thy servant heareth.'

'I can't take you any further, sir,' the captain explained. 'This road is blocked.'

Anthony shook himself awake and climbed down from the jeep, his suitcase under his arm, and bowed to the young American. 'Thank you, Captain. You have been generous beyond all measure.' It struck me that his years away had changed him hardly at all in some respects.

'Thank you,' I repeated to the puzzled soldier, 'please call by the Consulate next time you're free.' Then I turned, and followed Anthony, as he picked his way over damp cobbles to his sister's house.

He had the keys, but the locks had been changed and planks nailed over the door, and the windows' shutters were locked from within. He turned slightly at the hips, finding his footing; then, swinging his lame leg in a way which echoed in my memory, he kicked the door open. He was silent at first, but I saw him trembling. The house had been partially ransacked. Most of the furniture survived intact, dust-sheets hastily thrown over it, but the dust of years lay heavily everywhere. I wondered how long it had been since the occupants died.

There were bare patches on the walls where pictures had once hung. Every trace of ornament had been stripped. Anthony went from room to room listlessly opening drawers, mentally checking off a list of all the vanished contents. I came across him at last in the big traditional stone-flagged kitchen, even the stock-pot missing from its beam across the inglenook. He was standing with his head pressed against the door-frame of a cupboard or pantry, its door pushed open.

'Even the brooms,' he murmured. 'Where do I buy brooms in this god-forsaken city?'

I had no answer for him. Instead I tried to ask, 'How ...?'

It was a long time before he answered, and when he did it was without malice or bitterness, only pain. 'There was a war,' he said simply.

'Do you want a hand clearing this up?'

He shook his head, biting his upper lip. 'No. Thank you. It will take too long to trouble you, and I know where everything should be.'

'You can't stay here, Anthony, not while it's in this condition. You'll freeze.'

'Why not?' He was quietly defiant. 'All I need to find is a chimney sweep and some wood.'

I saw there was no point in disagreement. 'At least take your meals with me till this is all cleared up.'

He shook his head again, crossing his arms to tighten his greatcoat about him. 'I want to sort it out before Christmas, Hannukah, whatever. It'll keep me busy. It's a quiet time for Jews without a family.'

There was nothing I could do or say to penetrate his gloom. It was as though he were dried up inside, and adding water would only split his fabric. I tried to think forward on his behalf. 'David Altdoorp has arranged for a car from his daughter's flat near the Vondel, at ten in the morning on Christmas Eve, to ferry his guests out to IJsselstein. I'm invited. Will you want a lift?'

'No, thank you. I shall make my own way out, on Christmas Day. I ought to think about how I trace a painting.'

'There'll be no public transport . . .'

He was suddenly vehement, more with weariness than rage, I think. 'Jeremy, if I can get a telegram accepted as urgent diplomatic information, and if I can fake my way on to a military aircraft, I can certainly make my own way twenty lousy miles across the flattest landscape on earth.' He slumped back against the door-post, his loss and frustration expended. 'I'm sorry,' he said, his voice hoarse. 'That was unfair. I'll see you on Christmas Day.'

Kit left for England that Friday, all the staff out on the snowy pavement cheering him off, the local staff waving and making ribald comments in Dutch. Bill planned to drive himself out to IJesselstein in his newly delivered toy. I stayed that weekend with Elena, unfolding in her soft selfish arms.

We agreed on the morning of Christmas Eve that we would hold the car until ten-thirty, lest Anthony should arrive (I was excited at the prospect of their meeting – I wanted to show them off to each other); but he did not do so, and we departed alone along with the chauffeur,

185

warm in sable wraps beneath a sky heavy with snow-clouds like dirty cotton wool.

The house was named after the small town of IJsselstein, a little south-west of Utrecht in some of the best farmlands and timber country in the Netherlands, easily the biggest estate in the area (and not, as I first surmised, after the IJsselmeer, the inland sea contained within the Northern Dyke, along whose banks, in Hoorn, Elena told me her father had been born).

I was glad we were well buttressed against the cold in the old Rolls-Royce (bought, she told me, to take her parents to and from the church on the morning of their wedding); for, as Anthony had said, it is some of the flattest country on earth and the year-end wind sliced over it like an analyst through a balance-sheet. In spring and summer it can be amongst the loveliest country I know, in the brightness of its cultivation; but in winter, the black earth under verglas sullen with waiting and ignorant of any possibility of a future harvest, its bleakness is unparalleled. I have been in wildernesses, yet they are not so oppressive, for their open wastes are proper to themselves, they are the way they were made to be. Here, however, in some of the best farmed land in the world, it is the presence of human habitation which creates the desolation, as though the achievements of man have gone into abeyance for the season, powerless against the time, all human aspiration broken. Black fields, black water, grey sky – all seemed of a piece with the destruction of the age, the proper country in which to celebrate the mutilated hope of Christmas after war.

My spirits did not lift when I saw the house, black and spread out like a gull dead in an oil slick. It was not even a century old but it looked old as the countryside about it, older than the immemorial hills of England, or the endlessly echoing Dutch nightmare of the sea. It had been built in the height of the nineteenth-century craze for medievalism, and was decorated with the curls and fig leaves of Flemish over-adornment. It was heavy, fussy, inelegant and cold.

The old man did not greet us; indeed, I did not meet him until dinner on Christmas Day. Adam arrived later in the afternoon, but that pale, nervous young man kept to himself. Elena and I passed the time twined in each other's company, and she came to me that night from her suite in the family wing.

There were flurries of snow on Christmas Day, and I wondered how Anthony would make his way here. I asked after Elena's mother. Her answer was off-hand.

'She died.'

'I'm sorry.'

'I'm not. Once I understood, I despised her. Except for the very old, people only die when they lose the desire or courage to go on living.'

I turned away from her, disturbed by her coldness and wondering if I would ever understand her. (I do not fully understand her still, although, having achieved great age myself, I suspect she may have been right.)

Anthony arrived that afternoon, on foot, to the horror of the servants. He had travelled to Utrecht by bus the previous afternoon, staying at an inn, and walked the eight kilometres or so from there.

'I'm fine,' he announced, almost cheerfully. 'I needed the clean air.' He went up to his room to change out of hot clothes and wet boots, while I went off in search of the others. I found Bill walking deep in conversation with Adam in the herb garden, and I realised with a shock that they must have kept each other company since Bill's arrival after supper the previous evening. I wondered what two such different young men found to talk about which engrossed them so deeply, but put it out of my mind, thinking I had been even more involved myself, in other ways, elsewhere. I asked them to introduce themselves to Dr Manet in the music room, and went to fetch Elena.

She was stretched out on the satin coverlet of her bed in a dark blue dress with little white flowers scattered over it (there was little gaiety in the house that day; the Dutch exchange presents earlier in December, and only the servants were churchgoers). She tossed her magazine to one side (*Vogue*, I expect), her small face serious, and asked, her dark bruised lips barely moving, 'Has he arrived?'

I bent over to kiss her and smooth her hair away from her high forehead, and nodded.

'That will be nice for you,' she said.

'I hope you'll like him too.'

'And if I don't?'

'You will – but even if you didn't, it wouldn't make any difference.'

'No. It wouldn't.' She was businesslike. She sat up and faced me, with what might have been suspicion in her eyes. 'He will still be your friend, and you will only think the less of me. Men are predictable, that way.'

I leaned my forearms lightly on her shoulders, my hands clasped behind her head, and whispered, 'That's silly. Nothing could make me think the less of you. You are the loveliest Christmas present I have ever had.'

She was cold and cynical and offended in response. She put out her left hand stiffly. 'Very well, then. Take your little wooden doll down to meet your puppet master.'

I could not break through her suspicion and reserve and, looking back, I doubt that anyone could have done. Anthony was at his most charming that afternoon, yet nothing made any difference. She sat like an Egyptian goddess, imperious and unyielding, her hands palm upwards in her lap, saying almost nothing while his gentle mockery unwound the afternoon.

He sat at the grand piano, touching the keys occasionally while pot after pot of coffee (real coffee) was ferried to him, smoking his small cigars and pushing his silver shock of hair away from his face. I listened as avidly as the others but my attention never left her, for throughout those days I carried the smell and feel of her with me wherever I went, melting in her remembered touch. Even in winter, even the freckles on her shoulders smelled of heat.

Adam asked him how he enjoyed teaching in the United States. 'Doesn't it depress you, the lack of interest from the students?'

'Not any more.'

The afternoon darkened, thickened and stroked by his talk. Bill asked him how often he played the piano.

'Not frequently enough, and very badly when I do, but it is the only pursuit I have which prevents my thinking of anything else. I also happen to believe that poor, maligned Pater was right, and that all art aspires towards the condition of music.'

He turned to the keyboard. 'Image of man aspiring, all right?' he grinned, and then began a piece I thought I recognised vaguely, at a furious speed, misfingering again and again, dropping notes or playing false ones by the handful. He stopped in mid-phrase.

'Even so, we say that music is the art in which form and meaning are one, in which the means of expression and that which is expressed are the same. That was the opening of the Beethoven Hammerklavier Sonata taken at the speed marked by the composer in the score. I played it very badly, admittedly, but no one has succeeded in playing it well at that speed. Beethoven was deaf when he wrote the sonata, totally deaf when he composed the sonata, but he wrote well enough for other instruments he had never heard – just like the most recently developed pianofortes – the double bassoon, for instance; so why did he mark this at a speed which everyone agrees is too fast? What is the relationship between art and the physical reality of the craft which expresses it? Why so fast? What did he hear inside his head?' He leant forward, darkness beyond the windows as the servants lit the lamps, and pared his voice to a whisper. 'And does it really matter?'

Elena broke the answering silence, very much the mistress of the house, and Adam seemed to shrink further into the gloom, his paleness the scarcely noticeable gleam of white bed-linen at night.

'Perhaps we should dress for dinner. I will have drinks served in the drawing-room. My father' (I distinctly recall the possessive pronoun) 'will join us for dinner.'

We drank in silence when we rejoined, till Elena led us into the dining-room, taking me by the arm, the others following behind us. The old man was already seated at the head of the long, dully-reflecting table. He did not rise as we entered, and I did not realise why until Elena ushered me forward to introduce me; he was confined to a wheel-chair.

It was a long walk up that room, gloomy with panelling stained black so it killed the candle-light instead of throwing it back to fill and warm the room, uncertain portraits muddy and brown, their varnish soured, on the walls. He sat at the end of the long table, his fine white hair lifted to points of fire by the candle-light; and as I approached a look of what seemed the most absolute lassitude and contempt formed on his proud, autocratic features.

He must have been a handsome man in his youth, and was not so sorely tarnished even now by his afflictions. It was a strong, square head with clear pale skin, a fine reticulation of veins only just beginning to break in his cheeks and across the long straight nose which fined down to an almost exaggerated point. His eyes shone cold and blue, the only conspicuously living thing about him, and even they might have been ice, to match the rest of him and the weather it seemed he had conjured up for our own especial dejection. He sat at the end of the table like an albatross or some such other bird of omen and passage, controlling his surroundings by the fear he engendered in the people about him. It struck me that the whole house seemed to have gone sour, the point of curdling in the creamy comfort of the country; as though here, in this chiaroscuro folly, some cancerous passion had turned in upon itself, feeding on its own entrails in intestine strife. There was power in him, and a kind of beauty. Once, there must also have been grace. All of it was turned at last, preying on itself like some great love without any adequate object. His greetings were cold as the room he sat in, and when they were done Elena and I took our places at his left and right, Bill and Adam beneath us, and Anthony stuck awkwardly almost out of the old man's sight beyond Bill. Below us all the room curved off into darkness unalloyed by the frail light of the candles or the silent issuing inwards of the servants with their trays.

189

I remember nothing of the meal itself, except that the food was fresh and therefore expensive and the old man's cellar obviously excellent. What I remember is his harsh, deep voice rasping into the darkness, filled with delighted malice at others' misfortunes (the cripple's perpetual weakness) and profound, unassailable unconcern for anyone about him. He might have been stone or fire, for all he cared for the world. Conversation, when it came, came between long silences.

'How are you finding our tawdry little capital, Mr Burnham?' he began.

'Cold. Interesting . . .'

'I can understand the cold. I understand you are employing my children.'

'I have resigned, father,' Elena interrupted.

His thin, translucent, hooded eyelids lifted fractionally as he examined his daughter anew, as though she were a hitherto undiscovered species or unreported tribe. 'Have you? Indeed? And Adam?' There was no mistaking the unconcern and disregard in his voice. It was Elena who replied once more.

'Adam doesn't work for the Consulate, father. Apparently he works sometimes for the Embassy at the Hague.'

'Does he now? Well, I suppose even a fool can stumble his way to the centres of power occasionally.' He turned to me. 'I don't know why your people waste their money, Mr Burnham. He worked for me once, but never again. I cannot afford to employ the weak, the woolly-minded, or the incompetent.'

Adam sat through it all with resigned calm, his eyes never lifting from his soup-plate. The old man seemed amused. It occurred to me with a shock how all of us were ageing; I called him old, yet he cannot have been much more than ten years older than Anthony; it was the collapse of his once strong body which gave the impression of someone who had outlived the tumult of centuries. He turned his attention to Bill.

'I understand, Mr Carstairs, that you have been making a nuisance of yourself with my staff. Now you have had your Consul importune me. We do not take kindly to such interference. However, Mr Burnham,' (here he acknowledged me with a wave of his knife; he ate fastidiously, as though everything which passed his lips reeked of corruption, as though nothing would ever give him pleasure again) 'I have already been in touch with your Ambassador. If you would care to send your man to see my people, they will sort something out to our mutual benefit.'

'Bill?' I began, but the old man cut me off.

190

'Not Mr Carstairs. Send Mr Harkworth when he returns from England.'

I bowed my head, not wishing to antagonise so powerful a man – and Elena's father – but angry at being instructed as though I were a child of little understanding. He ignored me, as he ignored the servants who shimmered in to do their duty. He was a man for whom the world consisted of his own attention. For the first time now it extended to include Anthony, and though nothing changed in his manner, demeanour or tone of voice, a darkness seemed to fill the room, behind the darkness of the night, a darkness which might be touched, darkness tangible.

'So you have come back, Dr Manet, to Europe, on my terms. I own I was surprised, that you would risk immersion in the maelstrom where so many of your people died. Are you not afraid you might be playing with fire? There is trouble again in Poland I hear.' (He was right; it has generally been forgotten, in the sentimental wailing for gallant little Poland, that that country has the worst anti-semitic tradition in Europe, was the location of the majority of the death camps and – even after the revelation of the Final Solution, which barely one per cent of Polish Jews survived – of the last great institutionalised anti-Jewish pogrom in Europe, in 1946; besides, I have seen this continent stumble into war over Poland once before, and I would not willingly see it again.) The old man's eyes sparkled, suddenly, like pale blue magnesium flares. 'Aren't you frightened of playing with fire?'

Anthony's voice was gentle, barely audible in the dark. 'We are told that a bush burned with fire, and the bush was not consumed.'

'Fairy stories, Dr Manet!'

'Perhaps, but I believe that some truths may only be available to us as stories. There are fictions more penetrating than any agglomeration of facts.'

'It was too great a fire, Dr Manet. Fire and wind and storm. The bush is damp and black and smoking. It will never bear leaves or fruit again.'

Anthony was unrepentant. There was a kind of nobility in his calm. 'We are also assured that the Lord was not in the wind; and after the wind an earthquake; but the Lord was not in the earthquake; and after the earthquake a fire; but the Lord was not in the fire; and after the fire a still, small voice.'

'Very small, Dr Manet. Very still. Do you still believe in your Lord, after what has been done to your stiff-necked, peculiar people?'

'If I had done so before, which I did not, I could not do so now, for he has exceeded the bounds of all malice.'

'What do you believe in?' The old man was playing with Anthony, toying with him, and I at least was tense with sympathy; but nothing could break my friend's supernatural calm.

'I believe in reason.'

'Really? After all we have learnt about the weakness and wilfulness of mankind, their murderous passions, their desire for absolute certainty, and absolution? You still believe in reason?'

'I still believe in reason. It is one of the very few things we have achieved against the empty, immeasurable spaces between the stars, the certainty of our own extinction and the futility of everything we do, against the time when the earth itself will be cold stone, turning in the pitiless forgetful night. There is a great truth which Pascal knew, but did not articulate: that reason, too, has its passions, which passion recks nothing of.'

It was over twenty years since I had heard him speak of belief with such quiet conviction, but nothing he could say could stay the old man's amusement or blunt the edge of his ridicule.

'How very poetic, Dr Manet. Such a pity that poetry is of so very little use to real men living in the real world.'

I saw Anthony tremble as he lifted his fork. He seemed to shake constantly in those days, as though he were palsied, and I wondered what illness or desolation racked him. Looking at the two men, so similar in the collapse of their figures, they seemed to me absolute and eternal alienated opposites, and I wondered how wealth could have created two such different men; one riddled with hatred, disgust and contempt, with all the thoughtlessness, selfishness and pride of which the rich can be so exceptionally capable; the other learned and gentle, often forgiving, usually amused, and now stretched out – as the other never would, never could be – on the inner and self-afflicted torment of his own intelligence.

Altdoorp seemed to hesitate before his next attack, and as he did so he appeared to sink in his chair, settling like sediment or foundations after long disturbance. 'But what it seems to mean, Dr Manet,' he said, and this time his malice did not dance but lay dully between them, no laughing matter, 'is that you teach people to whore, adulter and disrupt the social order while deriding those of us who do the things which must be done to make the money that pays their whoring. Isn't that true, Dr Manet? Isn't that what you do?'

Anthony hardly moved at all, merely lifting his great grey head to ask his antagonist to specify, to clarify his meaning. 'I do not understand you. I do not think I take your meaning.'

Altdoorp was openly contemptuous, 'Love, Dr Manet, love. So

much your poets, painters, singers seem to make of it, and all it is is theft. It is all stealing other men's wives and daughters, corrupting them, making whores out of the daughters of the city. If you steal a man's wife you steal his honour.'

Anthony looked away as he heard the old man out, and did not turn to him as he replied. 'Sometimes, most times, I think perhaps you are right. Sometimes it is to steal the honour of a man and woman. But there are times, I think, when it is only doing honour to the world and what there is of value in it, while others deride it, destroy it and fill it with disease. It is true that there can be honour among thieves, when honest men are grown corrupt and vicious.'

'Very pretty, Dr Manet, very interesting,' Altdoorp interrupted, plainly bored. 'But do you believe in sexual licence?'

Anthony played the ball expertly. 'I don't really know. I do know that I sometime's think it ought to come with the equivalent of a driver's licence.' Bill almost choked over the food he was swallowing. Anthony continued regardless. 'I'm not sure that what takes place between people and their cars ought to be a matter of public concern, unless they endanger other drivers or pedestrians. And it would never do to frighten the horses.' (Anthony spoke in the days when cars were rare, and rich. I wonder how he would have felt now everyone owns or aspires to one.)

Adam spoke for the first time, shyly, his paleness deepening if anything, until he seemed only like clouded glass. 'But isn't it said that the sins of the fathers will be visited on the children, even unto the seventh generation?'

The old man's response was quiet, but ferocious in its intensity. 'It is also said, correct me if I am mistaken, Dr Manet, that the fathers have eaten sour grapes, and the children's teeth are set on edge.'

There was uncomfortable silence for a while, till the old man scattered it with an irritated shake of his head and right hand. 'It is also said that of making many books there is no end; and much study is a weariness of the flesh. I am tired of scholarship. Come, tell me, Mr Carstairs, I understand you are hunting Nazis.'

I was almost surprised, until I realised that for once the old man's information was inadequate or mistaken. Bill corrected him.

'Not me, not really, sir. We have people at the Embassy who, under inter-allied agreements, are still hunting down war-criminals and collaborators – or at least the important ones.' I shifted uncomfortably in my seat, remembering what Elena had told me about her previous employment. I had never reported it. Bill must have known; he hired her. 'Unlike the Russians, we don't believe you can try everyone, unless you propose to imprison almost all Germany and half the occupied territories.'

There was a kind of bleak, wintry gaiety in the old man's next comment, as though he took pleasure in misery. 'I thought that was precisely what the Russians were doing.'

Bill shrugged his shoulders and continued. 'Some of my people at the Consulate keep an eye on applications for visas and traffic generally, looking out for wanted persons. I liaise with the Embassy on the subject.'

'Is that really all there is to it, Mr Carstairs? It sounds rather lackadaisical to me, even unwilling.'

Bill almost blushed, looking embarrassed, mumbling his reply. 'Some of us aren't altogether happy with it. The official policy is that we can't root out every criminal because almost all of them were administrators of one kind or another, and the countries concerned need them if they're going to recover after the war. It's a trade between justice and expedience that some of us think goes too far in the direction of ...' He paused. 'Realism.'

'I understand your feelings, Mr Carstairs.' The old man's thin lips cracked into a vermiform smile. Adam put down his fork and looked away. 'I also understand the official policy. What would you put in its place? The world must be governed as well as peopled.'

Bill reddened. He was young, after all, and recent revelations had shocked the young most of all (some of us have never doubted the human capacity for wreaking death and torment when opportunities arise); and he did not know how to take the matter lightly, or to deal with the clinical dispassion of this aristocratic old man. 'I think,' and he hesitated, 'I think we should be doing more to hunt down the bigger criminals, especially the ones who weren't so obvious, who weren't in the SS or the army or even members of the party. I think we ought to do something about the people who set up slave labour factories in the east. Do you know there are eighty thousand deported Dutch people still reported missing? I don't suppose more than five thousand will have survived.'

'Yes, Mr Carstairs, I do know,' the old man said quietly. 'I live here.'

Bill seemed to pay him no attention. 'The trouble is that, after the dock strike of '41 protesting the deportations was put down, the repression became total. The people who might have told us what was going on are mostly dead and the records mainly destroyed.'

There was silence again, as the table was cleared and dessert and coffee and port brought in. Altdoorp broke it after he had filled his

194

glass. 'I wish you joy of your endeavours, Mr Carstairs, but I feel I ought to warn you – if Mr Burnham has not done so already – as one who had to deal with the Nazis.' He waved back Bill's expostulation. 'I am an industrialist, and the men and women who work for me have to work to eat. We are only human after all.' (At that moment, in his case, under the flickering candle-light scooping his majestic face into abstract patterns of white and black, I honestly doubted it.) 'I feel I should warn you that the people you are pursuing are dangerous men and women. They have stopped at nothing before. They will not do so now. Be very, very careful. And be discreet.'

Talk almost ceased over fresh and candied fruits, over port and coffee (I cannot tell you the relief the coffee was; it is my one real drug, and I had ached for it; I wondered where he got it from, but pushed aside quibbling questions of legality). The old man talked desultorily with his daughter, of whom he was evidently proud and protective, and I realised whence her coldness came. She was lovely in the candle-light, her long swan's neck and small pale face rising from her low-cut black gown, and I felt again the pang of possession. The old man seemed to lose his way on occasion, and his concentration. I began to realise his secrecy arose from his condition; he endured the strain of ordinary conversation only by an enormous effort of will. I wondered how long he could hold his reason by effort alone; but I had not expected his decline to show itself so suddenly, as he snapped from an instant of confusion with a gibe which shocked us all, still tender from what armistice had revealed.

'You there,' he called, waving at Anthony, 'Rosenbaum, Hymie, whatever your name is, what are you doing here?'

Anthony contained himself with an effort of will almost as great as Altdoorp's must have been all evening. He set down his glass and napkin and rose slowly to his feet, his chair sliding out behind him, grating on the polished floor, and said in a small clear voice, 'I thought I was here to look at what might be a Rubens.'

The old man remembered himself with a start, but did not apologise. He was not the sort of man who would ever apologise or explain. He was born for success. 'Of course you are.' He clapped his hands and the servants broke back into the room, one of them standing attention at his wheelchair.

He led us into the library, Anthony limping at his side, a high-walled room haunted by dust, leather and the smell of ageing paper. He led us directly over to a small painting hung low in one corner above an escritoire. Anthony paid it no attention, however, his anger dissipated. He was staring at the painting over the fireplace, a life-size female nude. Even I, who have never cared for Rubens' pink, heavy fleshiness and opulence, knew at once it was beautiful and rare.

'Dear God,' he said, awe-struck. 'Bathsheba. I thought she was still in the Belgian Royal Collection.'

Altdoorp smirked. 'I bought it fifteen years ago. The sale was never made public.'

'She's lovely. The lithotypes do her no justice.'

'Hadn't you better come look at this?'

Anthony dragged himself back to the corner and bent over the smaller painting. He almost closed his eyes, peering through his long eyelashes (he had told me years before that it was a standard technique for filtering out the subject or meaning of a painting, to concentrate on its surface and workmanship). Then he pulled out a pair of spectacles I had never seen him wear before and examined the painting again. At last he straightened out, his right hand in the small of his back, stretching. He noticed us all looking at him expectantly and smiled.

'Well, don't expect an immediate answer. It is likely to take some time.' We were disappointed. I would have been defensive in his place, but he had no such qualms. 'At this stage I can only tell you the most obvious things about it. It's very good, it's a *Deposition*, and it's after Caravaggio. They're always after Caravaggio. And I wouldn't mind wagering it's from the studio at least.' He turned to Altdoorp, polishing his spectacles with his handkerchief. 'I shall need the purchase documents,' (the old man nodded) 'I shall need some time with the painting, and I shall need some time to myself.'

A look of self-satisfied cunning crossed Altdoorp's face. 'As you can see, Dr Manet, I have no need for another, smaller, inferior Rubens of dubious authenticity.' He licked his thin lips. 'If you should find it genuine I would be happy to consider selling it for, shall we say, a thousand dollars?'

Anthony stood silent, his arms crossed, considering the extra-ordinary offer of a bargain-basement Rubens before replying with a smile. 'Seeing the root of the matter is in me,' he said, 'let me tell you now the answer is no.' Then he was brusque again. He bowed to the old man, with a single 'Goodnight' for us all, wheeled, and was gone.

We all took our leave of the old man in turn, Elena last and longest of all, stooping to kiss his broken-veined cheek, and left him considering his paintings in the high library where the fire had long since faded, leaving it chillier than the chilliest heart of hell.

Afterwards, in Elena's bed, exhausted and content, I asked her the question which had troubled me all the day.

'You didn't like him, did you?'

There was a long silence before she answered. 'It isn't . . . It doesn't matter'; and then she turned away from me.

I rose early next morning to return to my room, for the old man had arranged a Boxing Day shoot for his English guests, which would mean an early start. Outside, it was the deep darkness of the hours before dawn. I scratched the sleep out of my eyes and lit a candle (it was a long time, I gather, before the generators had enough fuel to service the whole house). I ran a hand through my hair and, new to the room, asked Elena where her looking-glass was. She stirred in her sleep, stretching her long legs and rubbing her tiny, childish hands in her eyes. She was frighteningly young.

'There isn't one,' she said at last. 'There aren't any in the family wing. My father can't abide mirrors.'

It was a cold, wet, miserable day for the shoot. I had been right in guessing this was wild-fowling country; wood-pigeon mainly, with some duck. I was nonetheless marginally surprised that a man as rich as Altdoorp had not taken up breeding birds for the gun, for he owned woods which would have made more than adequate pheasant country; as it was, we saw few of them that day. It was, I think, the worst, most careless, most ill-organised shoot I ever did take part in. It was neither wild-fowling nor a proper shoot. To one brought up to the sport in England it seemed arbitrary, ill-advised; walks through rough country were interrupted by formal stands, chosen without any apparent logic or reason and with virtually no liaison between the guns and beaters, the gamekeeper standing idly and frustratingly by. At various stages during the day I had to calm the extremity of Bill's outrage, for – as he pointed out – if Altdoorp had wanted to dismiss, offend and generally show his contempt for his guests, he could not have done better than to lay on such an unnecessary and dangerous shambles.

At first, the guns were set to move in a diagonal line up the longest edge of IJsselstein wood. Beaters moved through the wood itself, led by the gamekeeper and Adam. ('The boy dislikes the sound of guns,' his father informed us with sour pleasure, his eyes invisible behind the dark glasses he wore against the wintry light. 'And besides, he is so fragile the recoil might break his shoulder.' I could believe it.) Altdoorp was wheeled up the innermost edge of the line, closest to the wood, from which position he would occasionally instruct us to make a stand, if the beaters started a flurry of birds. Anthony was placed next, then me, then Bill, and beyond him four of Altdoorp's richer tenants to make up the line. They greeted us suspiciously at the beginning of the day, like dolphins lifting their noses above water to the wind, or dogs sniffing each others' hindquarters. It was almost like being at a new shoot in England.

The day began with vacuum flasks of coffee and the exchange of hip-flasks of whisky, plum brandy and the oily, sweet Dutch genever gin, too aromatic for me. Most of the morning was a bore, the old man and Anthony monopolising most of the birds that were started, many of them right under their feet. I was slightly surprised by how good a shot Anthony was, the two lame men doing much slaughter. (He explained to me in one of the many breaks in the clattering of the beaters' sticks as the gamekeeper bounded out of the bracken for further instructions, that he had learnt when he was a boy on his family's estates in Pomerania.) We shared a single retriever, a good-tempered black Labrador bitch, though she did little work for me. There was little to interrupt the tedium, except for the sound I have always found enchanting, of shot rattling and raining back to earth, cracking like thousands of knuckles on leaves and heavy wet grass.

I was relieved when we broke for lunch, and spent some time helping to look for runners and other wounded birds (the few pheasant that morning had been low and fast, only winged by shot, tumbling to earth and running with a speed which astonishes the unwary), killing the injured by pressing in their skulls or slapping the back of the head with a walking-stick, the birds still heavy in the hands, still warm and their eyes and feathers bright, still flesh not meat, the big glottis sliding in the throat to cry or call no more.

When I rejoined the guns most of the game-pie and sandwiches had disappeared inside the Dutchmen, who were snuffling and snorting to each other – talking about sex, I imagine, as men all too frequently do when the spill of blood makes them feel masculine, speaking of conquests which, to look at their mountainous frames, they would not have enjoyed since youth, or which were entirely imaginary.

Bill was dissatisfied with his sport with even more cause than I, for at least I had had the chance of shots at the few birds Alt-doorp and Manet let past; but none except a few wounded had got past me.

'Do you think he's going to switch the line over this afternoon? Seems a bloody waste handing out Purdeys, then keeping all the birds to yourself.' (He was right; they were beautiful guns, the best of English workmanship; the guests' guns alone would have bought and paid for every shop in a village high street.)

Altdoorp had himself carried over, and answered the question. 'We won't have much light this afternoon, so I propose to make two stands, instead of passes: the first in the western spinney, the last at the apex of the wood. We shall switch the line round, excepting the tenants, who are here out of charity, to give you a chance. Dr Manet and I have not been very generous this morning.'

Bill brightened visibly and passed me his flask, its contents the only thing which could keep out the bitter wind across the flatlands, picking up moisture where the ground had turned back to bog or fen for the winter. Anthony rejoined us from his examination of the morning's bag. He shielded his eyes as the sun pulled free from cloud for the first time that day, glaring across without warning and dazzling.

'Two dozen brace of pigeons, three brace of woodcock, two geese and a pheasant.' Bill grinned. Anthony guessed why. 'But no partridge and certainly no pear-tree.' The two of us broke off alone together across the dark wood, following the keeper out to the western copse.

The wood was damp, the feet of most of the trees scarred by fungus, exposed roots rotting, leaf-mulch springy and slippery underfoot. Occasionally shafts of light tried to cut through but were trapped by humidity and broken by leaves, hanging suspended in the air, leaving the lower reaches murky. He seemed occupied as we walked. I tried to make conversation.

'You're shooting well today.'

'Thank you.'

'I must have a word with Amanda's father; have you to stay in Norfolk.'

'I should like that. How is Alan?'

'Gone for a soldier.'

'And you?'

'Better, much better. Sometimes I even feel alive.'

'Tell me if it's none of my business . . .'

I had expected him to guess all the time. 'It's none of your business.'

He smiled inwardly, and leaned against a tree trunk to light a small cigar. He had trouble with the match in all that dampness. 'Do you love her?' he asked once he had drawn.

'Am I so transparent?'

He did not answer.

I hesitated. 'I don't know any more, Anthony. I'm beginning to feel my years, but she's the first woman I've met since . . .' He patted me consolingly on the shoulder. 'She's the first woman I've met who I'm glad is who she is, instead of wanting her to be Amanda. I didn't put that very well.'

'You were fine. We'll teach you to write before we're finished.' (I am beginning to wish he had never said it.)

'I don't really know if I love her, not all the time, is the answer to your question. I think I may.'

'She is in love with you, I think.'

'I find that difficult to believe.'

'So do I.'

We both laughed, and broke into the clearing where the penultimate stand had been organised.

It was an unmitigated disaster. We could not see each other, any birds or the beaters, though we heard much, sound coming at us from all directions, bouncing off trees and the canopy of the wood without any sense of distance. Occasionally there was the hopeful cough of a gun, but no one added anything to the bag.

It was a disgruntled party that came out to cross to the apex of the wood, none more so than Bill, who was swearing steadily under his breath. Anthony and I ignored him, dazzled by the sight which met us at the edge of IJsselstein wood. The sun was low on the horizon, clear of cloud and burning with a pale, wintry fury, casting long shadows of trees and dogs and men; but before us the grass had bent over under its own weight of growth and dew, and the sun caught it at the brow of its curve and caught the water too so that the whole field looked alive with innumerable greens (quite literally so; try counting all the greens you can see on a summer's day) and sparkled, sparkled with thousands of brilliants or diamonds as though it were cloth with sequins scattered on it. I am not a poet, I am an ordinary, conventional man, and I can do the scene no justice. I knew from his stillness that Anthony was as moved as I, but when he made a comment it was matter-of-fact.

'Lovely, but if he keeps the line as it is the sun will be a problem.'

He kept the line as it was: Bill, myself, Anthony, himself, and his tenants. The sun was a problem. We stood at the apex of IJsselstein wood, in a diagonal line; the sun almost directly in our eyes. It irritated the dogs; Anthony called ours back, talking to her softly. The old man had his own, held on to by a loader. We waited, nine men drawn up against the coming dusk, listening to the calls and chanting of the beaters, the rattle of their sticks and the finally released barking of their dogs. There was nothing else at first, just pastoral sounds in the silence, like waiting for an eighteenth-century battle to begin. Then came the first excited clattering in the undergrowth, the first start, the first whirr of wings. The first pigeon flew dazzled out of the wood.

'Mine,' called Bill, and fired. It tumbled out of the air. Then it began.

They came like a storm-tossed fog, all ways at once. Everything was noise, and heating barrels, and the smell of cordite, and dying, falling, bouncing, or wounded birds, dogs running back and forth, small corpses speckling the ground. Then, with a silence as sudden as thunder, it was over. Anthony stood patting the flanks of the Labrador bitch, repeating 'Good dog, good dog', with the emphasis on the good.

We waited for the beaters to break out of the wood, waited for any last, as yet unstarted birds. We waited for what seemed minutes, but nothing came. I walked over to Anthony; he remained stooped over the retriever, patting it, smiling.

Then something came out the wood, low and fast. Bill released one barrel, then another. It flew on, too fast for us to do anything, out to Altdoorp's stand. Then it was rising, up into the sun. He tracked it and fired. It dived, stooping low, back for the wood. Altdoorp tracked it, shouting 'Mine', but it was flying wide, too low, too fast. For an instant we were looking down both his barrels, black holes as black as his spectacles. I went down. I heard Anthony falling behind me, and the report, all wrapped up together. When I turned over there was blood all over his face. He was laughing. I thought it was shock then, but now I think he knew exactly what had happened.

It looked worse than it was. Altdoorp had continued to track, and the murderous central funnel of shot had gone wide; only random pellets from the peripheral cone had fractured Anthony's face, punching blood to the surface. He stopped laughing as abruptly as he had begun and rolled over on to all fours, his long grey hair flapping forward, like Nebuchadnezzar eating grass, or Blake's Jehovah. He put one hand up gingerly to his left eye.

'It's all right, I think. Some pellets in the face still. I want to stop them working towards the eye. You'll have to give me a hand, Jeremy. I can't look up to see where I'm going.'

I helped him to his feet. He was trembling still, but it was hard to tell if that was fear or shock or the palsy which seemed continually to afflict him then. Certainly he was almost unnaturally calm. He waved back the other guns as they ran forward (I did not hear their cries or approach; after the vision of David Altdoorp's barrels, my attention and my world had fined down to a narrow patch of grass and air), annoyed by the fuss and alarm.

'How is the dog? Come here, girl, here.' He pushed one hand out gently, rubbing the thumb across the finger-pads, coaxing. I noticed her for the first time since it had happened. She had dragged herself away, bloody gashes and bruises in her flank, and lay stretched a few yards from us whimpering. I went over to her and, as I moved, little black pellets worked their way out of lodging-holes burrowed into my heavy tweeds, popping out of cloth and over grass.

'She's all right,' I said. 'She'll be all right. More frightened than hurt.' I rubbed her muzzle, trying to soothe her, but the keeper had arrived and with an air of sturdy efficiency he scooped her up in his arms to carry her home, nodding once in Anthony's direction, inquisitive. I nodded reassuringly and he set off without a word. Anthony was standing now, bent over, one arm outstretched, and Bill and I helped him limping back on the long walk to the house. As we went, he cradling his left eye with his hand, holding it open, keeping the peppered and perforated skin away, he said only one thing, and repeated it.

'Whatever David Altdoorp may say,' he grunted, 'keep his alienists and witch-doctors away from me. I want a proper doctor with a proper certificate on his wall from a proper college or hospital. No bloody voodoo.'

I did not know what he meant.

I discovered that evening. Adam Altdoorp had gone straight from IJsselstein wood to fetch the local physician, to the old man's evident distaste. The doctor spent a fair half of the evening pulling sphericles of lead from Anthony's injured face, swabbing the wounds, adding some stitches and doing his best to patch the whole mess up. At the end of it all the left side of his face was one continuous bruise, already purple and swollen. Anthony immediately commandeered an invalid's privileges (he was nobody's fool) and insisted on having his supper served to him on a tray, alone, in the library. The rest of us gathered in the gloomy dining-hall for cold cuts, soup and salad. What strikes me most in retrospect is that none of us did anything to upbraid the old man with his near-fatal negligence. Our silence was, I suppose, a homage paid to power, a desire to forget the entire occasion, and ignorance as to how to deal with his careless, insouciant manner. He reminded me of Procrustes making up a guest-bed for the night.

One small thing remained, however, to fuel my anger (I knew my job, and kept it concealed, despite the fact that an instant earlier on the trigger and it might have been I who lay extended in the library, picking at a cold platter and trying to read; it was almost an attractive thought). I noticed again, as I had noticed the previous night, and even at luncheon in the field, another example of Altdoorp's fastidious distaste for all the world outside himself and, perhaps, his daughter. Every morsel or mouthful served to him was served on his own special crockery, in his personal glassware, with his own individual cutlery, all brought to him by one appointed servant, never coming into contact with any dishes which might be used by other unsavoury mortals. There was something narcissistic in his desire to hold aloof from the world, as though he stood in fear of its infection and sought inoculation against time and the planet's inevitable corruption. It angered me; that this man, who in his disregard for anything outside himself had come close to killing me and had injured my friend, should parade his contempt for ordinary mortality seemed an affront to our common being (if not dignity) as men.

I held back my feelings, however, and chewed at my meal in glum silence. It was Altdoorp himself who broke it, sounding almost cheery as though the day had salved his temper and left him amused at the ironic foolishness of the world.

'I don't understand Dr Manet, I must say,' he mused with a vulpine smile. 'I obviously took him to be more intelligent than he is, and it is rare for me to over-estimate anyone.' None of us asked him what the devil he meant. 'He puts such touching faith in doctors of medicine, when it is palpably obvious that all doctors are frauds, knaves or fools. When did they ever cure anything except by accident or misadventure? And as for their precious, antiseptic hospitals, they might as well set up as undertakers and fit the patients for coffins as they arrive. I offered him the services of my own physician from Utrecht, but he would not hear of it.'

Bill asked the obvious question. 'What is so different about your physician?'

'Ah, there you have it,' the old man responded cheerfully. 'Most doctors address the failings of the body and material injuries, but true illness and damage reside in the mind. The patient has to want to be well. My physician employs the mind itself, by means of hypnotism, to line it up with the great forces of the world, the solar and lunar powers, the oceanic tides, to cure the ills of the flesh.'

He seemed to be perfectly serious. I understood what Anthony had meant. Bill showed his youth and inexperience in the service (though for once I was almost glad). 'I don't see,' he said, 'what the forces of the earth can do about a dozen shot-pellets in the face, unless he's carrying some powerful kind of magnet.'

Altdoorp was almost pitying. 'That is because you lack the requisite faith. I am not talking about folk medicine or faith healing. This is scientific, proven. Health requires an act of will, and with sufficient will there is no reason why any of us should not live forever. I, for one, intend to try.'

I wondered what sort of life he could hope for, tied eternally to his wheelchair, protected by servants and his wealth from the world's contamination, able, it seemed, to enjoy only the suffering of others. It was his hobby-horse, however, and he was unstoppable.

'Of course, it did not help that my son went running for the local fakir the moment it happened.' (I remember that exactly; just 'it'; he did not even have the grace to acknowledge it as an accident.) 'But then he is foolish in that way. He sends for the conventional hide-bound quacks the moment he takes a chill. I keep telling him he must exert his will. He has only to want to be well. What do doctors know? All they ever do is invent new imaginary illnesses for us to be frightened of. Dangerous to work down mines they say. Nonsense I say. I employ six hundred men who do just that every day of their lives, and who are none the worse for any of it. They want welders to wear smoked glass spectacles and they say that polio is incurable.' (I wondered if that was what had confined him to his wheelchair, but knew better than to ask.) 'What good are doctors, when they cannot even cure bad backs?'

His little outburst seemed to have amused but exhausted him. He lapsed back into a querulous, unfocussed silence, leaving us to eat and drink in peace. I noticed that Elena's eyes never left him, attentive to his wandering mind and whims, and wondered what immense force of personality there must still be in him to tie her so closely. His will was written in every stone of the house and the estate and their minute-by-minute running, and even, I guessed, in his firm; all bent to his desire and his opinion. The only power he had not subdued beneath his tyranny was the power of time itself, and that remained unacknowledged – although his body was no longer his to call his own – by the arrogance and ambition of his ageing mind. I noticed Adam, also, maligned and traduced, keeping silent watch on his father; but I could riddle or rune no expression in his features.

At last the old man recalled himself and decided it was time for us to join Anthony in the library, where coffee would be served. (At the thought of coffee my temper ebbed a little.) As we entered the cold, high room, a fire flickering fitfully in the grate and the lamps dimmed, he must have heard us where he sat at the escritoire before the little Rubens, staring at it, a book casually open in his left hand, for without turning to face us he spoke.

'It's very strange. Even with one eye useless and no stereoscopic vision to speak of, I can still see depth of field and perspective in this painting. Why is that, do you think? It must be a purely mental event, the mind reconstructing a learned format in a two-dimensional field, even when the eye can find no depth in the real world. How?'

Altdoorp ignored him. His mind still rode his hatred of doctors. 'I was just saying, Dr Manet, that I did not understand why you refused to see my physician.'

'Your galenist, you mean.' He turned to face us, disfigured and already yellowing. 'No, of course you do not. I know the paintings are the most valuable things in this house, but you would understand me better if you had ever opened the most useful. These bookshelves haven't been dusted in over a decade.'

Altdoorp rolled forward, ignoring his servant. 'Idle toys, Dr Manet, for the poor, the frustrated, the sick and the foolish. I have a real world left to inhabit. I have no need of idle dreams.'

'Then what are the paintings?'

It occurred to me with a shock that they were both prepared for this meeting, they had both been planning it. We were witnessing a squally, inconclusive chess match, debate, duet, between two grand masters who had longed for this bitter occasion. I wondered if difference and hate had first made them conscious of each other, till they were defined by their human opposite. I wondered what drove them together, their minds locked elsewhere in a sphere inconceivable to the rest of us who saw only turned pieces moved clattering across the chequerboard of the evening.

'They are my possessions,' the old man replied. 'They are the originals. You are here to prove they are, my hired servant.'

'Is your servant a dog that he should do this great thing?'

'Another book, Dr Manet? Books have no original worth speaking of. They are printed a thousand times over. All we have are copies. They do not interest me, Dr Manet. I am only interested in the things I possess so that no one else can possess them. I am not interested in what I cannot own.'

'Then you never will understand your servant.'

'I understand you perfectly well. You are all the same. Look at the picture behind you. A man who allowed himself to be tied to a wooden cross and have nails driven through his hands and feet and a spear thrust through his side, in the laughable belief that by doing so he would mysteriously save the world. Only a Jew would do anything so stupid.'

'Only a Christian would believe him.'

'I only believe in my own will.'

'And paintings. Only a fool would pay so much for pigment daubed on canvas.'

'I only paid paper for them.'

'Then you understand the value of printed words.'

'Books are not a fiduciary issue.'

'They are the only issue left between us.'

'Not books, only paper.'

I was lost. I think we all were. They had taken their gambits into realms of play where we could not pursue them. I piped up on behalf of normal conversation: 'Actually, Anthony, why didn't you see Mr Altdoorp's doctor? It might have been quite amusing.' The old man scowled. So, to my regret, did Elena.

Anthony was himself again, and lay aside his book, smiling crookedly, with a wince at the ache of his injuries. He was ironically formal. 'Mijnheer Altdoorp knows that I try to keep an open mind on most subjects. He also knows that I believe in testing ideas against experience ...'

'To hell with ideas.' The old man was vehement, gripping the arms of his chair till his hands were as white as his hair. Looking at his fiery whiteness, I could see whence Adam's unnatural pallor came. Anthony continued as if there had been no interruption.

'... again and again. He also knows I hate the habit of calling scientific those things which do not or cannot employ the scientific method. It is because of what I believe that I still use my grandmother's age-old prophylactic recipe against a chill, and was even able to tolerate Freud's charming poetic fantasies as the necessary fables of a working doctor ...'

Altdoorp interrupted once more. 'I thought you liked the man.'

Anthony turned to his opponent, with disdain. 'As a man, I loved him. As a troubled, harried, over-worked doctor I revered him. I hold no brief for him, however, as mythologist or theologian. It is the man I remember, who – like many I have cared for – was driven into exile or an early grave.'

Altdoorp finally lost his temper. Elena tried to restrain him but there was fire in his eyes, in his belly, in his nostrils. Little pearls of spittle spattered before him as he spoke. 'Weakness, Doctor, all weakness. It is the same with all of you who have no will. Strength, skill and swiftness are the masters of the world, and the devil take those who fall behind.'

There was something heartless in his catechism and his burning belief in his creed, but Anthony only smiled. 'The race, mijnheer, is not necessarily to the swift, nor the battle always to the strong.'

206

'Always, Doctor, always! You should need no reminding if you looked at the world instead of forever citing me scripture.'

Suddenly Anthony collapsed, like a sail when the wind turns, all spirit gone from him. He fiddled with the cord of his dressing-gown. Then he spoke, quietly and lost. 'Yes, always. I had almost forgotten. Yours is the world, mijnheer, and all that is in it, but I will quote you one last piece of scripture before the end of all between us. I will quote you this.' He paused looking over to the old man, who had recovered his composure and an air of triumph. It was a weary voice he spoke in, but a voice which echoed with a distant smile. 'And a certain man drew a bow at a venture; and smote the king of Israel between the joints of his harness.'

The accusation lay between them, a guilty barrier, like a dog turd on a drawing-room carpet. The old man heaved, and his servant rolled him away.

We were to receive no explanation. Anthony took up his book again. There was nothing for us to do but leave him, as the old man had, leave him consoling himself as he considered the strange combat we had witnessed uncomprehending. I do not believe he found himself entirely defeated. It may only be the random and untrustworthy eye of memory, but I seem to see him still, as we departed, looking up from his book to the painting over the dying fire with a look something like gratitude, as though it had reminded him of something he had been in danger of forgetting.

In the long reflecting telescope of memory there is something faintly ridiculous about the strange gavotte those two men conducted, something altogether different from the irritation I experienced at the time at what seemed bad manners and self-indulgence, both of them driving a partisan wedge of silence between Elena and myself. It is strange how time itself conspires to diminish them, for we were to discover in time that there was good cause behind their mutual dislike. We did not know that, however, during that damp depressive Christmas season, and I falsify to mention it. Our dislike and ridicule then arose because we did not know; now it grows because we are trying to forget. I am trying to set aside the knowledge of another place and season. I am trying to remain scrupulously exact.

I wanted to get out of the house. Bill, in his friendly, misguided way, suggested that I might stay on a few days, trying to ingratiate myself with David Altdoorp and keeping an eye on the recovery of my old friend, Manet. I could not bring myself to do so. I was still disturbed, I suppose, by the Ambassador's request that I keep an eye on Anthony, and I remember thinking that if I knew he were laid up and working at IJsselstein I would not have to spy on him, yet would still be fulfilling my commission by knowing where he was and what he did. There was more than that, however. The house itself disturbed me, and its owner's brooding, cynical presence. Part of me said, with the dispassionate analysis of a lifetime in the service, that David Altdoorp was old, ill, his mind and self-control wandering; it said that his company must effectively be under the control of others and that I had done enough by introducing myself to its nominal master. Another, less reasonable, part of me, however, replied that the house itself and everyone in it, in their steady celestial revolution round his will, were evidence of power, power absolute and probably malevolent. Most disturbing of all was the sway I knew he held over both his children. If I am entirely honest it was Elena's submission to his will that disturbed me, for like almost everyone else I took young Adam at his father's estimation, and ignored him as a pale, big-jointed, hypothalamic fool or weakling. I understood some of the rage the old man must have felt at finding himself with such a shadowy, insubstantial successor. Perhaps it was no wonder he turned the little delight and affection he was still (or ever) capable of on his daughter, who was at least lovely, straight and clean. She diminished beside him, however. She abandoned herself before him, abdicating her personality, all her emollient daylight hidden by his dark, eclipsing moon. I felt myself grown old in the old man's presence, as though I, as well as Anthony, were part of some plot on his behalf against a young world which even in the stricken silence after war had rediscovered my capacity for enchantment.

I could not burden myself with Bill's suggestion, and decided to leave the following day. I hoped, I suppose, fondly, that Elena would choose to disengage, detach, herself from her father, and follow me to Amsterdam. I realise now that my failure came from thinking of her – and all other women – as merely parasites, needing a man from whom to suck their being and necessity. I should have known better, but I could not see her for herself, moving with her own demands, desires and affections through fortune's shark-infested sea. I deluded myself, however, if I thought that anyone, even on short acquaintance, much less her mandatory sentence of propinquity and respect, could escape the old man's restless domination so easily.

On the morning of my departure he sent for me. I was in my room, packing, when the door slammed open, two servants beyond it in heavy black cutaways. I stopped my packing.

'Yes?'

They remained silent. Then one of them spoke wearily, with a contempt I realised was aped from the affectation of his master.

'You are required.'

I was frankly bemused by this operatic summons and slipped on a jacket. They parted to allow me into the corridor, then closed ranks behind me, like guards. Their presence behind me, just too close, propelled me forward. I did not know where we were going, but they pressed me on like drovers with cattle until I found myself in the long dining-room once more. It was a covered but bright, cold day outside; but the curtains had been drawn here and only stray fringes of light filtered in, disturbing the darkness and dusty air. He sat as I had first seen him, far away at the other end of the room, in his wheelchair. The servants did not follow me in, but slammed the doors behind me, the sudden thump startling the room, then vanishing without echo. I did not approach him, waiting for him to speak; but he sat in silence, too far away for me to see his eyes or to establish if he had noticed my presence. I began the long walk up the room, the padded click of my footsteps beating out the time on the polished floor like a dead march. Everything seemed to stand in darkness except the opalescence of his hair. His eyes were closed as I came near, and his head bowed. They both rose expressionless when I stood before him. He did not invite me to sit down.

'My daughter informs me you are leaving us.'

'Yes.'

'You will send Harkworth to see my people?'

'Yes.'

He nodded, distant, elsewhere. 'We will attempt to accommodate you. Is Carstairs leaving with you?'

'Yes.'

'Will you need a lift?'

'He has a car.'

The old man's thin lips curled up in a sardonic smile. I thought I could understand his amusement, but I am not so certain now. I thought he was amused that I had let Bill persuade me to travel in the little racer. 'So I understand,' he said. 'You must warn him to be careful.'

'He's a pretty good driver, I gather.'

'Is he? You should still warn him to be careful.' There was no change in him as he spoke. It was as though he had decided what he wished to say, irrespective of any comment I might make. 'People who work with me,' he said, 'people who work for me, are always safe. Remember that, Mr Burnham. It is the people who work against me who are at risk. People who work with me are safe in my protection.'

'My job is to help British and Dutch people work together.'

The platitude pleased him. 'Yes. It is, isn't it? You might remind your young man of that.'

I wondered what he meant, but I had no intention of interrogating or wrangling with him. He would have ignored me in any event, as he ignored the world, doing so once more now.

'I do not expect to be troubled by you again, Mr Burnham. You have been invited here so that I may show my good intentions to our latest occupying power, but if anything further should arise my office will take care of it.'

'I understand. Thank you for receiving me.'

'I had my own reasons as well, of course. Otherwise you would never have entered this house. I am a very private man.' He broke into his savage smile again. 'That much is legendary. I am glad to see you are not the kind of officious fool who interferes between a master and his hired hands.'

I assumed he was speaking of Anthony. 'It is not my place to intrude. The gentleman can take care of himself, I think.'

Altdoorp was generous. 'I take care of those who work for me. Mr Carstairs would be well advised to remember it.'

I did not know what Bill could have done to upset the old man, unless it be his unlikely friendship with the son, but I was too sick of the house and everything within it to care. 'I had better finish my packing. Goodbye and thank you again, sir, if we should not meet before I leave.'

'We will not.'

I turned to go, leaving him to darkness and his hatred of light and his own reflection, but as I turned he spoke again. 'Elena is old enough to know what she is doing, Mr Burnham, and strong enough too.'

'She is of age.'

'Indeed, and it is best that the young should re-invent the world for themselves, as I did; but do remember, Mr Burnham, that I keep a guard on everything I own.'

I left him there, brooding over his brutal kingdom, a broken statue of a man, his artificial twilight drawn up about him.

Both Anthony and Elena were distant when I took my leave of them, and I could not find Bill at first. I found him at last with Adam in the garden, which, like everything else that season, seemed to have run to seed, its topiary scruffy-haired and untrimmed, new shoots breaking

210

from the pollarded trees. Their conversation fell away as I approached.

'I'll be with you in a moment, sir.' He turned to Adam. 'Well, old man, I'll see you when I see you, I suppose. Good luck with the old fellow. You've got more chance than anyone, I suppose.'

It is only now, in retrospect, that I wonder whom he spoke of.

Bill was eager to get away and we left before lunch, his breezy little motor, piled high with luggage dumped wherever it would go, bowling us down the long lanes of Holland, across open fields under an endless snow-filled sky. (I prayed against snow, I remember, and my prayers were answered, although I developed serious back-ache from stretching round periodically, struggling to keep the luggage safe as Bill's accelerator pedal inched ever faster.) Only occasional barns and farmhouses interrupted the long horizon that day, except for groves of beeches, black with damp and cold, stiff against the light as hog's-back bristles.

'Lovely little motor,' he said as we distanced ourselves from IJssel-stein, with proprietorial pride. He must have seen my unconvinced expression, for he added, 'Not quite your style, I suppose, though, sir?'

I tried to smile against the tears the cold wind forced into my eyes. 'Not quite what I expected when I looked forward to being a Consul.'

He grinned. 'Oh well, we all have to shift as best we can, these days. Glad to be out of that place. Gave me the creeps. No wonder Elena's so tough, with an old man like that.'

I tried to sound disinterested. 'Yes, I suppose it follows.' I meant to ask about Adam, but did not get the chance.

'You seem to know that Manet chap quite well, sir. Known him long?'

'As long as I've been in the service.'

His look indicated that that counted as unimaginable aeons.

'I'm not that old, Bill, but I've known him twenty years and more, on and off.'

'Funny old bird. Couldn't get the hang of what he was saying half the time. Is he very religious?'

I laughed. 'I suspect he's one of the least religious people I have ever met.' (My memory tells me I was right. He used Holy Writ to tease the world and himself, with all their infirmities and imperfections. Much of his mind consisted of quotation.) 'I haven't seen him for years, mind you, not since he went to the States, but he does still seem to have a touching faith in books and people.'

211

'In that order, I gather, sir.'

'You may be right.'

We were silent for a while, tumbling through the cold, the early winter nightfall prefigured in the sky. At last I remembered the subject of my earlier curiosity.

'You seem to get on pretty well with Adam Altdoorp. I wouldn't have thought you had too much in common.'

'He's all right, sir. Decent enough sort of a chap. Not as daft as he might look. I suppose we have that much in common.' I laughed, playing the understanding superior. 'He's really quite tough, in his own little way. There's a bit of his father in him there.'

I could not see it, at the time. They seemed to have only their paleness and their delicate, clear blue eyes in common, but I kept my peace. We had to stop for a cart as a farmer shifted winter hay from a barn across to his cattle, huddled away at the dark time of year. Bill honked his horn good-naturedly, receiving a universal gesture in response. He leaned past the windscreen to call 'Let's not take all day about it!' but got no response at all. He settled back, watching the cart eagerly for signs of progress, speaking without looking at me. 'The only think I don't understand about young Adam, is why any chap as rich as he is isn't constantly surrounded by bevies of adoring girls.'

He grinned, and gunned the engine.

The last few days of that year were as quiet as I can ever remember them being. There was no work for me to do. Bill kept himself busy as usual, disappearing in his pride and joy, and I did not enquire too closely as to the purpose of his travelling. The only message came from Kit in London, asking for his leave to be extended, as his wife had not yet reached her term. I could remember how he felt, all his alarm and anxiety, and his sadness at knowing he would have to leave her and the child to cross the water. (I have always been grateful that I had my wives and children with me during my terms of overseas duty, but at that time, after the war, consular families remained confined to England; we became a bachelor, and surprisingly celibate in many cases, service.) I happily agreed to allow him to extend his leave until after the birth.

I spent my birthday alone that year; quiet, a little saddened at time's destruction and at the waste and detritus as well as the happiness and successes of an ordinary life, but not yet overly grieving. (I suppose that for the past few years, even when with my family, I have felt the same as on that day; a man with a past, but no great

212

future to look forward to; it is the future which keeps us going; it is the future which I have lost.) I went for a walk in the afternoon hoping to clear my head. It was the first day on which the city showed signs of returning to life. I came across a party cheerfully trying to shift a dead drunk, frozen after the previous night's celebrations (I had even seen a single firework curl upwards from my high bedroom window). The bars were open, steamy and filled with people sedulously drinking long, swelling glasses of foamy beer and munching on sausages. Even the indigent hawkers on the streets, selling off their few paltry possessions to buy firewood or blankets, looked a little more hopeful, less certain the world was entered into a conspiracy against them. The wind smacked my face until I suppose I was as ruddy as everyone I saw, well wrapped up in a heavy coat and muffler, blessing my military boots, the envy of less fortunate passers by. I was not conscious of where I walked that afternoon (I am not certain to this day), happy only to be witnessing something like gaiety returning to the streets of the city and wondering if, for once, for now, fire had had its day and was retiring its endless combat with air and earth and ice, resigning them to sunshine and the coming spring, that they might possess the world for a season. I think I must have walked through the old Jordaan district, tatty and destitute, for I remember passing a massive faceless fortress of a brewery, and I remember thinking how much the area reminded me of Jericho in Oxford (off-limits to undergraduates in my day, but the only way out to the cleanness of Port Meadow), both of them time traps catching the broken birth of the industrial revolution, heavy with disregarded canals and outmoded industry, their people still locked in the habits and pastimes of a worn-out working class. I remembered there had been riots here not fifty years before, when the government stamped out the traditional entertaining blood-sport of pulling eels apart, like something from the bear-pits of an older England.

I walked without destination or cause, my feet growing numb with cold, stopping off for rum and ersatz coffee when the wind became too much for me. I know that I slipped into a church somewhere, perhaps hoping to gain comfort from the New Year faith of the congregation; but I did not understand the words that were spoken (I grew to read Dutch quite well, but the accent and tune defeated me) and I did not even know the hymns. There was nothing to restore the comfortable memory of other earlier winter afternoons passed in my grandfather's church and, ultimately, cathedral; no sense of belonging or place. I walked out wherever my feet might lead me, and found myself at last in the Vondel Park, far out from the canal system, night covering over the sky, a few lamps already fitfully gleaming; and knew, I knew not why, that I was looking up to Elena's windows. I felt angry with myself, and guilty. I must have scowled, for the few walkers in the park hurried by me, heads bowed, avoiding my solitary, sullen intensity, till at last there was no distraction for my eyes, the cattle who grazed in the park gone to shelter for the winter, no cyclists now to chirrup their bells or swing legs forward in pleasure at their speed and skill, nothing to take me from my anger; and I knew that it had begun again, the annual vigil, the black dog of depression that fell upon me, as it has done ever since, in the days which led up to the anniversary of Amanda's death. I cursed myself, and Elena, and Amsterdam and the world, and turned away from one possible future to the warehouse which passed as my home.

Little remains in my memory of that dead, dull month. I know that I worked, as best I could, and I know that Elena returned to Amsterdam at last. She could not understand my mood or temper and I did little to enlighten her, warm in the certainty of my loss and self-loathing, wondering what the world would have been like if time had taken different turnings and she had been with me now. (She could not have been with me, and time has only one turning it can ever take. The world is what it is; what happens happens; I knew that even then, but ignored it, wrapped in my own self-pity.) Only Anthony understood. Adam Altdoorp, red-eyed and ungainly as ever, dropped a letter from him into the Consulate on the day before, the twelfth. I remember it simply saying that he had returned to Amsterdam, that he would be working in the Rijksmuseum library all the following day and would leave my name at the desk. I was welcome to call for him if I wished, or to arrive at his sister's house in the evening without any need for warning. I could not avail myself of his invitation, his covert suggestion I should not spend the day alone and that the time had come to face the world again, whatever the sorrows of the day. The time was unripe, and so was I, as Elena discovered.

She called on me that evening, in my high tower of melancholy; but I turned her away as though the past were her fault, my affliction her creation. I did not even tell her why. She must have gone from me feeling spurned and rejected without cause or warning or reason, and I knew I had done wrong.

It was the very fact that I wanted her for herself, and not as a shadow of the past, which so distressed me, as an act of retrospective infidelity. It was as though I feared I had allowed what happened to happen, with unknowing forethought, five years before, to clear my path for such an adventure. I knew it was not true, but I almost wanted to be

214

the dark corrupting hero of that dream, the murderous figure of my own imagination.

I wrote to her in apology, and we came together again – but everything was changed. Our outward disengagement from each other seemed to be belied by the urgency of our passion, clawing at each other like creatures of the night or sea-bed, but they were one and the same. We came together from need, not desire, a terrible urgent necessity as though we were seizing what we could, each from the other, whilst we could, without any care for the other's person or feelings. The worst of it was, we knew. We never spoke of it, but there were times when we could not bear to look into each other's eyes, lest we see the person standing there and be moved to affection or tears. We had ceased to be alive to each other, collections of bones and flesh which coupled in the long cold nights for our private satisfaction. I became obsessed with the particularities, the singular individuality of her flesh, in a bitter parody of the inquisitiveness of love. I knew every fold and crevice and tiny blemish of her, the tiny craquelure which cross-hatched the skin beneath her eyes when weary, the taut tendons of her arms and the lazy invitation of her legs in sleep or repose, and each unguent cranny of her receptive flesh. There was pride, too; not the lover's pride in another person, but in possession. Since she had left the Consulate we were open in our affair, and I took a kind of pride of ownership in the envious or disapproving glances of strangers at her icy beauty, the elegance and expense of her clothes, and her youth, despite my own contempt for myself, and in my own despite. We dissimulated for our own reasons and pleasure, but never admitted the dissemblance brought us pain. I knew that something in me grew corrupt, and faithless. I was a war of fire and ice.

I fulfilled my charter in those weeks by seeing Anthony every two or three days, but I could tell him nothing of this and he never asked. He was, perhaps, the one person I could have turned to for advice or help, the one man who would have understood and might have assisted to rid me of my own disturbance, to acknowledge the past and face the present as a man and not a mannequin; but I am a conventional creature of the world and to my pain and regret I did not know how to speak or ask. I was only able to display my new toy, my possession, with pride, inviting envy, surprise and acclamation. The opportunity passed me by. He thought that I was happy, as I wanted him and all the world to believe. I wanted them to think the old tree was pushing out new leaves, instead of rotted and damp and decayed, dressed only in new mistletoe, a climbing-frame decked out in later growths.

There was one time when I wanted to ask him, the day of Kit's

215

return from England. We met for lunch at Kit's restaurant in Spui-straat (we had come to know it as our Greasy Spoon or, simply, condescendingly, as Mick's). I could not bring myself to speak in the end. He seemed so calm and bright and unaffected by the uneasy hither-and-thithering of our world that I allowed myself to uncurl in his company, rather than raking hot ashes into fire, uncertain if anyone could control a conflagration. I remember only one remark of his that day, although I do not believe it was particularly addressed to me. He was trying to remember who first said that absence has the same effect on love as wind has on fire, fanning the great ones and extinguishing the small. 'I think it may be true,' he said, rubbing the bridge of his nose (in that instant we were young again, and in Venice). 'But it goes no way to explaining why I always seem to be a parting man.'

The rest of it has gone, vanished from my memory, although I have tried to recall it, riddling back and forward, trying to understand – but it has been swamped by the rest of that afternoon. He parted from me in the street, limping away into the pale hard brightness of the afternoon. I went back to my office.

Bill Carstairs was leaving as I arrived. 'Ambassador's on the telephone for you, sir' (I cursed under my breath, wondering what the interfering old fool wanted now). 'I'm off to Schiphol to pick up Kit.' I waved him goodbye and went through to the switchboard operator's cubbyhole as he called a final 'Cheerio', to ask her to re-call the Ambassador from my office telephone.

I was standing there, just off the hall, as he pulled away with a roar of the engine, deafening me, blotting out the Ambassador's querulous chirping, one of the girls tossing him something for Kit, a buttonhole I think.

'Yes, sir, what can I do for you?'

His distant voice piped with anger. 'What have you done with Dr Manet?'

'Nothing, except fed him.'

'What do you mean?'

'I've just had lunch with him.'

'Are you sure?'

I saw, I can still see, as if in slow motion, the girl's hands go to her face as she stood in the street, her eyes and forehead and hair all shining in the sun.

'Of course I'm sure. I paid the bill.'

'Well he hasn't been home for the last three days . . .'

Then I heard it. I had missed the squeal of tyres and the angry

216

honking of other drivers, the crashing of glass and the screams of pedestrians, but I heard the explosion, short, unechoing and almost physically loud, beating down upon us. I left the Ambassador yelling on the line and went out to the bright street where the girl stood weeping and screaming. Bill was already dead.

THREE

Sometimes, sitting here at my desk, looking out into my garden where the early roses are in bloom, working at my typewriter (I find a fountain-pen too tiring now; and my hands shake) as I have done these past few weeks, I can feel something in the room behind me; something which is not and should not be there, as alarming and uncanny as the face, seen in a mill-pond, of someone you know is not in reality there, or the glimpses sometimes seen or half-seen in a looking-glass of someone behind you grinning, considering your destruction and inescapable end in earth or fire. I have had such apparitions, such visitings, before, felt and gone before I am aware they are felt, leaving only doubt, desperation and fear. I do not know what they are or mean, but they have come to me for years. If it seems they come more frequently now, that is only, perhaps, because of an old man's uncertainty; the sense of being hunted by the hour-glass, by every flickering, shadowy minute and by each long remorseless day; perhaps it is only the fear that they will stop one day, after one last, unrealised as the last, visitation before the common end of men comes for me in their place. Certainly it is fear; fear which has little or nothing in common with the anxiety of the passing day. It is something else, for which I cannot find a proper name, something which laughs and threatens, something which conspires to persuade me – even though unsuccessfully so far – that the intuition this fear brings me is true, that there is something amiss and wayward, irreclaimable, about the world itself.

I felt it that day. Even now, thirty-nine years later, I find it almost impossible to disentangle the events of the next few hours. I know that in the end they all of them fitted together, but I cannot see where or how. It did make sense at the very end.

I have spent too much time with policemen in my long career in the service. Ours is not the best relationship to have with the agents of law. We almost always want something and, like all men offered the power of commission which that brings, they tend to flirt with their interlocutors, playing out the time like fish, before they land the compromise you ask. It is true of anyone with power, with the gift of something other people want – be it beauty, riches, escape or simply liberty – that the worst thing about our dealings with them is having to give them what they want in return, is having to play by rules they change as they proceed, is their exaction of obeisance before they will comply.

It was not like that on this occasion. Neither of us had anything we could give; there was nothing either of us could ask for or wanted. We had lost a human being, that was all, and they are irrecoverable. Nonetheless, I felt uneasy, sitting in the basement office at Amsterdam's No. 1 District police station, talking to the superintendent (his name was, ridiculously, Bosch). It seemed what had happened was simple enough. Bill had pulled away into the street, full of power and speed and pride in his motor, double-declutching up to fourth and hammering the accelerator pedal. He had roared away in a sticky stench of hot rubber and thick smoke. Then everything failed together, brakes and steering mainly. He had powered down the street unable to help or save himself, scattering other cars and passers-by like cardboard cartons, straight into the new, only newly replaced, plate-glass windows of the De Bijenkorf department store. It was the glass that killed him, shattering in long shards and splinters, pinioning and beheading him. Then the petrol-tank exploded. He died between glass and fire.

'Was he a good driver?' Bosch asked.

'Pretty good, I'd say. A little impulsive sometimes, like all young men; a bit of a show-off perhaps; but pretty experienced and sensible for all that.'

'I see.' He tapped his pencil across his knee, sitting one leg over the other on his desk. 'We have to examine the car, of course, to see if there is any evidence that it was tampered with, any suspicion of foul play.' He pursed his lips thoughtfully with a sad smile in his eyes. 'I sound like a cop in the movies. You must forgive us, Mr Burnham, if we seem a little officious. We are only just getting used to being real policemen again, instead of runners and traffic attendants for occupying powers. I want my people doing their job properly, by the training-manual if necessary, especially in the case of an accredited diplomat. I hope you understand.'

I nodded mutely.

'Did he have any enemies, do you know? Anyone who might wish him harm?'

There was something preposterous in the notion of that cheerful, reckless, charming man having any enemies, more saloon bar or smoking-room comedian, alive with tales of commercial travellers' derring-do, than formal diplomat or frightened spy. I thought of David Altdoorp for a second, but dismissed the thought. I could not believe he would trouble himself with anyone so insignificant as Bill, and I knew better than to make baseless aspersions against the character of a rich and powerful man.

'No one in the world that I can think of.'

Bosch nodded unhappily. 'Yes of course. I'm sure it was only an unfortunate accident, but we have to go through the motions, you see? Will you notify the family?'

'Yes, certainly. Will I have to identify the body?'

'No.' I was relieved. 'It won't be necessary. It couldn't be anyone else. We have all the eyewitnesses we need. To be honest, the body is too badly damaged, burns mainly, to be identifiable. If we should need a formal identification it will have to be done from the dental records. Do you have those?'

I bowed my head, closing my eyes, the remembered smell of cold and formaldehyde, damp, decay and vomit coursing through me once again. 'No. The Embassy has those at the moment. The personnel people there. I can get them if you need them.'

'Thank you. I will let you know if we should.'

The darkness shocked me when I came up into the antechamber to leave the station. It must have taken longer than I thought, the chaos of ambulance, firemen, police and doctor, for it was past six o'clock and the bar-lights opposite already gleamed into the night. The switchboard operator from the Consulate was waiting for me as I came up. It occurred to me that the other staff must already have gone home. I hoped that someone had explained what had happened and calmed them. I missed Christopher more now than at any time since he had gone on leave. I wondered what the efficient, anxious-looking woman wanted. I hardly knew her, except as a disembodied voice.

'Mr Harkworth telephoned, sir, from the Hague.'

I was tired and suddenly angry, no longer in control of events, no longer certain I could sort them out, no longer sure what end, if any, lay in store. I was intemperate. 'What the devil is he doing there?'

She was very good, almost unnaturally submissive, as though she sympathised. 'It seems the Embassy had a car waiting for him. There wasn't any way he could let us know from the airfield. He had been expecting Mr Carstairs.'

'Yes, of course he was. I'd forgotten.' I had forgotten the Ambassador's telephone call, too, and was both annoyed and concerned that

I did not seem to know what was going on about me any more.

'He said the Ambassador's called an urgent meeting for tonight. Mr Harkworth will be coming to collect you in a staff car. He said he would collect you from your flat, if you could wait for him there?'

I tried to be responsive and kind. 'Yes. Yes. Thank you for staying late to tell me all this. It was very good of you. I won't forget it. I suppose the others have gone home?'

'Yes sir. I got your keys out of your desk. I know it's not allowed, but I thought you'd want somebody to lock everything up, Mr Harkworth being away.'

'That was very good of you, really above and beyond the call ...'

She handed me the keys. 'That's all right, sir. I wanted to see you anyway, to ask about poor Mr Carstairs.'

They did not know after all. I felt a fool, and guilty of some dereliction, for not having arranged things better. 'No chance, I'm afraid,' I stammered out at last. 'He died on impact.'

She said nothing, but folded her hands before her, looking down at the whitening knuckles of her thumbs. Then she went away.

I walked home down the Oudezijds Voorburgwal, the plaster on its houses' stepped gables crumbling and peeling in the damp and cold and the reverberation of battle and war, the waters of its canal flowing shiny and black and quiet as pelts, convinced the Ambassador must have made some mistake about Anthony. I had lunched with him myself, after all, that very day, and he had said nothing about leaving his sister's house, or nothing that I could remember after the scurry and trauma of the afternoon.

When I arrived at Ruth's house there were no lights burning and the door was locked. I waited for a while, trying the door, knocking and calling, but no answer came. At last I tried the little tunnel alley cut through the side of the house, as through so many in that city, which led to the kitchen yard behind. It had often occurred to me that in sunnier times there would have been children playing in the alley with a big red ball, while housewives or maids strung their laundry in the yard or carried baskets of provender in from the street, as in the paintings of the Golden Age, if such an age had ever existed. Now, however, I fingered my way down its damp brick walls without any light to guide or help me. The yard was almost as dark again, surrounded on all sides by houses. I tried the kitchen door, its painted slats cracking and spongy to the touch, spillikins of timber flaking away. The lock gave way at once, to my surprise, making my heart race faster.

221

I found a lamp on the butcher's block table; then, crashing and stumbling between drawers, matches to light it with. He had done wonders with the house, scrubbing down all the floors and walls, stripping the woodwork and revarnishing it. He must have worked on it every evening he had been there, but he had not been able to rid it of that strange, indefinite smell, more dust and damp than anything, which speaks of emptiness in any habitation. There was a sense of something lost or forgotten about the place, as though its owners had been called away. There was still a half-filled coffee-cup on the desk in the study, the bed in his room remained unmade, the clinker remained uncleared in any of the grates. I went into his bedroom again, checking the wardrobe and under the bed. The suitcase was gone. I knew then that the Ambassador had been right and that Anthony, without a word of explanation to his friends, was missing. I knew how the Ambassador knew as well. Someone had been in the house before me, forcing the kitchen lock before me. Such of the books as had been left in the study had been riffled and gone through, and left where they fell on the nursery-chair at the fireplace. A few personal papers had been turned over and left open on the desk, residency permits mostly, for half a dozen countries, most of them out of date. I wondered at last what had brought this surveillance, myself included, on Anthony's ageing, unwell head. I wondered once again what kind of world it was we lived in.

Kit was waiting for me outside the flat when I returned, in a staff car with a military driver. He was huddled into his coat and regulation trilby, muffled against the cold. He began without pleasantry or introduction.

'I'm sorry sir, but we have to leave at once. We'll be back before morning, so there isn't any need to pack.'

'What is going on, Kit?'

The damp was hurting the shattered root of his arm. He rubbed at it with his remaining hand, but did not reply. The driver was pulling away from the centre of the city as quickly as he could, through the still nearly-empty evening streets towards the southern reaches and the main road out to Rotterdam and the Hague. I tried to check my watch by the light of those lamps which burned through power shortage. Kit rescued me.

'It's gone half past nine, sir. With a followng wind we can be at the Hague in an hour.'

I was dissatisfied. 'Not if the police catch up with us we won't.' The driver accelerated, as if in reply.

'They won't stop us, sir. Or if they do it'll only be to offer us an escort.'

He obviously knew more than I, but equally obviously had no intention of telling me anything. I tried to shock him into some kind of receptiveness by telling the news of Bill Carstairs' death.

'I heard about it, sir. The police got in touch with the Embassy while I was there. They were after his medical records, or something of the kind.' I realised I had been excluded even from that simple administrative series. Kit went on regardless. 'Sad. Stupid. He was a good officer. Such a silly bloody waste. He was daft about that car.'

He shut down into silence after that, the random lamplight of the city giving way to the darkness of the suburbs and eventually to the total blackness of empty open country, buffeted by winds, our headlights the only illumination, the throbbing engine the only human sound. Night journeys always seem to take longer. This one seemed to take hours, though in the end Kit proved not far from wrong; we were at the Embassy well before eleven. All I remember beside the cold is that at some stage I recovered myself enough to be polite.

'How are the mother and child?'

I could sense him smiling in the darkness. 'Both well,' he replied, 'though I was getting worried. Seemed hideously over-due but the specialist said not to worry; some women carry for longer terms. Little monster, the boy was. Nine pounds seven ounces.' I whistled, aiming for a mix between sympathy and appreciation. 'Greedy little bugger, too. Keeps everyone up half the night with all his screaming to be fed. Everyone says he takes after his father.'

'Have you decided on his names?'

'Yes, done that. Sarah wanted him christened before I came back. Seemed a bit unnecessary to me. I did my bit ten months ago, but you know what women are.' I did not, and in many ways never really have done, but most men seem happy to relegate them to the status of a cheerfully disregarded mystery, so I said nothing. 'Matthew William James. Not too happy about the order. William James was an American, wasn't he?'

'I don't think there's any possibility of confusion. Named after anyone in particular?'

'Both grandfathers, and all the men in my family have a James in somewhere. Comes from a long way back, the family whose family acres we married into, seven, eight generations ago. Lost it all later.'

'Wise choice.'

'Simple gratitude.'

Then we were silent again, for the duration of the seemingly endless ride.

When we got to the Hague all the lights in the Embassy building were burning, despite energy conservation regulations. (Not every good idea is new; we lived many of the fads of today all those years ago out of simple necessity. I have a vegetarian daughter and I have always resented paying small fortunes in restaurants to buy her the nut and carrot cake which was one of our staples during the years of rationing.) They had their own generator, of course, but I was still surprised. Kit led me silently into the high marble hall, its lights almost unbearably bright after the darkness of the drive. A young clerk was waiting for us by the lift cage.

'They're waiting for you upstairs, gentlemen, in the Ambassador's meeting-room.' He showed us into the lift and out to the office. It was too late now to ask Kit what I was supposed to be here for.

There were five of them waiting for us in the meeting-room, and two of them in particular took me by surprise. There was the Ambassador himself, Jasper Collins, his private secretary, and a senior-looking Dutch policeman. There was also Bosch, the superintendent from Amsterdam's First District, who must have been sent for immediately after he had finished with me; and there was Adam Altdoorp, red-eyed and blinking in the harsh electric light.

The Ambassador spoke first. 'Sad business that, at Amsterdam, Burnham. Very sorry about it indeed. Fine young man, by all accounts. Good officer too.' Bosch looked faintly disgusted by the eulogy. For some reason, I felt so, too. Having dispatched the dead, the Ambassador made his introductions. 'Jasper you know. This is Assistant Commissioner van Beinum of the Dutch Criminal Investigation Office. Superintendent Bosch I think you know, and Mr Altdoorp too.'

I wondered what calamity had brought such an unlikely group together, and I wondered most of all at the presence of pale, gangling, diffident Adam Altdoorp. I tried to dominate the room. 'Has a crime been committed?'

The Ambassador looked annoyed and an ounce frustrated. 'Sit down, Burnham. I'll explain as much as you need to know.' Kit and I sat down, at the end of the table. The Ambassador returned to his chair, turning it away from us towards the window, as though he could see through darkness down to the promenades and vistas below. His left hand played idly with his pen. 'As all of you know,' he began, 'Dr Anthony Manet has been missing for the past three days – although Mr Burnham here claims to have had lunch with him today.'

I was irate at his incredulity. 'I did have lunch with him. Check with the restaurateur.'

'We shall. Did he say anything unusual or indicative when you met?'

'Nothing out of the ordinary at all. If it hadn't been for Bill Carstairs' crash, I could have told you as much – which is, by the way, all I know so far about this affair, until someone enlightens me – on the telephone.'

The Ambassador smiled, coldly. 'You know he is genuinely missing. You went to his house this evening. The fact was reported to me. Why did you do that, I wonder? What were you looking for?'

I was surprised by the comprehensiveness of the fat old fraud's information. I tried to bluster over my uncertainty. 'I was looking for Dr Manet.'

He put me in my place. 'Even so, in the circumstances I think it would be wisest if you made a statement about your little luncheon-party. Perhaps Kit could take it down and pass it to the Commissioner?' He turned to face us all, resting his elbows on his desk and his chins on his hands. 'We are here, gentlemen, to find Dr Manet, and to do so as discreetly as possible. This must seem to all the world a perfectly routine missing person enquiry, but it must be attacked with rather more address and resolution than they are usually pursued with.'

'What is he supposed to have done?' I asked. 'He's hardly been here a month.'

Bosch replied, with some small show of sympathy, I thought, 'Nothing. Apparently it doesn't matter that we should know why we are looking for him.'

I was calm, but my anger at being treated like a skivvy and rushed around Holland at the dead of night without warning or explanation – and, mixed in, I suppose, my weariness and shock at the circumstances of Bill Carstairs' death – must have shown. 'Even so,' I suggested, 'I am supposed to be responsible for all British subjects in the Netherlands and it might be helpful if someone told me why we're looking for this one.'

'Shut up, Jeremy.' It was the Ambassador. He was still smiling. 'You, like everyone else in this investigation, will be told exactly what you need to know and nothing more. I hope I will never have to mention again, gentlemen, that this affair is covered by both our countries' security statutes and by our common security treaty. It is not a matter for debate. I do not want it even whispered abroad. I believe you have some information for us, Commissioner?'

The Dutchman straightened, square against the table, obviously and rather foolishly impressed by the company he was keeping. I suppose even Adam was a famous industrialist's son. He addressed us like a public meeting. 'We have notified our Customs and Immigration people and all the airfields, both public and private. Our people at the ports and the road borders already have photographs, most of them. The rest will receive them in the morning. Our people throughout the country have been issued with descriptions and warned to watch out for unusual events or happenings, particularly those in areas where a light aircraft could be landed.' That sounded like most of Holland to me. 'The sea and air ports have effectively been closed to him. My only worry is that the photograph is not as recent as we might like, but it will serve.' I remembered noticing that a snapshot had been lifted from one of the documents on Anthony's desk. 'Superintendent Bosch here has been assigned to lead the uniformed police investigation in Amsterdam. I think he ought to outline his plans himself.'

The Ambassador nodded his agreement and the big policeman unfolded, stretching his hands out on the table before him. He was sombre. 'I must admit that the nature of the investigation you have called for puzzles me,' he began, and I could have cheered that splendid figure, 'but that is not my business . . .'.

'You are quite right, superintendent,' the Ambassador interrupted urbanely. 'That is not your business.'

The policeman took a deep breath before continuing, leaving one hand on the table. 'We will of course institute spot checks on cars and lorries leaving the city, to supplement the work being done in the countryside, and at all the exit-points by our Customs and Immigration service. To be honest, I don't think that holds out much hope. What I can promise you, which may, is reliable, regular police-work. In particular, we need to track his customary movements. Mr Burnham's information will be especially useful there.'

The Ambassador jumped in again. 'See to that, Jeremy.'

Bosch continued as though he had not noticed the interruption. 'What I can promise you is that we will track his every movement, and enter, search and watch every place in the city he has ever visited. If he is still in Amsterdam, that is the only kind of search which can find him.' I began to warm to him, and to understand his dislike of occupying or arrogant friendly powers.

The Ambassador turned to me. 'It's unlikely he'll show up at a Consulate now, but I want all your stations warned. It is just possible that at some time after his arrival he may have approached one of your stations under a false name, or with foreign papers – which I believe he

has a right to – or both. I want your staff supplied with photographs –
the Commissioner can arrange it – and a complete check made of all
your records since he arrived. They may turn something up. Do you
have a system in place to arrange that?'

'Well, yes, but it was devised for tracking war criminals ...'

'Put it in motion anyway. I want Kit here to liaise between the
police, the consular staff and my people. You are to tell him everything
you do and about anything that turns up. Until this investigation
is over, any instructions from Kit or Jasper have the force of
directives from me personally. They will also liaise with Adam here.
Adam?'

He turned to the young millionaire with one hand extended. Adam
was quiet. We had to lean forward to catch his voice. He dominated
the gathering by the very softness of his speech, yet his blinking
weakness took the edge off that power.

'We've heard about the ports and air-strips. The real problem,
however, is road transport. It's impossible for the authorities to check
every vehicle, at least with any certainty. My father's people will take
care of that.'

I was contemptuous, wondering why he was here at all. 'What can
your father do?'

He smiled shyly. 'My father, and Jordaens-Altdoorp, are still very
powerful. The union representatives in our lorry fleet have been given
a description of Dr Manet. They are instructing union shop stewards
nationwide tonight. By morning we'll be in a position to make sure
every lorry-driver knows about him, and to turn him over to the police
if he hitches a lift. Perhaps just as important, we should know in a day
or two if anyone's given him a lift already, and where to. If he has got
out of the country we need to know. Our shipping fleet people are
doing exactly the same.'

He blinked, and looked as though he wanted support or appro-
bation, but none such came. 'As to my own people,' he continued,
'about a third of them are back on the streets as criminals of one kind
or another, black marketeers mainly.' (The Commissioner looked
disapproving; Bosch was only stony-faced.) 'They have their own
sources of information. I'll let you know if anything turns up.'

I did not understand what he was talking about, but I knew better
than to ask. I asked something else instead. 'What if he doesn't use any
kind of transport? This country is half land border, most of it farm-
land and woods. What if he just walks across?'

The Ambassador turned to face me down, with an air of quiet
triumph. 'He might do that, of course, but if he does we've put

227

additional guards across the border. They have instructions to shoot if he doesn't stop at the first command.'

I was silent; shocked, mainly. I could not understand what Anthony could have done. I was not intended to, as the Ambassador made plain, closing the meeting. 'This operation has Most Secret status. I want no alarm, I want no noises bruited in the market place. The easiest way to ensure that is by treating it as a perfectly normal, quite usual investigation – a search for a missing person; a celebrated academic. That is how it must appear, gentlemen, if it appears at all. Please remember, however, that while this search lasts it takes absolute priority over any other matter. Goodnight. Thank you for sparing us your time.'

Kit and I were driven back to Amsterdam in silence. He said two things only on the journey. The first was to offer to arrange for Bill's remains to be returned to his family in England. I agreed. The second was more curious, and puzzled me. He said, tugging at his empty sleeve, 'I wouldn't have gone away if I had known. I don't understand it. He seemed such a reasonable man.'

Next morning, the chaos began. It was to continue throughout February. We put the Ambassador's instructions into effect. I suppose the additional work at least had the effect of taking the Amsterdam staff's minds off the shock of Bill Carstairs' death, but it only put greater pressure on Kit and me.

Kit grilled me for two hours that morning and passed his notes to the police, who grilled me all over again throughout the afternoon. I was informed I was not to leave the confines of the city without first informing my assistant or Superintendent Bosch. They wanted to know everything about Anthony, about his sister, about his movements. Only Bosch treated me with any respect or understanding once the restaurant staff had reassured him about the innocence of my lunch appointment with the missing scholar. The rest of them seemed to be enjoying their new-found importance and urgency too much, as policemen all too often will (it is that which makes them a danger sometimes to the public order they are supposed to protect). Even the Commissioner was ludicrously disappointed and sullen after not finding Anthony waiting to be arrested at his customary desk at the Rijksmuseum library that morning.

By the end of the day I was exhausted, and distressed. I resented the lack of trust my colleagues had shown in me, I was alarmed for and curious about my friend's sudden departure, and I felt used by everyone about me. I went home to bathe and change, and then – I do not know why, unless it be that I sought company and relief from the febrile events of the past two days – I walked out to the Vondel Park, and Elena's.

I almost did not go into Elena's building. Doubt and self-disgust held me back; but at last, folding the evening out of my eyes, I went up to her flat, out of habit, out of laziness and loneliness and need.

She answered the door in a silk peignoir, dark blue with fern-like patterns all over it in black; it hugged and stroked her body as I had done, restless, shifting, sealed to her skin.

She had been crying, I thought, and her dark blonde hair stood up a little as though she had swept it away in anger and frustration with her strong, long nails. I must still have looked exhausted, carrying the burden of death, doubt, disillusion and my own self-pity, for she caught her breath at the sight of me and our eyes met for the first time in what seemed like an age.

'Oh love,' she said, grieving, stretching her strong hands out and putting her arms about me. I might have been stone for all the response I could make. Part of my spirit sat defeated inside me. I could not speak, and my eyesight failed.

She took me by the hand and led me into the drawing-room. A fire was burning in the grate. I collapsed before it, slumped and upset as a child defeated or questioned in play. I felt safe in her presence, as though we had never grown apart and never been distanced. I wanted a home, any home at all, and it seemed as though I had found one.

She sat beside me on her knees, saying gravely, her dark eyes tender in the firelight, 'I heard about Bill's death. I wanted to call.' She took my face in her fingers, understanding, and my skin sang under her touch. 'Was it very terrible?' she asked. I could not speak, and she folded me in her arms, cradling my head between her soft, heavy breasts. Then she sat across me, and reached down to kiss me, all over my face, with butterfly kisses. I do not remember how she managed it, the tussle with clothing and fitting. I remember only the warmth of the fire down my side, and her moist, expectant flesh, and her little cries of longing as we came together. For a time I was all silence and forgetting.

I had begun to believe I was a carrier of death, infecting but unaffected. Nothing else could explain the chain of destruction I thought I saw about me. I had generated an unspoken belief in a failing I carried within me, which threatened to destroy everything I

229

cared for. I know it was not true, and I believe I knew it even then, but I wanted to blame myself and I wanted to discover some terrible, impartial, heedless affliction which explained the powerlessness I had increasingly come to feel. Perhaps part of me reached out to match and share the insanity of the world I saw about me. I do not know. What I do know is that such dark dreams were held in check by the close obsession of her skin and her imponderable eyes. It was many kinds of relief to wake beside her at dawn, unconscious of time before or time to come, finding her whole, replete.

She stirred a little when I rose. I showered and went to the kitchen to make us both coffee. She was on the edge of awakening when I returned. I sat on the bed and shook her gently by the shoulder, noticing again the clear gold haze her skin became in the pure Dutch light of early morning or evening.

'What time is it?' she muttered, her face still crumpled, like a child's.

'Much too early, but I have to go. I want to be at the Consulate early. I brought you coffee.'

She smiled wanly and accepted the mug, propping herself up in the bed. 'Something important?'

I hesitated. 'Not important really, no. Just a bit of a nuisance. It means we're going to be overworked.'

'When will Kit be back?'

She did not know of course. 'He got back last night, which is something. He'll take care of repatriating Bill . . .'

She placed her free hand on mine. 'I was sorry about that. I was in De Bijenkorf myself, but I couldn't get through the crowds and I thought you would be busy.'

'Yes, I was.' It troubled me that my reaction to the news that she had been in the store had been a sudden fillip of alarm, retrospective worry for her safety, I supposed. I thought I had disentangled myself more than that, but need was overcoming reason. Even so, I was confused and did not know how to answer her next question.

'When will I see you again?'

'I don't really know.' Her gold skin darkened as though a bruise were growing. I thought of Anthony's damaged face, still swollen but no longer discoloured, the stitches cut, leaving little scars in his skin like the loose ends in coarse-woven fabric. 'We have a missing person enquiry to deal with. It isn't very important, but the police are keen to be seen to be going through the motions – which puts a lot of pressure on us. It's silly really, but I have to see it through.'

'Is it someone very important?'

I smiled. 'Hardly. Not in your estimation. It's Anthony Manet.'
'Your friend?'

It felt like an accusation, but I reassured myself it had not been intended as one. I lied fluently. 'The British Council has reported him missing. It seems he's missed all kinds of appointments and he's left his house. I don't understand it myself' (that much was true). 'He's old enough to look after himself. Still, they insist on jumping us around like jack-rabbits in March. I could try to get a weekend off. We could go out into the country. Not this one maybe, but the next.'

She was sleepy still, and absent-minded, dreamy. 'That would be nice.' She was thinking of something else; it was Anthony. 'Wasn't he working for my father? He will be furious. Nobody breaks a contract with him. You ought to talk to him. He might be able to help.'

I wanted to ask her about her brother but knew I must not; so I left her, promising to call, the confusions and wear of the day beginning to cover the simplicity of the dawn and the previous night.

I took a tram back into the centre of town and went to the flat to change. By the time I got to the Consulate early, Kit was already there. I wondered if he had slept at all.

The day was turning from its pristine clarity, clouding over, presaging rain, and a cold wind had struck up, skirling dust and paper in the streets and even thickening the atmosphere of the high, light rooms of our offices. Kit looked tired, his arm still troubling him. He looked up from the papers he was working on, acknowledging my arrival.

'I've been going through Bill's files,' he explained. 'You don't seem to have had much fun out at IJsselstein.'

'David Altdoorp isn't the most congenial host, no.'

'I see I'm supposed to get in touch with his private office. Well, that should be easy enough. In a funny way the Manet affair makes it easier.'

'Does the old man know Adam is working with us?'

'Good God, no. Nor must he.' He withdrew inside himself, as though he had admitted too much. He was pensive when he continued. 'In a saner, less conditional world we could have gone through Adam from the beginning, but there are complicating factors. You've seen what the old man thinks of his son. I'll have to go through the usual channels. Still, it's nice to know we can get the old firm on our side. One small achievement for the tangled world of diplomacy.' He did not smile, but stared out of the window, his fine intelligent features expressionless. 'Going to be a filthy day. Filthy, bloody city. I hate it.

Be glad when we're done.' He was businesslike again. 'Any idea why the old man didn't take to Bill?'

'None. Unless it was that Bill seemed to get on with Adam.'

'Well that's hardly surprising . . .' He checked himself, and I felt a wash of anger colouring me. Even Kit was concealing things from me and I could not ask him why.

I knew the service. I had grown in the service. It had brought me position, and rank – and some power – and I knew its ways. I had come where I had come by being steady and dependable and never making a fuss. Now, however, it had decided there was one area in which I was not dependable. I knew it was wrong, for I learnt my lessons well and young and have always been the colourless conventional service man; but I knew as well that if I made any commotion now it would be taken as evidence that my masters had been right, and that there was an area in which my emotions were unsafe and uncontrollable, that I was somehow losing my grip. I had to let them lie to me, conceal things from me, if I was ever to regain their absolute trust, so I struggled on in silence, doubt and confusion. I suppose it must have worked, for though the mills of the service grind very small and slow, they would have prevented my forthcoming elevation if I had failed them in any way. The Call Me God, the cross of a Commander of the Order of St Michael and St George, came through in the following New Year's Honours List, on my forty-sixth birthday. I waited another ten years for the K to tack on to the front of it, the ambition of all diplomats, the honorific Sir of a knight of the kingdom.

So I did not press Kit at all on that or almost any other day, trying to recognise his hesitations, withdrawing when he seemed uncertain, sympathising with his tricky position, for I had been in something like it once myself and I did not want to be accused of the same mistakes, gross errors of judgement, as Arthur Howard.

That day brought in the first wave of 'leads' as the search got under way. The Dutch police provided the first redoubt any possible sighting had to pass and, even now, I do not envy them the labour they went through. Most reports came in from the ports and from lorry-drivers. Late in the first week there was a scare when a driver who had been on a long-distance run to Italy (he had had to skirt through France, the Swiss route still closed, the dispute with that government about wartime enemy traffic and the seizure of their overseas funds still unresolved; Switzerland was starving that winter, and has never forgotten the ignominy of its submission) finally returned. He reported he had given someone answering to Anthony's general description a lift as far as Rotterdam, where he was collecting cargo. He had

232

dropped the man by a Norwegian vessel, which had subsequently sailed for Lisbon. It was the first time we really became involved in the procedures of the search. I got in touch with our people in Lisbon, who had had good relations with the local authorities for nearly six hundred years. They were waiting when the vessel docked, and arrested the man. It was a missing SS colonel.

Throughout this time, however, and thereafter, the search continued in Holland unabated. Any number of bewildered old men were stopped on the streets and in the villages, at the ports and airfields of the country; each one checked, each one interrogated, each one thrown back into the world without a word of explanation. The worst time of all for me came when Bosch collected me one morning to take me to the city morgue. A body had been found bobbing in the Amstel, downriver of the city and I was expected to identify it. I protested loudly; they had his photograph, I said, there were others in the city who had met and known him; but I knew that Bosch was right. It was becoming evident throughout the investigation how solitary a life Anthony had been leading. Except for two weeks at IJsselstein, when he was largely confined to the library, he had hardly seen anyone at all. He worked in the Rijksmuseum library, he shopped for food, and he had called on me when he felt the need of conversation. I was the only person in the country who could be really said to know him. I went with Bosch to the mortuary.

I did not recognise the corpse. I am not sure that anyone would have done. It must have been in the water for a week or more. I had not realised the corruption water could wreak on flesh. It was as though evolution had turned its clock back to the water creatures who first clambered out on to land to make this white, puffy, inflated, greening thing which bore so little, so distant a resemblance to a man. In a way I was almost disappointed, for as the search continued we all became more aware of the hopelessness of the task. There were millions of missing people in Europe that winter; and in the unresolved turmoil which had followed the war, administrations still new and untried, it was easy to disappear. Bosch's people in Amsterdam had the worst of it, I believe, winnowing through the city again and again, not even certain that the man they sought was there, a figure almost unknown to the local population to whom he might have been a trick, a ploy, a figment of the police imagination. I almost pitied Bosch, who came to see me one grainy, monochrome afternoon.

There was no visible change in him. He still looked the picture of the burly, friendly local copper, more desk-sergeant than superintendent. His uniform was still crisp and starched, his manner still open and avuncular, but something invisible had changed. He was tired. He was becoming hopeless.

'None of it works,' he said, simply, not asking for sympathy or support. He was stating fact, bleak fact. 'He doesn't seem to have done very much. Eat, sleep, shop a little, work. The people at the local butcher, baker, greengrocer, grocer, all say he was charming, quiet, unassuming, better at Dutch than most foreigners but happier in English or German. He would exchange a few words, but never about himself or his family or his work. He was a pleasant sheet of paper with nothing written on it. Same at the Rijksmuseum and the bars and restaurants he went to. Always alone unless he was with you. Nothing to hang on to, nothing to hold, no quirks of character or action. We've even tried the brothels, without any success at all so far.'

'What about IJsselstein? He was there two weeks.'

'Nothing. After the shooting accident – which should have been reported by the way, but we're ignoring it – and after you left, he seems to have withdrawn inside himself. Most of his meals were served to him on a tray. He doesn't seem to have talked to anyone much. We've interviewed everyone now except for David Altdoorp, and Mr Carstairs, of course.'

I was intrigued, but remembered to thank him again first. 'You were very helpful over the Carstairs affair, superintendent. We won't forget it. If there is ever anything we can do . . .'

He waved a casual hand, disclaiming credit. Only human things seemed really to matter to him. 'How did his family take it?'

'Not well, I gather. Kit's been dealing with it mostly – Mr Harkworth that is.'

He nodded. 'It's only to be expected, I suppose. I think sometimes all of us feel no one should die any more, now the war is over.'

I was in no mood to trade philosophy with him, and I still had losses of my own to nurse. I was more interested in David Altdoorp. 'Why not David Altdoorp?' I asked. 'You must at least have seen him.'

He shook his head. 'Mere policemen never get to meet David Altdoorp. No one gets to interrogate him. Very few people have even seen him. You're very lucky. His office told us he had nothing to tell us about Dr Manet. It seems he never concerns himself with his paid servants.'

'I can imagine him saying it.'

The policeman raised his eyebrows. He was obviously interested. 'What is he like? We hear so much, it's impossible to know what to believe.'

'There isn't a lot to tell. He's a very distant, cold, old man, about sixty, I suppose ...'

'Sixty-one,' the policeman interrupted.

'He looks a lot older, though. He really isn't very well – has strange ideas about doctors, has his own healer of some kind in Utrecht – and of course he's crippled.'

Bosch was surprised. 'I didn't know that. They haven't let that out. Perhaps that's it. I never did believe the other story.'

It was my turn to be interested. 'What story is that?'

'You don't know it?' I admitted my ignorance. Bosch explained. 'He's very rich, as you know. He owns the biggest private industrial concern in the country – property, food, shipping, transport, steel and finished manufactured goods – everything. He was born rich, an only child, and made himself richer. Most of the fortune was built up during the First War, I don't know the details. They say he has a passion for business, very tough, loves nothing more. He crowned his career by buying the old Jordaens firm. It was only then he married, in his late thirties, in celebration. His wife died young, after a long illness, some kind of breakdown. They say it made him a recluse, turned him in on himself. I find that hard to believe. I'm not sure that any man that powerful, that passionate about power, would be so sentimental.'

'So that's it. I still don't see why you didn't insist on an interview.'

'I don't think you understand. He is very powerful, Mr Burnham. There are a lot of people who run big companies, there are very few who own them as well. It is the largest active personal fortune in the Netherlands. He runs it like a private estate. He owns an enormous amount. Not just his company either, whisper it who dare. He owns people too.'

I did understand. I had been a servant of power too long not to. Men like David Altdoorp might as well be forces of nature for all we can do about them, with their powers of reward and patronage and their ability to strip others of their livelihood, like a tornado across a dirt-crop farm. One thing remained to puzzle me, however. 'Why does he hate his son so much? And where does Adam fit into all of this?'

The policeman shrugged. 'Who can say? A lot of fathers don't like their sons, usually for not being replicas of themselves ...'

'They look very alike.'

'Interesting, but not what I meant. The other thing, of course, is that though Adam isn't very much to look at, I doubt that he's terribly obedient. The old man wouldn't like that, I think. As to the other thing, I think you ought to ask your own people. I know very little about it myself, probably less than you.'

235

He knew I could not ask. I did ask, however, for permission to leave the city for the weekend. I told him I wanted to take a friend to Haarlem. He smiled. 'That would be Miss Elena, I suppose?' I had not realised how thoroughly he conducted his interviews. I was embarrassed for a moment, even a little ashamed. He was understanding. 'She's a very pretty girl. I don't think that should cause any problem. If anything comes up, I'll deal with Mr Harkworth.'

I was glad he had made it so simple and straightforward. I could not have borne asking for permission from or explaining to Kit. I told him after Bosch had given me his agreement.

I had seen Elena only once since the night after my return from the Hague, and then only briefly, in a tangled knot of limbs and desire. I had told her I would try to reserve a staff car for the weekend, but she had only laughed, saying 'I do have a car, you know. We are rich.'

I had left it at that, and I understood what she meant when I arrived at the flat by the Vondel Park that Saturday morning. It was a pre-war, dove-grey Hispano-Suiza with an engine which could have powered a tank.

'My father bought it for Adam on his twenty-first birthday.' (It was only long afterwards that it occurred to me that must have been after the German invasion; I still wonder who its original owner had been and why he needed to sell.) 'But Adam wanted nothing of my father, so he gave it to me instead. I'll drive.'

I was unconvinced at first, but she drove well, with style and dash and – most of all – speed. We must have turned every head in the outskirts of the city that morning as we sped by, a pretty girl in a huge sporting racer, her ageing beau at her side. Her enjoyment – of the day, of her speed, of the things she owned – reminded me surprisingly of her father. I could imagine a similar self-confidence powered him; and, shrinking as she roared round corners or passed other, poorer, slower cars, a similar disregard for ordinary mortals.

It is only about a dozen miles to Haarlem from Amsterdam and it took her no time at all. The town seemed barely to have awoken when we arrived and stationed ourselves, the envy of passing admirers, at the very edge of the Grote Markt.

'I've booked us into a hotel,' she announced cheerfully.

'So have I.'

'Well, yours will simply have to whistle. Shall we have breakfast before we check in?'

There was no denying her. We went into the most expensive-looking of the expensive cafés in the square and ordered chocolate and

236

boterhammen rolls filled with honey and raisins. Beyond the steamy windows, on a day still curling and alive with mists, stood the great church I had recognised with a shock at our approach, with a sense almost of déjà-vu from having seen it in so many paintings, and the statue of Laurens Coster, whom the Dutch call the Father of Printing. I tried not to think too much of churches as we ate and drank, with all their remembered weight of funerals, christenings and marriage; still less of printing. I wanted for a day at least to forget about paper and printing and books and research, and the sour fear I had begun to feel about Anthony Manet's fate.

She was magnificent when we checked into the hotel, driving doubt and disillusion away. It was small and central and plainly very expensive. 'My father owns it,' she explained, as we headed through the oak and plate-glass doors.

She looked like a princess as she stood at the desk in her blue-fox coat and boots, and my memory stirred uneasily once more. It settled as she rapped on the desk. The clerk was obsequious, bowing and clasping his hands.

She was curt. 'Elena Altdoorp.' He checked the reservation. I cannot swear as to what ensued, but I think the exchange began with the clerk asking something like 'And this is Mr Altdoorp?' He must have known very well it was not. I think she told him not to be impertinent. We got the best and biggest room in the house, looking down the little anachronistic street at the front, with its jutting attics and pinnacled gables, out on to the Grote Markt. She had them park the car. (Later we went to the smaller, rather dingy place I had tried to book by post, consulting my guide-book like any other tourist, to cancel the reservation. They had never received my letter. Elena was amused and slightly uncomprehending about the whole affair. She could not understand why I worried about hoteliers; she never had. There seemed no point in explaining that it would never have done for the British Consul-General to be sued for non-cancellation of a reservation. I would have claimed immunity, but it is better not to have to.)

What I remember most about the day is rain and laughter. It alternated between absolute downpour, the black skies opening up like hoses, and a steady penetrating drizzle. Elena's coat was reduced to rats'-tails. My shoes and trousers were a lake. None of it seemed to matter. We toured the Bavokerk, releasing clouds of vapour from our clothing, trying not to giggle at the local burghers and their wives who had popped in out of the rain and who shot us disgusted glances. It was exactly like the paintings. I almost wished we could slip back,

237

unnoticed, three centuries, to before the troubled times we lived in, but part of me knew the world could not be different, and was not so different then. People still died. The world still suffered under rain and fire.

We had lunch at a restaurant on the Binnen Sparne, watching the rain and river flow, water fading into water, eating hardly anything at all. That afternoon we made our way to the Frans Hals House, laughing at all the dour group-portraits of local worthies whose unchanged descendants we had mocked that morning, proud in our immorality. Then she began to ask me, for the first time, about Amanda. I could not answer her, washed away in a sense of my own unworthiness and wrong-doing. She fell into silence with me, like a stream, swirling us.round the remaining galleries. Outside afterwards in the cold blinding rain she hugged me and asked the question I had feared. She asked me if I had ever thought of marrying again. I could not speak, but held her closer to me, hoping to drown her questions and my guilt. I must have hurt her in silence, for that night she was almost unresponsive, unmoving. I was too obsessed by her body to care.

We drove back to Amsterdam still silent the following morning, my turn at the wheel. She had shown no interest in breakfast, the car or me, and there was nothing I could say to console her. I left her on the steps of her building. I left at once; I could not have endured to stay, for if I had stayed I believe she would have started weeping, and I had had enough of rain. It was as though the world had become an aspect of my feigning.

I have thought back on that time again and again since then, and wondered how much would have changed if I had given her the answer she wanted. I know it was impossible, for I could only have answered if I had been another man and a man she might never have come to love, or love as much as her father's ruthless education would allow. Nonetheless, there have been times when I wished the world were other than it is and we could cancel its destruction. I shut myself away when those times come, ignoring the callous laughter ringing in my ears and in my mind, telling me, mantric, in litany, that the world is what it is and there are no objects within it beside material things. There is no gain or fortune in weeping for the world.

I know these are the contours of the world, I know them as certainly as I know the falling features of my face grown old. I know them like my own smell, sharp and nitrous, when too long absent from water, or the flicker of my shadow at my feet, the dark attendant attached to me these three-and-eighty years. I know the world for what it is and have never been a fool before it. It has repaid me for my patience and my honest understanding. I have never been poor, or forgotten, or harried, or lost, as those forgetful of the world have been. I have never been amongst earth's exiles or refugees. I am an ordinary, honourable, English man. It is a person which has served me well.

I have seen enough destruction not to want to face it. I have seen enough pain not to want to share it. I have seen anger and hatred and ignorance and fear be masters to the world too long to stand against them. I know what the world affords its creatures, and I have always known my place.

I have been as well served as a man may be by such simple understandings, such phosporescent flotsam in the wake of foolish people's dreams. I have had everything a man can hope for. I have been well married, and happily, twice. I have had four children and three will survive me. I have my grandchildren, my house and my income. I have my health, or as much of it as any man my age can reasonably expect. I have earned the respect of my colleagues, and the honorific titles and trinkets of the state I have served. If I have sometimes also experienced defeat and doubt and loss and shame, I have had no greater portion of them than any man can expect in the turmoil, transience and change of a long lifetime. It should not be any cause for regret at this great age, landed from the troubles of the open sea. What I have been and what I have done is no greater cause for disturbance than any man may have, and greater than for most a cause of delight. There is no cause for me to wonder what might have been, for the world will go its way, and none of us shall be changed. There are only the elements we shall be broken into, when we are past all caring.

I avoided her all the following week, which was in any event a week of trouble and dismay. Fresh leads had been reduced to a trickle of confusion, errors, misunderstandings, lies. I had not realised till then with what passion men enter into quests. Bold for adventure and glory, as though the world were a darkling wood and they were knights of chivalry, they were desperate for the credit of having entrapped our minor, shadowy, unexciting quarry. False sightings, mistaken identities, sheer mendacity littered our trail. The police investigated them all, but with growing disillusion. Bosch even once admitted that we should face, or at least prepare ourselves for, the possibility that Anthony was dead.

'Who knows?' he explained, one dreary overcast morning. 'There is so little we know about any other human being. So much of our lives is conducted beneath the surface. We are deep waters all of us, and other people swim only in our shallows. For all we really know he might have fallen in with black marketeers, or become involved in the trade in stolen paintings, or in falsely attributing them. There may be a woman in the case. Who is to say, for all we really know, that he has not been the victim of a gangland slaying or the revenge of a husband or lover? This is the most crowded country on earth, yet there are still fields to bury a man in, dykes to brick him in, quarries to cover him in, and rivers and lakes to drown him in. No one really seems to have known him. Who, besides yourself, and that how deeply, would really miss him? Who, besides a foolish policeman like myself, would traffic and tramp for endless days, or even years, to find him or discover what became of him? Perhaps he simply grew tired, in the end, of the world, or of being himself. We are our own greatest burdens. We can never be rid of ourselves. Who is to say he has not engineered his own destruction? Or perhaps he has simply disappeared. He has money, he has papers, he has no family. It would have been quite easy. If he really wanted to vanish forever – instead of merely to change his life, as most of the missing do, for a time, without thought for the future – it would be almost impossible to find him. We could discover him only by luck.'

I could not disagree. We could only follow our orders, pursuing a man, for reasons we did not know, bound on a journey we could not guess at. We did our jobs, as best we could.

I spent most of the next weekend with Kit. We went to the museums, we walked the town, we even ate in restaurants beside Kit's own. I was trying to clear her from my mind. Out of cowardice, like the ostrich, I hoped that if I did not attend to her she would forget me. Although I tried, it was more than I could properly do for her. The sound of her voice, mocking, tender, wordless with pleasure, the precise dark blonde of the hair at the nape of her neck, the fold and shadow of her inner thighs, the arch of her instep and the curve of her cheek – all haunted my imagination, as did the long line of her back and her sharp freckled shoulders and the mole at the base of her spine. As I fell asleep her private smell drifted into me, and her hot salt taste.

I used Kit and I used my work to fill the time and fill my mind. I was trying, whatever came, to play the understanding, unflustered, sympathetic chief. I wanted Kit to see me as the man I was; the entirely impartial diplomat, sealing his emotional life from his work, stable, and to be trusted. I hoped, I suppose, with time and assiduity to break down his resolve and the alarm of my superiors. I hoped to cut into the exclusion zone erected around the reasons for this enquiry. I wanted what I have always wanted; I wanted to know what I was doing.

I asked after Kit's wife and child. I gave him paternal advice. I talked about his career, and the posts and promotions he should aim for. I talked about paintings and houses and property values. I talked about schools for his children and investments for himself. I exchanged the reliable information of a man of my class and my generation. He gave me only one thing in reply.

'I wanted to warn you anyway, sir. It's one reason I was glad to spend some time with you. I'm not supposed to know myself, but Jasper Collins genned me in. We can expect a surprise visit from the Ambassador in the early part of the week.'

'What on earth for?'

Kit sounded as cynical as I felt, though only a diplomat would have known for it came out in the tone of even-tempered boredom diplomats affect. 'It seems he isn't entirely happy with the progress of the search for Dr Manet. I understand he believes that things will liven up if he spreads himself about a bit.' (I smiled; if that man had spread any further, all Holland would have been engulfed.) 'It appears he plans to galvanize the troops. Something of that order.'

I was grateful for the information, and prepared myself for trouble and a little sport. I have always known how to humour my superiors whilst making it evident to them they have failed, and that no one could be working better or harder than the people who worked for me or, indeed, their boss. What I was not prepared for was to sit at my desk on the Monday morning and to have an other than official letter delivered to me by one of our girls. It was in Elena's small neat cursive script. I was told it had been delivered by hand.

As soon as the girl had started down the stairs I went to my window, craning out to look down into the street, but I could see no sign of Elena with her strong gait and air of wealth other people parted for. To my eyes the street that rush-hour Monday might as well have been empty. I supposed she had paid to have it delivered. She paid for everything.

The note itself was brief, but I was troubled and could hardly bring myself to read it. I wanted her all the time, but I wanted more to be rid of her. Curiosity overcame fear. All it said was 'Dear Jeremy, I have to leave Amsterdam for a week. I so much want to see you. I shall be here at the flat until after lunch. Please come if you can. Elena.'

Perhaps I should have gone, then. Perhaps everything might have changed. I am falsifying to think it. Then, all I felt was anger, anger that she should make such demands on me – as though I had made

241

none on her – anger at my own weakness. I felt self-righteous as only the guilty can. I felt the injured, innocent party. I felt put upon, aggrieved and hounded. I screwed up the note and threw it away. I thought no more of it after that, for there were other things on my mind. Kit came in from his office, straightening his empty sleeve, pressing his fingers along the forward crease, to tell me that the Ambassador had already arrived.

He did his best, and did his best to be discreet, and did quite well, as ambassadors go (things have got much better, I gather, as the service has grown poorer; ambassadors are less aloof and uninformed about the real endeavours of their staffs); but I could almost have dictated, three weeks in advance, how every minute of his visit would be spent. It was supposed to be a casual, random, informal and unexpected tour, and Kit and I remembered to look surprised, presenting the expected air of anxious pleasure. He toured the building, chatting to the most lowly and humble, charming them with his magnanimity, his interest and his common touch. (I must give him credit for that: he had worked hard and successfully at acquiring it; he could have given lessons – and perhaps, looking about me, old and disgruntled, at some of our whippersnapper leaders, should have done.) He affected to be ignorant of the missing person enquiry, and it was a professional delight to watch the carefully modulated interest and attention blooming on his face, nodding gravely as a junior clerk explained the systems and the workload undertaken to date, or a typist-secretary explained the filing system and how every possibility or enquiry, including those from all our subordinate stations, was cross-referred and indexed and constantly checked and updated. The system looked good, and I knew the Ambassador felt disgruntled about it; he had been hoping to have the opportunity to demonstrate his power, as well as his prodigious size, by jumping on us, his humble servants, in a froth of disappointed anger. He had no call to do so, and he knew it. The system was good. Kit Harkworth had designed it well and with care, and serviced it like the master he was to become. I liked to think (and I believe I did so rightly) that I had had no small part in its successful functioning. Experience had taught me that much could be gained by leaving an effective administration intact and running, without interference or comment, save for praise. I had also learnt that good staffs (which means intelligent staffs) want intelligence, acumen and skill from their bosses much more than they want energy, noise or interference. It is not necessary to act often or loudly; it is only necessary that one's interventions should be swift, effective and dextrous beyond the ends one's people could achieve. If a man's hand has still not lost its cunning it is not necessary to prove it every day.

I had learnt one other thing by then as well. As soon as I had been informed of the Ambassador's arrival, I sent one of our clerks round the corner to Kit's Spuistraat restaurant with a bundle of cash and strict instructions that the owner should go out at once to buy the freshest produce available on the black-market and cook the finest meal of his career. Visitors must be fed, and in the service must be well fed. It is not so much that our masters required or expected it, as that they would have been disappointed if it had not been so. I have never taken that risk. No one, whatever the range and power of his pride and grandiose self-respect, can bear a grudge as long or as effectively as a bureaucrat.

I had planned wisely. As the morning drew to an end and we sat in my office drinking tea (Nilgris; he liked it; Kit and I both insisted on decent tea, fresh-brewed; we did not keep an urn; a distant cousin in the India trade kept my family supplied) the Ambassador turned the subject to the question of lunch.

'I've invited Bosch. I'm sure you can arrange something, a cold collation, perhaps. It seems the Americans have flown the Assistant Commissioner – flown, mind – to Arnhem, for some training course or meeting. Sounds most unlikely to me.'

We waited for Bosch, then walked round to the restaurant. The Ambassador was pleasantly impressed (so was the owner). On the way, he tried to pay us what passed for a compliment.

'Jolly good work your people are doing. Glad to see it's not affecting their normal work. Can't imagine what possessed London to farm out so much of the supplemental stuff to a Consulate. Should all have been in the Embassy. Suppose you people have some clout I haven't been informed of. Not so good a show. Still, jolly impressive. Pity they still can't seem to find him.'

I noticed that Bosch looked briefly angry, as though on our behalf. He tried to explain a little of the problem as we ate.

'I sympathise with your people, Mr Ambassador. They face the same difficulties as we do. They with paper, we on the street. We can check and check again, sift every piece of paper, track every movement, watch every habitual haunt – and get nowhere if the garment of his absence is seamless. We need something to come loose, the smallest thread of information. If and when it does, we can tug and tug, pull and pull, unravelling the mystery till it leads to him, revealed in its final winding. We can expect nothing, however, until we find that small stray thread. That is what has evaded us.'

'Very poetic, I'm sure, superintendent,' (the Ambassador was dismissive) 'but it doesn't help me. My instructions are to find him and in that respect you have all lamentably failed me.' (It was always a personal matter with him, as though the world were designed to spite him; it never occurred to him that we might be depressed or disillusioned too.)

Bosch tried to explain, as he had tried to explain to me. 'This is supposed only to be the most important of the missing persons investigations we are conducting. We are ordered not to make a fuss. That itself causes problems ...'

'Solve them.'

'I cannot without causing a stir. There are tens of thousands of people – in Amsterdam alone – wanting to know what happened to relatives who disappeared during the Occupation. We are supposed, officially, to give those enquiries priority. We are supposed to liaise with the Allied authorities, here and in Nuremberg and Berlin. I cannot downgrade them further without drawing unwelcome attention to this investigation.'

'The others really don't matter.'

'They do to my fellow-citizens.' We were all silent for a while, embarrassed by being reminded about our peculiar position, the invasive nature of our role and occupation. The policeman recovered himself. 'What I am trying to say is that it might not even be necessary to upgrade this investigation, with all the possible consequences, if we could find some other way of guessing Manet's probable behaviour. If there were only some rough edges to his personality we could take a grip of them, and build the investigation on them. It is so wearing at the moment because we have to check everything, however harebrained or spurious. We would increase our chance of success if we could reduce the number of avenues we are required to patrol.'

The Ambassador was unyielding. 'Well, Burnham, it seems it's your fault. Why can't you tell us more about him? He is supposed to be your friend.' (He made it sound like treason). 'Excellent liver this, by the way. Haven't eaten calves' liver in Lord knows how long.'

I thought carefully before I spoke, hesitating, defensive, for I knew he would find what I had to say – what had begun to glimmer into my mind over the weekend as I trotted round galleries with Kit – merely irritating.

'We might try Antwerp.'

'What in heaven's name for?'

The others were all attentive now. 'I can't swear to it, and I might be quite wrong ...'

244

Bosch was firm. 'Don't worry about that now. Why Antwerp? Did he mention it to you?'

I felt foolish. 'No. No, it isn't that at all. It's just that I was thinking about what you said the other day about really knowing Anthony – Dr Manet, that is. I gather he's a very good art historian. He's made something of a speciality of documentary attributions. When I first met him, twenty years ago, it was a brand new field. He helped invent it. That was one thing which occurred to me. The other was that he's always moved in mysterious ways. He's never quite where you expect him to be. Even his going to America surprised his friends; he really didn't like the place that much. The very first time I met him was in Venice. The painting he was working on was in Dresden' (it occurred to me with a pang that it was probably ashes by now, after the most criminal Allied folly of the war). 'When he'd finished in Venice he didn't go back to Dresden, though. He went to Vienna.'

'What has all this got to do with Antwerp?' the Ambassador barked, exasperated.

Bosch, however, was intrigued, and silenced him. 'Please. Go on, Mr Burnham.'

I plunged on, though part of me felt that what I was saying was ridiculous. 'I told you he told me he had come to work on the attribution of one of David Altdoorp's paintings, a Rubens, a *Deposition*.'

'Yes, I remember. We confirmed that with the Altdoorp children.'

'Well, when I first met him in Venice he was there because the painter, who was supposed to have done the painting now in Dresden, had lived there. He was checking the contemporary records.'

Bosch encouraged me, one hand unfurled, as though I were a young quarrelsome colt. 'And Antwerp?'

'Well, wasn't Rubens born there?' I asked unhappily, staring down into my glass (wine, not beer; Kit's special reserve). 'I think his house is a museum now. If it's still open, if it's survived, after the war. I said he was a surprising man, full of . . . always doing unexpected things. It just occurred to me he might have gone there. He wouldn't necessarily have told anyone, if the idea just came into his head.'

Kit was unconvinced. 'What about the three days he was missing from the house – two and a half days – before he had lunch with you?'

I had no answer for him. 'I don't know. I just think it's a possibility. It's just that it occurred to me we were behaving as though he were just like us. Behaving the way we would behave in his shoes. The thing is, he isn't just like us. We wouldn't have done this. There isn't a hue and cry for us. It occurs to me that he doesn't even live in the same kind of

245

world as us. There isn't an office he had to go to every morning. There's no one he has to report to. He takes on his clients on his own terms. He doesn't even really have a home, where people can look for him, where they will always take him in, where there are people he loves.' I was silent, unwilling and unable to add anything further.

Bosch was quiet, but quite definite. 'I think we ought to check. It's only an outside possibility, but it's the first time anyone's suggested anything based on the kind of man Manet is, instead of what he has or might have done.'

The Ambassador was unconvinced. 'It sounds pretty preposterous to me.'

Kit rallied to my defence. 'I think the superintendent's right though, sir. I think we have to check. We have to try. We've got nothing to lose, after all. At the very worst, he will still be missing.'

The Ambassador heaved a sigh. 'Very well. Have a word with Jasper, will you Kit? See what our people over there can do. It can't get worse than it already is, but I don't want the search to slacken in Holland, superintendent. If he is still here I want him found. I'm not best pleased that almost every hopeful lead we've had so far has come from Adam Altdoorp's people.'

We walked slowly back to the Consulate, Bosch accompanying us part of the way, where the Ambassador passed a little time being pleasant to my staff and building up his reputation before returning on the fast drive to the Hague.

As we were walking back, at the point where the superintendent took his leave, he held me by the arm, holding me back while the Ambassador and Kit strolled on ahead.

'Thank you,' he said, simply.

'What for?'

'For giving me some idea of him as a man and not a case. I had never thought of him before, in the terms you described.'

I tried to smile. 'Superintendent, I know him as well as I know anyone, and I probably know him as well as anyone still living does, and yet I've begun to believe I don't really know him at all.'

They were bad days in Amsterdam. Everything had come down to the present, and that is hardly bearable; we need our fond entanglement with, our strange attachment to, the future. Hope lies in the future tense, and life in auxiliary verbs. We all knew the investigation was failing. We could not foresee it having any outcome. Most of all, I knew that for reasons I had not been given, because of circumstances I

246

could not understand, if it failed, I failed with it. I was angry and I was anxious. I had come too far in the service to be able to face with equanimity the prospect of a life chained to an unchanging office, without promise of promotion or title. My ignorance itself, of the causes for our search, was a kind of indictment of me, a confession of my own turpitude. I almost came to hate the man; but something nagging at the corner of my personality prevented it, as though I owed him something, as though we had been too long entwined to break the unknown bargain or contract which had kept us friends despite time and distance. The worst thing of all for me was the uniformed police, the ordinary bobbies doing their duty on the streets and canals of the city. Their very existence became a kind of accusation, an implacable implication of guilt. It sounds ridiculous now, but I became self-conscious about policemen. I avoided them, all the time, crossing roads and turning corners to avoid them. One I could not avoid, however. Bosch reported to Kit every day, and though his failure was some consolation ('It was the other man what did it, sir') I could not help wondering just how much he knew. I wondered how much everyone else knew, and I loathed the unexplained participation of gawky, bulging-eyed, big-jointed, almost-albino, ugly Adam Alt-doorp most of all. I wanted to know what I was supposed to have done, I wanted to know where my failing lay. How had I offended? How had I transgressed? I knew that ignorance was no defence, but I wanted to defend myself and my actions. I had never done anything to harm my service, my country, or my career. I wanted to hear the charges that I might answer them. I wanted to be told.

At last, uncharacteristically, the anger boiled over. I could retain it no longer, or the calm exterior which has served me so well so long. I was unfair, I knew the delicacy of his position, but I took it out on Kit that bright, almost hopeful, Thursday morning, pregnant with the first faint promise of spring. I called him into my office and told him to sit down. He looked tired. I think we all looked tired at that time. He hardly gave me a chance.

'What is it sir? We're very busy ...'

'For God's sake, grow up.' He sat uncomfortably, shifting on his seat, staring at me and playing with his empty sleeve. 'I have some very simple questions to ask you, Kit, and I want you to answer them. I am asking them as your Consul, and as your superior and, I had rather hoped, your friend. I won't be shut out any longer. I want you to tell me what Anthony Manet is supposed to have done. I want to know why we are looking for him. I assume that will tell me why you all distrust me so much.'

247

He was adamant. I admired his courage and resolve. That is untrue; I admired his professionalism. 'I'm sorry, sir, but I have written instructions not to answer such questions – from London.'

'That is ridiculous. I am trying to help. I am the Consul, and I am being prevented from doing my job.'

He responded in exactly the right way, like the skilled negotiator I had trained. He responded with anger. I had not taught him that the anger should be real, but it was. 'I simply don't believe you, sir. I don't believe you don't know. I think you are a part of it but it seems you have a spotless record, so you have been given the benefit of the doubt. I don't know if anyone really believes you, but I do know that this ought to have been the simplest and cleanest of operations, no foul-play, no fuss. Son or no son, I would never have gone away if I had believed – if I could possibly have believed – that Bill, with what I must assume was your connivance, would cock it up so completely.'

He did not wait for me to dismiss him, but stood up and left. If I had been the kind of man the heroes of novels are cut from I would have called him back, I would have been angry, I would have berated him till he broke, fond and apologetic, spilling out information. I am not made of stuff such as that, and he would not have spoken; he was, like me, too much a part of the service. Whatever the difference in our backgrounds, it had made him as much as it had made me. I was, in any case, no longer angry. I was frightened. I could think of only one thing. If that was what Kit, my witness in Holland, believed, then what must London have thought?

After that, everything moved much too quickly, with one of the peculiar characteristics of speed; although I was aware of how fast we were moving, everything seemed to take much longer. I did not know it then, but the end began when Kit came through into my office just after nine the following morning, the last Friday of that February. We were both quiet, edging about each other after our previous meeting, and I had another reason to be sombre; I had found another note from her, delivered by hand once more, when I had returned to my flat the latter evening. All it said, the latest in a long line of accusations, was 'You did not come. I am returning in the course of Friday. Elena.' Kit's message was almost more distressing.

'Jasper Collins has just been on. Panic at the Hague. Something's come up and they want us all over there right away. Bosch will be giving us a lift.'

We did not speculate on the purpose of the meeting as we sped towards the Hague past flat black fields, heavy with water, soon to be ready for sowing. We had nothing to say to each other.

Bosch laid on a car for the three of us and we arrived just before ten-thirty. The Assistant Commissioner and Adam Altdoorp, however, had both been delayed and Jasper Collins informed us apologetically that the Ambassador refused to start without them. He also refused to tell us what the meeting was about. We spent the rest of the morning kicking our heels, Kit and I in a silent fury, Bosch with his customary stolid Dutch equanimity. I was further incensed when it became apparent that the Ambassador had a lunch-engagement he had no intention of breaking. Collins would not listen to my protests or Kit's cynical mockery. The rest of us had gathered by two, but it was getting on for three before the Ambassador could bring himself to join us in his meeting-room (sky-blue, stuccoed) on the first floor. He did not even give me the opportunity to protest at the delay.

'Well, so much for your fantastic Antwerp theory, Burnham. He's made a proper fool of you, and no mistake.' His tone switched suddenly to one of eager concern. 'Commissioner, you have the results of the tests?'

He was answered by a nod and grunt, and the creak of the Commissioner's aching uniform. It encouraged him to continue.

'Manet's still in Amsterdam. Mr David Altdoorp received an envelope from him yesterday morning at his house at IJsselstein, postmarked Amsterdam, this Monday evening.' He looked round the table, hoping to elicit some response, but found none. 'We didn't inform you Amsterdam people immediately because we wanted the Commissioner to arrange some tests – apologies to Superintendant Bosch – hence the delay.' He half-lied easily. 'Could you run through the results, Commissioner?'

The big man leaned forward and took a file from his portfolio. The case looked surprisingly dainty in his hands, and the file dispropor-tionately small. He flicked through it and settled to his exposition. 'The envelope, a large brown manila, standard office issue, was posted at the Central Post Office in Amsterdam at some time between the five and six o'clock collections. It contained a lengthy report on a painting of Mr Altdoorp's, confirming that picture's authenticity. It also included two invoices, one for twenty thousand United States dollars as an attribution fee; the others, covering expenses, cancelled alter-native employment, loss and discomfiture, in the amount of one hundred and twenty-five million, one thousand nine hundred and twenty-three United States dollars and fifty cents.'

Kit, Bosch and I had all burst out laughing before he had completed

249

the figure. The rest of them looked at us as though we were alien conspirators. The Commissioner continued regardless.

'There are supporting invoices for the one thousand nine hundred and twenty-three dollars and fifty cents in three currencies - dollars, pounds sterling and Dutch guilders. The British and Dutch invoices have conversions attached.'

Kit spoke for the men of imagination in the room. 'Well, I suppose he must be alive to pull a stunt like that.'

He was ignored. The Commissioner continued. 'There is a brief covering letter, confirming completion of Dr Manet's undertaking with Mijnheer Altdoorp, and requesting that the invoices be settled by two separate cheques, the smaller amount to be drawn to the credit of the bearer, the larger to Dr Manet by name; the cheques to be sent care of poste restante Amsterdam, where they will await collection. Needless to say, we are watching the post office.'

The Ambassador turned on me, still unamused. 'Well, that's it, gentlemen. So much for Antwerp. He has made complete fools of you all.'

I got in before Kit. 'One moment, sir. How do we know the parcel is genuine? I haven't seen it. I would guess I'm the only person here who could authenticate his handwriting.' The Commissioner tried to butt in, but I rode over his spluttering. 'Even if it is genuine, it's four days since it was posted. How do we know he is still in Amsterdam? How do we know he posted it? Every policeman in the city is sick of his photograph. Why wasn't he picked up on the street?'

The Commissioner got to have his say at last. 'The envelope and the papers are genuine. We have checked the handwriting against specimens found in his late sister's residence. You will have the opportunity to confirm the authentication in due course. At the moment they are still out at our finger-print laboratories. Every test already made is being replicated. For your information, the only markings are the fingerprints of Dr Manet, Mr David Altdoorp, Adam Altdoorp and the gloves Adam Altdoorp put on once he realised what he was handling. There are vestigial traces of other prints, multiple sets. We have confirmed that one of them belongs to the postman who Mijnheer Altdoorp pays to collect the mail from his box and deliver to his house. We must assume the others belong to postal workers, sorters, and the stationer who originally sold it. Criminal Investigation are looking into it, Bosch. Your people need not be involved.' I thought I felt a flicker of the usual enmity between uniformed and detective forces. The Commissioner had only one more thing to add. 'As for your other questions, we do not know that he is still in Amsterdam, we do not know that he does not have an accomplice who posted this letter on the very day you suggested he was in Antwerp. We are here to decide what to do next.'

For the first time in far too long I felt the relief of real, externally-directed, anger. I protested my innocence. 'Now wait a minute. If I were Manet's accomplice why would I suggest Antwerp when I knew this envelope was on its way to prove me wrong? Why should I draw attention to myself?'

Jasper Collins replied, presumably on the Ambassador's behalf. 'Perhaps Bosch's men were getting too close. Perhaps you wanted to buy him a few days' time.'

'Don't be ridiculous! Why me? Because of the accident of our acquaintance?' (It should have felt like a betrayal, but it did not; more a relief, a flight from responsibility.) 'I don't even know what you want him for. Why me? Why not golden boy Altdoorp? If Adam's father really doesn't know he's working on this investigation, why did he hand the package directly over to him?'

I was exhausted by my forensic outburst, and I could sense the suspicion of me which remained. Adam Altdoorp only added to it, his voice as soft as ever and his sore eyes blinking.

'My father does not know that I am taking part in this enquiry. He does know that I do some work for the Embassy. He also knows that Dr Manet is missing and that a routine enquiry is under way to discover the whereabouts of a vanished Briton. When the package with its ridiculous invoice came, he thought he should hand it over. He also thought that to do so would help cement his relations with the British authorities – which, as I recall, you yourself helped to establish, Mr Burnham. He asked me to run this errand for him. He often has me run his errands.'

He had the advantage of being and sounding perfectly reasonable. There was nothing I could say.

The Ambassador rapped us back to attention. 'The question is, gentlemen, what do we do next?'

There was silence for a time. Kit spoke first. 'As I see it, we don't have much option. Bosch's people simply have to start all over again and search the city thoroughly this time. Adam's people will have to get back on the streets and pick up any information they can.'

Bosch squirmed in his chair, surprisingly sinuously, shaking his head in disbelief at Kit's simple-mindedness. 'It can't be done, it really can't be done. We have tried everything that is humanly possible, everything legal and some things less than legal. All we could do is to do the same things all over again. It's been a month now and we still haven't succeeded. You have to face the fact, gentlemen, that in a modern city if a man chooses to go to ground, especially if he has intelligent and reliable accomplices, there is virtually nothing you can do to trace him unless you are prepared to pull the city down brick by brick. The Germans couldn't do it. Neither could we. We can go on doing what we have done already, both ourselves and Adam's people, but if he and his accomplices haven't broken yet I can almost guarantee they never will. We are still in the realms of hypothesis and conjecture.'

There was silence again. Then I began to laugh. They looked at me as though I had gone mad, but I could not help myself. At last I choked myself into a fit condition to speak.

'I'm sorry, but don't you see that it really is very, very funny? I should have thought of it sooner, but if I had you wouldn't have believed me. Can't you see it? Isn't it obvious? This letter is a joke, a joke pure and simple, at our expense. Anthony's laughing at us. If he is still in Amsterdam, and if he has accomplices, then he is well aware of what we have been doing to find him, and he knows we have failed and will go on failing. Can't you see he's laughing at us? That he's saying the more we do the less chance we have of finding him? We want to find him, and yet he evades us at every turn. I will bet good money that if we want to find him all we have to do is stop trying.' Their disbelief was manifest. 'I swear it, I really do. It's Friday afternoon now. Call off the search. Call off everyone. Let him pass wherever he wants, unimpeded, and I will wager he will have reappeared by Monday morning. I know him. I am the only man here who does. I swear that if you admit defeat, if you surrender, he will reappear of his own accord.'

The Ambassador's response was more curious than menacing. 'Are you prepared to wager your career?'

'What do you mean?'

'I mean that you may be right; but if we do as you say, and if he does not reappear – if we discover we have lost him, by your accident or design – I swear you have no future in the service. Are you prepared to wager your career?'

I hesitated, and I was lost. I had been convinced of the certainty of my intuition but my presumption faltered. Adam Altdoorp saved me.

'You know,' he informed us softly, 'I rather think that Mr Burnham may be right.'

It took another two hours of wrangling to persuade the disbelievers, and it cost an unconscionable amount in overtime payments to clerical staff to put it into operation, but we managed. I did not know who Adam's people were or how he informed them, but I later gathered it had taken half the night to pass the message down all official channels of communication. By then Superintendent Bosch, Kit Harkworth and I were back in Amsterdam making our independent arrangements. Most of what I felt was relief. It was the nearest thing to a success I had had in months. The price exacted was that Kit and Bosch would be available at all times if I needed help, and that I was to take Anthony to them as soon as I reasonably could (I had pointed out that I might have to persuade him), if he reappeared. The rest was left to me, but most of all to him. Anxiety inevitably reasserted itself, aided by Kit's caustic leave-taking. He remained sceptical to the end.

'If this works, Mr Burnham, I shall still always believe you were involved.'

'What if it doesn't?'

'Then I shall want a new desk when I move into your office.'

I woke next morning to a cold, bright, sharp day; a day on which, more than any so far, it was possible to believe that the earth was turning and that winter and war's retribution would one day have an end. I did nothing. I read. I pottered. I tried to rearrange the furniture. All the time, however, fear began to rise in me, a kind of quiet desperation. If I had believed in prayer I would have prayed, and my heart leaped when, at lunchtime, a knock came at the door. My room was filled with light from the high sky and glittering waters of the canal and I did not recognise my visitor at first. It was the uniformed doorman from Elena's building. I was almost sick with anger that she should once again pay to harrass me so. Her note was brief, saying only 'I'm sick of this. Come. Please.' It was unsigned.

I dithered a little, but I knew this for a crisis. I had already risked everything, any future I might care for, and I realised I had to end this; I had to be rid of her now. I scribbled a note and pinned it to the door. All my hopes were held in seven words: 'Anthony, Back soon. For pity's sake wait.' Then I followed the doorman.

He had brought the Hispano-Suiza and sped me across the city to the Vondel Park. He let me into the flat using the pass key. She was standing in the centre of the drawing-room, the curtains drawn shut, as her father's always were. In the light of the standard lamp I could see she was dressed in a damp, scruffy towelling robe. Her face was blotchy, purple, snotty and ugly from tears. She wore no make-up and her hair stood up in stiff little spikes. She stood ugly as an accusation and gave me no chance to begin.

'I should have known, I should have known all along,' she started, words tumbling from her bloody, bitten lips. 'I should have known that you were weak. But you were powerful, I saw that. My father taught me only powerful men are attractive, but he warned me about weakness too. I saw you had power but I didn't see that you were weak. I thought you were nice, just nice, the nicest powerful man I'd ever met. The only nice one. I should have known.'

There was nothing I could do to halt the flow of her recrimination. I stood rooted, stricken.

'I tried to talk to you. I tried to tell you. I tried to ask. So many things I tried to ask. I wrote to your office to ask you to come here so I could ask you all the questions, so many questions, but I knew as I wrote it I needn't have bothered.'

Her voice had risen to a thin parody of itself, but she steadied herself now, stilling her hysteria. She faced me, clutching her shoulders, rocking slowly back and forth, trying not to cry, and spoke in a voice of terrible, reasonable, reasoned pain.

'It wasn't the marrying, it wasn't just the marrying. Do you have any idea what it is like for a woman to give her body to a man who can't even bear the thought of having children with her? Did it never occur to you to ask about my periods?'

What could I say? We were shyer and more reticent in those days, and I was selfish. Amanda had always dealt with things like that before, and knowing her not to be inexperienced I had closed my eyes to it and trusted.

'Don't you understand? Do you still not see? I had an abortion four days ago and I couldn't even ask for your comfort. It isn't true what they say. It isn't nothing at all. It doesn't leave you undamaged. Go now. Never come back.'

With the placidity of hindsight I can see it was the shock of what Elena had done to herself and our inchoate, unformed child which taught me I could not imagine growing old alone, and that I still wanted children. It led directly to my marriage two years later to Angela Sutton, a proper conventional marriage to a good and decent English-woman who made a marvellous consular wife. It led directly to the birth of my two other children, Nicholas and Pamela. (It is Pamela's son, Mark, I began to write this memoir for – he is two years old – that he might read it when he comes of age in the unimaginable new century when I and mine and all our pains are so much dust and vapour.) It led to the hard times, working in the most broken parts of Europe; and Angela's unfailing, gentle, amused support through the

254

years of exile in London; and the late happy flowering as Consul-General in Monaco and California.

It led to all of those, but I did not know it then. I knew nothing at all, evacuated of sense as I had rarely been before. I think I must have taken a taxi home. The taxis were coming back on to the streets. I cannot remember it at all. I must have made a fire. I must have tended it, but I do not remember doing so. I remember nothing until after darkness tumbled in the afternoon, all light extinguished except for the firelight at my back.

Then I began to cry, for myself, for Elena, for our child, for Bill and Michael and Amanda, for Tom my brother, for Arthur Howard and Jane Carlyle and Anthony's forsaken sister; for everyone I had seen or known destroyed by this ridiculous, futile world; but mostly for myself. It was true evening when I stopped weeping.

There was a knock at the door. I answered it. Anthony stood wedged against the door-jamb, looking older and sicker than any living man I had ever seen, his big brown herring-bone coat flapping loosely about him. His eyes were closed, and his voice cracking.

'This is my son,' he said, almost stumbling into the room, 'who was lost, and is found; who was dead, and is alive again.'

FOUR

I had drowned my guilt in self-pity, just as, even now, I shifted to use what I knew to be a happy future to assuage my remembered, present, shame. I had no emotion left in me; no curiosity either. I did not even interrogate or upbraid him. I let him sit there, on the floor before the fire, his cough hacking and sawing the evening air. I waited for him to explain. I left myself in his hands. I was smooth as wax; free for any impress he might choose to leave.

He pulled out his hip-flask from the big loose folds of his coat and offered it to me. I took a swig gratefully, then another. I do not think I tasted it, but I think I knew it was extraordinary. It had none of the rough filthiness of most of what we drank in those days. Instead, it seemed to steal into the stomach and system almost without my noticing. It was liquid anaesthesia.

'What is it?' I asked at last.

'Liquid compassion,' he answered, pulling off a mouthful himself. 'The last of my supply of 1914 Armagnac.' I must have shown some surprise (it was, even then, about the most expensive brandy you could buy – when you could find it; almost all Napoleons were already all but fraudulent) for he said with what might have been a smile, 'I have my methods, Watson, and I might as well drink it while I can.'

He stretched his legs out on the rug before the fire and put his arms up on the seat of the chair behind him. He looked terrible; his skin grown sere and yellow as leaves; his once-clear eyes the opacity of impure glass, clouded by air and silica. He began to speak, in a hoarse low voice.

'I owe you an apology. I owe you several apologies. It can't have been very pleasant for a man of your calling and reputation to be under a cloud so long. I could have told them their suspicions were foolish – but then, if I had been in a position to tell them, there would have been no suspicions. I hadn't even meant to be in hiding. I just wanted to get away at first, to think and work. I wasn't missing. I came to lunch with you; but that was the day we realised how desperate everyone had become, and it seemed best to see it through. I was beginning to worry, about how to end it. I gather I owe that to you. I understand it was you who suggested calling off the dogs.'

I nodded dumbly, not even caring how he knew.

'The stupid thing,' he continued softly, 'is that it should never have happened. If I had had the good manners to die on schedule, none of this would have come about, and you would have been quite safe; if only I had left off first, for manners' sake.'

I did not understand, and asked him what he meant. He looked surprised; even, at first, a little suspicious. Then he seemed to understand something, a missing character in some code he was working on. His voice was sympathetic.

'They really didn't tell you very much, did they?'

I could not even generate anger. I stated a fact. 'Nothing at all.'

'Then I am sorry. It must have been baffling.' I tried to smile, to indicate that he understated my confusion. I registered what he said next without any shock, without any sorrow. He showed no sorrow for himself. 'I am a dead man, Jeremy. I am living on unrepayable time. Stomach cancer. It was diagnosed eight months ago. I was supposed to be dead by Christmas. That would have solved everybody's problems. I was meant to be the longest stammer in history.'

I could not remember to be polite. I contrived to be honest. 'Aren't you frightened?'

'What is there to be frightened of? It's only death. It is no bad thing to die.'

Even now, in my extreme old age, I have not achieved such equanimity. He, I think, spoke nothing but the truth. It is how I like to remember – it is how I would like to remember – him, extended in the gloom of evening, his white hair flopping over his forehead, scattering ash from his small cigar and brandy fumes, unafraid and unashamed in the shifting flicker of firelight; but there are too many other memories overlaying it, and the light thickens, and that cellulose image is vanquished by fire.

He reached into his coat once more and pulled out two long thin slips of paper. 'I will explain,' he promised gravely, 'I will tell you everything you want to know. Before you are another morning older there will be nothing left of mystery. But now, tonight, the Concertgebouw play Mahler. I have two tickets. Will you come?'

It sounded strangely like a dying wish, the last request of the condemned man. I was too exhausted to refuse him. I was too evacuated to protest.

It was raining and we took a tram. I was glad, for the Concertgebouw hall was, as it still is, in Van Baerlestraat, close to the

Museumplein and the Rijksmuseum and Stedelijk where Anthony had worked and where the police had waited for him in vain. It is much too close to the Vondel Park, and I do not think I could have brought myself to approach the area on foot.

It was the first time I had heard the orchestra, that night; the first of many in the hall which is their home. It was the loveliest noise I had ever heard. I was not to hear the equal of it till I finally went to Vienna in the season, and heard the Philharmonic making music in their operatic pit. Later I discovered it had been part of their first short season to celebrate the end of the war. Many of their musicians were dead, but the spirit which had sustained Willem Mengelberg before his fall from grace must have moved out on the waters of the Netherlands, recovering a band who could have been auditioning as angels.

They played the little Mozart *Nocturnal Serenade* first. I had never heard it before. It was shapely and gentle and melancholy and pure. It was a kind of benediction. It came from a world before the horrors we had witnessed; a world which had still known famine and oppression and war, but in which music like this, formal, assured and certain, had had a place. To those who had known it, it must have seemed a world worth fighting for.

After the interval (Anthony was silent throughout it, nursing a brandy as I sipped a beer) they played the Mahler Ninth Symphony. The young never believe me when I tell them it was the first orchestral Mahler I had heard. Except for the inspired championship of the Concertgebouw, he was almost unknown when I was young and middle-aged; even then, thirty-five years after his death. Certainly the concert programmes of England were not sullied by the temperamental Austrian. I suppose, if I had taken to the city and the people, I might have heard some in Berlin conducted by Klemperer himself before he too was forced to flee; but I did not have that honour till many years later, in London, when both of us were old, and I went to his final concert, and almost believed the 'Resurrection' Symphony.

I cannot say I understood the music then. I knew it was beautiful, and there were moments of inspired simplicity or irony I understood at once, enchanted with the loveliness of the earth, and embittered by its follies. I did not see, however, how all of it fitted together. I did not hear the mad, tormented certainty that it is the very beauty of the world which makes it painful, for we know the loveliness we must lose. Perhaps it was my mood, unfit for further revelations. Perhaps it was an unwitting sense of self-preservation, for I do not know what I would have done, then, all those years ago, if I had understood, if I could have read, the final movement's horrible, outraged and anguished leave-taking of the world; its certainty of waste and desolation; its merciless contempt for hope. I was spared that much, but as the orchestra swooned and swooped through one passage which particularly defeated me I turned to Anthony and found him weeping, uncontrollably. He did not move. There was no sound. He was not racked by sobs and the ugliness of grief. I doubt if anyone else noticed, but the tears rolled down his cheeks, splashing silently on to his shirt-front and coat. It was as though an awful, useless pity welled up and overflowed. Pity will not save the world.

Finally – when it was over, after the tumult, the shouting, the applause, when the rafters no longer rang – both orchestra and audience stood and they played, simply for the dead, without thought of country or creed, the Funeral March from Beethoven's 'Eroica'. Anthony could bear no more, and slipped out of the hall. I met him afterwards in the foyer, in the only entirely silent crowd I have ever found myself a part of.

It had stopped raining. Anthony folded up the lapel of his coat and drew it about him.

'Would you mind if we walked? I know it's a long way, but it's such a long time since I walked the city.'

I nodded. I could not mind if he wanted to breathe the air and watch the water flow. I suggested only one exaction: 'We could talk.'

He nodded in his turn and we set off on the winding journey home amongst the anonymous crowd. He was silent at first. It was almost dark, with only a few of the street-lamps burning. Then another fit of coughing broke him, and he settled himself to speak.

'Have you any idea,' he began, 'what the last fifty years, and the last twenty years in particular, have meant to people like me?' I could not answer him, but let him speak on in his eccentric, ruminative fashion. 'The only particular gift I was born with was a gift for languages, and the ability to read – rarer than you might think, especially amongst academics. I was also born with money to fall back on. There were enormous numbers of people like me – an entire liberal, learned society. We came close to being the dream of a Europe without borders. We travelled and studied where we wanted. We shared our information. We offered each other hospitality. Perhaps that was where we went wrong, where we became misguided. We, in our very persons, were evidence that nations were only an administrative convenience, of no real relevance to an international community. It has taken two world wars to prove us wrong. We believed it was possible to be human, simply human, without the atavistic necessity to belong. We had a strange apocryphal vision of the world. We said we would light such a candle of understanding in its heart as would never be put out, but it is we who have been extinguished.'

I do not think I really understood what he was saying, and I am not sure I do now; but I did know that we came from entirely different worlds, so I took it all in, letting his sad voice unwind in its own fashion until he had told me what there was to know.

'I lived,' he continued, 'by my peculiar facility for language. You will remember how I worked, for publishers all over Europe. The rise of the total states destroyed that possibility and robbed me of my markets. There was no work for me in Russia, as a foreigner, a capitalist and a Jew; in Spain, as a liberal; in Germany – well, you know what they did to my books in Germany; even gentle, chaotic Italy, whose bark is traditionally so much worse than its bite, which – despite giving us the word ghetto – had no terrible tradition of antisemitism or xenophobia, could find no place for me in the end; I had no future in occupied or Vichy France; I could, I suppose, have survived on the fringes of the provincial yapping of literary London – friends like MacNeice and Bowra offered to help – but it would not have given me time; time to read and think and work. I saw it coming. It was what drove me to the generous plains of Kansas and Dakota and the high hills of Utah.'

I responded to the mockery in his voice, and mocked him myself. 'It doesn't sound very like Harvard Yard to me.'

'No.' He tried to smile, but nothing came. 'I exaggerate. They were generous however, to a home-sick and intransigent exile, and I was safe, unlike many others. In many ways, almost the worst part of coming back to Europe after so many home-sick years, was to find myself suffering from the most literal nostalgia – the pain of coming home. I saw at last what had happened. I saw what people like me had allowed to happen.'

I asked him the question any of my compatriots would have asked him that winter turning spring. 'Why didn't you come back? If not to fight, at least to be with us? We needed men like you.'

There was a look of rueful sympathy in his eyes. 'I tried. I did try. Your man in Boston was very charming but he told me, once he had established my various nationalities and the divided loyalty of my family in a former war, that I would be arrested as a hostile alien the moment I landed in Britain. I saw no point in passing the war shifting hay in a camp near Ely. The American army doctors took one look at me and asked me not to waste their time.'

We had crossed the fringes of the canal system. More lights were working and I saw he was pressing heavily on his game leg. He was tired, as well as ill, and the strain was showing. His yellowing face shone in the lamplight. Far away, in the reaches of the Amstel, a tugboat honked its horn. He recalled himself from my question.

'The worst thing about it all is that we let it happen. We did it ourselves. Osip Mandelstam was murdered; Garcia Lorca was shot; most of the Physics faculty from my time in Göttingen, the ones who escaped, are at Stanford or Princeton; Thomas Mann and Hermann Broch live on in unquiet California; Sigmund Freud died dispossessed; Walter Benjamin shot himself, an hour from the Spanish border, rather than fall into German hands. People like me; my friends. The worst thing of all is that we did it to ourselves. Maxim Gorki became Stalin's lap-dog; existentialist philosophers sang for scraps from Hitler's table; Croce and Lukács were seduced by power; Richard Strauss and Wilhelm Furtwängler waltzed our enemies to their untroubled dreamless beds. People like me. It wasn't only David Altdoorp who murdered Ruth, and all the others like her. I did too. Everything I have done of late I have done in the knowledge of my own guilt, my own complicity. Do you know what Czernin said about the fall of the Hapsburgs? He said, We were bound to die, but we were free to choose the manner of our dying, and we chose the most terrible. So did my world. For me it began when I failed to do anything about the killing of Jane Carlyle.'

I was startled by the mention of her name. I admit I had almost forgotten her, and the troubles which attended our first meeting, in the travail of the years. It was another thing he had said, however, which had attracted my interest.

'Is that what all this is about?' I asked. 'David Altdoorp and your sister?'

He seemed to be looking a long way off, into the future or the past, and his voice was equally distant when he finally spoke.

'I had a sister,' he began, but hesitated, unable to go on, lost in the distance again. It seemed an effort for him to return. 'For you, and for your people, it begins with Ruth, and the unchangeable fact I loved her. After the war, the First War, she was all of family I had left.' He tried to make a joke, but it rang hollow. 'I even liked Pieter, despite his being an advocate.'

Both the night and we were too far hidden from the face of day for me to care about discretion. I asked the question which had always puzzled me. 'Why did she marry a Dutchman?'

This time he did smile, remembering. 'Thanks to wanderlust and persecution, members of my family at one time or another have spoken almost every European language, except Dutch. Ruth always used to

261

say she decided it was about time someone learnt, just in case; but the answer to your question is very simple. He was a good man. She loved him.'

I was sceptical, I suppose. 'It's a big step to take, for love.'

He was not. 'Oh yes, it is; but it can be done. My people have something of a tradition of it. I know nothing in the scriptures lovelier than the words of her namesake.' His voice was calm and clear as he quoted: 'Intreat me not to leave thee, or to return from following after thee: for whither thou goest, I will go; and where thou lodgest, I will lodge; thy people shall be my people, and thy God my God.'

For a while thereafter he could not bring himself to speak, as we paced the long wet flagstones of the Rokin. I let him lead us where he would. I wanted to hear him talk. In the darkness between two street-lamps he began to speak again.

'Ruth worked as a secretary, for the planning director of David Altdoorp's largest manufacturing subsidiary – everything from trucks to pots and pans. It was a good job, and a blow for emancipation in its time, until the Occupation came. They were already in danger thereafter. They were Jews, and Pieter, as a lawyer, protested the arrests and deportations as soon as they began. He was a brave man. I find it worth remembering there were many like him, and that thousands of good Dutch people, of every religious persuasion, endangered themselves, and died, because they could not stomach the evil they saw about them. Even so, Ruth and Pieter might have been safe – he was a distinguished man, though he never acquired much corporate business – until Ruth began to suspect something at her place of work. She began to suspect, and later she knew, that Jordaens-Altdoorp had set up factories in Poland and was manning them with – frequently Dutch – slave labour. David Altdoorp, and his greed, lay behind many of the deportations from Holland. You know, as I do, that the identity of such manufacturers was one of the best kept secrets of the war. Ruth did not know what to do. It was not as though she and Pieter could do anything, but she did not want these people to go to their deaths unremembered, unacknowledged. She could not write to me, in enemy America, but I do not have an especially Jewish name and the family still possessed one apartment in Frankfurt. She wrote to me there, and her letters passed uncensored. After the war, the concierge's family posted them on to me in the States. It took some time for them to be forwarded from Harvard, which was the last address they had for me. It seems some time in 1941 her employer began to suspect her. The last of her letters is dated November the 21st, 1941. After that she and her family disappeared and I cannot be certain of their fate, beyond the certainty that they are dead, as dead as my Russian cousins. It must have been a little after the time Adam Altdoorp began to suspect what was happening and refused to work for his father's company any more.'

I began to understand. 'You have the letters?'

'I have the letters. They are the only documents in the case against David Altdoorp. None of the witnesses have survived. They are all that can guarantee David Altdoorp swings.'

I thought I had comprehended it at last. I thought I could see why the Embassy was so desperate to find him, before he could be bribed, especially having been Altdoorp's guest and employee, and before he died. I thought that only one thing remained to puzzle me. 'The only evidence? What about Adam?'

He explained patiently. 'I think you underestimate David Altdoorp's power, personal as well as financial. Even if Adam could bring himself to testify against his father, his testimony would not be accepted by the court. It would not be possible to allow the evidence of a man who stands to become a millionaire on the execution of the accused. No, what matters is documents, and Ruth's letter are the only ones left. All the ones within the company, and I doubt that many were kept, seem to have been destroyed or mislaid.'

'I see.' I nodded wisely. 'No wonder the Embassy was so keen to find you and have you testify, before ... before anything happened to you, or someone got at you with a bribe ...'

He stopped, and looked at me as though I were wearing a chamber-pot on my head. Then he began to laugh. It seemed like loud, echoing laughter, but in fact it was nearly silent, and there were tears in his eyes. He fell upon me, embracing me, folding me into his coat. 'Dear, dear Jeremy,' he said, 'I do love you. I really do. Never, never change. Promise me you won't.' He stood back from me and took me by the arms, looking into my eyes at last. I was embarrassed by his closeness, and I wish now I had not been and that my education had not prevented me from his comfort. 'Don't you understand?' he asked. 'They want to stop me testifying.'

I could not believe him, yet I knew it to be true. He began walking again, and the story came out.

'He is rich, he is powerful, he is able, he is an employer, and he is not a communist. Here, now, those things are important enough to save his life. How long do you think it will be before even Krupp himself, David Altdoorp's old friend and business colleague, is released from his American prison and sent back to run his empire on the Ruhr? Even if you have not been told, you know it is true. You know it is the policy for administrators and businessmen. David Altdoorp has done what he always does, and did under the Germans too: he has used his fortune to buy his freedom. I must have seemed a patsy to the authorities. I didn't make a fuss; I went through the proper channels; and they knew they had only to delay to silence me On top of it all I walked into the dragon's lair, and came to Amsterdam.'

I was monosyllabic with shame. 'Why?'

'Because I am a historian, and because I believe in examining the terrain, the background, the circumstances. It has always been my method. I·wanted to see the man, and he invited me. I suspect he had always suspected. There are other matters between us. And I wanted to settle Ruth's affairs.'

'Why didn't you come to me? You could have told me.'

I think I knew what his answer would be, and that it was true; but it did not stop it hurting. 'I could not tell you because I knew what you would do. I knew you would not compromise your career. I knew you would fall in with the official line, retailed to me in London, that I should consider very carefully, for the sake of peace and the Dutch people, before doing anything rash. It seems your superiors feared the exact opposite, but I know you better than they. That was why they put Kit Harkworth and Bill Carstairs in charge of the operation. They miscalculated everyone.'

I could not help asking, now it seemed I was to be faced with the truth, 'Then why did Bill Carstairs die?'

He looked at me shrewdly. 'We don't know for certain he was murdered. Now the occupying power has changed it isn't necessarily Altdoorp's way. Nonetheless, I suspect he was. The old man has enough mechanics who can fix a car without it showing up afterwards. He'd already tried to buy me, perhaps even frighten me, though we shall never know if the shooting was an accident. There was a motive for Bill's death, however. As I said, everyone miscalculated. Kit Harkworth toed the party line, but he went on leave, confident in Bill and his good sense, not knowing Bill utterly opposed it. He wanted me to testify. In the circumstances, it was a good enough motive.'

We seemed to be approaching the truth. 'Is that why you went into hiding?'

'Not really. Adam had heard whispers that something was likely to happen, and I wanted time to think, and work. I did have a contract with David Altdoorp, remember. I didn't really mean to be in hiding, merely unavailable. I even came to lunch with you. Then Bill was killed, and the Embassy panicked, all at once. I didn't want any part of you, after that.'

264

I was baffled. 'What does Adam have to do with this?'

Even he was surprised. 'Dear God,' he murmured softly. 'They really didn't tell you anything, did they?'

I was bitter. 'Nothing.'

He looked sideways at me and asked, 'Does the word Standfast mean anything to you?' He read the suspicion in my face. 'It's all right,' he assured me. 'I know all about it. You won't be giving any secrets away.'

I remained wary. 'Well, I wasn't directly involved with Intelligence. That was more Kit and Bill's line of country ...'

'I know that.'

I told him the little I knew. 'It was the name for our principal group of agents in Amsterdam ...'

'I know that too. Adam Altdoorp ran it, for the last eighteen months of the war. He was Standfast. Bill was his runner. Bill was keen for me to bring David Altdoorp to court. Adam, at the very least, didn't want me to be bought or pressurised. I've been in one of his safe houses in Amsterdam for the past month.'

I was upset by Adam's duplicity as much as anything. 'I don't understand it. He's been helping run the search for you. The Ambassador kept going on about his people.'

'So I gather. We thought it was rather elegant. You mustn't underestimate Adam, Jeremy. He is, in his quiet way, almost as strong as his father.'

Everything began to fall into place; the friendship, otherwise so unlikely, between Adam and Bill; our complete failure to get any scent of Anthony; Adam's unexpected support for me at the last meeting at the Hague. We had been had.

'I thought at first,' Anthony continued, 'that the search wouldn't last long. I assumed they would assume I was dead. When it didn't happen I sent the attribution to the old man anyway – with the results you know. The search became a nuisance. I had only gone away to think, in the first place, unharassed, and unaffected by guilt. Everything got out of hand, so I have to thank you for the chance of slipping back. I wanted to talk to you anyway. You are the only person who would really do.'

I suppose I was disgruntled. 'Why not Adam? You seem pretty thick with him.'

'It isn't surprising, really. I taught him for a year, at Harvard. His father pulled him back when war broke out. He wasn't brilliant, but he was able and enthusiastic; one of my better pupils. I've always suspected his father sent him there deliberately.'

'Why should he do that?'

'He has his reasons.'

It was evident he was not yet prepared to explain his curious relations with David Altdoorp. I chided him, in the guise of a question. 'Do you always put such trust in your former pupils?'

'Not trust, no, but I keep in touch with the better ones, as best I can. It's a much more pleasant relation, for both parties I think, once the element of power is removed. Anyway, I could hardly put my trust in your Ambassador.'

He smiled, but it did not work. He had tried, but nothing seemed to lift his spirits. It was as though he had done the impossible thing: he had become all pain, and survived; what passed for a personality and moods flickering over that emptiness, without ever invading or affecting it.

We had come into Dam Square. All the lights were burning here, though darkly. A drunk was picking his way homeward. Scraps of paper skipped and scraped across the pavement, the morning's headline already fading. The wind was lifting. Air thickened into fine drizzle. Then the rain came down again. Anthony took me by the arm and ran me into the nearest bar. Something occurred to me while he was ordering our drinks (some local fire-water, so unlike the hip-flask of our own dear don). He asked me what the matter was.

'It's only just occurred to me,' I told him, 'that I haven't eaten all day. I'm famished.'

He did smile now, and ordered me sausage and pickles. They were unwilling to serve us food so late, but he unfolded notes till they agreed. We ate in silence for a while, at a little table by the lace-curtained window, near the door. Occasionally it would break open as one of the drunker patrons seated at the bar stumbled home, or a night-worker came in for a lunchtime bock. The place was crowded and filled with steam and smoke, though there was little noise or conversation. It was late and this was a serious place. I was surprised at first that it should be so busy, but glad. It was the most hopeful sign I had yet seen that the city was coming back to life, returning to some kind of weary normality. A whore in the corner eyed us over professionally. Anthony waved her away with a sad slow shake of his head. He brought me more sausage, and both of us drinks, and settled back into his chair, lighting one of his small cigars and screwing his eyes up against the smoke. When he had done, and wiped the stray ash from his shirt-front, he turned to me, speaking with the voice of a man consoling a man much younger than himself, more full of kindness for

266

me than for himself. I wished afterwards that I had been to at least one of his lectures.

'Let me tell you a story,' he began. 'There was once a certain man ...'

I entered into the spirit of his narrative. 'Was his name David Altdoorp, by any chance?'

He shook the dead match in his hand, as though to indicate that that was neither here nor there. 'There was once a certain man,' he continued, 'born in Hoorn in the Netherlands. He was born into a prosperous family of merchants and landowners, and he was an only child. He was also born with immense business acumen and a passion for power. He grew, and grew quickly, the most able and ambitious industrialist of his generation. He shared one inestimable advantage with that generation, which he made better use of than most. When he was thirty, the Great Powers of Europe went to war. Throughout the hostilities there remained products and supplies which the combatants wanted which were only, or best, produced by their enemies. Krupp's German fuses for Vickers' British shells, and British cloth for German field uniforms, were two of the more blatant examples. Obviously, such trades could not take place openly between enemy powers, so Holland became the accepted entrepôt for their covert exchange. It was the making of a certain man, and turned financial stability into a trading and industrial empire. At last, the war over, came the summit of his career. The old Jordaens group of companies, one of the largest private conglomerates in the country, had been grievously mismanaged for generations. The trading companies, though fundamentally sound, were close to insolvency. The family, most of it of matrilineal descent, was desperate for cash. A certain man crowned his career by buying them out, amalgamating their companies with his, and creating the most powerful private trading group in the Netherlands. He attached only one precondition to his purchase. The surviving Jordaens male heir had a daughter. She also was an only child. It seems the family had lost all its energies. She was seventeen years old, and the time had come for the man to marry.

'It was the grandest wedding of the season, and marked the acceptance of the upstart parvenu from Hoorn. It made him in polite society. There was only one thing which might have clouded that acceptance, and which he discreetly failed to mention to anyone. He was already syphilitic.

'He infected his young bride, who did not know what had happened to her until the first medical examination of her pregnancy – by which time it was already too late to abort. I do not know how much her husband had to do with the timing of that medical. I do not think she fully realised what had happened to her until her son was born and her doctors informed her of the implications of his congenital infection. Then something inside her snapped.

'She called her son Adam; I think because she believed she was guilty of his damnation, his fall from grace. She never really seems to have blamed her husband.

'The development of modern medical techniques and drugs saved her young son's life and stabilised his condition. Money bought him years, but he could never be cured. The disease was structural in his make-up. It was too late in any case for her husband. He developed a hatred of doctors and conventional medicine, and he was always afraid of drugs. The fact that he has survived so long, albeit crippled, in something like his right mind, is perhaps the greatest tribute to – and corroboration of – his belief in his own invincible will. Even so, the tertiary stage of the disease has clearly begun.

'The young woman herself was sent to the Ehrlich Institute at Frankfurt. She stayed with my family, old friends of her family, most of the time she attended it. Blessedly, she was cured. Most of what was achieved during that time was accomplished on the advice and by the intercession of a brave and intelligent Englishwoman: a dear friend by the name of Jane Carlyle.

'The young woman remained in a state of mental collapse after her physical cure was effected. Jane arranged to send her to Freud in Vienna. Freud was honest. He did not think psychotherapy could cure her condition, for he believed it was an entirely rational response to the circumstances she found herself in. Only time and her own efforts might cure her.

'There then began a heroic struggle on the young woman's part. For the sake of her son she struggled to regain her composure and her stability. It seemed to begin to work. At last, she went south, to recuperate in the sun, amongst people who did not know her, in Venice. It was in Venice that you met her, and I met her again, partly at the instigation of Jane Carlyle. You knew her as Eva van Woerden, but her name was Eva Altdoorp – Eva Jordaens before she married. The rest is a matter of simple arithmetic and simpler biology. We became lovers. Elena Altdoorp is my daughter.'

He drained his glass and turned it round and round in his hand, watching the oily traces of alcohol ooze and smear. What could I have said? What should I have told him? He gave me no opportunity, becoming quietly peremptory, his dark brown eyes investigating mine. I recognised them now, in her, as I had always unconsciously recognised her mother.

'Say nothing,' he told me. 'I know that neither of you have been as happy together as you wished. I wish you both only what may be best. She is my daughter and you are amongst my oldest, and my few surviving, friends; but she is old enough to ruin her own life, if she chooses; as are you. What I do not know if I can do, is to ruin her life for her.'

I could think of only one thing to ask. Even now, after all these years, I do not know why, I think it was a selfish question. 'Does she know?'

He shook his head, his thick, heavy hair falling into his eyes. 'Not unless David Altdoorp is a liar as well as a monster. He will never tell her now, I think, for he has won. Before . . . all this,' (he made an empty defeated gesture with his free hand, seeming to include the bar, the city, the world) 'he wrote to me only once. I destroyed the letter. It was full, understandably I suppose, of hate. He threatened Elena with bastardy, and to destroy the reputation of her dead mother. He said he would say he was infected by his wife. He threatened to destroy the memory, as he had destroyed the person, of the only woman I have ever loved. I did not know what to do. So David Altdoorp won. He has a healthy, loving daughter, to take the place of his damaged, legitimate son.'

My self-pity rose again. I hated him for that moment, wondering how different the world might have been if he had only been able to withstand the power and wealth of David Altdoorp. It was foolishness; it is I who have always been the servant of power. 'Why didn't you stop her? Why did you let her go back to him? You could have fought him then.'

He shook his head, heavy with weariness, trying to explain. I think he knew that I, of all people, should have understood. 'By the time we became lovers, in Venice, his hold on her was too absolute to be broken, as his hold is now on our daughter. He also possessed her damaged son. I tried, that spring; and I hoped, more utterly than you can imagine; but when Jane was murdered, alarm and shock and fear, and fear of discovery, and shame – shame that I could do nothing to right so conspicuous an injustice – drove her back to him. He destroyed her. He nearly destroyed me.'

'How did she die?'

'Two months after Elena was born, of the Jarisch-Herxheimer reaction to the dead spirochetes in her system, and the arsenical properties of the neo-Salvarsan used to treat her. She died of her cure.'

269

He sat in silence for a while, thinking of her destruction. He was very calm. He did not brood. It was simply that the world had become unbearable. Then he spoke again, trying to explain once more. 'There was another thing as well, another reason I could not save her. It was near-bankruptcy which had driven her into his arms and his control. It was the spectre of poverty which had led her to destruction. She had grown to fear it more than anything else; more, even, than her husband. He was rich. I was poor.'

'You have never been poor.'

He nodded, sympathetic. 'Not absolutely, I grant you. Not poor as the mendicants, the unemployed, the maimed, of this and other cities are poor. I have never had to beg or return to the ancient, honourable, rabbinical trade of tailoring, for which I am more grateful than I can say; but in your terms, Mr Burnham, I have been poor as long as you have known me. Most of my parents' money was invested in Germany. I was wiped out by the Great Inflation of '23 and '24. When I met you I was almost bankrupt. Why do you think I sold my grandfather's house? Why do you think I worked so hard, when Europe still allowed me to? What sent me to America? What makes me hire my services to men like David Altdoorp? Why do you think that for eleven years now I have not written, much less published, a book?'

There was nothing I could really say. He told me only things I should have already realised. In the end I was peevish. 'You travelled First Class from Venice, I recall.' I had not thought the past would hold us to account.

'That is true.' He was unapologetic. 'I did travel First Class to Vienna. I could not have borne to weep in public. I have grown stronger-willed since then.' He paused a while, thinking back from that quiet, hazy bar. 'It was her voice I have never forgotten,' he said at last. 'It may seem strange or stupid to the world, but it does not to me. In destroying her he destroyed what might have become one of the finest voices of her generation.'

'Was she really so good?'

'The first time I ever heard her sing – before her marriage, only seventeen, still not fully formed, still in need of training – I thought I had already died, and this was heaven. After Adam was born she never sang again, except the once. Then you brought us the news about Jane.'

He rose, pulling his coat about him, strewing ash as he stubbed out his cigar. He rifled in his pockets and, finding what he wanted, pulled out a little paper parcel. He held it out to me.

'Smell it.'

It was coffee, real coffee, ground that morning. 'You are a master.'
He was almost shy. 'I meant it as a present.'

'Then come with me. I have a kettle, and I have a Primus.'

We went out into the clean air of the empty square. The rain had
eased. There was a policeman on duty, but if he noticed who we were
he followed his instructions and ignored us. There was something else.
One of the barrel-organ grinders who fill the city streets in springtime
and summer, playing popular tunes or mincing out waltzes, had
stationed himself in the corner of the square closest to the bar, his usual
stand outside the nearby brothels doubtless depleted or otherwise
engaged for the night. The bright colours of the organ were reduced to
shades of dark and darker grey by the thin street-lighting. I did not
recognise the air he was cranking out at first, and when I did I could
understand why he did so little business. I had expected some popular
tune of the day, perhaps slanted towards foreign visitors, of victory or
sentiment. Instead he played the opening bars of the 'Eroica', over and
over again. Anthony could not escape it at the last.

He stood motionless, listening. To this day, I wonder what dream of
youth and hope it recalled to him. I did not expect his comment when
it came.

''Tis the God Hercules,' he quoted, 'whom Antony loved, now
leaves him.' Then he took me by the arm and led me home.

We passed out of the avenues of lighting on the way back to my flat, the
waters of the canals as black as silence between the rows of houses and,
beyond, the pool of the Amstel where men worked late into the night
unloading the city's necessary supplies, and the waters of the river
running like lemmings to the sea. He had to rebuild the fire when we
got home (he was always good at simple, manual tasks, moving
without unnecessary fuss or labour) while I pumped the Primus for
coffee. The flat had grown cold and we kept our coats about us as I
brought the tray over to the fire, settling the enamelled pot on the
grate. Anthony resumed his former position, on the floor, his legs
alternately stretched and pulled up like ungainly pylons. He poured
the last of the Armagnac into our mugs.

'Heresy, I know,' he whispered, 'but when amongst the un-
believers . . .'

As we settled, he took up his tale once more. 'In the end,' he
explained, 'there is something inessential about the details, even of the
corruption of his flesh. He would have found another way of destroying her, and probably me as well. People like David Altdoorp will
always need people like Eva, and Ruth, and me. People to play with

271

and destroy. Our destruction may be the price we have to pay for the temporary freedoms we are allowed.'

I am not sure I understood him, even then. He had passed into deep and dangerous waters where I had no wish to follow him, full of speculation and uncharted ideas. I set it down here only as I remember it, a victim of my memory.

'I think I am glad Elena does not know,' he continued. 'What could I tell her? What advice could I give her? How could I prepare her for the world she must inhabit? She cannot possess, not even for a season, the countries I resign. I come from a peculiar people, and I was born into an interesting time. It seemed possible the old squabbles of race and creed might be forgiven. It seemed we might be men.'

He drew at his mug and turned to face me. 'Do you know what my favourite story was, when I was a child? I didn't understand it, but I loved the sound of it, I loved the words. I used to pester whichever of my parents was at hand to tell it to me, over and over. It was the story of how a group of learned men came to the great Rabbi Hillel one day, while he was reading from the Law. They said to him, Hillel, you are known to be the wisest and most learned of us all. Tell us, in the great body of the Law, is there one commandment, one Great Commandment, a just and pious man may follow all his days, holding it before him as the desert traveller holds a shining picture of the city of his destination, or the wise man the image of his family, and know that he will walk in the path of righteousness? Unfold us the Law, Hillel.

'Hillel lived about a century before the birth of Christ. This question was and is amongst the greatest debates of Judaism, and it is where the blasphemer Jesus belongs in our tradition, if not yours – not even really mine; I come from too many traditions.

'Rabbi Hillel thought for a long time. Then he spoke, saying, There is one great commandment such as you seek embodied in the Law, requiring two things of us equally: Praise God; do nothing you would not wish done to you in return.

'Then they praised him, as the wisest of the sons of Adam who are gifted to expound the Law. Perhaps it was because they praised without thinking that they did not hear the words which followed, invalidating churches and dogma and fanaticism with eleven simple words, words which, if we believe in language, should have extirpated the tyrannies of faith in a chime of syllables, for Hillel had not done speaking. What he said was, That is the whole of the Law; the rest is commentary.'

He poured us both more coffee, stretching his weary, recalcitrant limbs and the body which had betrayed him. 'That is what we tried to

272

remember,' he continued. 'That is what was forgotten when Stalin and Mussolini began to rewrite the histories, and when the books were burned at Göttingen. The world chose to forget, as it has always forgotten, forgotten the honour and independence of truth and of its servants, be they the unhonoured mathematicians of the Arab world or Maimonides the Jew, who rebuilt philosophy while the Middle Ages slept. Who remembers now Augustine was a black?

'We denied intellectual ownership, forgetting that we ourselves were owned and that the world is what it always was, the plaything of demonstrable power. I have no reason even to believe, as once I did, that in their rancour and rage and vengefulness at the events of this miserable twenty years my own stiff-necked people will do any better.'

I realised that in his way he was reading the funeral-rite over an entire way of life: his own, and that of people like him: the people of a liberal, human, European culture which has finally disappeared. It would have been impertinent to intrude on his grief, even if I could not understand it.

His eyes closed, and his head bowed, as he rose to his peroration. 'Sometimes I have thought we were only characters in a nineteenth-century novel. The world may have been simpler, Aristotelian, in the past. That wise man believed that character is action, and all liter-ature agreed with him; but we have grown at last to a state where character overflows action, and replaces it. We have excess of it. We strove to be ourselves, and to be men, whatever the world might be or do, in despite of all its actions. It is our characters, not our deeds, which have destroyed us. Sometimes I have believed that Pope was not cynical enough, and that it is most people who have no characters at all, and that this is the only way to be happy in the world, matching what you are to what you do, or can do.

'We were teachers, all of us, in our different ways, and we taught our charges that a man's a man for a' that; we taught them with Schiller and Beethoven that all men were becoming brothers; but we did not teach them what they most urgently needed to know, if only to understand us. We did not teach them what a man is.'

He was silent for a while, staring into the fire, its multi-coloured tongues folding and unfolding. 'Perhaps we did not know. We had forgotten that our leisure to think and to teach were bought for us by the powers of the world. We thought we had been given freedom when we had only been given licence. Perhaps those of us who turned and fawned on the powers who destroyed our world were only more honest and intelligent than the rest. Men and the world, which is a world of power, can never be unscrambled.' He smiled inwardly, a smile of

273

disillusion. 'We could not even build a place for Jane Carlyle to fill, and she was rich. Do you know what she was, and what all she wanted was?'

I found it difficult to speak of her after so many years, but found words in the end. 'She told me once she wanted to be a diplomat.'

He smiled again. 'You misunderstood her, I think. She translated mediaeval Latin poetry, quite brilliantly. It was her occupation, and she wanted more than anything to teach the skill to young people worthy of her; or to work, like you, close to the manuscript collections. If there had been places for women like her – as there are beginning to be – she might have ended her days in the Proceedings of the British Academy, instead of in a Venetian sack. And as I say, she was rich.' He paused in the flickering light, drinking his coffee and smoking his cigar, letting ash drop into the grate. His face was drawn, and his eyes were masked, as he said, 'I have never dared ask you before. What became of John Younghusband?'

'His brother died. He inherited the title. The fascism didn't last very long. It was black magic next, as I recall, to no little scandal. The last I heard he got involved with Huxley, the writer, and was taking drugs. He lives on the rolling acres, quite at peace with the world, and very rich.'

'Yes, of course. He would. And happy? You forgot to say if he was happy.'

'I would imagine so. It is easy, if you are as rich as he is, and commit yourself to doing nothing.'

Anthony nodded. 'How simple. In the end it is always simple. I had a sister, who was murdered, with tens of thousands of others, by a man I can hang by the simplest of actions. Revenge could be no simpler. I have a daughter, whom I watched in that man's house, who is devoted to my sister's murderer, and who, although I hold no brief for millionaires, simply could not exist outside the security of the world he has built for her. There are only two other factors. The Washington-London thesis that we can expect no better from men as they actually are, and that the workers of the world, as much as the indentured scholars, cannot survive without people like him. And there is the knowledge that the world which Ruth and I grew up in taught us to despise revenge, and to put forgiveness above retribution, or even justice. The world which made us is in ruins, but if I act in anger, as though vengeance were my prerogative, I would be casting a blazing brand on its funeral-pyre. In the end, the world being what it is, I do not know what will be gained by any possible action. That is why I went away: to think; to decide. The only thing left to me is the ability

274

to choose, unbiased and unharassed by any other. It is why I had to get away from you all. It is the only freedom I have.'

'Have you decided?'

'Yes.'

'What have you decided?'

He reached into the inner pocket of his coat and drew out a small packet of envelopes, secured by a rubber band which he rolled over his wrist for safekeeping. He riffled through the envelopes, extracting one and taking out the letter it contained.

'I want to read you something. It is the postscript to Ruth's last letter.'

It was in German, which he knew I spoke. I suppose it was the effort of following a language in which I was growing rusty which has forged it so indelibly in my memory. What follows is my own, entirely inadequate, translation.

'Beloved Anthony, by the time you get this we will already be forsaken or dead or both. Pieter has been very good. He has managed to explain it all to the children. I think they understand, but I hate their having to understand. I was never as clever as you, little brother, and I never learned as much, but there is one thing I have learned I want to tell you. It is the numbers who suffer which seems so horrible now, and which will still seem horrible later, but the numbers do not matter. Multiplication does not matter. There is no arithmetic of pain. The most suffering in the world, the most pain we can possibly imagine, is the most pain any one person can feel. There is no cure for that. I think there never will be, in a world where things like these can happen. I do not know why I am telling you all this, unless it is because of the pain I know you will be feeling now. I want to stop that pain, little brother. I hope I can help a little, if it is true that ghosts can reach back from the grave. Your loving sister, Ruth.'

He folded the letter away reverently, and returned it to its envelope and the envelope to the pile. Then he took the whole packet between his forefinger and thumb, holding them against the firelight, and threw them on to the flames. Their number smothered the burning at first; but then their edges began to blacken, and their hearts to fade, until they were as black as the barks of the trees from which their substance had been made, and broke apart, all carbon and ash, returned to oblivion by fire.

As we watched them crumble he whispered, 'Rien ne va plus.' Then he stood up, pulling the folds of his heavy coat about him, and began to leave.

As I watched him parting, some nameless futile pity and anger broke in me as though we had become each other. 'Why not, Anthony?' I called after him. 'Why not act? We could find fresh evidence. Why not? Why?'

He turned to face me, pocketing his reading-glasses, and for a moment he was the old Anthony I had always known, unvanquished and inviolate, his dark eyes liquid with fire. 'Because you would not see it through. The evidence is in the paintings, for anyone able or willing to find it, but you would not see it through. You have been my bargain with the world, Jeremy, and I have fulfilled my pledges, even if I think in the end my kind were bought too cheap.' He softened, and looked at me once again with the strange expression I had not identified twenty-three years before, and know now to be pity, and said, in a still, small voice, 'Besides, I told you once before. Sometimes the price is much too high.'

He started down the stairs, and I followed him to the street-door, watching him disappear, his syncopated footsteps silent on the cobbles of the rain-swept street.

Kit Harkworth came for me the following morning at seven-thirty. He looked as though he had been running all the way. He was panting. 'I've been a bloody fool,' he croaked, as he lurched about the room. 'It has to be Adam Altdoorp.'

I took him to the house on the Oudezijds Voorburgwal, back to Anthony's sister's silent home. This time both the doors were locked. (Later we discovered Anthony had jammed a chair under the handle of the forced kitchen door.) Together we went to fetch Bosch and I explained the position to both of them. He summoned two of his men and broke the door down. Afterwards, the doctor told us Anthony must have died between three and four in the morning, in his sleep. I remember very little about finding him. I remember noticing he had removed the rubber band from his wrist. I remember Superintendent Bosch standing with his head and forearm pressed against the frame of the bedroom door, punching the wall. I remember the few books still scattered, broken-backed about the study, like mute, gun-shot birds, struggling to break free, still trying to fly. It was not until afterwards I discovered it had been his daughter's birthday.

The Ambassador, of course, was delighted. When I told him about the letters, even I was returned to favour. All that remained to assure a satisfactory conclusion to the affair was to ensure it was clear he had died of natural causes. He had done, but there was a fuss even over that. The certifying doctor, the one man to behave honourably throughout the whole sad affair, refused to list stomach cancer as the cause of death, saying the actual cause was rare enough to be shown truly, for the sake of the medical literature. A post-mortem was performed, and it was ascertained that he had suffered indeed from terminal cancer of the stomach, with major secondary growths in the throat, lungs and duodenum. He had been on the verge of total renal collapse, and his spleen looked like a colander. There were fatty deposits in his arteries and round his heart which would have stopped a beer-truck. He should have been dead months before. Any one of them might have killed him at any moment. The actual cause of death, however (and it appeared on the certificate) was, quite simply, exhaustion.

He died intestate and without known family. Kit took care of the formalities, but I know no next of kin ever came forward. The last time I was in Frankfurt, nearly twenty years ago, I looked for his apartment building. It had been bulldozed and replaced by a particularly brutal modernist shopping-centre. (I do not know how we are supposed to trust architects, in the age which has given us Albert Speer.)

Anthony was wrong, tragically wrong, about the evidence of the paintings. The story did begin to come out, in the early 1970s, when some of them were sold. It transpired it was not the authenticity of the paintings which was in question, but of some of the purchase documents, or the prices actually paid. Perhaps that is what he had meant. The former owners seemed to have all died or disappeared between 1940 and 1945. By then, however, the old man had succumbed to the final indignity of his condition. He was irrecoverably insane, and there was never any question of a prosecution. It was a miracle and, as Anthony had said, a tribute to his unshakeable resolve, that he lived so long. He died in 1974. The company had long since been restructured. Adam died before he was thirty, blind, crazed and crippled by syphilis. Elena survived, the sole inheritor of a tainted fortune, until last year; still alone; still unmarried; still, I believe, the unwitting and unconscious battle-ground for the unquiet spirits of both her fathers. She died last December, and it is only now that I realise her death provided the trigger for this book, the release for the memories which have so utterly unbalanced it, invalidating it as the memoir I had intended.

I claimed Anthony's body myself, for want of anyone else to do so. There was an error in the procedures at the last, and both Bosch and I had to go to the morgue to sign for him. I have sworn since then that I will never again enter a mortuary until it is I who lie chilly and bleaching on the slab.

He had not been reassembled since the autopsy. His rib-cage had

277

been sawn open, and the ribs stood up like old wrecked spars. The major arteries protruded like the cut ends of hoses and his guts lay heaped in a neat pile beside him. The stomach, collapsed by two long incisions, was black and the size of a melon. All the blood had drained into his back and he was the unnatural whiteness of death. His eyes had fallen in. All over his body, strips of skin had been peeled back to search for budding sarcomas. The last time I saw him face to face he had none. He was the final, absolute, surgical, nakedness of man. I tried to be grateful they had taped back on the top of the skull. We were not faced by the six and a half pounds of white and grey tissue which had once been the residence and location of my friend.

I had thought at first of having the body returned to England and buried close to Jane Carlyle, but I did not think he would have thanked me for a Christian burial. He had never been devout, nor even a believer, so there seemed little point in consulting a rabbi. In the end I had him cremated. Earth did not seem a proper element, and I did not see him as mulch for roses. After talking it over with Bosch and Adam, the three of us took his ashes out by trawler from Rotterdam one fresh spring morning and poured them, five miles out, into the restless, cosmopolitan waters of the sea. Somewhere, Adam had found a Dutch translation of the Jewish prayer-book, and read the Kaddish over the sinking mercurial clinker. Bosch, unannounced, pulled a single white carnation from his portfolio-case and cast it aft. I had not known what to do about flowers. From his big hands the gesture did not seem ridiculous. We watched it fall behind us, weighting with salt-water, until – whether through distance or drowning I cannot say – we could see it no more. It seemed the least, if only the least, we could do in taking leave of what had been, I persist in believing, a kind of greatness.

I have betrayed myself. This is not the book I intended to write when I sat down in the first full hope of spring, the last I ever expect to see, to account for my actions and my time.

I have been re-reading these pages, and I see that what was intended as a witness to the tumult of the century, and the possibility of contentment within it, has resolved itself round two brief episodes in my life, of little moment and lesser import. Perhaps my mistake has been to weave a continuous narrative, for my tale has run away with me, demanding its own emphases and importance. I should have known, after all my years in bondage, to papers, to minutes, to protocols and accords, that truth does not lie in stories; truth lies in the quotidian dreariness of diaries.

This story lies. This is not the colour and pattern of my life. These people – and their history – played only passing, unremembered – till now – bit parts in my days. Although he was my friend, as these things are, Anthony's fate was no great matter, his passing no great loss. He and his kind were always wrong. They put their trust, and their concern, in people. The world is quite other, altogether different, much greater than we are; it inheres in the intricate network of actions which pass between people, and not in people themselves; it is the whirling, uncontrollable, gaps between us; it is energetic space. We do not really matter.

I have always known this. I am an ordinary, conventional man. Even now, as I sit here at my desk by the open window looking into the garden where Tom, my grandson, Alan's youngest boy (he is eighteen years old; last Christmas he failed to get into Oxford, the fourth consecutive grandchild so to fail, and unlikely to be the last; I do not know what we have come to – what are the fathers doing?) is raking the lawn and burning grass and clippings, the sour-sweet smell of smoke drifting into the study, even now I know that this is real and the proper matter for a life, the small gestures of family, career and success. There is more truth in this than in Anthony Manet's chimerical dreams of truth, intelligence and eternal love. Nothing lasts forever. Nothing is absolutely true. It is not given to us to know everything which can be known. It was the old dream of scholarship which damned him, which recognises (perhaps more truly than any) but cannot endure, or change, the world.

Even so, now that he has drifted into my attention once again, as I sit here watching the boy, handsome and strong in his youth, flirting and laughing with his pretty, charming, vacuous girl-friend, I feel a little pang of longing for the world he came from, and which I sometimes passed through, or touched at a tangent. I have always liked the young; I do not know what diminishes me now. The young of my class and even, increasingly, their elders, all children to me, begin to offend me. They know so little. They are so small, so stupid, so arrogant, empty and assured, without even the wealth or empire which gave us our assurance. They travel without tasting. They look but do not see. They do not realise it, and if they did, they would dismiss it as the raving of a foolish, fond old man, but they look ridiculous.

Why have I so betrayed myself? I have heard great argument and walked amongst famous men, and this was intended to be the subject of my memoir, as a happy and successful family life was intended to underlie it. Why have I betrayed myself, my family, my times, to

279

recount the insignificant doings of these anonymous souls?

I cannot say. It is as though some explanation or understanding lies beyond the edge of conscious reach, as though there were some significance here I cannot grasp, something I should know.

It cannot be the conscience which creeps over me now the heavy-headed roses are tossing in the breeze, the first faint hint, the hesitant understanding, that it may be I who have been the betrayer. I cannot believe it. I am not guilty. I am not responsible. I did not educate Arthur Howard in foolishness. I did not murder Jane Carlyle. I did not rain incendiaries on my wife. I did not riddle David Altdoorp with corruption or infect poor, defeated Eva. Whatever he may have said at our last parting, I did nothing to Anthony Manet and I made no bargain with him. I gave him no hope his world could teach me anything. I told him nothing more than the truth of the working of the world. I did not deport his sister Ruth. I did not vote for Hitler or Mussolini. I pulled no trigger on Giacomo Matteotti. I did not invent the world I live in. I am not responsible for Anthony's end in water and in fire. If I have not been the best, I have not been the worst, of men.

So why should it come again? – the sense that this account, in more ways than I know, is true? That everything I lived for was illusion or dream? I have only been a creature of the world. Now it comes again, stronger than before, as the smoke comes drifting in, the sour-sweet smell of betrayal and waste. It is behind me again, in this room, as the half-caught reflection in the looking-glass or mill-pond, and I know it for myself, unrecognised down all these years, the emblem and servant of my master. Wood-smoke is sweet and the afternoon is bright, but night always comes, the unanswerable night, when I lie awake riddling past and future, aware of the end as of the muddle of things. What is the world I have inhabited? Is it true that we and all we know shall not be changed? Are all our elements refined? Have we done well or ill in service to the world, when no other conceivable world could be achieved? Was this all we could do or work with? What is the end of fire?

These are the questions which disturb the night, against the night which always comes. I know they have no answer, and that no better could be had; but that certainty does not settle these final castings of the runes. What is the end of fire? Can no one tell an old man, frightened of the dark and his own extinction, whether or not it is true that in the real world dragons never die?

Mephistophilis
Hampshire, 1984